Terreldor
The Long Path Home

Chris M. Hibbard

Terreldor
The Long Path Home

Vol. III

Adventures in Terreldor

1st Edition
Copyright © 2013 Chris M. Hibbard All Rights Reserved

TP

Terreldor Press
Houston, TX
http://www.Terreldor.com
publishing@Terreldor.com
ISBN 10: 0615844855 (tpo.)
ISBN 978-0615844855
Published by Terreldor Press

To receive release notifications for new books by Chris M. Hibbard, email publishing@Terreldor.com with "Adventures in Terreldor" in Subject line.

Printed in the United States of America
First Edition

Terreldor Press   http://Terreldor.com

Contents

Part III

Part IV

For an interactive map and visual tour
Visit http://Terreldor.com
To receive email notifications of new Terreldor Press releases
send email to: publishing@Terreldor.com

Acknowledgements

I would like to thank my wonderful wife and children for their patience, understanding, edits, interest in this series, and for their outstanding support.
I would also like to thank Tricia for volunteering to proof, provide insightful suggestions, and point out countless errors in the manuscripts from which this series was born.

Thank you.

Notable Characters

Right and Honorable King of Terreldor: Wade Harrington
Princess: Schelli Harrington
Princess's Steward: Lady Sally
Captain of the Guard: Andrew Williams
Lieutenant of the Scouts: James Underhill
Duke of Enthicia: Cornelius Ward
Sphotch: Imprisoned Lyssiltik

Capt., Good Ship Explorer: Capt. Knemoller
Cabin Boy: Jaren
Portsmouth Innkeeper: Mr. Salomon
Pigeon Keeper: Bob Tiller
Protagonist: Mark Adams
Mark's Brother: David Adams

Portsmouth Delegation

Asst. to the Head Delegate: Robert Eastman
Delegation Secretary: Stephen Gravy
Chaplain: Patrick Davis
Military Liaison: Lt. Phillips
Medical Officer: Dr. Maher
1st Troll Delegate: Norman Tlaghiri
Farming Advisors: Tim Brotstetter
Nick   Brotstetter

Notable Merchant Families

Hapsteads	Separatist Trade Guild, NW Enthicia
Neerfals	Separatist Trade Guild, SW Enthicia

Influential Families in Portsmouth

Tlaghiris

Norman Tlaghiri:	Portsmouth Delegate
Sarah Tlaghiri:	Norman's Wife
Yenem:	Elder Son
Yureev:	Younger Son
Sisheen:	Norman's cousin

Arnolds

Jonathan Arnold:	City Mayor (retired)
Kale Arnold:	Arnold's Son

Ahrens

Thomas Ahrens:	Councilman, Father
Bishop Ahrens:	Eldest Son
Tom Junior:	Youngest Son

Adventures in Terreldor

Journey to Terreldor
Terreldor at War
Terreldor: The Long Path Home

availability and details at Terreldor.com

Part I

1.0 Testify

Trolls don't get seasick. As I stood on the deck of the Good Ship Explorer, salty breezes twisting my hair, I contemplated this possibility. Sarah, a troll woman taller and stronger than most human men, seemed completely unaffected by the choppy and often dangerous surf as we sailed over the Shelf. Thomas Ahrens provided a stark contrast; he ate nothing until we reached land. In fact, he struggled to hold down the water he drank.

We had favorable weather the rest of the way. I spent my time relaxing topside, admiring the ocean view. I thought about the progress I'd seen since arriving at Portsmouth. There was a long way yet to go, but recent events had done much to improve my expectations. I finally felt things were headed in the right direction. When I looked up to see Sarah comforting Thomas as he leaned over the rail—sick again—I recalled how large some of the latest changes had been.

Seeing the tall, brawny man accept comfort from a troll wasn't even a possibility a short time ago. Still, Sarah and Thomas were unlikely friends. Not only was there tension between our races, Thomas was indirectly responsible for her husband's death. Only weeks ago, he had been one of the most vocal of the human farmers opposing the trolls owning land. His accusations against Sarah's husband had ignited a chain reaction where his son was nearly killed in a fire, but for the sacrificial rescue Sarah's husband made. Before his body had even been buried, Sarah had forgiven him, and Thomas had sworn to take financial responsibility for her and her sons. Weeks afterward, the three of us were called to testify an Engdynlor, on the events related to her husband's death.

A new family seemed to form, and Thomas's household accepted Sarah and her sons as their own. I wished all the human families at Portsmouth had become so accepting. Thomas's eldest son, living within Portsmouth's city limits, had no love for the trolls, while Kale, the grown son of the former mayor, had been disowned by his father for his change of heart toward the trolls. After the sacrificial rescue, Kale was forced to accept trolls as his equals, and yet, he fled from the great social experiment in Portsmouth, leaving the town where his family had lived for generations, rather than live beside them under his father's animosity. I felt a pang of sadness for Kale and the truths he'd almost embraced.

Months back, sailing down to Portsmouth, I hadn't paid much attention to the scenery. It was a mistake I was resolved not to relive on the sail north, back to Oyster Bay. I paid particular attention near the end of our first day, as we reached the first islands of the Broken Coast. I was surprised again at the beauty of these small islands. Those closest to Portsmouth were the largest, and most beautiful. Most had no visible beaches, and seemed to rise right from the ocean, fully covered with plant life. The top of one island was hidden in cloud, or perhaps a large plume of smoke. The wispy column looked almost as if it were a tornado, connecting the larger clouds to the island. I asked the ship's captain if anyone lived on any of the archipelago's islands.

"Someone may, my boy, or so I've heard." When I pressed him for details, he made an excuse to return to the cabin. He was a large man, with a thick beard and thicker accent. He sounded, I recalled with a laugh, just how I would expect a pirate might sound, though he was far from the marauding type. On this afternoon, he seemed unusually abrupt. On my trip to Portsmouth, or simply *the Port*, as he and his crew called it, he'd been very friendly, even offering welcome advice on the political atmosphere I was soon to join.

The long hours I spent on deck gave me time to reflect on all that had happened in Portsmouth. Soon after Norman— Sarah's husband—died, I was called to Engdynlor to testify at Sisheen's trial. Sisheen was Norman's cousin, and it was he who had maliciously started the fire that had claimed Norman's life.

Thomas Ahrens and Sarah were also called, and each of us was invited to stay in Engdynlor as guests of the King. Thomas's invitation was something of an enigma. He was also being charged for the part he'd played in the events leading to Norman's death, while at the same time, serving as Sarah's guardian-protector, as the trolls' tradition required traveling women be so accompanied.

When we'd reached the dock to begin our journey, I was happy to see Captain Knemoller directing his crew. By then, Portsmouth was sending items back to Oyster Bay. The economics of trade didn't allow ships to return with empty cargo holds for long. As it was autumn, the human farmers had squash and melons and corn to spare, and so they sold their surplus to shops and tradesmen in Oyster Bay.

As we boarded, Captain Knemoller yelled for one of his sailors to take over for him, and came to welcome us aboard. Directly after showing Sarah and Thomas into the ship's small cabin, he congratulated me on my work.

"What work are you talking about?" I'd asked.

"Why, the work you're doing with the trolls, behind the Port." I remembered how easy it was to misunderstand him. "You're changing things, for sure," he said with a lopsided grin.

I wondered what he'd heard of the delegation. His face turned somber when he offered condolences for my *friend who passed*, whom I took to mean Norman. I asked if Jaren was on board, but was sad to hear he'd gone fishing in Oyster Bay and wasn't on his crew.

Other than the day we sailed over the Shelf, the voyage was peaceful, and I didn't feel a touch of seasickness.

After four days at sea, our trip was over. We were welcomed at Oyster Bay by a large crowd, led by a troop of heavily armed soldiers, and to my surprise, Princess Schelli. The King wanted to show the people at Oyster Bay how committed he was to the work at Portsmouth, and so there was a ceremony arranged to receive us.

Schelli led a parade from the docks to the inn, as an honor to the delegation and our work. She rode on top of a decorated coach, standing between myself and Sarah. Most people hadn't heard of Sisheen's criminal trial, and few knew we were traveling to testify in court. It certainly wouldn't have helped the people's sentiments toward the trolls.

Schelli was delighted to finally be involved with the

delegation. Her youthful age did nothing to detract from the fiery certainty she held, that she must be part of the work at Portsmouth—the trolls' last hope to find peace. Only months after the war, she was impassioned to help bring our two peoples together, and in doing so, to heal a rifted kingdom.

She was a year or two shy of my fifteen years, though I wouldn't have guessed by the way she spoke or acted. She was stately and graceful—whenever her steward, Lady Sally was watching. Her red curls were bunched up and hidden in some complex formation, beneath her ceremonial tiara. Her eyes shone with excitement, focused on Sarah as we approached.

She was loved by the entire kingdom, and I was certain her love and acceptance of the trolls would have a great effect on many. She stood on the coach during our cut-short parade, waving to the large crowd. The way their glowing faces greeted her, it was as if they were cheering their own daughter. It was early afternoon, and the warm breeze from the harbor along with the sun's rays, were just enough to balance the cool autumn air. The trees lining the road were in peak fall colors. I couldn't imagine a more beautiful day.

Suddenly, I was nearly blinded in one eye by something glinting over the crowd. Then, a flurry of motion, and chaos burst out all around me. The coach jolted, I fell from my seat atop the coach, and landed on several people in the crowd. Someone pulled me away from the coach's rear wheel as it rolled by me. I stood and shielded my eyes from the sun, struggling to see what was happening on the coach. It did me no good.

The coach sped off, down the lane roped off ahead of it. All at once, soldiers appeared from everywhere. *Were so many here a second ago?* I wondered to myself. Then I saw Sarah, on the other side of the road. Soldiers rushed to her from every side, and forced her head down; she was swallowed from sight. *No*, I tried to scream, *Leave her alone.* My mouth wasn't taking instructions from my mind, it seemed.

I tried to claw my way through the confusion to find her. Through waving arms and fists and faces, I negotiated my way to the tight collection of soldiers. One seemed to recognize me, then another. Wild-eyed, the first soldier grasped my jacket with both fists, and pulled me *hard* to his chest. He spun a tight half-circle, then shoved me toward the center of the clustered soldiers, yelling all the while, "*Cover!* Heads down, *heads down.*"

Sarah and I were forcefully cajoled into a small shop, as the soldiers used their bodies to shield us.

"Where is the Princess?" I demanded.

"In a safe place," an older guard replied.

"What's going on?" I asked, though no response was offered.

Thomas was in the shop with us, and I tugged at his coat.

"Do you know what happened?" I asked.

"Something bad. I think an arrow flew past me, right before I was thrown from the coach," he replied.

"*Thrown?*" I asked incredulously,

"Yes, I suppose so. If there was an attempt on the Princess's life, I'm sure her security detail wouldn't assume I'm to be trusted—not as long as her life is threatened."

"So they just *threw you out?*" I might've understood, but I didn't have to like it.

"You'll come with us," the older guard announced. "The Princess's security has been confirmed. You will join her now."

Sarah, Thomas, and I were rushed—once again, surrounded by a tight cluster of soldiers—to another building, then through its corridors to a stable, to another royal coach, waiting to carry us to Thraen Kholl. It was both larger and sturdier—and, if I knew my mentor, the Captain of the Royal Guard at all, it would be reinforced against arrows.

As we walked to enter the coach, I recognized one of the soldiers posted guard nearby—it was none other than my mentor, the Captain. We embraced, then shook hands. His demeanor was strange to me. He looked worried, or perhaps weary. His expression was one I hadn't seen before, and he seemed older. It must have been my imagination, but his hair looked for once more grey than black. His eyes shifted with apparent suspicion.

"Captain, what's happening?" I asked.

"In good time, son. Let's get you into the coach, and out of Oyster Bay. There's a troop of soldiers waiting to escort us to Engdynlor."

When Sarah, Thomas, and I followed the Captain into the coach, I found the Princess and her steward, Lady Sally, sitting beside her. I tried to shake Lady Sally's hand, but she pulled me in for an embrace.

"*Mark*," she exclaimed, nearly crushing me, "I'm so glad you're safe."

As I sat across from her in the large coach, I saw in her eyes a thin veil of calm covering a storm of emotion. She hadn't been in the other coach, earlier. Whatever time she was separated from the Princess, she surely spent fretting over her safety.

The Princess bristled. "I don't see what all the fuss is about. The arrow never even came close to me."

"All the same, your highness," the Captain answered, "we will take the precautions I believe are necessary." It was the most contradictorily I'd ever heard someone speak to the Princess, discounting her father.

"Captain," I reminded him, "*what* arrow? What's going on?"

"This information can't go beyond this group," he said, briefly locking eyes with each of us in the coach, "until there has been a full investigation. I believe there was an assassination attempt on one of you."

No one said a word in response. I looked to the Princess, but her expression seemed far less concerned than I expected.

"There were at least three involved—a conspiracy. Any one of you could've been the target."

"I understand the Princess, or even Sarah as a target, but why Mark or me?" Thomas asked, nodding to me as he spoke.

I introduced the Captain and the Princess to Thomas and Sarah. The Captain nodded towards my friends from Portsmouth, and continued.

"All four of you are known for your commitment to building a community where trolls and humans live together. Since the war ended, this is the largest source of contention we have left."

"I would have guessed anyone who opposed the King would have sided with the duke in the war," I offered, still shocked someone might want to hurt Princess Schelli.

"If I thought otherwise," the Captain started, "I wouldn't have allowed the Princess to leave Engdynlor. According to my responsibilities, I must assume the Princess was the primary target." He turned to her shaking his head. "Two assassination attempts in one year—I'm afraid your father and I are going to have a long talk about your future travel plans."

Princess Schelli opened her mouth, and judging by her expression, I expected a shrill rebuttal, but she remained quiet. She was wise enough to know her words would have no effect on him. Lady Sally clasped her hands within her own, and held them to her mouth in a worried gesture.

"But Captain," I insisted, "what was the *attack?* How do you know there were three attackers?"

Before he answered, he cautioned us once again not to repeat any of the details.

"There was one attacker," he said, resolutely. "He had at least two coconspirators. One used a large mirror to blind the coach's driver by reflecting sunlight at him from a nearby rooftop. The other pulled a string of shields across the road, which the driver ran over, jostling the coach badly. The three actions happened nearly simultaneously—they acted together, and they were *practiced*, I would wager. Of the three traitors, we apprehended only one—the man who held the mirror. He's traveling to Engdynlor in another coach, bound in chains and under heavy guard." The Captain's eyes narrowed and his voice dropped a full octave before he continued.

"He was a soldier from the King's armies—*he fought for us in the war.*"

"Why?" I asked.

"Time will tell," he said, thoughtfully, "but I fear we may find out too late. Until we find everyone involved, each of you is in danger."

We rode in silence for several miles. I took a second look at the Captain. Inside the coach, his hair color appeared once again *mostly* black, but his expression had only grown more worrisome. The wrinkles around his eyes and forehead seemed more pronounced. He was a little older than my father as far as I had guessed, but since we'd uncovered the duke's plot before the war, some days he seemed ancient. I turned away, not wanting to speak yet.

Seeing Sarah sitting among humans highlighted the differences between humans and trolls. Thomas was a large man, tall and strong, but beside Sarah, he seemed puny. His mop of dark hair and overalls, coupled with a week-old beard, made him almost as unexpected a sight in a royal coach as Sarah. Sarah's skin, where it showed, was the common mottled green of the larger trolls. She had two sons, one whose skin wore the same assortment of greens, and the other, covered in the assorted shades of brown also found in their people. Sarah wore the traditional garb worn by many troll farmers and mothers. Her dark hair was cropped short, whether for style or convenience, I did not know. She sat beside the Princess, and the contrast was almost comical. Princess Schelli was laughably small in comparison. The many ruffles of her white dress that seemed so stylish while she waved to the people in Oyster Bay only moments ago, seemed to be a detestable nuisance to her, sitting on a wooden bench in the coach. Her skin was fair, completing the image forming in my mind. Beside Sarah, she looked like a doll.

Sarah wore a concerned expression, as if she felt responsible for the attack. Eventually, Lady Sally broke the silence, and pulled a basket of food from behind her seat. Thomas's eyes grew wide, his gaze, along with my own, drawn to the basket

"Perhaps you can all help me dispose of this food. Don't ask me why they packed so much for us."

Soon she was passing all sorts of food around—jellied tarts, fried chicken, roast beef sandwiched between pastry bread, hard cheeses, and fresh fruit. A gentle breeze blew the clouds away, and the afternoon sun warmed our coach. As we rode past scenic pastures, our collective mood relaxed a little.

At first Sarah and Thomas seemed shy in front of the Princess and the Captain. I was surprised to see how differently they acted in the presence of these, my dear friends. I tried to relax the group by joking with them, but if it helped any, I couldn't tell.

I wanted to talk to the Captain about so many things, but knew I needed to wait until we were alone. Thomas wanted to hear the Captain talk of the war, but he soon saw the topic made Sarah uncomfortable. The ride to the palace stretched out as each of us tried unsuccessfully to start a casual conversation. Finally, Thomas settled for asking Sarah questions about troll ceremonies and customs, and the rest of us were content to listen.

Princess Schelli compared everything Sarah said with her troll friend from her early childhood. She made comments like, "Oh, that makes so much sense now," or giggled, "...just like Hrinda used to say it." I wondered how she remembered so much from so long ago, and how many of her memories were accurate. Finally, Sarah asked the Princess for the name of her troll friend's deceased mother.

"You know, I don't remember—I called her Auntie. Sally, do you know Hrinda's mother's name?"

"Yes," she replied, turning to Sarah. "Her name was Issilbhem. Why do you ask?"

Sarah's green eyes widened with excitement. She said something in Chrutghy, the common tongue of the trolls, which to me, sounded like a sneeze.

"*I think I knew her*," she said excitedly. "Your friend, Hrinda—she's at Portsmouth right now."

"Are you sure?" asked the Princess, hope gathering in her eyes.

"Not until now, but yes, I am sure. Hrinda is a common name for girls, but Issilbhem is not common at all."

"But—who is she? Who does she live with?" I asked, doubting such a coincidence had occurred and no one had learned of it yet.

"Well, as I said Hrinda is a common name. But even so, your friend changed her name, probably fearing someone would recognize her as the troll who lived in Engdynlor. She might even have expected her new family wouldn't like to be reminded of this fact. There is a young lady at Portsmouth who goes by the name Sreehabem in our Chrutghy, though she was once called Hrinda. Thomas, you might know her as Linda. When she chose her name in your tongue, she picked a name that sounds like Hrinda."

"Young Linda?" Thomas asked in surprise. "The girl who watches Tom junior?"

"The very same," replied Sarah, smiling. "I knew her mother was named Issilbhem, and she died some years ago, at the hand of humans. She lives with a kind family, and takes good care of her adopted siblings. She is a sweet girl—a young lady, really."

"Oh, I must see her, I really must," the Princess insisted. "Surely my father won't stop me from visiting Portsmouth now." The Princess was so excited, she told us of her plans to visit Portsmouth for most of the remaining ride. She told us her plan to convince her father to let her go, and what she wanted to say when she first met her old friend. The Captain rolled his eyes now and then, but held his tongue.

Finally, as we entered the gates of Thraen Kholl, Sally quieted the Princess enough for others to speak.

One more welcome surprise was waiting for me once I reached the castle Engdynlor—my brother David was hiding in my room. It felt so long since I'd seen him, as if years had passed, though it had only been a few months.

We hugged each other, slugged each other on the shoulder, then laughed and hugged again. He'd been invited to Engdynlor to watch the upcoming trials. It was the first incidence involving violence between trolls and humans since the war trials.

Early on the morning after I reached Thraen Kholl, David and I went for a walk outside the city walls. I steered us toward the babbling brook the Captain had taken me to, not so long ago, though it felt like a distant memory. I knew we'd go to Crystal Caves if we had enough time away from the trials. *Surely we can take a few days to rest before we return*, I thought hopefully.

David asked how I thought my assignment had changed me, and what I felt about leading the delegation.

"I almost feel *old*," I told him. "I never expected to do such grown-up things in all my life, let alone while I'm still a teenager. But I also feel—younger," I said, which surprised both of us. I remembered how I'd felt when I told Sarah her husband had died, and when Eastman first tried to bully me out of the delegation.

"Well, you'll always seem younger to *me*," he joked. It was only by eighteen months, but he'd never let me forget he was the older brother.

"Sometimes I feel like the job is too big for me," I went on. "I feel like I'm only a child. Other times I feel like I could conquer the world to make the delegation succeed—but it never lasts long. Whenever I meet another person who really hates the trolls, I start to think we can never live in peace."

David laughed out loud at me. I punched him in the arm, covering my embarrassment with a sneer.

"That's exactly how I feel," he said, rubbing his arm. "*Exactly.*"

I laughed back at him. We thought we were men. We were still boys, but boys with the responsibilities of ten men. To this day, I think if I'd really understood how much was at stake, I would've been frozen with fear, unable to accomplish a thing. Perhaps I understood well enough, but in my eager naivete I believed I could do no wrong.

The weather had chilled somewhat from the previous day, and noting it, I realized once again what a great convenience I'd taken for granted back home, to have a daily weather forecast. Degrees of temperature and precise minutes of the clock held little value to most of Terreldor's inhabitants. I looked for the entrance to the trail I'd followed from the road only months ago, in vain. We were not far enough from Palace Engdynlor to find that path. The threat of winter was in the air, and I thought I smelled a rainstorm on its way. I scanned the horizon for dark clouds and shivered; perhaps we should head back. David's conversation distracted me.

He told me of the progress he had made with his delegation in the icy heights of Golden Mountain. He asked the merchant families whom had remained loyal to the King throughout the war, if they would consider operating a new trade route with new products. David hoped to find several trade families interested, so no single family would have a monopoly over the new products.

Most cities had a few ice boxes, in either the shops selling expensive meats, or in the homes of the richer families. With the new supply of ice from Golden Mountain, the King's economic advisors predicted most homes would soon have ice boxes. Only the largest merchant families were interested in trading in ice, and even they were wary of the large investment they would need to spend on ice storage buildings in the larger cities of the kingdom. There would be no payoffs on the ice trade until spring came, and the initial investments needed to be made during the winter, when it was best to transport the ice.

To lower the guilds' risk, David sought permission from the King to restrict the trade of *eltsstatch*—or snowsnake— pelts to the merchants investing heavily in the ice trade. The pelts would have immediate payoffs; they were already in high demand in several cities.

This was how a few loyal guilds began to interact with the Lyssiltiks, high on Golden Mountain. The trolls received the tools and lumber they needed to hunt and reap further from their village, and once again raise their own meat. Back at Engdynlor, Sphotch had helped the delegation even before he had intended it. His choice in meals showed which foods his people could eat. As soon as they could afford it, the Lyssiltiks on Golden Mountain had begun to buy imported food for the first time in known history.

I saw changes in my brother since I'd seen him last. Letters were not enough for two brothers used to sharing a room together. I might have imagined it, but it seemed he'd grown an inch or two, to my disappointment. He already stood a full eight inches taller than I; I didn't know if my pride could accept him outgrowing me further. His hair had always been a shade darker than mine, but the lack of sunshine he found himself exposed to high in the frozen mountain peaks had taken effect, and his hair could now be called truly black. His mannerisms seemed less obvious, as if he'd given less concern to the thoughts of those around him. I decided I was glad for the changes in him, vertical advances and all.

Before long, we headed back to Engdynlor. David had only arrived at the palace the previous day, and he was just as tired from his journey as was I. The following morning, we hardly felt more rested. Tired as we were, we were too late to catch a nap after breakfast; Sisheen's trial was soon to begin.

I was called as a witness, as were Sarah and Thomas. No one addressed any jurors during the trials, but I noticed a mysterious host seated behind the King: a double row of chairs filled with men seated in the dark shadow of a thick veil and curtain. *They might be a jury,* I thought to myself. They watched silently during all the proceedings. I wondered if they were the King's advisors, or Honor Knights, or both.

The King seemed always an intimidating presence, but seeing him presiding over the trial somehow inspired me with confidence. I'd only spoken to him a handful of times, but each time was momentous in my memories. He spoke with a deep voice, in deliberate tones every time I'd heard him. I almost expected the seats to rumble when he talked.

The trials were short compared to the war trials. Again, only the facts were allowed in the King's Court, and questions the King asked of the witnesses. The entire proceedings lasted less than half the day. The King ruled Sisheen was guilty of breaking his parole, endangering a child, kidnapping, attempted murder, manslaughter, and willfully obstructing a government delegation. Four of these convictions were each enough to buy him a death sentence, but when the King passed judgment, he declared the kingdom had tolerated enough trolls' deaths at the hands of humans.

The King sentenced Sisheen to a lifetime imprisonment, which I was told is very rare. Sisheen interrupted the King's ruling, pleading for a death sentence. The King continued his ruling, but paused long enough to explain his life was not being spared for his own sake, but to benefit the kingdom he had worked so hard to destroy.

"You owe both our peoples a great debt," the King told him. "In prison you will have an opportunity to begin to repay that debt. I perceive the effects of your deeds may have already begun to change you. If so, you may find atonement in helping bring peace between our peoples."

Within weeks, Sisheen was telling the King's historians and scientists all he could about troll history, culture, anatomy and medicine. Eventually he learned to write in our language, and discovered he enjoyed it. He began to record the oral history and legends that had been passed down by his people for centuries. Some of his writings would become required reading for those in government who would work with trolls.

There were two other trolls I suspected had taken part in

Sisheen's attempt to burn down the barn and kill Tom Junior. Since Sisheen refused to testify, I had no evidence against them. Both were paroled citizens, and I thought of sending them back to Thraen Kholl for obstructing the delegation, but even this option wasn't as easy as I'd hoped. One of them had married and was no longer under the same restrictions as other paroled citizens. They remained a worry to me, and had often spoiled my sleep. Even if I'd known I had only a short while left with the delegation, I doubt it would have brought me peace.

On the next day, Thomas was tried. Sarah, Sisheen, and I were called as witnesses. Again I noticed men sitting in the seats at the unlit back of the room, behind the King.

Thomas's trial was just as short as Sisheen's. The questions were so accusing, I wondered if the King was planning on sending Thomas to jail. As he read his judgment and sentence, the King told Thomas he knew he was a changed man. Even so, he convicted him of several serious crimes: endangering children, arson, inciting a riot, and reckless destruction and endangerment. Thomas hung his head as the King read his decision. I saw fear and shock on his face while the King judged him, and I held my breath, also surprised. After all, Thomas was a guest in the King's house, and even welcomed in Oyster Bay by the King's daughter.

Thankfully, Thomas received a suspended sentence for the crimes of endangering children and inciting a riot. He delayed portions of the punishments he earned from his other crimes, but ruled the rest of the sentence would be enacted immediately.

For arson and reckless destruction and endangerment, he would compensate Norman's family for the monetary hardship he put them in. The King listed the monetary damages, and they included all the things that Thomas had already pledged to supply: a salary for Sarah to live on and use to raise her children, a home for the three of them, and an inheritance for Norman's children when they came of age or Thomas died.

Then he announced the suspended sentence would be enacted at a later time of Sarah's choosing. If Sarah had worried Thomas might break his promises at some time in the distant future, she knew after his sentencing there was no cause left for concern. With Thomas's obvious change of heart, and Sarah's trust in him, the King's sentence was hardly necessary, and I wondered why he added Sarah's clause. In the end, I decided he wanted to give Sarah the opportunity to forgive Thomas every day, each time she was reminded of her husband's death.

1.1 Reviews

The same afternoon, David and I went to my room to plan another trip to Harringtonwood, or at least to Crystal Caves. Before we unrolled a single map, the Captain arrived and delivered an important message.

"The King has called a Delegation Review for each of your delegations."

"What does that mean?" asked David, almost defensively.

"It means he would like to question you on the progress of your delegation, the policies you've implemented, and other actions you've taken as *head delegates*."

"Have we done something wrong?" I asked, hoping to conceal the concern in my voice.

The Captain mimicked my worried expression as he answered, "This is what your Delegation Review will show." Then he relaxed his face into a smile and spoke as if he were letting us in on a joke. "Don't worry. Reviews are a standard policy for any delegation the King sends; it doesn't *necessarily* mean you've done anything wrong." He winked.

"You had me worried," I sighed.

"Still, this is not a light matter. Your responsibilities are great, and you will be asked difficult questions about the decisions you've made."

David interrupted, "So is the King unhappy with our work, or not?"

"If he were, he would have made it clear to you before now. He's not one to let you continue in your mistakes when something so important is concerned. Think of your reviews as a way of helping you become better, or of helping you grow as leaders."

His words didn't bring me any comfort. "When will they be?"

"Now. The King doesn't want a prepared presentation, just your honest answers."

"*Right now?*" I asked. "For both of us?"

"Yes. I was sent to *bring* you, not *warn* you. If you don't hurry, you'll keep the King waiting."

We both followed him to the room we'd left less than an hour ago. I sat near the door, as David was led to sit where Thomas sat, in front of the King's throne-like chair. The room certainly looked as if we were on trial. Again, the mysterious audience sat in the dark end of the room, clothed in shadow. The King came in shortly, unannounced. Everyone stood. The Captain finally took a seat with the others in the back of the room. *They're the Honor Knights,* I thought to myself, certain I was right.

I was pulled from these thoughts as the King welcomed David and explained it was time to review the progress of his delegation. Finally, we sat again and the King began his questions.

The Captain's warning wasn't enough to prepare me for the seriousness of the review—it sounded almost as if David were on trial for Sisheen's crimes. At first I was glad David's review was before mine, but as it progressed, I became anxious. He asked David difficult questions, such as: "Why did it take so long to make initial contact with the Lyssiltiks?" and "Did you put the kingdom at risk by going out to search for them?" and, "How will your policy on the ownership of glacier ice be enforced?" and, "What punishment do you recommend for merchants who try to steal ice from the glacier?"

David sounded uncertain of some of his answers. Some of the King's questions were obviously concerning things David had never thought of before. Before I knew it, the King thanked David for his time and service, and asked him to exchange seats with me. Nervously, I took the lone seat at the front of the room.

I felt a chill run down my spine as I sat. I shivered for a quick second. The King began asking me questions as I struggled to answer them the best I could.

"Why did you remove Robert Eastman from the delegation?" It threw me off—I hadn't thought about Eastman for a long time. Didn't the King already know why I sent him back to Thraen Kholl? What lies did he tell the King about me?

"I—he...um..." I wasn't doing well so far. I swallowed hard before I continued. "He wanted to make the trolls a servant class to the humans."

"What accusations did you make against him?"

I tried to remember exactly what I'd said to Eastman when I sent him away. Suddenly, the words were there, falling right out of my mouth.

"I warned him he was very close to treason, but I didn't accuse him of it. I accused him of trying to overthrow me as head delegate. When I said these things, most of the delegation was there. In my written testimony against him, I accused him of lying about me, based on what the other delegates told me. I accused him of attempting to turn the trolls into a labor class, although it's possible he was ignorant of what his policies would have done, or I and the other delegates evaluated the policies badly."

"Did you do anything to incite Mr. Eastman's anger against you? Did you provoke him?"

"Not unless it was this one thing I said; right after he told me the entire delegation wondered why I was appointed as head, I told him, 'you'd have to second guess the King if you wondered too long about that.'"

I heard a chuckle behind the curtained rows of seats, and I was certain it came from the Captain. The room was so quiet, so *serious*, I fought back a smile and wondered if it were truly possible to recognize a voice from only a chuckle.

"And why did you tell him this?" the King continued.

I hesitated, contemplating making an excuse. I'm glad I didn't contemplate it long. "I was angry and hurt, and I wanted to hurt him back." The King didn't even pause before his next question.

"What policies did you set as head of my delegation?"

"I added a non-voting member to the Portsmouth City Council. I made a policy preventing the county council from meeting without a member of the delegation and trolls present. Other than these, I made suggestions and additions to the delegate's instructions, and I organized events where trolls and humans could learn about each other, but none of those were policies. I guess I set only two policies…"

Why didn't I set more policies? I wondered to myself. I thought of the important policies David made to ensure profitable trade for the trolls, saving many of them from starvation.

"Was there anything you could have done to prevent Norman's death?"

"Yes, sire." I thought I heard a surprised gasp from David, still sitting near the door. My answer even surprised *me*. But I'd already said it, and immediately I knew it was true. Under a great weight, I went on. "When Sisheen tried to start a riot after Norman's house was burned, I instructed soldiers to watch over Sisheen. I didn't realize until later it was also *Sisheen's house* which had been burned. I should have made sure the soldiers found him."

The King gave me a bothered look and waved his hand dismissively. "Irrelevant. The soldiers knew Sisheen was staying with his cousin as well as you did. Anything else?"

My heart rose as I heard the King's response. Maybe there *was* nothing I could have done. Could I have known to order soldiers to follow Norman, just in case Norman found his cousin first? No—there was no reason to think it would have helped prevent the fire at the barn. Could I have ordered a search for Thomas Junior after Norman's home was burned? My heart sank again. Yes, either of these might have prevented Sisheen from trying to kill Tom Jr.

"But Sire, I didn't even order a new search for Tom Junior." I sounded as if I were pleading. Before I went on, I tried my best to lower my voice. "If he'd been found by the soldiers before Sisheen reached him, Norman would still be alive." The King's face grew stern.

"Mark," he replied, gravely, "the men and woman who lived in Portsmouth County their entire lives hadn't found him yet, and there were already soldiers helping in the search. You are not at fault." He paused a bit, as if to let his point sink in, then continued, "Remember, this is a Delegation Review, not a trial."

The King asked me many other questions. Some of them showed me things I should have done differently as head delegate. The King was a wise and frightening interrogator.

When I'd answered the last question, I felt certain I'd be punished somehow for my many oversights and mistakes. I was sure I'd be replaced as head delegate.

After we stood and the King left the room, the Captain returned from his place in the curtained rows of chairs, and walked us to my room. When we got there David and I collapsed onto the edge of my bed.

"You handled yourselves very well," the Captain said. "A review by the King is never easy. He needs to collect all the facts, even the ones no one is comfortable sharing."

"What are you *talking* about?" I moaned. "It was *a disaster*. I had no idea I did so many things *wrong*."

"Did the King *say* you did something wrong?" the Captain replied.

David chimed in. "Well, he didn't *say* it…but his questions didn't leave much room for doubt. He brought up so many things I'd never even *thought* about—things I *should* have thought of."

The Captain laughed at us, mockingly. "Did you think you're as wise as the King—and can see the future?"

"Of course not," we exclaimed. "What does *that* have to do with it?" I added.

"Well, why do you expect you should have thought of everything the King did—especially when he's had weeks and months to review your actions, with full knowledge of their results?"

I wasn't sure I understood what he was saying, and I told him so.

"The King has known of your actions from your reports to him, and from those of your fellow delegates. He's had plenty of time to reflect on them, and their outcomes. *And*, as I implied, he's wiser than the two of you. He's wiser than me, too, for what it matters."

"But the things he brought up," I said, "they would have been ever so helpful if only I'd thought of them at Portsmouth."

"And what did I tell you the purpose of the Review was?"

I tried to remember exactly what he'd said when he came to fetch us. David answered first.

"You said we should think of it as a way to help us do our assignments better."

"That's right," replied the Captain. "And as a way to grow into better leaders. You're expected to *learn* from the King's questions. You will be given notes of what you were asked, and of your answers, too."

"So we're not in trouble?" I asked.

"No, not at all. In fact, I'd say the King is very pleased with the both of you. If he thought you were so unteachable you couldn't grow from his feedback, this would not be so."

The Captain stood and told us we'd need to get ready for a special dinner. The King had called for a banquet in celebration of a new beginning with the trolls. At first, I thought there wasn't much yet we could celebrate—but from the King's view, this was a very significant time. If his citizens could accept it, the kingdom would enter a new era—a relationship with the trolls they had never seen before. I knew the Captain was very hopeful the New Rule would soon come as part of the kingdom's changes.

We had arrived at a very important time, when the kingdom was at the brink of great renewal or great ruin—and if I had to be honest, ruin seemed the more likely of the pair.

At the time I didn't fully understood its importance, or my role in it. Sometime during the Delegation Review, or while I was getting ready for the banquet, understanding found me. Our names might become part of their history—people might talk of us for centuries to come.

That night I felt nervous on the way to the banquet. David was quieter than normal, and I asked him why. His thoughts were the same. We walked into the banquet when a page told us it was time. We were announced as we entered the banquet hall, and the entire crowd stood and cheered. We were ushered to seats at the King's table at the front of the hall, and stood there waiting for the King. Sarah and Sphotch were announced, and they stood near us. Sphotch half-leaned into his *chair*, a solid block of glacial ice with a narrow ledge for a seat. When he later sat, he pressed his upper body and head into the high back of his icy chair.

I was glad I wasn't in David's place, sitting next to Sphotch the entire meal. I later learned Sphotch had bargained for more comfortable living conditions before he agreed to attend the banquet and act politely. He was still cooperating with the King...*mostly*, and there were no other Lyssiltiks available to represent their people at the banquet. Perhaps deep into winter, the King might receive true ambassadors from the trolls on Golden Mountain.

Finally, the King and Queen entered and were announced, but we remained standing. The King thanked us for attending, and for celebrating with him the re-birth of the kingdom. If I hadn't already realized the significance of these times, the King's speech spelled it out clearly. He spoke only for a few minutes, but made his concerns and hopes, and their importance to the kingdom, known to all. Those who wanted to follow the King by sharing his values had much to take in from his speech. The King ended by telling us how we could help their reborn nation to grow.

"When you meet those who still bare hate for our newest citizens, remind them our new friends at Portsmouth and on Golden Mountain are not our enemies. They never were. Our enemies are those trolls and humans who wanted our peoples to remain enemies forever. The traitors who followed the...*duke*," he said reluctantly, "and the trolls who joined him—*they* are our enemies. Our goal is to defeat them—in their ideology, now that the most heinous of them have been defeated in war. We want to bring about their worst fear: a kingdom where humans and trolls live peaceably together as equals. Maybe this will be enough to motivate them, until the love of that which is right and just replaces their hatred. I pray it shall be."

He ended by thanking the soldiers and delegates who were working with the trolls, and honoring David and I as his delegate heads. The banquet was not in our honor, and I was relieved to see far fewer eyes cast my way than during the previous banquet I'd attended.

The crowd clapped and cheered. Finally, the entire room sat and the feast began. Even though Eb cooked all my delegation's meals, they were plain compared to what was served at this banquet. I'd forgotten the difference until the banquet started. David had become accustomed to even poorer meals; his delegation was fed by an army chef.

The food was delicious and I ate too much of it. I hoped the other banqueters were more interested in watching the King, or Sarah and Sphotch, than watching me. When the entertainment began, I was already feeling sleepy. *Why did I do this again?* I thought to myself, remembering the last banquet.

The entertainment was a long line of musicians who played a sad sonata for us, using very unusual instruments. Each musician had two large bells, and two crystal glasses set before them. Their hands moved swiftly, ringing their bells, and rubbing the wet rims of their glasses to make them sing. It was the most curious concert I'd ever heard, but it was also one of the most beautiful. I ordered two cups of coffee in attempt to stay alert. They almost helped.

By the time the banquet was over and the banqueters were walking by our table in a long line, the coffee took its effect, and I felt almost shaky. David introduced me to several of the new merchants who had been trading eltsstatch, or snowsnake furs. I was surprised to see Eastman and his wife in the line of banqueters. I grew nervous as he approached us. As he shook my hand, I could see a change in his face. The anger was gone, and a quiet sadness had replaced it. He silently mouthed the words *I'm sorry*, then quickly stepped past me, following the line of banqueters.

David must have noticed my confused expression. Between handshakes he whispered, "Who was *that*?" I shook my head slightly to let him know any explanation I would give him would have to wait.

The line seemed to move faster than I remembered from the other two banquets we'd attended. The King and Queen left through the same doors they'd entered a few hours before. As the rest of his table began to leave, the Captain told David and me to follow him. To our surprise, he led us to the same side-room where the King first assigned us as delegate heads a few long months ago. The Captain wouldn't say why he led us there, though of course we asked him on the way.

Upon entering the room, we were shocked to find a small crowd of men seated, facing us. There were two stools before us, and the Captain motioned for us to sit on them. He continued past us, and took a seat next to the King, who I'd just noticed in the front row of seats.

I glanced over the men before us, but did not recognize many of them. A few in the front row were very old. David whispered a half-formed word of amazement, and I strained to see what had surprised him. I knew I'd found it when I saw his mentor, Lieutenant James Underhill in the group.

At first I wondered if we were going to be questioned further on our delegations. Then I thought we would receive a formal judgment from the King—some type of evaluation of how we'd performed. Finally I remembered the shadowed men who sat in the trials and reviews, and I knew why we'd been brought before these men. They were surely the *Honor Knights.*

I sat frozen, wondering if David had realized what I had. The King rose, as did the other men. David and I stood also, knowing it was something expected of anyone who saw the King. I *didn't* expect him to tell us to be seated while he remained standing.

"As you might have guessed, Mark and David, we are the Honor Knights." Though I already knew this, I couldn't help but to let out a little gasp as he said it. The King went on.

"As you have surely deduced, we are revealing our membership to you because your apprenticeships have come to an end. You have both learned what your mentors meant to teach you, and you have demonstrated your commitment to our kingdom. More than this, you have proved to be capable of command and humility, of honor and maturity, of strength and restraint. You are eager to live by the Three Tables which guide our LifeGrowth." David stole a sidelong glance at me, wearing a shocked smile. Only then did I remember he didn't know I was an apprentice. I gave a knowing smile back to him. The King paused for a second, also smiling. Did he know what we were thinking? It wasn't the first time I'd wondered.

The King continued his speech. "You will not be asked to swear any oaths tonight; you've already sworn them when you became apprentices. If we didn't trust you to honor those oaths, you wouldn't be here. There is no elaborate ceremony tonight, no feast in your honor. As you know, there is no public honor bestowed on you by our order; it is hidden even as you serve. But tonight you are welcomed; you are introduced to the full knighthood. We celebrate your passing into our fellowship, and we congratulate you on your service to our shared goal of the New Rule. For even if we don't live to see it fully introduced by a kingdom reborn, we live in the New Rule every day. Our actions are defined by it; our lives are lived out as its citizens. With each one we touch, with every person we teach, the New Rule kingdom expands a little, and it grows closer to becoming the material kingdom around us. We share this joy and this labor with you, our newest brothers."

The Captain stood and instructed us to kneel. When we did, the King drew his sword and placed it on our shoulders. He called us his brothers and his sons. He told us to stand, then shook our hands. The other knights stood and gathered around us. The Captain crushed me with a great bear hug, as David's mentor whisked him off to introduce him to someone. The Captain introduced me to his own mentor, who had trained him so long ago. The old man asked to see the knife I had taken from the Captain, who had so long ago taken it from him. Before he gave it back to me, he ran his thumb carefully down the edges of the small blade, lingering over the nicks and dents from one of the Captain's more recent lessons.

It was a long evening, though it often seems fresh in my memory. It was one of my proudest moments, and one my mind has revisited in detail many times since.

1.2 New Knights

By the time we walked back to our rooms, I was ready to collapse. I fell asleep in my clothes, too exhausted to change. The next day David and I woke early, considering the late hours we'd kept the night before. David's first words were, "I never suspected you were an apprentice *too*." I only smiled. "I should've known the Captain would be an Honor Knight," he went on. "After all, he was probably the most important person in the kingdom during the war."

When I remained silent he asked if I ever wondered if he was an apprentice.

"I suspected it." But he read my eyes too well.

"When did you know for *sure*?" I felt lighter as I realized there was no longer a reason to keep it secret.

"I found out when we thought you and the Lieutenant were dead. The Captain got permission from the King to tell me. He hoped it would bring me comfort."

"*All that time?*" He looked hurt for a moment, then smiled. "You're a better actor than I thought." He slugged my shoulder, still smiling wide.

"How did you miss it, when we both were given delegations to lead?" I chuckled. "You must've known your assignment as head delegate was given to you because you were an apprentice. It's not like the King has a hundred delegations all around the kingdom right now."

"What did the delegations have to do with our apprenticeships?" David asked.

"Didn't you know? We needed to show we could lead men before we could become knights. It was our last test—as apprentices, anyway. Now that the delegations are off to a good start, I guess it was enough to convince the knights we were capable. During our reviews, don't you think the men sitting in the back were Honor Knights, judging our actions?"

"Yeah…I guess so. I had to go first, you know. I didn't have as much time to sit back and contemplate who all the people in the room were."

"All right," I replied, "I'll give you that one. But how didn't you know our delegation assignments were related to our apprenticeships? Unless—*oh*. They knew if they told you, you would have guessed I was an apprentice. *They thought of everything.*"

We talked on for hours in David's room—about our apprenticeships, our mentors, and about finally being knights. At that point we were ready to stay in the kingdom forever.

We both assumed the King was wrong about us going back to our own world. After all, the time we'd spent on our delegations had nearly doubled our stay already, and the King had predicted our visit was half over before we joined them. Sometimes I wonder how long our desire to stay would have lasted.

Later that morning, David's mentor came to visit us. He explained we would attend a special debriefing later that day.

"There are some very practical things you need to learn as new knights. There are common things, such as who might deliver instructions to you, to whom you can give your reports, and how you can request an audience with the King. Then there are some…special arrangements to be made for the two of you…" his voice trailed off while he looked like he was grasping for words. "You are…*unique* knights." My ears tingled each time he called us knights. He was the first person to do so after the King. I pulled myself from my daydreams when I realized the Lieutenant was still talking.

"Because you are from another place, and also because specific actions on your parts were predicted in some of our historical documents—"

"You mean the prophecies?" I interrupted. I'd nearly forgotten them. Surely the things we'd done as delegation heads would prove or disprove we were the ones the old documents spoke of.

"Oh—so you've heard of them," said the Lieutenant, looking at me. "I wasn't sure."

"Well," David asked, "did we fulfill their predictions, or not?"

"You'll have to wait until the briefing to find out—though it's not because you can't know. I simply don't want to cloud your understanding of what the King has to say to you later today."

"The King is going to be there?" we both asked in unison.

"Yes." He told us little else, and left by congratulating us again on our knighthood.

When a page came to fetch us after lunch, I was already busy planning what things I would do when I returned to Portsmouth.

It was a strange time. My memories of home, my parents and younger brother, were never far from my thoughts. My emotions rocked between homesickness, and a terrible burden to see our work with the trolls finished. Some days I worried we'd never find our way home, while others, I worried we'd be sent home before we were finished.

On this day, with my new membership in the knighthood had steeled my resolve to stay the course. I wanted to get back to work.

While we followed the page, I set aside my thoughts of Portsmouth. My mind raced, wondering what the King would tell us. The page led us completely around the castle, nearly returning to where we'd started, but on another floor. At one point we passed through a set of heavy doors, locked and guarded. There were other doors, unlocked, which I noticed *could* have been barred and locked, but were not. Finally, a pair of guards let us through one last doorway, and we were in the King's royal suite. We were led to a small room by a guard who told us it was *the King's private meeting chamber.* We crowded our way in, passing the Captain and David's mentor, and were seated in front of the King. The King actually stood to shake our hands, then patted our backs and congratulated us once again. He returned to his seat and let the Captain begin to tell us some of the basic information Lt. Underhill had mentioned earlier.

We learned, as knights, we could request a private audience with the King at any time, should we feel it necessary. He told us how we could do so, and some other minor details about the knights' communications. We were told how we would receive assignments, both publicly and privately, and even how we would eventually send coded messages to the King and other knights.

When the Captain was finished, the King asked if we had any questions. Too excited to wait, I asked, "What about the prophecy? Did we do the things it predicted?"

"You certainly did," replied the King with a wary smile, "more accurately than even *I* had expected." When he said no more, I went on.

"Which things? Can we read the prophecy pages now?"

"Ah…I don't think that would be a good idea." I hoped he was joking.

"What—why not?" David asked, disappointment plain in his voice. "I thought all knights could read them."

"You have access to them," said the King. "In fact, the Captain tells me you've already discovered the room in which they are kept." I thought back to the secret door we found in the levels beneath the palace. I remembered a stack of large papers on a shelf and wondered if we had really been so close. But the King was speaking again. "I don't think it would benefit you. You see, your recent actions fit the prophecy pages so well, there are few left who doubt the prophecies predicted your coming to our kingdom, and the actions you've done *and will do* here. If you read them now, you will be filled with doubt concerning their age. It's enough for you to know they are written about you."

"*What?*" I asked incredulously, "I couldn't read them before, because I might not do what they predicted, and I can't read them now because I actually *did* what they predicted?" The Captain glared at me. *Did you forget who you're talking to*, his eyes seemed to say. "I mean…is that right, Sire?" I added, trying to cover my short-tempered outburst.

"No," he replied with a cautious look. "As I said, you *do* have access to them. But I wanted you to know I don't think it would be helpful to you; I think it would cloud your mind with doubt. You must decide for yourself whether you read them or not."

That left me silent. David asked, "What about battle skills, the stealth training, and things like that? I thought we'd learn more…*physical* skills before we were made knights."

The Captain answered him, "Normally you would be correct, but each knight's skills are different, and yours are as unique as your early memberships."

"Do you mean our ages?" David asked.

"Yes. Never before has our order accepted apprentices so young as you two. However, your accomplishments are also uncommon. Your memberships were fully earned."

"But why did we have less battle training than the other knights?" I asked. I was worried he might tell us we weren't really full knights yet. Before speaking, the Captain first looked at the King, who simply nodded.

"The King felt you two are unique in your knighthood. He believes you will return to your own world where the skills of battle and stealth will not play an important role. Other skills of our order will be vastly more important to you." When we both looked at him with curiosity, he elaborated.

"Philosophy, negotiating, face-reading and lip reading, leadership, and service—you will be instructed in these and more as you work on your next assignments. You see, for the King, the Knighting Ceremony was a bittersweet event. He believes you'll be returning in a relatively short time."

The King added, "If I'm wrong, there will be plenty of time for battle training. But if I'm right, you don't have enough time left before you leave us."

I could hardly bear to hear him talk of us going home. It teased my hopes, but also disappointed my ambition to becoming a respected member in his service—like the Captain had become.

"Sire," I asked, "how are you sure we'll return soon, when the Captain—and maybe others—aren't so sure?"

"You mean others like yourself?" asked the King with a knowing look. I felt embarrassed as he went on. "The Captain is free to interpret the prophecies as his reasoning and experiences lead him, of course—he isn't obligated to see them as I do. He lacks a...*certainty* I have about them." If this was meant to satisfy my curiosity, it failed miserably.

"How do you explain your certainty," I asked, adding a meek, "sire?" in attempt to sound less demanding.

The King answered my question with another, an option I didn't have when speaking with the King.

"How can you explain anything you truly believe in?"

His reply didn't make sense to me for a moment. I thought about things I believed in that were obvious to everyone, but these didn't fit. *He must mean some other kind of belief, something others doubt.*

David piped in while I was still mulling over these thoughts. "So if we don't have time to learn more sword fighting, were our delegation assignments somehow more important?"

"Infinitely more," replied the King. "You've learned skills and accomplished tasks which will outlast any battles in which you might have fought." I wondered if he'd meant to infer we wouldn't be doing any more battling. If it was so, it was fine with me.

"And that brings us," added the Captain, "to your first assignments as knights."

"Yes. I suppose it does," said the King. "You've become knights only hours ago, and already it's time for your first assignment. A knight's first assignment is always given right away, partially to drive home this point: an Honor Knight never stops growing. Your new assignments will teach you this lesson, and another. You'll learn what it feels like to pass your positions on to others, a task we must always be ready to do. You will return to your delegations in Portsmouth and Friendship Hall to choose and train your replacements. If you choose a head from outside your current delegation, you'll need to recruit him before leaving Thraen Kholl."

He must have seen our eyes widen. "Yes, I know, this was

not your expectation. But training someone to take your place and relinquishing your authority is our highest aspiration, as we look forever forward to the day of the New Rule. This is what the New Rule means to us—to pass our positions on to others."

His words shocked me, but not as much as I would soon shock him. And yet, I felt strongly what I was about to say was right.

"Sire? Can we appoint *anyone* to replace us? Anyone at all?"

"You can. But your actions as head delegate are open to my review, and I can undo them if I feel I must. Why, do you already have someone in mind?"

"Yes," I replied. "But I'm afraid my choice will be unacceptable to you."

"You cannot choose your own mentors," the King said to both of us. "I have other assignments for them."

"It's not my mentor I choose, Sire," I replied.

"Who, then? Why do you think I won't approve of him?"

"It's your daughter, King. *She* should lead us into an era of peace with the trolls." His eyes seemed to grow without moving, as if my eyes were playing a trick on me. He remained motionless. "Who could be a better example," I went on, "of treating trolls as equals? Who loves trolls more than the Princess?"

"*Mark!*" Finally the Captain found his voice. "I hope you don't find this a time for *jokes*."

"No sir, *I do not*," I said with more conviction than I knew I had. I blushed hot red, but would not be deterred. "No one is as motivated as she is. Her heart is the very heart you want your kingdom to have, Sire."

"But she's *a child*," the King replied. He sounded as if he were talking to himself, even trying to convince himself.

"Are you forgetting her safety?" added the Captain. "You haven't forgotten your reception parade in Oyster Bay, I hope."

I had no answer to the Captain's objection, so I responded to the King instead.

"Weren't there doubters who said we are children?" I asked, gesturing toward David and myself. I looked to David for moral support, but he looked away, a smirk hiding just below the surface of his expression. Apparently my choice wasn't as obvious to him.

"We'll talk of this later," replied the King with a faraway look. For a moment, there was an awkward silence no one seemed willing to break. Finally, the King spoke again. He handed us each a rolled sheet of heavy parchment, saying, "Here are your Reviews. You will have questions about them, but study these reviews for a while before you ask. For some of your questions you know the answers already—though you may not yet know it. We'll meet again in two days' time."

He had a faraway sound, as if he were distracted by many thoughts. Maybe he was arguing with himself over sending Schelli to Portsmouth. Or *maybe* he already regretted trusting me to choose my replacement.

My replacement. No sooner did the Captain lead us from the room, did I realize I couldn't imagine leaving the delegation. How could I leave the job unfinished?

There was no true peace in Portsmouth, not while the military was present, enforcing it. Ever since the incident with Norman and Tom Junior, I had nightmares of the townies leading a revolt, complete with torches and pitchforks, to destroy the troll camp, and run them out of town. They frightened me most, because I knew they were possible, even likely.

What would happen if my fear became true? Would the

trolls, realizing this was their last chance to survive, fight back? Would there be a short-lived war, wiping their people out forever?

Giving it away...The King's words reminded me of something on one of the Tables. I pulled out the pocket version I'd made, and found what I was looking for on the Table of Maturity. The mature characteristic *Leader* was followed by these words:

Teaches and allows room to grow, to choose right. Leads to loyal relationships. Gives away authority when possible, trains others to take place. Gardener leader.

The childish characteristic *Authoritarian* was listed near it:

Controls others through fear, leads to resentment and disloyalty. Holds onto control. Watchmaker leader.

And so I learned it was an unhealthy urge to hold onto my position forever. As the Captain and the King had told us, knights don't stop learning when they become knights, they continue on the path of LifeGrowth all their days. My first assignment as a knight would teach me to give my leadership position away. I'd once thought only the generation of knights who led in the New Rule needed to give their positions away, but I knew the King meant to teach us it was a characteristic valued by all the knights. It was part of establishing the New Rule in our own lives *now*, not merely a fixed point in the distant future.

At first, I hadn't understood what the King meant about having the answers to our questions, but soon I realized I'd already answered one. It felt odd to have knowledge I didn't know I had. I wondered if it could really happen again.

The Captain gave me a strange look when he left us, but did not speak. David and I walked back to our rooms. I followed David into his room, instead of going to my own.

"How do you think we'll be able to train others to take over for us?" I asked him immediately. He seemed frustrated by my question.

"I was just thinking of that," he eventually replied. "I thought I'd try to make a list of the things I still need to do, and train someone until they have the same list."

"You mean, you'd tell them the things you have left to do, then just...hand it over?" That didn't sound like training a replacement to me. It was more like leading the delegation *through* someone else.

"No, I *won't* tell them what I plan to do next. I'll train them until they're able to figure it out on their own. That way, when they can guess what my next steps are, I'll know they're done learning from me."

"That's a strange way of looking at it," I said. "I like it. But they won't plan things *exactly* the same way as you would, even when they are fully trained, right?"

"Yeah," replied David, "I was thinking that. I guess the King doesn't look for us to do things exactly as he would either. What's *close enough*, though?"

"Maybe we'll have a better idea after reading the King's reviews."

David looked down at his hand, still holding his review rolled in a cylinder. We opened ours at the same time, and began reading them to ourselves.

I was surprised at the first comment I read...and the second, then the third. I felt *naked*, reading the King's comments on what I'd worked so hard to accomplish. It was as if he'd read my mind, as if he knew my every fear and insecurity. Every time I'd doubted myself, every time I'd felt inadequate as the delegate head, the King seemed to know about it, and how it affected my actions—and several times, how it *didn't*. It was an uncomfortable feeling, worse than embarrassment or shame—it was unnerving.

"I...uh...think I'll read mine alone in my room," I said, breaking the silence. David turned away from me, hiding his face.

"Yeah," was all he said in reply. I took a guilty consolation in knowing his review seemed to affect him in the same way. In the privacy of my room, I wondered how I could have done so badly as head delegate and not known it. Then I remembered what the Captain had told me about shame and guilt. Both emotions were results of *pride*; *conviction* was their healthy counterpart. These were listed in all three of the knights' tables, so it was a lesson I knew I should make all effort to learn. I read on.

It was painful to read. Once I told myself I wasn't a perfect delegate, and I needed to know which areas to improve, it was only slightly easier. I was exhausted by the time I'd reached the end of the review, though it wasn't long. Buried in what I saw as my list of shortcomings, I read encouraging things too. In fact, the King had pointed out many good things I'd done.

The summary of the review read as if he was extremely pleased with my efforts—in fact, it ended with a heartfelt congratulations and short note of thanks, handwritten and signed by the King. How could he be pleased with what I'd done, when there were so many negative points he'd listed? The first part of the review read like I hadn't done anything right—or did it? Maybe I was still too prideful to read it accurately. I remembered what Lady Sally had once told me, *"The King corrects those who he merits worthy. He disciplines those who he trusts to work with him. How else can we be a part of what he's trying to accomplish in the kingdom?"*

I was still struggling over these points, hours later. It had been a long day, and I found I was hungry. I waited a while to give David plenty of time to read his review, then asked if he was ready for dinner.

We ate in the kitchen, as we had done many times with Eb. After dinner, the Princess came into the kitchen looking for us.

"I hoped I'd find you here," she exclaimed. Immediately I remembered what I'd said to the King about her. Would the King have told her what I'd said? She gave no clues of having heard of it. She invited us to visit with Sally and her.

In her quarters, Sally was setting a dessert table for the four of us. "Welcome! Come and eat. I hoped to cheer you with some tasty desserts."

"Cheer us?" I asked.

"Why?" David added.

"Didn't you receive Delegation Reviews from the King today?" she asked, smiling.

David and I looked at each other, hurt. "Did you hear what was in them?" I asked.

"No, *never*," she replied in a more serious tone. "*No one* else gets to see them, as far as I know." She looked at us and saw our discomfort. "I heard, in general terms only, the King was very pleased with both your delegations." She found no relief in our expressions, if she sought after it. "You don't understand...*any* review the King gives, even a *shining* review, is difficult to receive. I've had my own reviews, on my many assignments in the Princess's instruction and care. The King sees things so clearly, so expertly, he finds things we rather he didn't. Even so, they *are* helpful. Wait a day or two—you'll see." She sighed heavily. "I know from experience receiving your first Review from the King is challenging—even painful."

I felt better at hearing this. It was nice to spend the evening with them. They were good friends, and I'd forgotten how much I missed them both. I tried not to think about my suggestion to the King about Schelli going to Portsmouth. I ate more sweet, rich foods than anyone should eat in a month.

David and I returned to our rooms, but I didn't want to sleep yet. We talked for hours. I questioned him on everything I could think of concerning the ice trolls, and their differences from the green and brown trolls I worked with.

David explained how the King instructed a doctor and a team of doctors to study Sphotch as soon as he began to cooperate. While Sphotch first suspected the King was looking for physical weaknesses to wage war against his people, his real intention was to offer them medicines. We already knew Sphotch's skin was not warm to the touch. The scientists were astonished to find Lyssiltiks are not warm-blooded creatures. While it sounded logical to me, it astounded the King's scientists. They never expected such a large being, let alone a fellow apparent primate, might be cold-blooded.

Despite their similar appearances, the King's scientists considered them to be no closer to the other trolls, biologically speaking, than to humans. Their method for digestion and even survival remained a mystery. Eventually by studying their diet, they found the pine needles the ice trolls ate contained a substance that wouldn't easily freeze, even at very low temperatures: a kind of natural antifreeze. The same substance was found in the blood of the ice trolls and snowsnakes. When they tested Sphotch's blood later, they found the substance was nearly gone. The traders who were contracted to supply the mountain delegation soon began to bring fresh pine needles to Sphotch, in case it was harmful for him to go without them. In time, the chemical's level in

Sphotch's blood rose much higher than when they'd first drawn his blood.

It was well known to the mountain delegates by then, but when David first told me the ice trolls never drank, I was shocked. I should have guessed it; all the water they'd ever seen was frozen. Instead of drinking, they ate snow. In fact, they used clean snow to do any washing they needed. We'd known Sphotch began drinking water as soon as he was taken from the snowline, but he had never shared with us how unpleasant he found it.

In the spring, the new ice merchants would begin selling their dense glacial ice. They were laying up stores of it in the icehouses they'd built in the larger cities around the kingdom. From these stores, they could deliver ice to any city or town but Portsmouth. The King had made provisions to build a road from the southern end of the Plains Road all the way to Portsmouth, but it would take years to complete. In the meanwhile, I hoped the road would supply some of the Portsmouth trolls with labor jobs, should too many arrive at Portsmouth. David had hoped the ice might be shipped to Portsmouth from Oyster Bay, but its great weight meant shipping costs were too high to turn a profit.

I went to sleep exhausted and glad for the welcome distraction David had given me, from my worries with the delegation.

1.3 To Convince a King

A few days later, I knew both Lady Sally and the King were right. David and I were given an opportunity to ask the King questions about our reviews. By the time my appointment came, I'd already answered many of my own questions. As Lady Sally also predicted, both David and I felt better about our reviews. To this day, I cringe a little inwardly, when I think back to the King's insights into my most private thoughts and fears. After all these years, I still feel no pressure to share them.

In the remaining days before we left for our delegations, I was given the chance to convince the King his daughter was the best person for my replacement. Before we met, I was intimidated, but before we'd finished, I was shocked by my determination and conviction. I found myself speaking to him in a manner I never dreamed I could—respectful, but contrary at the very least.

"Don't you realize how taxing this assignment has been for you?" the King asked at one point. "It will be even more so for the Princess."

"I disagree, Sire. She's easily as smart as I am."

"Intellect has little to do with it—she's not *old* enough."

"She's nearly as old as I am. Did you agree when others said *I* wasn't old enough?"

"I'd be lying if I told you I was comfortable sending you," said the King. "I knew it was right, but I lost sleep over it. It will be harder for the Princess than it was for you."

"Are you sure? In your review, you told me the riskiest part of the delegation is over. The people at Portsmouth are on the right track."

"Aside from a child, appointing a *female* as head delegate is—*unprecedented*," the King finally blurted.

"Does it make her less capable?" I asked, taken back.

"It makes the job harder. If she were equally capable at an equal task, it would not be so. But if she is equally capable and her task is made more difficult, then she is less likely to succeed."

"And what makes the task more difficult, Sire?"

"The men of the delegation will not welcome a female leader, royalty or not."

"They will be following their King, not his daughter." I remembered the revelation I had before I truly believed the delegation might follow me. "She will be following you alongside them."

"I can only lead where my people will follow. I don't know if they're ready to be led to this place you've dreamt of. I'm not sure *I'm* ready," said the King.

"Aren't you?"

The King sighed heavily.

"She's my *daughter*, Mark. I don't want to see her go through the things you went through—it was painful enough to watch *you* go through them."

That gave me pause for thought. Did I really believe she could do it?

"But she loves the trolls so much, Sire, and your people

love your daughter. How can they fail to follow her example?"

"*Many* will fail. They will think her naive. They will call her too innocent to understand how barbaric the trolls are. And as much as the kingdom loves you, it didn't help much in Portsmouth."

"The people *love me*? They love their Princess!"

"You might be surprised. For much of the kingdom, you and your brother are boys of legends. Rumors have spread—you're more famous than you imagine. Enough so, I'm very glad you're loyal to me." It was the second time his words shocked me.

"Why?" I asked. "What does my loyalty have to do with it?"

"If not for your loyalty, someone might have stolen you away after the war, and tried to install you as king."

"No one would do this to you—it's *impossible!*" I answered, dumbfounded.

"You missed my point; you're loved enough by the people that someone could have *tried*." I failed to see the compliment.

"But—Schelli's such a good example for the people, and so many people would follow her example if only they could see her—*I know this is true*, Sire." I wasn't putting my thoughts into words very well.

"Is that all?" chuckled the King. I looked up at him, surprised at his sudden levity, so soon after such a heavy mood. "You feel she has to be seen by the people more, and act as an example to a greater number of them?"

"Yes. You should have seen her at the reception parade at Oyster Bay. The people beamed to see her sitting next to Sarah. It was a great idea you had."

"It wasn't my idea—it was my daughter's; she alone

convinced me to let her be a part of the welcoming ceremony. I was afraid it was too dangerous for her, too much possibility of riot. But let's back up a moment. You said you are convinced she should become a more visible example. Is that why you'd like to choose her to replace you?"

"Of course," I replied. "What's so curious about that?"

"Don't you see? She doesn't need to lead the delegation to be a more visible example. She only needs to *be more visible*. She could visit both delegations. She could even visit the larger cities, acting as a goodwill ambassador for trade with the trolls. She could—". The King stopped as he saw my expression change from worry into a wide grin. "You have something to add, perhaps?"

"I just wasn't thinking clearly enough. This is what I had in mind all this time. I thought she could do those things as the head of the delegation. Those aren't really tasks the head delegate would do, are they?"

"No, they're not," replied the King in a relieved voice.

An unpleasant thought returned to my mind.

"What about the assassination attempt in Oyster Bay? Is it safe for the Princess to travel?"

"Not yet," he replied. "She won't be able to travel until our investigation is complete, and the other conspirators arrested. But tell me, does this mean you've changed your mind, for your choice of your replacement?"

"Yes it does. I'd like to name the Princess, the delegation's *Ambassador of Goodwill Relations*."

"Well, then you'd better get to thinking about your replacement as head delegate—*and* how you'll transition your responsibilities to the new head. You'll also need to define the roles for an *Ambassador of Goodwill Relations*. While you do, don't forget her *parents* will need to approve any of her responsibilities beforehand."

We talked a little further, and I left his chamber. Later, I learned the King had taken so long to talk with me not to *argue* with me, but to learn why I disagreed with him on such an important topic. He knew if he forced me to pick someone else, he might kill the passion driving me. "If you can by any means afford it," he once told me, "never kill the passion of those you lead. They'll never accomplish as much doing it *your way* as they will with their own passion to guide them."

I took the King's suggestion seriously. I thought long and hard about the person who should replace me as head delegate. No matter how much thought I gave it, my mind kept returning to the Chaplain, Mr. Davis. In the end, I decided he was the right choice. I wrote to him and asked if he would accept. In his reply later the same day, written in the fine print of a pigeon's scroll, he refused. I began to draw up my plans for handing the position over to him anyway, certain he would change his mind—which he did, before I could even return.

1.4 Back to Port

Before I left Engdynlor, I was resolved to find out more about the prophecy pages. My brother, always ready to disagree, argued it was a test for us. Since the King told us we were *allowed* to read the pages, but didn't *want* us to, David argued, it was the same as if he'd forbidden us. He argued that our oaths prohibited us from doing anything we knew the King didn't want us to do. I reasoned the King merely thought it wouldn't benefit us. In the end I returned alone to the hidden room in the deepest of Engdynlor's halls. I discovered the King was right. I was immediately surprised, then doubtful, and finally angry with myself. The last page read as if we'd written it ourselves.

I never told David I'd read those pages, and in time I came to regret I had. My doubt *did* cloud my judgment. I saw it would have been easier if I had trusted the King and not read them. I nearly drove myself crazy wondering if my doubt came from reading the pages, or if it was already present when I ignored the King's advice on the matter. Once some doors are open, they cannot be shut.

David and I never took a third trip together, to Crystal Caves. We left the palace on the next day a ship was scheduled to leave Oyster Bay for Portsmouth. I would sail with Thomas and Sarah, and David felt no need to linger at the palace. The Captain accompanied Thomas, Sarah and I to Oyster Bay, though the Captain and I didn't ride in the coach. We rode on horseback, as I wanted to ride Yashel again, and we wanted privacy to talk freely.

As soon as we were alone on the road, I turned our conversation to the assassination attempt back in Oyster Bay.

"Who was behind the attack?" I asked the Captain.

"The prisoner was quick enough to tell the soldiers who found him—though he wouldn't name their target. They call themselves *the kingdom's shield*. They claim they are the only ones who will protect the kingdom from the trolls. It's why they used a string of shields to disrupt our coach, back in Oyster Bay. They intended to entangle the horses, to bring them down. It seems the conspirator who pulled the shields across the street was slower than intended."

"And they were veterans—from the King's Army?" I replied, questioningly. I already knew the answer. Perhaps I felt I would find it easier to accept if I heard him say it again.

"Yes. All three were members of the Third."

"Were they attacked by villagers in the southern plain, after the last battle?"

The Captain paused, and I saw anger in his expression.

"They were."

He needed to say little else. I remembered the surreal irony of the Traitor's worst trick. He'd deceived the towns of southern Terrezia into believing the King had surrendered to the trolls, and given them rule over humans. In this way, many towns were tricked into rebelling against the King. These towns attacked the Third Army on sight, after the war was over.

"How many are they?"

"We don't yet know. I have a few…associates, who are posing as men sympathetic to their cause, in all the towns of the southern plain."

It was obvious to me he spoke of other Honor Knights. I wondered why he didn't say so plainly, now that I was finally a full member. Perhaps old habits die hard.

"When can we be sure they won't attack again?"

"I am confident the assassination attempt was aimed at the Princess, not you, or Sarah, or Thomas."

"*How* confident?" I asked. While the Captain accompanied us to Oyster Bay, I knew if he believed an attempt on the Princess's life was likely, wild horses couldn't drag him from Engdynlor.

He smiled at me with a gleam in his eye. He knew my thoughts.

"Fairly."

We rode in silence while I contemplated what another assassination attempt might look like, on the road to Oyster Bay.

Eventually, the Captain changed the subject. He told me there was a knight who had missed my induction ceremony, stationed at Portsmouth. Apparently *Bob the birdman* belonged to our order. To say this surprised me would be a great understatement.

"But I met him twice already," I objected. "He didn't show any interest in me at all."

"You didn't expect him to tell you he was a knight, did you?" I shook my head. "Or maybe you would expect him to keep you from getting to know him…"

"But how could he make sure I wouldn't *want* to get to know him?"

"Did you?"

"Not at all. I felt uncomfortable every minute I was near

him. He seemed pretty angry when I took his room from him."

"You took his *room*?" the Captain asked, a little stunned.

"Well, he was using both an office and a bedroom in the small inn. To get two rooms, the owner of the inn made him agree to give up his room to other guests."

The Captain laughed out loud. "Well, I guess he was feeling a little creative. Take nothing from his disliking you. He was purposely rude to keep you from getting to know him—*most likely*. He's not normally so easily offended."

"Really? The innkeeper didn't seem too happy about having me there either."

"Well, I can't make any guarantees about the innkeeper," he said, smiling wider.

I laughed at myself. *Imagine—he knew I was an apprentice knight all along.*

"So why tell me now?" I asked.

"Why tell you the lowly birdman is actually an Honor Knight? Because you, my friend, are going to learn the quiet skill of managing a loft of homing pigeons."

"I'm going to *what*?"

"Oh, it's a pleasant occupation, I'm told," he said, still smiling. I waited. "All right, then. Bob will teach you how to run a loft of homing pigeons as your public assignment. Privately, he'll be training and mentoring you in your next stage of LifeGrowth." He saw my eyes grow wide at the word *mentoring*. "Don't worry," he quickly added, "you won't get rid of me so easily. I'll be your mentor for a long time to come. Bob will be working with you while you're at Portsmouth."

"What will I be learning about next?" I asked.

"All the things we deem most important, in case the King is right and you're leaving us soon."

"Such as?"

"Were you sleeping when I told you last?" he said with a smile. "You will learn to read people's expressions better, and to read lips. He'll teach you *philosophy of negotiating*, and more on the importance of leadership and service. And don't be surprised if he requires you to learn quite a bit about homing pigeons, too."

"Really? Why?"

"Believe it or not, he's very passionate about them. Don't laugh!" he said, unsuccessfully trying to hide a chuckle. "How could he perform his job well if he weren't passionate about it?"

"Why would the Honor Knights need a pigeon keeper?"

"Well, let me put it to you another way. Do you think our order would find it valuable to have a member with direct access to the fastest communication in the kingdom?" I nodded soberly. "Our order has averted war before, due to a member in his profession."

Passionate about pigeons? I thought. I remained unenthusiastic.

1.5 Beach Row

When we arrived in Oyster Bay, we found our ship had been delayed by a full day. The Captain decided to show Sarah, Thomas and I around town. Oyster Bay was a large city, with an eccentric flair. We sampled foods in little shops, and saw crafts for sale in a district the Captain thought Sarah might like. She could see little use for the things they sold, so we left for a place called Beach Row.

Beach Row was unique in all the kingdom. It was a long strand of shops, built right on the beachfront, though *that* part was hardly unusual. It was a strange kind of merchant, however, who chose to build his shop in a place which guaranteed its destruction every few years, with little or no warning. Nevertheless, the shops seemed very profitable, judging by their furnishings and prices. They were well constructed, using the same techniques as buildings meant to last a hundred years. Most were small, but some were nearly as large as the delegation building back in Portsmouth. Sarah was shocked when she learned of the shops' collective fate.

"*Surely not*," she'd exclaimed.

"I've heard it's true," Thomas offered.

"I assure you it is," replied the Captain. "The foundations

of hewn stone remain, but most shops are carried away into the ocean entirely."

"What about the families who live in them?" asked Sarah.

"No one may sleep in Beach Row," said the Captain, "by decree of the mayor. The shops all close when a storm is on its way, or when a surprise storm begins. The storm front washing through these buildings is like a great a wall of water."

"What about the ships in the harbor?"

"They are brought into dry-docks, far up from the beach, during the worst weeks of the storm season—late winter to early spring."

Soon after arriving, I decided calling the buildings of Beach Row *shops* didn't do them justice. There were art galleries, small but magnificent as any room I'd seen in Engdynlor. Vintners sold expensive wines, and tailors made custom clothing while their customers shopped. Jewelers and antique dealers offered impressive items of high value…most of which were packed up each night and hauled off the beachfront, as late in the fall as it was. We looked like beggars, compared to the richly clothed people going in and out of the shops. Many of them gave us a wide berth as they walked around us, eying us suspiciously—especially Sarah. Beach Row seemed to me a contradiction: the fanciest and richest customers dressed in their best clothes, strolling along packed sand while they visited doomed shops. Another surprise was the constant buzz from the criers. They were hired by the shop owners to lure customers into their shops by yelling about their wares. It seemed like a cross between a carnival and a snobby society gathering.

When we walked by a cluster of restaurants I saw something that caught my eye. As I stopped to look, the Captain explained the restaurants served the finest and most exotic foods from around the kingdom. The item I noticed on one menu—proudly displayed in a gilded frame set with jewels—was *cutlet of snowsnake*. The Captain laughed when he saw what held my attention, and pointed out to the others the new import from David's delegation. As he did, the crier recognized us by the Captain's words.

After cocking his ear our way and listening a while longer, the crier rushed into the restaurant and returned a minute later with the chef and owner.

"Sir, are you Captain Williams, of His Majesty's Royal Guard?" asked the owner.

"I am, sir," he replied with an air of exaggerated flair.

"And are you the young man we've heard so much about, the Captain's loyal assistant and servant of the King, Master Adams?" I'd have been more flattered if he hadn't used the title *master*, which was meant for children.

"That's me."

"Oh, you *must* honor my restaurant with your presence," said the owner.

"I will cook you such a meal, you'll think you've died and gone to heaven," the chef added proudly. "You'll taste the best foods from the farthest corners of the kingdom, as only my staff can prepare them."

"You may know us by reputation," said the Captain, "but we are humble servants of the King..." He trailed off as I wondered what he was implying.

"And you could do us no higher honor than visiting our establishment and sampling our fine menu. The King's money is no good here; you are our guests." *Ah, money.* I guessed the menu prices would be a difficulty, even for the Captain.

"Well?" the Captain asked me. "What do you think?"

I turned resolutely to the owner. "I assume our friends are also welcome? They have the honor of leading the rest of our kingdom by example; they are some of the first subjects from our two peoples to live peacefully together." I watched the owner and chef react as they each gave a sidelong glance toward Sarah, and eventually nodded slowly, though with insincere smiles.

"Of course your friends are welcome to join you. We've heard much of your...*progressive* policies in Portsmouth, and we welcome them as loyal subjects of our King." The owner sounded anything but earnest. *Still*, I thought, *I'll never have another chance to eat a meal like the chef promised.*

"In that case," I replied, looking back and forth among our group, "we would be honored to be your guests."

"*Excellent*," the owner replied excitedly. Please return just as you are in a half-hour. We need a little time to arrange for your table and begin preparing your meals."

The Captain thanked them, and we continued along Beach Row.

"Do you realize what you've gotten us into?" asked the Captain, smiling.

"What? Is their food so strange I won't like it?"

"No, I'm sure the food will be delicious—most of it anyway. But I have an idea we're in for a busy evening."

"What do you mean?"

When the Captain only smiled, Thomas answered my question. "I think he means we'll be the center of attention during dinner."

The Captain added, "You'll probably feel like you're in another banquet at Engdynlor—only we'll all be dressed quite differently from the other diners."

Sarah looked uncomfortable. "Will you be all right?" I asked her.

"I think so...I don't know how well I'll fit in though," she replied fretfully.

"Don't worry," the Captain responded, "I think we'll stick

out just as well." When Thomas asked what he meant, he went on. "The people who shop here aren't merely the richest people from the Bay, or even the kingdom, they're the most extravagant of the rich—and those who wish to be associated with them. Most of them are concerned with social activities more than any events of true meaning."

To hear him describe it, I imagined they were something like spoiled movie stars. When he said their support of the King's policies were mostly limited to words, I began to wish I'd denied the restaurant owner's invitation.

Distracted, I trailed behind the others. The evening had cooled, and salty gusts began to bite through our jackets. We spent the rest of our wait in an art gallery. The paintings and sculptures were impressive. Most of the paintings were extremely realistic and detailed—I had to check twice to be sure they weren't photographs. In one corner, an entire collection of ocean-themed paintings hung. Two of them immediately stood out. They looked gloomy, and were painted entirely of dark blues and grays. One showed the last islands, at the southern tip of the Broken Coast island chain. The other showed an imaginary scene which looked somehow familiar to me. I wondered if I'd seen something like it once before. It looked like a part of an island was floating in the sky, surrounded by swirling clouds. Unable to shake its eerie familiarity, I asked the gallery owner for the painting's name. He rudely backed me out of the corner, until I nearly bumped into the Captain.

"Please stay closer to your father," the owner said, walking briskly away. I looked up at the Captain, but he only offered a lopsided grin. As I wandered off, the owner's rude words rang in my head. They reminded me of my home, and how impossible his advice was to me. My emotions twisted from one extreme to another as I realized how much I missed my family. I felt suddenly small and helpless, but I imagined my father would want me to act bravely. My mind flashed back to something the King had told me so long ago.

"We are responsible for keeping our emotions under control. That doesn't mean we can stop ourselves from feeling them, but it does mean we can stop ourselves from making a decision based on them."

What does it mean now? Should I deny my feelings? I tried to remember what the context was when the King had spoken those words. As I concentrated, it became clear to me.

I'd been worried for David at the beginning of the war. The Queen helped me see we were better off for having such a close relationship, even though it came with fear at times. I thought about my father, wondering if I'd ever caused him such worry.

My mind stumbled upon an old memory, of a week David and I spent at camp, years ago. On our second night there, a powerful storm had blown through, toppling many trees and even damaging some of the cabin's roofs.

The next morning at the mess hall, the camp director told us some of the activities would be cancelled. The road connecting the camp to the outside world was blocked by many fallen trees, and likely wouldn't be fully cleared until our parents came to pick us up at the end of the week

At the time, it seemed the director was being a little dramatic, but he made a point to tell us all our parents had been contacted. They had already been informed: none of us had been harmed, and we would be able to go on with most of the activities they'd planned for us.

David and I spent the entire day fishing, since the small, swollen lake had been too muddied for swimming. I returned to my cabin that night, tired and ready for sleep. When David and I reached the mess hall the next morning, we were shocked to see my father there, waiting for us.

He wore a broad smile, though he looked as worn as his disheveled clothes. His pantleg was torn at the knee, with a nasty scrape on his shin, and he looked half-soaked, but his expression told us he was excited to see us.

"What's wrong?" I asked.

"Do we have to go home early?" David added.

"What, and take you away from all the fun you're having? I wouldn't dream of it."

David and I glanced at each other, then back to my dad.

"I got the day off work, and felt like having breakfast with my sons. There's nothing wrong with that, is there?" he chuckled.

He sat beside us, at a table with the rest of our bunkmates. He didn't add much to our conversation, and I remember feeling more than a little embarrassment over having the only parent who visited our camp.

"Hey dad," I started when the thought occurred to me, "how did you get here? I thought the road was blocked with trees."

With the hint of a smile, he replied, "It was—but not anymore."

I didn't give it another thought until that night, back at the mess hall. My father was by then back at home, and I was peeling potatoes—punishment for pushing another camper in the lake. I overhead one of the counselors talking to the camp director, just outside the kitchen. I slowed my peeling and breathed shallowly, not to alert them I was listening.

"Did you make it all the way to town?" the counselor asked.

"Yes," the director answered, "though I barely had time to turn around and get back."

"What? How could it take so long?"

"Bob and I went. We took the four-wheel-drive jeep and two chainsaws, and still had to stop every mile to saw and clear downed trees from the road."

"I thought that parent who drove out here this morning said he cleared the road," the young counselor replied, questioningly.

"He gave us quite a head start. In fact, we wouldn't have made it halfway, but for the trees he cleared last night."

"Last night? I thought he just drove up this morning."

"He *arrived* this morning. He must have spent all day yesterday, and most of last night cutting and rolling logs, and dragging branches off the road. You wouldn't believe some of the messes he negotiated that old pickup of his through."

"And he had no help?"

"No," the director said with a laugh, "just his truck, his saw, and a whole lot of determination. I'll tell you this; the visitor we had in our mess hall this morning—*that* is a father who truly loves his kids."

My face flushed warm, and I held my breath.

"I don't understand—didn't you call him just after the storm? Didn't he know his boys were safe?"

"Son, you don't have kids of your own yet, do you?"

The counselor must have shaken his head.

"Well, when you do, you'll understand."

I didn't truly understand what they were talking about that summer. In fact, standing in the finest gallery in Beach Row, I didn't understand it fully, but I *began* to understand.

My face flushed in embarrassment once again. How did I act, at the camp mess hall, sitting beside my father? Could he tell I was embarrassed to sit beside him in front of the other campers? Did he feel disappointment at realizing how I felt? Did I ever thank him for spending all that time and energy, just to come and sit with us and the other campers for a lousy breakfast?

As a young teen, I considered my father a strict man—far too strict in my youthful opinion. After that day at camp, I never looked at him in quite the same way. I didn't become a more obedient child—not for some time—but even with the pale understanding of his labored visit I had at the time, I appreciated him more. When I suspected I was forbidden to do as I liked for no better reason than to irritate me, I compared it with my memory of that long trip to camp.

A deeper appreciation took root in my soul that night in Oyster Bay. I resolved to never again trade a shared moment with my family for so cowardly a thing as embarrassment. It was a vow I worked hard to keep. I even succeeded at it from time to time.

I felt all the more childish for it, but I closed my eyes and thought to him as if he could hear me. *Dad, I'm going to make it back. I'll do whatever it takes. I will come home.*

When I looked up I realized I'd nearly stumbled out of the store. I faced the large sculptures on display in the gallery's windows. I'd almost toppled a massive tower of glass, which I first mistook for a pillar of ice. From the angle I first saw it, I thought it was a piece of glass meant to look like an enormous jewel. As I circled it, I saw something else.

It reminded me of a glacier—and yet something moved inside—tiny figures within the glass. They were mere wisps; like strings of cloud frozen in a block of ice. I turned again and watched some of the figures fall into focus. Were my eyes playing tricks on me? The ghostly images were tiny ice trolls.

Amazed but also doubtful, I turned again and saw other shapes coalesce into more Lyssiltiks, just at my limit of focusing on them. I stepped away at a new angle, and saw the shape of the entire sculpture resembled an ice troll, hunched over. I walked one way, then the other, watching the glass transform back and forth from the hunched troll to the shape of a glacier. Stepping one way, then the other, I finally bumped into Thomas. He too, was interested in what had captured my attention.

"Did you see Lyssiltiks in the glass too?" I asked him. He nodded.

"Now take a look at the sculpture over *there*," he whispered in near awe, pointing.

I walked closer to the piece he spoke of. I saw its price written on a small label at its base; it was a lot of digits. I wondered if the boat we sailed on from Port was worth as much. It was another glass sculpture, but while the outer portion was clear, the center was dark red and black. Moving even a little, I could see the center transform into dancing flames. I searched for another angle, for another meaning in the sculpture. Finally, I saw it. Not far from the edges, imbedded into the fiery interior, I found ash, and what looked like splinters of wood. They were brown, but I hadn't seen them at any other angle—*how did the artist do it?* In the center of it all, was a large form nearly filling the sculpture's center. It was a man—no, it was a troll. His arms were stretched out high above him, right out of the smoke and flame. I stepped closer, and saw an image come into focus in the clear glass at the troll's hands. It was a smaller troll—no, it was a human boy. My eyes opened wide as I turned back to Thomas. I saw his eyes were red, and he rubbed at his nose. Uncomfortable, I moved back away from the sculptures. When Thomas had composed himself, he approached the gallery owner.

"Can you tell me about that red sculpture there?" he asked, nodding his head in its direction.

The owner barely turned his head to acknowledge Thomas. He told him the price, which was high. He added, "It's by one of our newer artists—her latest piece. It arrived just this week."

"Did you say *her* piece?" asked Thomas.

"Yes," the owner replied, not bothering to look directly at him. "She works only with glass. Amazing detail is hidden within each of them. I don't suppose you found the troll in its center?"

"Yes."

"Well I'm not surprised, most do. Did you see what it's holding?"

"I think you mean...*whom he's* holding," Thomas said in a low voice.

"Maybe I do. What is it to *you* how I speak in my own gallery?" He finally turned to give his full attention to Thomas, irritated with him.

"*He's mine*—and the one holding him is his savior." Thomas seemed to grow taller as his voice grew to fill the shop. Others customers turned nervously toward the commotion.

"What are you talking about?" asked the owner, stepping back a little. He'd seen the images in the sculpture without knowing who they represented. The piece of glass told the story of the moment which had become a turning point in Thomas's life.

"Never mind," Thomas growled, "I won't disrespect his tale by telling it to the likes of you. Have it packed up and ready to be shipped to Portsmouth at dawn."

"*For you?* Are you going to display it in your *farmhouse?*" mocked the owner, looking up and down at Thomas in his worn clothes.

"Yes, but if it's all the same to you, I'll be paying you with *gold*, not vegetables." He turned on his heel and yelled angrily over his shoulder as he stormed out the door. "I'll have the bank's man over to see you first thing in the morning. My name's Tom Ahrens, and I just bought your finest sculpture. Have it at the docks by dawn, if you want your gold."

I passed the owner, standing motionless as I followed Thomas. Sarah and the Captain followed shortly thereafter. Sarah seemed as though she might have been quietly crying. Thomas hadn't said a word to me, but when Sarah appeared, he rushed to her like she was a troubled sister. I pondered at the change in Thomas in the past few weeks.

"Are you all right?" he asked her.

"It is so beautiful. I wish my boys could see it."

"They will, they surely will," is all he said. Soon after, the Captain quietly mentioned we'd be late for our dinner if we still wanted to go, and we walked the short way back to the restaurant in silence.

Later, when I wrote to David describing the sculptures, and how Thomas bought the one which told the story of his son and Norman, he was shocked. He wrote back to tell me of an apprentice artist who'd ridden up the mountain with the ice merchants, and wanted to live with the ice trolls. She'd said she wanted to learn of their ways. Worried for her, and for any trouble she might cause with the trolls, he'd sent her with a trusted soldier, to meet the trolls and visit them for a week. He didn't want to discourage interactions between the Lyssiltiks and civilians when there was so little of it already. It turned out she was a talented sculptor who'd heard of their ability to slice the glacial ice into large blocks. The same young woman learned the ice trolls have their own artists, who work their craft with ice.

She learned their skill of working the ice in sculptured halves, cut to fit so closely together, they were easily melted together with a little friction or pressure, so no seam could be found. She'd planned to do the same with glass somehow—

and apparently succeeded. I later found she'd heard of the disaster at Portsmouth after returning to Oyster Bay, and had just finished Thomas's sculpture after we'd arrived at Engdynlor for the trials. If our ship hadn't been delayed, or if the trails had been scheduled a week earlier, Thomas and I would have never learned of the artist, or her wondrous sculptures.

David's letter telling of her seemed strange to me. His attitude and description of her made me wonder if he'd been angry with her for staying with the trolls, or if he worried she might hurt his mission somehow.

The Captain's prediction proved true; the dinner was long and tiring, with as many tables arranged to face ours as possible. And just like a royal banquet, we were greeted by a long line of well-wishers, or more accurately, those who wanted to say they'd once shaken the commander's hand. We were very late returning to the inn where we'd left our things. I lay in bed, thinking of all the fancy foods we'd tried, too full to fall asleep yet.

I thought of all the many dishes I'd sampled, hardly taking a bite from each of them. The chef took it as an opportunity to showcase all his best dishes on our table, each artfully arranged for all his most respected customers to see. I felt bad for Sarah, who found most of the dishes unappetizing. The chef made some kind of raw meat sausage for her, but it seemed more like an afterthought than a main course for an honored guest.

We all tried the snowsnake, which tasted horrible. Thomas felt it had been over-seasoned to hide its natural, though foul, flavor. Each small plate of eltsstatch meat came with a tiny swath of its tanned hide, with its thick fur white as snow. It served both as a souvenir, and proof of its authenticity. In time, receiving the tiny patch was what I enjoyed most from the meal.

Early the next day, we boarded our ship and set out for Portsmouth. I had no idea Oyster Bay had so much to see when I'd passed through it before. Even so, I'd seen enough of it after only a day. The Captain showed us off, and inspected the crate with Thomas's new sculpture. It was packed tightly in a large wooden crate filled with some kind of leaves. As Thomas expected, it was delivered to the docks at dawn.

"How did you know the gallery owner would take you seriously?" I asked him.

"One thing I've learned about items with high prices: their seller is always eager to deliver."

The ride back was uneventful, but this time I had a renewed interest with the islands of the Broken Coast. Remembering the paintings from our night in Oyster Bay, I looked forward to seeing them again. On the last day of our trip, I paid careful attention to the islands closest to Portsmouth, until a storm blew in and chased me into the galley.

Returning to Portsmouth, I felt *different*. No one on the ship knew I'd been knighted, but it didn't matter. It was late afternoon when we arrived, and I decided to stay a night in the inn. Dinner was welcome, my first hot meal since we left Beach Row. As much as I enjoyed the food, I also wanted to talk with Bob Tiller—*the birdman*—to ask how and when we would meet. While spending the entire meal across the table from him, he showed all the hospitality of a cold fish.

When I tried to strike a conversation with him over the dishes, he only asked me to meet him in his office. Following him up the curving staircase, I realized I'd be forcing him from his bed again. When he opened his office door, I saw he'd already set up a small cot. The room was so small, I had no choice but to sit on it, while Bob sat at his desk.

"You'll meet me in the loft after tonight," he began abruptly, "until you learn the basics of pigeon racing."

"Pigeon racing?" I asked, surprised. My mind was focused on more important things he might teach me.

"Yes. You *are* to learn pigeon racing as your primary task."

"But…" I began, then immediately thought better of it. "Is there any chance we might be overheard here?"

"No. We can discuss anything pertaining to our order. To everyone who sees us working together, you are my apprentice in the art of pigeon racing. Privately, I will also train you in your next lessons as an Honor Knight. Your mentor tells me I can expect you to work hard and learn quickly."

"Um…isn't the pigeon thing our *cover*, so you can teach me about more important subjects?" I hadn't forgotten what the Captain had told me about Bob, but my mind rebelled at the idea of learning pigeon keeping when I only had enough time left in Portsmouth to hand over my position in the delegation. If I'd known my new teacher at all, I would've known my words were a deep insult to him. He reacted like he'd received a slap in the face.

"*More important—what do you think…*" he sputtered, and then drew a deep breath and calmed himself. "Did you consider your assignment as head delegate *only a cover?*"

"Of course not. It's the very purpose of my assignment."

His voice was cold in his reply. "Then kindly treat your training as pigeoneer in the same manner. Not everyone appreciates the importance of my trade, but by the time you leave Portsmouth, I can guarantee *you* will."

We'd met for only moments, and I'd already insulted his lifelong passion, and also—I later found—the chosen profession of his entire family tree, across many generations. I wished I could start over.

"I'm sorry sir; I didn't mean to offend. I guess I know very little about...pigeoneering." Finally, he smiled and softened his glare.

"It's all right. I know most people don't know enough about pigeons to appreciate them; it doesn't really offend me. However, it gave me an excuse to test your reaction to an immature leader."

When he saw my expression, his smile grew larger and he surprised me with a booming laugh. "And," he added, still chuckling, "it isn't really called pigeoneering; it's just what I like to call it. Others in my trade call it pigeon racing."

He began to explain a little of his profession's history. Starting as a child, he'd learned from his grandfather, even though his father was also an expert. It was always done this way in his family, so the pupil had the most experienced teacher possible.

"You'll have to settle for me. I have only thirty-seven years of experience with pigeons."

"*Only?*"

"My grandfather had trained for twice as long when he instructed me. I still haven't matched his level of mastery in breeding desirable traits into the birds. I hope to catch up to him in my lifetime."

I paused to try to arrange my thoughts respectfully. "I...uh...I didn't know there was so much to learn about pigeons."

He returned my uncertain expression with another hearty laugh.

"Look how polite you are when you think about it! I think rather you didn't know someone could take so long learning about a single type of bird." He laughed again, and I laughed at myself. I wasn't doing a very good job of being polite if he saw through my words, and read my impolite thoughts. I was left wondering how he'd guessed my thoughts, not feeling at all comfortable about it.

"Am I still being polite if you can see through to my real thoughts?"

"That would depend entirely on what you're thinking. If your thoughts are polite then there's nothing to see through. If your thoughts are arrogant and judging, then you're only *acting* politely. He paused long enough to see my face drop, then added with a wink, "Most people won't be able to tell the difference. They're too ready to hear what they want."

I smiled sheepishly. *Did he just call me arrogant and judging?* His face was kind, and full of warmth. When I knew him better I learned this was his way: to be friendly and utterly frank at the same time. He cut through all pretense and said exactly what he meant, whether it was praise or correction. He didn't act angry when he pointed out something wrong or immature I'd done. Neither did he act excited when he complimented me. It seemed almost *too honest* to me. It certainly took a while to get used to.

We spent an hour or two going over the very basics of pigeon care. I went to bed exhausted, wondering how much I would remember.

Part II

2.0 Settling In

When I left for the delegation building the next morning, it was Bob who took me there. We rode a small cart with a spring-mounted bench up front. The back of the cart held some bulky items under a tarp. I heard curious noises coming from under the tarp during the rougher parts of our ride.

The morning was cool, much more so than I expected. Most of the ride I contemplated asking Bob to stop so I could get my coat from my luggage sack. I rubbed my arms and doubled over, leaning into the wind. I could still smell the salt air, but I knew it would fade as we approached the delegation. I wondered how long we had before the first snowfall.

When we arrived at the delegation building, Bob surprised me by getting out of the cart first. As I hopped off the other side, I walked around the front of the cart to invite him inside, thinking he was thirsty or wanted to rest. Not seeing him there, I continued around to the back of the cart, where he was unloading something from under the tarp. To my surprise, it was a cage of pigeons.

"And here are your charges," he said merrily.

"What?" I stammered. "What do I do with *them*?"

"Just like we talked about: feed them and clean up after

them, give them clean water every day—"

"But you didn't say I'd have to do it on my own," I objected. He gave a curious look and I remembered he was my teacher. "Where will I keep them? They can't live in that cage, all four of them."

"I had a loft built for them in the building's attic while you were gone. And here is your book of codes." He handed the birdcage to me, and also a notepad, feed bin, water tray, and a sack of crushed grain. I was so overloaded I couldn't see where I was walking. I trudged toward the entrance, grumbling silent thoughts not even the birdman could guess. "Remember what I told you," he said as he tossed my luggage to the ground and climbed back onto the cart. "They *depend* on you." He was off without another word.

Angry, and feeling no particular need to hide it, I marched into the building with my load of pigeon gear. I left my luggage sack where it lay, and struggled to open the door. As soon as I walked in the building, I heard a loud *Surprise!* fill the front room. I turned sideways to see past my load, and found the entire delegation standing around me. Thomas and his family were also there, and Sarah with her two boys. A few seconds later, they broke out in laughter. The pigeons were flapping wildly in their cage, causing me to drop their feed sack. I nearly tripped over it. I was certain it wasn't how they'd expected me to appear when I walked in.

"Thank you! What is this all about?" I asked, flustered nearly as much as my pigeons.

Mr. Davis, the Delegate Chaplain stepped forward. "We wanted to welcome you back," he said. He gestured toward the others in the room adding, "We heard the Delegate's Review with the King went well, and we wanted to celebrate with you as soon as you returned."

I must have turned white as a ghost. *Did they get a copy of the*

King's Review? I wondered in a panic. As soon as Mr. Davis saw my expression, his face went blank for a moment.

"Yes, Mark. The King sent out a *public* review to all the delegates, outlining the basics of how the delegation *as a whole* is doing." His emphasis of those key words probably wasn't enough for most people to notice, but they spoke volumes to me. I felt the color return to my face and wondered how shocked I'd looked.

"That's wonderful," I said, slightly more relaxed. "We should all be proud of our work here; the King is very pleased with your progress," I looked toward Thomas and his family, and added, "*and* with the progress the citizens of Portsmouth have made." Of course they knew this, but I could think of nothing else to say.

The Lieutenant stepped forward and picked up the things I'd dropped. "Let me help you put these away, so we can sit down for the party," he said.

"Party?"

"Oh yes," said Stephen, the delegation secretary, "everything's ready. We have the discussion room all set up."

"Oh, I can manage most of this, lieutenant. Would you mind grabbing my luggage sack outside the door?"

In the end, he carried my luggage and half the pigeon supplies at once. We went up the wide stairs to my room. It wasn't until we'd reached my door that I realized I'd never seen the building's attic; in fact, I didn't even know it *had* one. I set the bird cage down and opened the door so the Lieutenant could drop my bag inside.

"Um...do you know how to get to the attic?" I asked him.

He smiled. "Well, I didn't until you left for Engdynlor. Then I had to have some men come and install *that*," he said, pointing to the ceiling back toward the staircase. I hadn't noticed it though I'd walked right under it. There was a large frame built into the ceiling over the hallway. I didn't recognize what it was at first, even with the piece of rope hanging from the large rectangular frame, but then I understood. It was a pull-down staircase. The Lieutenant pulled on the rope until a large, full-length wooden staircase reached down to touch the floor of the hall. It looked like it weighed a ton. It was nothing like the pull-down staircase in the house I grew up in—it didn't even fold. I wondered how he would get it back up into the attic.

He led the way, carrying most of the equipment. I carried the cage and watering tray. When we reached the top of the stairs, we were at the center of the attic. I saw a complicated-looking mechanism at the back of the rectangular hole in the attic floor, and pulleys and weights I imagined helped pull the stairs up, though I couldn't quite see how. Suddenly I noticed something I'd taken for granted; *it wasn't dark*. There were no lanterns or candles I could see. I looked to where the light came in. There had been changes made to one end of the attic, where the peak of the roof hung over an outside wall. Where there once was only a flat outside wall under the roof's peak, there now was a small structure built, with light shining through.

What is it? I wondered, as I approached the strange wooden structure. Of course, it was the pigeons' loft, with small compartments for a half-dozen birds. There was the one-way entrance Bob had told me about, and something else that let in light. I could see the loft actually hung outside the building some, hanging over the back of the building. There was a pipe with a valve hanging down from the roof, to fill the water trough, and overflow out of the building to keep it fresh and clean. I set up the food bin and filled it with grain.

I was nearly blinded with light when I looked through a vent built into one side of the loft. There were two tiny walls on both sides of the loft, where it hung outside the attic. They were built entirely of tilted boards, so air could move in and out of the attic, while keeping rain from entering. Something outside those boards reflected sunlight inside and lit the attic well enough to see by, though no one would call it *bright*. I wouldn't be doing any reading up there, but I also wouldn't need to mess with lanterns or candles, provided it was light outside.

The Lieutenant cleared his throat. "Maybe you should set up your pigeons' things later?"

"Whoops, I nearly forgot about the party—sorry. Let's go." I followed him down the staircase and stood aside as he lifted it up into the framed hole in the ceiling. I hurried back down, and the Lieutenant followed in a more formal gait. When I walked into the meeting room, everyone cheered again. I told them again how happy the King was, how much he appreciated each one of them. We sat down at the long tables to enjoy a freshly baked cake and crisp apple cider. When most people had eaten their food and began talking, I cleared my throat and loudly asked if I could speak to everyone for a minute.

All faces turned to me. I told them I had an important announcement to make about the future of the delegation.

"Did the King give us a new charter?" asked Dr. Maher, the delegate's physician.

"No, not exactly. I know this has been a strange delegation from the start. I know it's been a lot to ask of you to report to someone of my age—something never been done before. But the King is wise and has his own reasons." Some smiled warmly at me, and others looked uncomfortable. All of them meant well, but some were embarrassed while others seemed somehow closer to me when I mentioned it. Later I would wonder what I could tell of a person's personality by whether they smiled or shifted their gaze in that moment. I went on.

"The King was pleased with my role of head delegate. Even so, he has another assignment for me, and has called me away from the delegation." Their expressions turned to one of shock. Some looked sad, and Sarah looked as if she might cry. Thomas looked almost angry. Then they all seemed to talk at once.

"Why?" "You're not leaving us now, are you?" "What's wrong with the job you're doing?" "Where are you going?" "Who will take your place?" "It's not *the birdman*, is it?" They all spoke at once.

"Please," I started, holding my hand out toward them. "It isn't about the job I've done, or any problems the delegation's had, or anything else like that. And *please*, let's not start questioning the King *now*. He needs me somewhere else. He only planned for me to head this delegation until it got a healthy start, which you know well we *have*. The same is true for my brother, in the delegation to the Lyssiltiks. The King is calling us away to another assignment, but not immediately. He wants me to choose the new head delegate, and work with him until I've handed off all my responsibilities. And no, it isn't Mr. Tiller, *the birdman*, though I will be visiting him regularly while I'm still here. The King wants me trained to send messages by pigeon, perhaps for my next assignment."

Another barrage of questions: "He does?" "Why?" "Where will you be going?" "Who *will* replace you?" I took a deep breath and replied as best I could.

"When I was still at the palace, I wrote Mr. Davis about my replacement. He eventually agreed to head the delegation when I leave. We'll be working together for a little while before he takes over my role." The room looked a little more comfortable at hearing the news.

"Mr. Davis?" I asked, "Do you want to add anything?"

"Only to thank you," he replied. "I know the King has already thanked you for your work as head delegate, but I wanted to thank you on behalf of the other delegates. You're right; it was difficult for most of us to adjust to such a young leader, but you made it easy for us. It was a pleasure working with you. You are a wise and patient young man."

I blushed as the rest of the room clapped their hands and some even shouted heartily. I wondered how much of the Chaplain's compliment was born of kindness, and how much was based in fact. I thought back to what Bob had said about being polite and only *pretending* to be polite. *But he didn't word it that way…how did he say it?* I wondered, distracted for a second from the crowd before me.

"Thank you," I replied, trying to draw their applause to an end. "I appreciate all of you, and will miss you very much."

Finally, our farming advisors spoke up. "Well, you aren't leaving yet," said Timothy.

"So let's not cry on your cake!" added Nicholas.

We enjoyed the rest of the afternoon. Early that evening I brought a candle up into the attic and arranged the birds and their things. I wondered how much time I would have to waste with pigeons. *At least it's quiet work, and it might let me spend a little more time with the delegation,* I thought. I went to bed more relaxed than I'd been in a long time.

In the weeks to come, I spent less time with the Chaplain and delegation, and more time in town with Bob. The delegation passed my resolution to name the Princess our Ambassador of Goodwill Relations, only they decided to call her a Goodwill Ambassador. We had a long discussion about what her duties would be. The delegation kept trying to simplify her role, while I kept trying to add to it. It seemed to me, they didn't expect her capable of much.

"Look," I finally told them, "I know some of you might not think the Princess is capable of doing this much, but I tell you *she is*. She's a very strong person. Let's remember what our delegation is about…it's not really about *trolls*." Suddenly, I had their undivided attention.

"If we can teach the kingdom to treat trolls as our equals, but not women, we'll have failed at the very thing the King values: equality." I let that sink in for a moment before I went on. "And I know she's young; even *younger than me*. But she's not as young as some of you remember. Most of you haven't seen her for years. She's not the same person she was even a few years ago. She has a passion for helping our kingdom see the trolls as equals. You should have seen the parade at Oyster Bay. Wasn't it amazing Sarah?"

Sarah had replaced Norman in the delegation. She nodded her reply, but I prodded her for more details. "How would you describe the way the crowd looked at her?"

Sarah paused thoughtfully before clearing her throat. Hearing such a deep rumble from a woman still surprised me.

"The way they looked up to her—I would say they love her. I felt almost like one of them—like a human—when she sat beside me in the parade."

In the end, the delegation added about half of what I thought the Princess was capable of. They agreed to revisit her role in one year, and add to it, if at all possible.

Winter was coming and preparations were being made. There was a community dinner at the delegation building's new mess hall, celebrating the first day of winter. Before it became too cold to eat outdoors, the soldiers had built the large dining hall, attached to the delegation building by a covered walkway. Thomas used the party as an opportunity to donate the glass sculpture from Beach Row to the County Community Center, which is what the delegation building would become when it was no longer needed to house us. Thomas, his son, and his "adopted troll sons" would grow up without resenting each other, seeing the kind of man Norman was. It was a bittersweet occasion, and would remind us of Norman's great capacity for love and commitment to finding peace between our people.

I slept at the inn several nights a week to avoid the cold ride into town. The pigeons' traffic trickled near to a halt, but Bob insisted they could reach Engdynlor through anything short of a blizzard. I received a letter from David, re-sent by pigeons at the palace.

He was having a difficult time training his replacement. I wondered why, when things were going so well for me and Mr. Davis. It was as if he anticipated anything I wanted to try and teach him. I had no doubt he could just as easily been training me.

When I finally realized the difference, I decided to write him. "We were both mentored to take on certain of the King's values," I wrote. "What about your replacement? Does he have the heart of the King?" When he replied, he said he couldn't believe he hadn't seen it himself. He'd been trying to get his replacement to guess what needed to be done next, and all the possible ways things might go wrong. Once he tried to impart the things his mentor taught him, he saw his replacement was going to be well prepared. He had a harder time at it than I did, and he learned how much harder it is to teach a value than it is to teach a rule or set of orders. I found a deeper appreciation for the Captain and his abilities.

Meanwhile, Bob continued to teach me all his favorite bird facts, and quiz me on them:

"They lay…how many eggs?"

"Only two. And they hatch eighteen days afterward."

"They weigh only…?"

"About a pound."

"How long are they?"

"About a foot, but their wingspan may be over two feet."

"And how fast can they fly?"

"Faster than the fastest horse can run."

"From how far will they return?"

"From as far away as we carry them, they always return home to their mates in their loft."

One day when I was helping him build a new wall of pigeonholes for his loft, I asked him how they were able to find their way.

"Do you have to let them see out, when you carry them far away?"

"Ah," he replied, with a twinkle in his eye. "You'd like to know *how*, would you? Everyone wants to know *how*."

He turned back to his work for a moment, running a hand plane over a spruce plank in the loft over his head. Eventually, he set down the plane, dusted off his hands, and ran his fingers through his thinning, sandy hair. Not a few wood shavings fell to the floor.

"That is a question my family has studied for centuries."

"Truly?" I asked incredulously.

He shot me a sarcastic smirk. *"Truly."* Another pause, then finally, he asked, "How you do *think* they do it?" It was a subject I'd speculated over quite a bit.

"I think they must have some kind of compass, built into their heads."

"Nerves sensitive to magnetic pull, eh? That's a good hypothesis, but it's also wrong."

"Really? How can you know?"

"We've carried them on long trips, with no view of their route, with weak and strong magnets near them in all directions, even shifting simulated polar directions—and they had no effect."

"And they don't have to see the sky or sun during the trip?" I guessed.

"Correct. We've carried them in utter darkness, and simulated false paths of the sun in pitch black boxes. These too had no effect, though my experimenting ancestors expected it was the answer they sought. They believed pigeons somehow memorized enough of the topology they travelled across, to piece their return trip back together. They too were wrong."

"Well," I countered, urging him on with my hurried response, "how then?" My demeanor did nothing to speed his reply. When he finally answered, I nearly missed what he said.

"They hear their way."

"They *what?*" I was certain he was mocking me.

"They can hear sounds so low, they bounce off the landscape, and the homesick pigeon is able to build a topographical map of the land as it travels, both before and after they are released."

"Come on," I said, laughing. "No one can *hear* where they are."

"Oh, you're so certain, are you?" he mocked. "Well, they do indeed hear where they are. We first noticed heavy winds shifted their bearings, and we know light and magnetic waves aren't affected by wind—but *sound waves* are."

He went back to his work, but when I didn't, he turned back to face me.

"There are always low sounds moving over the world," he began, "too low for us to hear. When we've interrupted these sounds by masking them with louder low sounds we created, they were not able to find their way home. We have interrupted the sounds while we carry them, and when we release them. Either can cause them to lose their way."

I went back to the small boards I was hammering to the wall, pondering this. My mind wouldn't accept the idea.

"*How* low?" I asked. "And how did you know you were making these low noises, if you couldn't hear them?"

"Do you know anything about sounds waves?"

I admitted I didn't—close to nothing.

"All sound travels in waves. Short waves are high, long waves are low. The lowest sounds you can hear are from waves that cycle about twenty times per second, but there are sounds much lower than this. We call them *infrasounds*. Giraffes, elephants, and whales can speak to each other using infrasounds we can't hear, but pigeons can hear much lower than even they can make. The sounds are so low, they can't come close to fitting in a pigeon's ear—so long they need to take flight and fly in a large circle to collect enough of the sound wave to read it, then study how it's affected by the topology."

"Oh, you're joking, right?" It sounded ridiculous.

Bob only smiled. "I assure you, I am not."

"Then how do you know if you were making...infrasounds, if you can't hear them?"

"Math." I knew this couldn't be his entire answer, so I faked patience and waited for his explanation.

"If we can pluck a cable, or strike a metal bar that makes a high note, and a low note, then can't we predict what size metal bar and how tight a cable we must use to make an extra-low note?"

I grimaced, but eventually nodded.

"When we create a sound that is so low, it takes ten full seconds to complete a single wave cycle, it masks any pigeon's ability to navigate over new terrain. This is the length of wave they use to find their way home over unknown landscapes."

His explanation kept me working silently for a while, but it didn't last. I grew curious again, and eventually asked him how far *exactly* pigeons had flown to reach their home.

"As far as we are able to carry them."

"But how far is *that*?" I asked.

He sighed, then replied slowly and patiently. "We've released them from places all around the kingdom. As far away as we've released them, they have proved able to return. They've accompanied nearly every scientific voyage out to sea. They've returned even when the ships which carried them didn't."

I wondered if they had a limit to how far they would travel to find their homes. Perhaps the kingdom was too small to test their ability.

"Well, how far away *is it?*" I asked.

"Pigeons have flown from the place where the jungle meets the water at Athangust, all the way to the far shores of the Northern Forest. They reached their homes long before the ships carrying them returned."

Hearing of the southernmost portion of the island gave me a shudder. My strange memories from that fearful place seemed like a distant dream. It seemed so surreal, so impossible, I asked Bob what he knew of the Animal Coast.

"I've only heard tales. I've never seen it myself."

"What about the people who released pigeons from there? Were they were your relatives?"

"Yes. But they released their birds at sea, and left. They believed dangerous animals lived in the jungle."

"Why? What animals did they hear of?"

Bob slowly shook his head. He knew nothing of the legends or rumors they might have believed, nor what they might have suggested lived in those woods. He saw I was unhappy he couldn't confirm any more doubtful memories of my few days there.

"I only wish I could know how many things are real *here*, but impossible in my home."

"And you say trolls are only myths in your homeland?"

I nodded soberly in reply.

"With all the stories of weapons in your land, you seem to come from a very violent place. Maybe you killed all your trolls in war."

"Still, we'd have *records* of them."

"Would you?" he laughed. "How long do you think a kingdom can keep records before they are lost?"

When I thought about it, I realized I didn't really know. *How old were the oldest records we had?* I knew the Japanese had records passed down for a few thousands of years, and the Jews had passed down their Tenach for thousands also. If petroglyphs or hieroglyphics were included, perhaps we had even older records.

"A few thousand years maybe?"

"If they're *very lucky*. Even then, they probably aren't universally accepted as accurate. So, where do you think your myths come from, if not remnants of lost records?"

I nodded slowly, still wondering. My mind lingered on the strange beasts in my faintest memories. I'd mentioned them in my letters to David. His memories of those first days after we'd arrived were no clearer than my own. We'd talked about this in long letters, supposing what it might mean. Eventually I convinced myself the parts of our minds where memories are stored weren't fully working just after our amnesia.

"Tell me about your replacement." Bob's words pulled me back from my distant thoughts.

"He's doing just fine. He already has so many of the King's values as his own, it isn't much work at all. I'm sure he could have been the head all along. He should be training *me*."

"Well then, why isn't he?" Bob asked.

"What?" I tried to read his face. *Could he be joking?* "The King told me to train my replacement, not the other way around…"

"Does that mean you can't learn from him? He's probably four times your age. Is it possible he's learned some things that could benefit you?"

"I'm sure he has. But…" I didn't know how to reply without sounding arrogant. *I* was the head, not the Chaplain.

"Did you think the King believed you were the only one in the entire kingdom who could have led the delegation?" he asked. I didn't like the direction his questions were headed.

"Well, um…*no*," I stammered, "not really."

"Maybe instead the King had other plans than finding the only or best person for the job. Maybe he had more than one goal in mind."

"*Did* he? What else was he trying to accomplish? Did he only want the prophecies to come true?"

"I doubt it," Bob answered. "The King is wise; he rarely works toward one goal at a time. It's maddening to guess at, isn't it?" A sly smile crept over his face. He was taunting me.

"I always seem to underestimate him, no matter how hard I try not to." I played Bob's words again in my head, trying to find what hidden message he wanted to show me. Something rang true when he first spoke, but it had already slipped from mind.

What idea did he suggest? I thought. *First, he said the Chaplain had things to teach me…then, I'm not the only person who could have done the job, and finally, the King has more than one motive. Did the King send me to learn from the Chaplain? Is it a test I already failed?*

"What did the Chaplain do before he was a part of this delegation?"

Bob told me things about the Chaplain I never would have

guessed. He was a wise man, with vast experience in leadership and mentoring. My mind wouldn't take hold of the thought yet.

"Did the King really send me to learn from the Chaplain? Or am I here to learn from you?" I asked.

"Can you learn from only one teacher? Didn't you learn from the Captain, the King and Lady Sally all at once? Or did you think when you begin to *teach*, you can no longer *learn*?"

"Then it's true? Is this why the King assigned the Chaplain to the delegation?"

"I don't know. I'm only trying to discover why you've refused to learn from the Chaplain, a wise man with much to teach. Don't you think this should concern me?"

I felt defeated, as if Bob had told me I'd failed my first assignment as a knight.

"Yes, I guess it should," I finally replied, wincing at the implications of my words. "I have a lot to think about. Do you mind if I finish with the loft the next time I come?

"I think I could live with that," he said warmly. "You be careful, now," he teased, "not to think yourself into a corner." I wondered what he really thought of me, and if I would ever truly know. He helped me clean the area where I'd been working, and I left the inn for the delegation building. I used the small cart Bob had bought from the innkeeper, pulled by a horse lent to me by Thomas Ahrens. It was the same cart Bob drove when I'd first returned to Portsmouth, but the road seemed rougher on that day, despite the cart's springs.

2.1 Teaching Stories

I thought about Bob's words the entire ride back to the delegation camp. *How did I miss something so obvious?* Bob was right. I might need to hand the details over to the Chaplain, but I became convinced he'd been more qualified than me all along. The Chaplain had been so patient each time we met, and this ate away at my confidence, or at least gave me a new sense of humility.

I imagined the Chaplain laughing at me behind my back. *Would he do such a thing?* I wondered. *Never;* he was far too kind. More likely than not, he was saddened when I overlooked the easy lesson.

When I went to his desk that afternoon, I made every effort to act humbly. The other delegates were out, with the exception of Mr. Gravy. Chaplain Davis sat behind his desk, looking somewhat uncomfortable in a heavy coat. His desk was furthest from the woodstove, but he'd never complained. I hesitated to disturb the peaceful silence in the room.

"So what do we talk about today?" he asked when I sat near his desk. "More on the troll's food supply? The boars and deer we imported seem to be doing well, and we expect a mild winter. I think the trolls can begin to hunt them in the spring."

"No. I think it's taken me long enough to realize it, but I really don't have anything I can teach you." My mind flashed back to my memory of the Captain's story of his own mentor, and I hoped I would not be misunderstood.

"What do you mean?" he replied. I thought I saw a twinkle in his eye betraying his words. "There are still important topics we haven't finished." I felt a slight tension in the room. Secretary Gravy, I imaged, wished he was somewhere else. He cleared his throat, very quietly, as if to remind us of his awkward discomfort.

"Yeah, I know," I said quietly, still thinking of the uncomfortable delegate behind me, "but that's only *information*. I could simply leave you notes on those things, or you would learn them through the other delegates. I have a feeling you know most of it already."

"Well, what *do* you mean then? Are you ready to return to Engdynlor?" His words weren't deceitful, though he knew more than he was saying. He sounded hopeful, or expectant.

"No, Mr. Davis, I'm ready to learn from *you*. I need to learn what you have to teach, things I should learn and take with me when I return home."

The old man smiled and leaned back in his chair. His posture seemed to say *finally*, but in a kind, fatherly manner.

"Do you mean when you return to Engdynlor?"

"No. I mean when I return to my *real* home, in a faraway land."

"Well, I don't know *how far* it is…some might say it's not far at all. But that isn't important now. I'm not the wisest man in the kingdom, but I do think I can help you discover some things you might find useful, *back home*."

It was an odd way to word it, I thought at the time, but I would understand his meaning soon enough. This was how I began yet another training program at Portsmouth.

More immediately, I was curious by the way he talked about my return home. I tried to get the Chaplain to tell me what he knew of my world, and how he'd learned it. He certainly had theories, I could tell, by the way he spoke of it. I doubted he heard much on the subject from the King or the Captain. As many times as I asked, he only smiled and told me it wasn't important.

The Chaplain's training was hard for me to understand at first. It began with a test.

"Let's see if you can answer a riddle. Your answer will determine how we will proceed with your training." I agreed, hoping I would solve the riddle easily, though I had no idea what it would mean.

"An older lady, a dear friend of mine from Oyster Bay, was walking home from Beach Row, admiring a window crystal she'd just bought."

"A what?" I interrupted.

Nonplussed, the Chaplain replied, "It's a decorative crystal." Seeing I was unsatisfied with his answer, he went on. "It had a thousand facets to catch the sun, and threw rainbows all around the shop where she bought it. She returned to her aggregate—"

"What's an aggregate?" I interrupted once again.

"Oh, an *aggregate building*. They're common in large cities, wherever there are more people than open space. Imagine if the delegation building was much larger, and many people paid to live in it."

Oh, I thought to myself, *an apartment building*. I nodded, and the Chaplain went on.

"While she was hanging the crystal in her window, she saw a man in the alley getting robbed. After the victim handed over his money, the robber brutally stabbed him, and the poor man dropped to the ground. Though she didn't mean to, she let out a shriek. The murderer looked her way, and she was certain he saw her staring back.

"Here's where the tale gets strange," he said. "Instead of reporting the murder, she immediately walked down the hall to wish her friend goodnight, and give her a small gift. The riddle is: why didn't she report the murder?"

It was a strange story, to say the least. Not one element in it made sense to me. I thought for a while, going over the story in my mind again and again. *Why not report the murder? Why go on like it never happened?* I could think of no rational reason, so I gave the Chaplain an irrational one.

"She was senile. Though she saw the murder happen, she couldn't remember it a few moments later, and went on about her life as if it had never happened." The Chaplain smiled warmly at me. I was sure I answered correctly.

"Excellent," he said, patting me on the back. *"Not even close."*

"What?" *Was he mocking me?* I wondered.

"Don't worry, Mark," he chuckled. "You passed the test. You see, this riddle is only easy if you are psychotic. If you have no moral compass, you may fear a murderer, and yet hold no resistance to committing murder yourself. The old woman, you see, was criminally insane, and I was her counselor.

"If she reported the murder, she'd expose herself as a witness, and add risk to her life."

"If she doesn't," I interrupted a third time, "she runs the risk of living near a murderer. She might be next."

"Yes, but it's surely a very small risk."

He paused, and when I remained silent, he went on.

"And now, I must ask another question. What was the gift she gave to her neighbor?"

I wasn't merely unable to guess—I saw no possible way anyone could know the answer. It seemed wholly removed from the story, and I told him as much.

"You passed again," he replied. "You see, the present she gave to her friend was the very same window crystal the murderer saw her hanging in her window. If the murderer returns to kill the witness, he would see the crystal in her neighbor's window, and murder her neighbor instead."

I was dumbfounded. "The answer makes sense to me," I told the Chaplain, "and yet I never would have guessed it."

"Yes," he replied simply, "you are not criminally insane."

Having passed his dubious test, he asked me to return the next day, and promised to have another story for me to consider. When I did, he explained the next stories he told would not be riddles or tests.

"What are they then?" I asked.

"That's for you to discern," he told me. "Once you've memorized a few, you may have a better understanding."

At first it seemed he wanted me to memorize a series of random stories he recited. They were interesting, but often had unhappy endings. He made it clear the stories were fictional, and he refused to tell me what he meant to teach through them.

Even more unusual, he wouldn't let me write them down. I had to remember the stories and deliver each of them back to him in my own words. I honestly believed he wanted to teach me the skill of storytelling, or possibly better memory skills. I'd underestimated him before, and I was convinced I wouldn't do so again.

It was a full week before a pattern emerged: craftily hidden morals on misplaced priorities. This was my initial understanding of them, and it was partially correct. From the very first story, I expected to find moral lessons in them, but they were so well hidden, I'd given up looking. Each seemed to instead teach some random lesson, such as a year in their history, or a complex trade, or even political reform. Summarizing any of them by their moral, and comparing it to their full tale, I found they seemed on the surface, almost unrelated.

One story told of a young boy who was too concerned with earning the approval of other children. After an hour of describing the boy's sad upbringing, Davis painted the picture of a horrid death, lost in a blizzard. The boy risked the storm, convinced braving his way through it would impress his young friends, who cared little for his well-being.

Another story was about a rich man who was fair and generous, but died a lonely man nonetheless, because he hadn't left room in his life for relationships. Yet another told of a man who helped many, by spending most of his time serving others. He made a difference in a lot of people's lives, but was never able to impart the lessons he'd learned to others. The great causes he'd labored over all his life— each of them ended with his death.

The lesson in the last story Chaplain Davis told me, took me all day to find. When I gave my answer to the Chaplain that evening, I clearly surprised him.

"It normally takes a while for these things to become apparent," he said after a long and thoughtful pause. "How did you find your answer so quickly?" I could only shrug in response.

The story told of the life of a very rich man. At the age when successful men are their most productive, he sold his many parcels of land, and all his other possessions. He released businesses from contracts with him for a fraction of their value. All this he did to buy one thing he held to be invaluable. His friends and neighbors called him a fool, for they did not value his prize. He neglected any plans for his future and lost everything to obtain this one thing. At the end, Chaplain Davis asked me if the man in the story was a fool, and what it was he valued so much.

"No, he's not a fool," I'd told him. "He's only zealous. He's the silent duke, and the one thing he wanted most, is to pass on what he has to others."

Then the Chaplain told me this was the one thing *I* held as most important in life.

"I know now," he added, "you can become a capable leader—for this is a leader's heart, to give away what he has." I was shocked to hear him say these things. Was I speaking with the Chaplain, or the Captain?

"Why this sudden revelation?" I asked. "What does this have to do with the story of the silent duke?"

"That's the point," he told me. "This story wasn't written about the silent duke. It was *you* who made it about him." This was when he finally shared one of his true purposes in telling me these stories.

They were ambiguous by design, and each seemed as if it might teach several lessons, though not fully or effectively. To find a lesson in them requires interpretation. In hearing my responses, Chaplain Davis learned as much about me, even as I learned from the stories. The stories take on different meanings, depending on who interprets them. The same interpreter would be expected to find different morals in the same story, at different points in his life. Perhaps most importantly, the faster a person chooses a moral, the more important it is to him.

It wasn't an exact science, the Chaplain claimed, and the storyteller had to know the interpreter somewhat, for the process to work.

By telling me his full collection of stories, Chaplain Davis could draw up a long list of values, both good and bad, ranked according to how important they were to me. He claimed the ranking was more accurate than I could supply if I were asked plainly.

"Your subconscious doesn't lie," I remember him saying, more than once.

At the end, the Chaplain shared his results with me, and this was the true value of the stories. He encouraged me to find any portions of his findings I disagreed with, either in theory—as in *I know I should hold* this *as more important*—or in practice, such as *I'm sure I don't hold* this *value so important.* Each reaction showed either an area in which I needed further teaching, or a lesson I'd *learned,* but hadn't yet put into practice.

Then the Chaplain showed me his written copies of each story. I was shocked to find values I recognized from both halves of the Three Tables, but had forgotten completely they were mentioned at all. Those values, good *and* bad, were lowest in the ranking the Chaplain worked out for me.

It was a humbling exercise, and one I never forgot. I asked the Chaplain for permission to write copies of his stories, and share them with my mentor, the Captain. Chaplain Davis was quick to agree, but warned me not to share them with everyone, lest they lose their ability to test a person's reactions.

Finally, Mr. Davis told me there was only one story left: the story I had to tell him. He insisted I write it down before I told it. Though I tried to convince him I lacked the experience, I eventually agreed.

"One thing you need to know," he cautioned me. "Understand your characters can't all have the same moral maturity as you. This is harder than it seems." It didn't take him long to see I didn't understand him at all.

"There are six levels of moral behavior, on three different planes. No man can understand a plane of morality above the highest plane in which he operates." I wondered how long it would take him to speak plainly enough for me to understand him.

"Fine, let me explain," he went on.

He described the three planes of morality as: *others, self,* and the *beyond-self.*

"People who spend their lives in the *others* plane," he went on, "obey moral codes out of selfishness. They begin with a motivation of a fear of punishment. They eventually learn the second level of morals: to anticipate reward. Any animal can learn these."

"What next?" I asked, encouraged they might all sounds so easy.

"In the *self*-plane, we deal with ourselves, and it also holds two levels of morality: a healthy desire to conform or be accepted, and the morals of adhering to democratic rules that govern all."

For a moment I thought these were as high morals as there could ever be. I hoped his last plane wasn't something I couldn't understand.

"In the last plane, the *beyond-self,* we recognize morals are larger than ourselves. It contains *universal, self-evident truths,* which go beyond what immediately benefits us individually. Lastly, there is a moral of *ultimate love and truth,* a moral that is not motivated by any fear at all. If you desire to tell a story of characters of different moral planes, make sure they are consistent, and are each motivated by a specific plane, not seeing across all three."

I have reflected on these theories of his over the years, and plumbed untold corollaries and insights from this short description. They did not, however, alter the story I wrote for the Chaplain in Portsmouth. I believe he used this opportunity to plant in me the seeds of thoughts I would consider many times over a lifetime.

I did write a teaching story for him, and when I recited it to him, he promised he would add it to the story-lessons he passed on to others. To this day, I wonder how many he'd collected in the same way, from the people he'd taught and mentored over the years.

During all our time together I learned very little about his life's story, though he learned much of mine. What I did learn was entirely unexpected. He was once a soldier in the King's army, and went by another name. A narrow escape from death left him badly shaken. He left the army when he was given the opportunity, and eventually became an inventor. He became wealthy selling his inventions, though he made no attempt to prevent others from reproducing and selling them, and none of them were very complicated or advanced. One day he found someone had used one of his inventions to bring grave harm to another, and again he was shaken to his core. He went on a walking journey, abandoning his business and former life. When he returned, he'd changed his name from Patrick Ulrich to Patrick Davis. Since then, he'd dedicated his life to the same teachings as the Honor Knights, though he had no knowledge of our order. He'd learned them from another, though his teacher wasn't a knight either. He never spoke of his life as a young man, only the things he'd done after joining the army in his early thirties.

Almost everything about him began to puzzle me. He was warm and friendly, always compassionate, and he rarely spoke of himself. I wondered what secrets he held. In the few weeks we spent going over his stories we became fast friends in spite of his reservations in his personal history.

When I returned to my room that night, I found a letter waiting for me. The pages of the letter were not folded, but wrapped with paper, and tied with string, like a package. When I picked the packet up, I recognized the flowing script of the Captain's hand.

He didn't write often, but when he did, I could be sure it was something important. I rushed to lock my door, and tore open the letter. It was long indeed; longer than any other letter he'd written to me.

My attitude soured, as I perceived the mood in which most of the letter was written. It read more like a diary than a letter, and I wondered if the Captain had further motives than informing me of what had passed.

He appeared obsessed. His words were often scribbled, as if his hand struggled to chase after his mind while he wrote. He was consumed with the *kingdom's shield*, the rebel group who made an assassination attempt on our party, back in Oyster Bay. It seemed he considered it his own failure that such a group existed in the Kingdom.

He wrote of his associates in the southern towns of Terrezia. They had worked diligently to uncover the network of the *shield's* membership. They were a few dozen men who bound themselves to the fate of the troll's demise.

The last cell of the movement was the most difficult to uncover, and one of the men acting on behalf of the King died in his service, carrying out an order from the Captain to root out their last members at whatever cost was necessary.

I meant at the cost of the traitors' *lives*, the Captain wrote, *not his own.*

It took a heavy toll on the Captain, though he was concerned only for the family of his spy who had died to carry out his last assignment.

"I can finally breathe," he wrote. "I am convinced the last of the *shield* has been uncovered."

The King had been convinced much earlier, and thought the Captain had been acting irrationally, to suspect more members. Time proved the Captain right, though the extra worry had cost him.

I worried for the Captain. It was a feeling I wouldn't soon forget.

2.2 A Quiz

One morning not long after I'd completed my story for the Chaplain, I woke from my bed to the sound of rustling paper. Looking across my room, I saw a page had been slid under the door. There was a chill in the air. We'd had a few warm days after a near-blizzard, and most of the snow had melted. On this morning, however, I could see my breath in cold puffs before me—far too cold to chase after whoever left the message.

The large sheet of paper had a tiny pigeon scroll tied to it, and on the scroll was written a single line of random-looking symbols. I'd started to teach Thomas Junior how to take care of the pigeons, and I assumed he'd been by the loft already and found a message from Bob. The boy knew any message sent by pigeon was meant for me.

Bob and I had begun to send our own pigeons back and forth from my loft at the delegation building and his at the inn. I took out my *book of codes* as he called it, and began to transcribe his message, using the very last page of my codebook.

Each page of the notebook had a long list of random symbols. Each of the symbols matched up with a letter of the alphabet or a frequently used word, both of which were repeated many times on each page. He had an identical notebook, and we always worked from the same page. Once we encoded or decoded a message with a page from our code books, we both destroyed the page. When he first taught me to use this strange process, I asked why each page had to list the alphabet so many times, and why some of the letters were repeated in each alphabet.

"For the same reason we use symbols for short words," he had explained, pointing to random symbols used for words like *it, the, and, or.* "If we didn't, someone intercepting the message could begin to guess our code by the number of times a symbol is repeated."

I saw hundreds of symbols, but couldn't find the same one twice on any one page of the codebooks. A broken arrow-looking symbol might mean the first use of the letter *O* on one page of the code book, or the second use of the word *or* on another page. Before he taught me how to use the codebook, he made sure I knew it was a state secret. I swore no new oaths as none were required; he needed only to tell me secrecy was required of me by our order.

Encoding and decoding the messages was so slow and laborious, I couldn't do it if I was the least bit tired. We kept our messages as short as possible. Sending coded messages was very rare, due to the horrendous amount of time it required, but it was also a skill I was required to master.

I decoded Bob's message in my room that morning, trying to guess the rest of the message as I worked to save even a little time.

"Meet me…at the…*loft!* Come any…any*time* you like to…tomorrow!"

At first, I was happy to decode the message so quickly, but my happiness was quickly replaced with irritation.

"*Anytime you like,*" I said aloud, "*Meet me in the loft?* Where *else* would I meet him? Why does he waste my time like this?"

Even then I knew better. He wouldn't waste my time on purpose. Bob must have been trying to teach me something, but what? It hardly mattered to me that morning, sitting in the cold at the tiny desk in my room. I reminded myself of something the Chaplain had once told me: *patience isn't learned on a schedule.*

When I met Bob the next day in his loft, he handed me a new pair of codebooks. When I flipped through them, I saw they were empty.

"What are *these* for?" I asked, but I'd already made a guess—one I hoped was wrong.

"They're for you. It's *your* turn." He wore a taunting smile, which I'd learned meant an assignment was coming I would not enjoy.

"My turn for what?"

"Well, training you to turn codes has used up a full set of my codebooks. It's your turn to make a pair." His smile only grew.

"Does that mean my code training is over?" I asked, hopefully.

"Yes it does—and your *pigeoneering* training as well."

"How do you know I'm ready?" I asked. I knew I would be required to decode thirty letters a minute to pass his test. "I've never decoded anything in front of you..."

I watched his eyes roll up and to the right, a sign he'd taught me shows someone is recalling from memory. I knew it was intentional, since he'd been trained to hide this and other *tells*, as he called them.

"'*Anytime you like? Meet me in the loft?* Where *else* would I meet him? Why does he waste my time like this?'" he mimicked my voice, far from his gravely baritone.

"What? You were *there?* You were *spying on me?*"

He threw a handful of hay at me. "Think of it as giving you a test without the benefit of knowing you might fail. It *worked.* Forty-two letters a minute. Not bad for someone who didn't know there was anything to learn about pigeons a few weeks ago."

Though he might have been convinced otherwise, I came to enjoy taking care of the pigeons after my initial objections to cleaning their roosts. I told him so.

"I'm pleased to hear it. By now, a person would either enjoy them or hate them. Not everyone falls into the former." He flashed another smile.

"Did you train Eastman how to care for your birds—or how to use a codebook?"

"Well, let's see," he replied, mocking but still light-hearted. "The code is a secret of the Honor Knights, so, *did I teach it to him?* Hmmm…"

"All right, then—what *did* you teach him?"

"Mostly how to clean bird droppings from the loft. He knew something of our code, though he should not have. When I never mentioned coding a message, he got less and less patient, though he tried to hide it. He couldn't bring it up, because he shouldn't have known about it in the first place." Bob wore a mischievous smile.

"How did he learn about it?"

"Who knows? Maybe he found a dead pigeon who never reached its home." It was my turn to smile. Only Bob would use *who,* in describing a pigeon.

"What if he guessed how the code works?" I asked, wondering if it were possible.

"A code that never repeats a symbol is called a non-repeating cipher, and it is impossible to crack. Even if he knew how the code works, it wouldn't do him any good unless he had the right codepage to decode it. And once a pair of code pages is used, both pages are destroyed, never to be duplicated again. You'll see why when you fill them out yourself."

When he showed me how to fill out the codebooks, I understood how no two pages in a book are ever the same. He had a set of oddly-shaped dice. Every side of each die was inscribed with a piece of the symbols used in the codebooks. The dice were colored and had ten sides each.

"Just remember, 'red, orange, yellow,'—and *no repeats*."

Those were the only two rules to filling the books. When I rolled the dice, I put the three symbol pieces from the three dice together into a symbol. I recognized the way they belonged together because I'd spent so much time decoding Bob's messages and looking up the thousand symbols. I rolled my first symbol right there in the dim light of the loft. I entered it into the first box of the first page of both books. Twenty-six letters with each vowel repeated four times, and a dozen short words, over and over again on the page. I tried to estimate how long it would take to fill, but gave up in desperation.

"What if I roll the same symbol twice?"

Bob smiled. "That, my young friend, is the *fun* part. You have to check for redundant symbols as you fill out each page. You skip any roll that makes a symbol you already used. Otherwise, it would be too easy! After all, there are only a thousand symbols, each to be listed once per page." His mischievous smile crawled over his face again. He knew how long it would take me to fill the pages of the books.

I thought of the code a little more. "So even if someone knew exactly how the code works, they still couldn't figure out what it says?" I asked. As soon as I said it, I felt foolish. He'd just explained this to me, and it wasn't the first time. But his patient reply reminded me of his heart, and for all his peculiarity, for the kindness he'd eventually showed me.

"Exactly right. It's why we go through such painful lengths to fill each page. It would be much easier to write only twenty-six symbols per page, but there would be many repeats. If there were several one-symbol words in the message, it would be easy to guess which symbol in the message represents letter *A*."

"Ah. Which is why we have symbols for all these short-words," I trailed off, pointing to the page.

"Yes. These are the most common short-words a code breaker would look for. If Nigel—should that fallen knight still live—had found one of our messages, he would know which short-words we *don't* have symbols for. But because we don't repeat symbols in a given message, he'd only be lucky to guess a few short words at best, and they would be meaningless without any context. If it's a *really* secretive message, we don't use spaces."

I spent a minute reflecting on the code and wondering why Eastman wanted to learn it. Perhaps he *had* found a message.

"What ever happened to Eastman?" I asked.

"I hear he's doing translation work for the Mountain Delegation."

"*He's stationed in the Winter Palace?*" I asked, immediately worried for David.

"No, he's stationed in Thraen Kholl. He works with Sphotch, under Engdynlor."

I relaxed at hearing David wouldn't have to deal with him. He seemed like a changed man when I last saw him at Engdynlor, but I still wouldn't want him on my delegation.

"Now that we're done with the codes and pigeons, what do I learn next?"

"I don't know. What do you *think* you'll learn?" Bob

replied.

"*What?* Why don't you know? You're still my teacher…"

"Not anymore, I'm not. Now that your assignments here are done, you'll be given a new assignment."

"Really?" I felt a little sad. Bob was a different kind of teacher, but to my surprise, I found myself missing him already. "Then why did you have to certify me in decoding? What will I ever use all this knowledge for?"

"You'll need it soon enough. You'll send messages by pigeon on your next assignment."

"Oh. When will I find out what it is?"

"Right now."

"I thought you said I'd find out what it is *later.*"

"Actually, I said you'd be given your assignment *now.*" Was he trying to test me again? He'd taught me to recall pieces of recent conversation verbatim. He claimed it was paramount in negotiations. It didn't take long to remember the words he'd just said, and I saw he was right. The way he'd worded it, I expected to go back to the palace and receive my assignment.

"Well then, what is it?"

"As soon as you're ready to listen, I'll tell you." Again, he smiled at me patiently. I took the hint and sat down on a stool in the loft, and waited silently. My mind raced—would it be another learning assignment, or an assignment to return home? Bob couldn't reply soon enough for me to hide my impatience.

"You and your brother are to meet at Engdynlor, and will soon leave on a journey by sea. Other than that, you'll have to wait until you speak with someone who knows more than I do."

I fell into wonderment over what my next assignment could be. *Surely it wouldn't be anything so difficult as leading a delegation of adults*, I thought.

"There's something else, Mark," Bob interrupted my thoughts. "This will be the last assignment you are sent on…by the King."

"What?" I asked, suddenly concerned. *"Is something wrong with him?"*

"No. The journey you and your brother next take, will lead you *home*."

"My *real* home?"

Home again—I could hardly believe it. Another set of memories washed over me, along with a fresh set of emotions. I thought of all the things I so badly missed: m*y parents, my younger brother, my home, my* room—*electricity!* It all felt far away, and so very long ago. I felt younger when I remembered my real home, much younger than I felt that day, sitting in Bob's loft.

"There's some rush to get you back to Engdynlor, I understand. In fact, you've been asked to leave as soon as you have a few days' worth of work left on the codebooks, so you can finish the job on the ship to Oyster Bay. My guess is your ship has already left the Bay, and is on its way here."

"That soon?"

"That soon. You'll need to say your goodbyes in the next few days."

I'd be leaving before the Princess had a chance to visit Portsmouth and meet her old friend. It was a reunion I'd been looking forward to seeing.

"I'll miss you, Bob." Only when I told him, did I realize just how true this was. Randomly, I wondered why I called him Bob and not *sir* or Mr. Tiller.

He watched me through faraway eyes and said, "I'll miss you too, son." The air around me seemed to thicken, and every sound became soft, like after a deep snowfall. It was an awkward moment that seemed to stretch on for an eternity, and then it seemed it had never happened.

"Well, don't waste the whole day here!" he said in a gruff voice, sweeping the moment out of the loft along with the old hay and pigeon dung. "You'd better start making arrangements with the delegation, and letting your friends know how soon you'll be leaving."

I thanked him quietly and headed back to the delegation.

On my way to the stable, I saw Jonathan Arnold, the old Portsmouth mayor. He'd been on the opposite side of the street, but crossed over when he saw me. He walked with swift resolution as he approached, then blocked my path with his wide stance.

"Well, I hope you're happy," he said, nearly shouting. "You ran my boy out of town just to make things easier on your troll buddies."

I was in no mood for his foolishness. Did he really believe *I* ran his son out of town? I walked onto the street and stepped quickly around him. I tossed a hasty reply over my shoulder.

"Not now, Mr. Arnold, I'm in a hurry." I thought to myself, *with all the people I'll miss in Portsmouth, I'm glad I'll never see him again.* I looked forward to the day not far off, when I wouldn't have to guard my words and bite my tongue around this foolish, hateful man.

"Oh, that's how you'd like to leave it, is it? You run my boy off, rip him out of our family, and don't even have the decency to *face me?*"

Hot anger flashed within me. He was no longer my responsibility. His accusations were pathetic—blaming me for what he knew *he* had done. I froze in my tracks and turned to face him, knowing already it was a mistake.

"Decency? You shout about *decency?* What decency does a

man have who blames a boy for his own crimes? Who turns his own son against him and is too big a fool to admit it? Who hides in his own fears of what he's done and…and how many lives he's wrecked, but still hasn't the brains to *do something about it?*"

He fell back a step, as if he'd been slapped in the face. His eyes went wide, then narrowed as fury overcame him. He reached out and struck me hard with the back of his hand, right across the mouth. I couldn't believe how fast he'd moved; it was over before I could react.

He struck me so hard, I fell onto my back. My mouth was warm and tasted like salt; my nose was numb. I didn't fight to hold back any tears—there simply weren't any trying to escape from my eyes. I glared at him with pure hatred and lit into him once again, this time while my tongue and lips tingled numbly.

"Is that how you solve your problems, with violence and hate? Now your hatred has spread to me, and what will *I* do with it? I won't keep it. I give it right back to you. Go live in your hatred, and may it keep you from all the others you'd like to spread it to!"

I picked up the codebooks and charged on, silently wishing him dead. I didn't look back to see him again. I knew he'd struck me hard, but I resolved not to check until I was alone. By the time I'd reached the stable where I'd left Thomas's horse not an hour earlier, I was afraid to check. *What if he broke my nose?* I wondered.

I pulled the horse from her stall, leaving the cart in front of the stables. I didn't stop to talk to anyone on the way out of town. I rode as fast as the horse would carry me.

2.3 What Violence Begets

Thomas Arnold, I thought, *why did you have to find me today?*
When the town was well behind me, I felt my throat tighten
and my eyes burn. I wondered with cool detachment why I
hadn't felt like crying while I faced him. Perhaps I was too
angry…or maybe I was getting older. Rather than think of
what I'd just said to him, I pondered why I'd never seen a
grown man cry when he was frustrated or angry, but I'd seen
grown women do it. I'd seen teenage bullies cry, and even
older boys who weren't bullies at all.

Why is that? I wondered. *When does a man no longer need to
work at holding back tears when he's angry?* Soon I allowed my
thoughts to turn to the things I'd said to Arnold. *What if it
comes true? What if he lives in hatred the rest of his life?* I tried hard
to push the thoughts away.

I wanted to ignore the pain growing in my mouth and nose,
but it was getting difficult. I spit on the ground and tried not
to look, but saw blood from the corner of my eye nonetheless.
I jumped off my horse when I reached the delegation building,
and ran up to the washroom to clean my mouth and nose, the
codebooks still under my arm. Before I finished, there was a
knock at the door. I hurried to answer it, and found a very

concerned Chaplain Davis.

"*What happened to you?*" His brow was set with anger and surprise, both at once.

"Nothing," I said at first, but I knew he wouldn't leave it at that. "I said some things I shouldn't have, I suppose."

Mr. Davis gently grasped my shoulders. "Who did this to you?" he whispered urgently, "Was it that *birdman*, Bob Tiller?"

"*No*, he's my *friend*." *I'm not a man yet*, I thought randomly, and tried desperately to keep my voice level.

"Well then, who?"

"It was Arnold. He blamed me for Kale leaving and I got angry—too angry." Now the Chaplain seemed angry, but not at me. *He must not understand*, I thought to myself. "I didn't hold back. I said every angry thing I'd ever thought about him. I said such horrible things…" I stopped when my voice caught in my throat.

"You did, did you? It's bad enough for him to attack you—but to attack a representative of the King?" He let me go, patting my cheek as he turned and left. *Ouch*.

When he reached the end of the hall he shouted, "*Gravy! Phillips!*" Secretary Gravy opened his door right away. "Go and find some ice or snow, quickly," the Chaplain said.

It was winter, and ice was easy to come by. The ground wasn't covered with snow just then, but there was plenty piled up in well-shaded areas north of most buildings. Lieutenant Phillips appeared, apparently halfway through shaving. With soapy foam covering half his face, he thrust an arm through a thick wool shirt as he stomped down the hall toward us.

"*Lieutenant*," the Chaplain went on, "Jonathan Arnold assaulted our head delegate. They had a verbal exchange, and Arnold attacked him. Do you know what to do?"

"Yes sir, I do." His voice was cold and his gaze fixed steadily before him. He rushed past us, shoving his arm through the other half of his shirt as he stormed out of the building.

What's going on? I wondered. *They* must *have misunderstood me.*

"*Chaplain,* he didn't attack me...he just...I made him *so* mad. I said things I shouldn't have. I told him I hoped he lived alone with his hate for the rest of his life."

"Did you strike him, or attempt to strike him?"

"*No!*"

"In all likelihood, what you said was justified. Either way, we'll talk about your *verbal exchange* later. Here, let's go and sit in the kitchen." Chaplain Davis waited for me to walk ahead of him down the stairs. I clutched the rough-sawn handrail, unexpectedly light-headed. When we reached the kitchen, Stephen Gravy came in with a large pack of clean snow.

"Come," Davis said to me, patting a stool beside the long table, "have a seat here."

Davis tried to pack my nose with snow, while the chaplain washed his hands. He told me to put some snow in my mouth, and it stung. Davis told me to spit it into a bowl set before me.

"This is going to hurt, I'm afraid." The kindly Chaplin reached into my mouth with both hands and grabbed my lower teeth *hard*. He pulled and yanked on my teeth to straighten them. I let out a moan. He held them firmly with his fingers for a few seconds, then told me to spit again. Once more he reached into my mouth and held my teeth firmly. He left Stephen to feed me clean snow, and told me to keep a clump on my mouth and nose until he returned. The pain began to spread across my face. I wished they would both leave me alone. The way they treated me led me to worry.

The Chaplain soon returned with Dr. Maher at his side. The doctor looked into my mouth and nodded back to the Chaplain before he turned to me.

"I'm afraid some of your teeth were knocked loose. I'm going to have you bite down on some clay, then rinse your mouth." First he reached into my mouth and pressed hard on my teeth, just as the Chaplain had done. My eyes watered, it hurt so badly.

"And here's the clay," the doctor said. "We need an impression of your teeth while they're where they're supposed to be."

He handed me a wet, blue-grey lump. If smelled like rich, dark soil. I hesitated before I put it into my mouth. It tasted just as it smelled.

I bit down on it cautiously, hoping it would hurt less. It was soft and light, not like any clay I'd touched before.

"No, wait...wiggle the clay loose," he continued. "We don't want it to pluck your teeth from your mouth, do we?" I spit the clay lump out onto my hand and Dr. Maher took it from me.

"My teeth are loose? They don't *feel* loose."

"Well, they're not *really* loose—I just meant they've been moved around a bit. Your gums swelled up so they don't *feel* loose, but your teeth were in the wrong place. The snow will help the swelling go down, and I'm going to have this clay fired. The rest of the day, you'll need to keep snow in your mouth, or this piece of clay I'll soon bring back to you. Oh—and I'll bring you something for the pain, too."

The doctor's manner had calmed me considerably, and soon Stephen brought me more clean snow. I didn't have long to worry before the doctor returned.

"Here, rinse your mouth really well with this," he said, handing me a small cup with some kind of syrup in it. "It will make you tired, but it will also take away some of the pain." I took the cup and spit out the soupy snow melting in my mouth.

Ouch! It burned like fire, but as I swished it around, the pain began to lessen.

"Spit it out now, Mark. Try to spit it *all* out, or you'll be asleep before you know it." I spit the medicine into the same bowl as the snow. When I tried to speak, my tongue wouldn't work—it was just like getting a filling at the dentist. The doctor signaled me to stop.

"Don't talk just yet; there will be plenty of time for that later. Be very careful, and don't eat anything either. This is a strong medicine, and you could bite your tongue up pretty good without feeling it."

I tried to answer, but he held a finger to his lips. I nodded.

"By tonight you'll be able to eat a little—nothing with much chewing though. It won't kill you to wait until then to talk, will it?" He smiled. After what I'd said to Arnold, I thought it was probably better if I didn't talk for a while.

I tried to bite my tongue just a little. *Can I really chew it up without knowing it?* I wondered.

"*No chewing,*" Dr. Maher ordered, and I nodded back to him. He opened his bag and pulled out some cotton swabs and another bottle.

"You've washed up yourself, I see, but let's just try to make things a little cleaner." He hesitated long enough to worry me. "This might sting a little."

He put more of the same medicine on a cotton ball and wiped my nose and upper lip. It stung just as badly as when I rinsed my mouth, but again, it didn't last long. Then he opened the other bottle and used his cotton to wipe it over my nose and lip. By that time I didn't feel a thing. He promised he'd check on me later, and turned to leave. As he passed Stephen, the bowl of snow caught his eye.

"How old is this stuff?" the doctor asked him.

"It's from the storm, last week," he replied.

"*Last week*? I have no idea how clean this snow is. I've just disinfected his mouth; I can't let him put *that stuff* in there."

He turned to me again, and laid his hand on my shoulder. "Little change in plans, Mark. Pack some snow wrapped in a towel on the *outside* of your mouth, and keep the clay bit in there at least thirty minutes each hour until dinner time. The bit will be ready soon—it's being fired right now."

Not able to speak, I simply nodded. It had been a long day. *Am I really going home?* I wondered, remembering my conversation with Bob no more than an hour or two ago. When he brought the clay piece back, he pressed on my teeth one last time, and made sure they fit into the impressions in the clay. My teeth marks were deep, and filled with some kind of gummy syrup, maybe molasses. The doctor warned me to be careful when wearing the *bit*, and not to bite down hard on it. By the time the medicine wore off, I was almost glad for the pain to return—at least I could talk and eat.

I ate a small bowl of noodle soup. I was still tired from the medicine, and went to bed early. *What will happen to Arnold?* I wondered guiltily. I dreamt of him hitting me, over and over again. When I woke it was early morning, and I was glad to be rid of the dreams.

I went right to the mirror after waking, to see what my face looked like. It wasn't as puffy as when I'd looked in the mirror the previous night, but the bruising was far worse. I padded down the steps to the office room we all shared.

"Good to see you up and around." It was Stephen Gravy, the delegation secretary. He lifted his face from his desk when I entered the room, then winced when he saw my bruises.

"Thanks for all your help yesterday. I felt like the doctor made too much of an ordeal of everything."

"Do you really think so?" he asked.

"Mr. Gravy, you didn't hear what I said to him. I probably

deserved it."

Stephen suddenly looked old. He removed his glasses and rubbed his brow.

"That's not the point. We're here at Portsmouth to represent the King. This is even more obvious for you, as the head delegate. Forgive me for saying so, but as far as our law goes, you're still a minor. You're responsible for your own actions certainly, but we have laws that protect women and...well, *minors* from those who would do them harm. If he admits you didn't strike him first, or even worse, didn't strike him *at all*...well, then—things won't go so well for him."

Why did I let my mouth run away from me? For a fleeting moment, another thought flashed through my mind. *Serves him right.* I chased the thought from my head. Any punishment he received would probably make him a bigger enemy to the trolls—and the delegation. I tried to imagine how this might be resolved peacefully, but I found no answer. If he was a dedicated enemy of the delegation, he would be an enemy of the King as well.

"Why couldn't I have held my tongue for another day or two?" I said under my breath.

"Why? What difference would a day or two have made?" Stephen asked a little suspiciously. I realized I hadn't told anyone the news of my leaving.

"Oh, I just received my orders. The Chaplain and I have still been meeting, but not about the delegation; we've been done with the hand-off for some time. I'll be leaving Portsmouth by the end of the week."

"What? Why didn't you tell us?"

"I only found out yesterday morning. No sooner than I got here, the doctor had my mouth full of medicine and mud."

"Oh—I see," said Gravy, and shifted uncomfortably. "I guess we knew you'd be leaving soon. We'll all miss you very much," he said sincerely. Then his eye turned almost cunning, and he added, "Can I make one suggestion?" I nodded, eager to hear a solution to my predicament. "If your new assignment—whatever it is—is important enough it won't be delayed, then Jonathan Arnold will be on trial before you leave. What I suggest is: pass your title as head delegate to the Chaplain *now*. Then your last days in town won't be taken up completely by the proceedings of Arnold's trial, and you can make preparations for your next assignment."

I knew I'd be busy filling out the identical pair of codebooks. In a way, they *were* preparations for my next assignment. As I thought through it, I realized Stephen's suggestion might be the only way I could complete my codebooks before leaving.

I quickly agreed, and asked if he knew where the Chaplain was.

"I think he's in his room," Stephen replied. "He was up very late last night. He didn't get back from town until after you went to bed."

"Thank you, Mr. Gravy." He nodded back to me and went back to his work.

I returned to my room and began filling out the codebooks. It went so slowly, I thought it might take weeks to finish. As I worked, the coding became a little easier. I guessed if I continued to work faster, it might take only a week to complete. Before I'd finished my first page, there was a knock at the door.

"Just a minute," I called, closing both books and scooping up the dice.

"Time to check on your progress," I heard from the other side of the door. *Already?* I thought. *I've hardly had time to start.* Then I realized the voice at my door wasn't Bob's, so whoever it was had no knowledge of the codebooks. I opened the door to find the doctor patiently waiting.

"How's my favorite patient?" he asked.

"I'm guessing I'm your *only* patient right now," I replied with an awkward smile. *Ouch,* I thought, *remember not to smile.*

He had me sit at my desk, and pulled from his bag a tiny mirror on a stick. "Let's see how your gums look." With my mouth open wide, I had nothing to say. "I saw a lot of loose teeth during the war," he continued. "Yours are the first I've seen since then." I wanted to ask where he was during the war, but he was still peering into my mouth with a studied look.

"And…we're done. Everything looks much better. I don't think your mouth needs any special treatment today. Just try to keep it clean and rinse a lot."

"Thanks, doctor. I really didn't think it was worth all this fuss."

"Oh you didn't, did you? It was only worth *the fuss* if you mind having horribly crooked teeth for the rest of your life. Didn't you see how they were arranged when you got back from town yesterday?"

"Honestly, my mind was on other things. I guess I was looking more at my cheeks and nose."

"You'll look roughed up for a few days. After that, the swelling and bruising should be gone. If you find yourself in a similar situation in the future, you might be well advised to *duck*." He winked at me and left with a quick *goodbye*. I only got into the rhythm of rolling and writing a few symbols before there was another knock. This time it was Chaplain Davis.

"Mr. Davis, please come in. I was hoping to talk to you this morning."

"Yes, I'm afraid I had a very late night in town. Bob the birdman was very helpful. He agreed to send a bird off to the palace at night, which he rarely does."

Oh no—Bob knows everything now, I thought in a panic. *What will he think?* I remembered to calm myself. The Chaplain could know nothing of Bob training me in anything but pigeon care.

"Um...what did he say?"

"Hmm? Who, the birdman? Oh, he said he didn't like to send a bird out so late, but he could make an exception if it was very urgent. One thing was odd though—he wasn't very cooperative until I gave him the message. Of course, he chopped it down to almost nothing, to fit on one of those little scrolls. Until he read it, he was insistent he should wait for first light. I guess with all your time there learning about his pigeons, he's taken a liking to you."

"So what did your letter say?" I asked anxiously.

"Well, the King had to hear of this. I know you aren't blaming Jonathan, but you've got to understand this involves more than your own preferences now. If a former mayor strikes a representative of the King, there could be grave consequences if it were to go unpunished. I filed the report for you, as you weren't able to get around yesterday."

"Did you say it wasn't until night, when you sent your message?"

"I did. First, I was busy with the Lieutenant, making arrangements for Jonathan's trial, and his...care until then."

"What do you mean?"

"The Lieutenant arrested him. He will be kept under guard until his trial, which will take place here, at the delegation. I was busy working with the town council over the details. Only then did I send word to the palace."

"What kind of details did you work out?"

"Well, politically, there were some very important decisions to be made. Jonathan Arnold lives in Portsmouth proper.

The victim, that would be you, lives in our camp, here in the outskirts of the county. Though the violation was committed in town, you were on your way home on delegation business. That was a bit of a stretch, but since your assignment to learn about pigeons came from the King, and it came while you are still the head of the delegation, it is technically delegation business, so it is within the delegation's charter and jurisdiction. We get to try the case here."

"I'm not sure I follow you," I replied. It certainly sounded more complex than I expected. "Why is it so important where it's tried?" I worried I would be found guilty of antagonizing Arnold, or declared an unfit delegate.

"Don't you see? *The jury!* The jury will be selected by the judge—we'll have to talk about that—but the jury will be selected here, in the county. That means the jury will have to include *trolls* to be a fair representation of the county's people. This is a precedence of enormous proportion. Now all the trolls who have been recently granted citizenship will be eligible as *jurors*."

Understanding finally began to seep into my mind. As I grappled with the weight of the trial, I wondered who the judge would be.

"What were you saying about the judge?" I asked.

"Yes, that's what I wanted to talk to you about. Bob said something about the new assignment you received yesterday. He told me you read it in front of him…"

"*What?* Oh yes, my new assignment," I replied. In all the excitement, I nearly forgot I hadn't told anyone but Stephen. "I'll have to leave for Engdynlor very soon—by the end of the week, most likely."

"Yes. Well," the Chaplain started, "the head delegate would normally sit as judge on this case, but obviously, this creates a dilemma."

"But if I handed the position to you *now*," I interrupted, "we would have a solution."

"Heaven knows I'm not anxious to take over the delegation, but this trial would go much smoother…"

"And I've already come to the same conclusion…with a little help from Stephen. Yes, I'll hand over the position immediately. I guess we should call a meeting downstairs to have Stephen enter it into the official record. In fact, there's a lot of writing I need to do before a ship arrives to take me to the Bay. I had no idea I'd be leaving with so little notice."

Mr. Davis looked concerned. "I'm sorry you'll be leaving in such bitter circumstances. I would have liked to throw a nice party to show you off, and wish you well on your next assignment. With the trial going on this week, I'm afraid it would be impolitic of us." Then he turned to me and rested his hand on my shoulder. "I'll miss you, Mark. You've proven not only to be a capable leader, but more mature than many adult leaders I've known."

"Thank you, Mr. Davis. I'm glad I was able to see some of the things you have to teach me. I wish I had more time…and I wish I hadn't said those things to Arnold. I held my tongue all this time, but in the end, I did more damage than if I never held back at all."

"Maybe there's a lesson in there for you; one last lesson to take with you from *this place*."

My eyes widened in surprise for a quick second.

"Do you mean I shouldn't have held it in?" Just then I remembered the first lesson Bob taught me, when I'd first returned to Portsmouth. *Is it good enough to hold back angry, or prideful, or selfish thoughts?* I asked myself again. Certainly I'd rather not have the thoughts at all, but what else could I do with them if not bottle them up or let them out?

"Anger is a meal that grows more bitter as it stews. The

same could be said for unforgiveness, or jealousy, or a lot of hurtful things. It's best not to cook them at all."

"But how do I keep from cooking them?" I asked. "What else do I do?"

"That, my young friend, is a lesson you are still learning."

"You won't tell me the answer?" I asked, surprised.

"The answer isn't one to be told, it's one to be *learned*, when you are ready." Then the Chaplain added with a wry smile, "I'm still learning it myself."

I changed the subject, agitated, but also distracted by the urge to return to my codebooks. The Chaplain smiled warmly at me when he got up and left. He wished me well and said he needed to prepare for the jury selection. Looking back, I know there was no way my thoughts escaped him. He knew I was frustrated by his answer, and left to give me time to think.

2.4 Visitors before the Trial

I spent the rest of the week filling my codebooks: rolling the three dice, checking to see if I'd used the symbol yet, then writing it in one book, and finally copying it in the other. I knew it would be tiresome, but I was shocked at the amount of time I had to spend re-rolling and checking to see which symbols were already used.

Halfway through the first page I was convinced there was an easier way. I drew up a large chart with all the thousand symbols, and crossed out the ones I'd already used. When I rolled a symbol I'd crossed out, I simply used the next symbol in the chart. It was an easy way to tell which symbols I'd already used, and I didn't have to keep re-rolling. I imagined how long it would take using the old method to roll the last few symbols for each page—what a nightmare! On the third page I started feeling guilty, and I asked Bob if my new method was cheating.

"Congratulations—you've passed the test with flying colors," he answered excitedly.

"What test? What are you talking about?"

"No one could fill out the codebooks the way I showed you—it would take forever. Before you get too irritated, let me explain the two goals of this test. Not only does it test your ability to think of new solutions to a problem, but we also hope to find a better way of making codebooks. Your method was found many times before, and we've only made one small adjustment to it. When you roll a symbol you already used, you must pick the *next* unused symbol one time, and pick the *previous* unused symbol the next time. You take turns, you see?"

He could see the disappointment in my face. "Do I have to redo the last two pages now?"

"No," he answered with a chuckle. "The most important part to filling codebooks is: both codebooks are identical, and secondarily, symbols aren't repeated. I will have to check your work on both those requirements."

I sighed in relief.

"Don't forget to destroy your tables when you finish a page," he added sternly. "Now tell me this: how many pages did you fill before you found this method?"

"Um…half the first page."

"Well then, congratulations *again*. Some coders have completed one, two, or even three pages before they realized the faster method. You've done well."

Inwardly I beamed at his recognition. Somewhere in the back of my mind I wondered if I put too much value in Bob's approval.

I spent my time filling the books: roll, write, write, roll, write, write, over and over for the next three days, while the jury was selected and the initial trial formalities were performed. I had no idea the full trial would be so long. I wasn't called until it was time to give my testimony.

I had a surprise the day before the trial's examinations began. By this time, I was sick of working on the codebooks. I was just about to complete a page when there was a subtle knock at my door. When I opened it, I was astonished to see the Princess and Lady Sally.

"Well, aren't you going to invite us in?" she said with a giggle.

"Oh, yes—come in, come in! I'm afraid I don't have much room in here," I replied in a daze. I motioned Schelli to take the seat at my desk, and Lady Sally sat on the edge of my bed. They both wore clothes common for a wife and daughter of a farmer, and this was partly why I was shocked. It seemed as if two worlds had collided.

Schelli reached out and touched my nose as she passed by me.

"Does it hurt…much?"

Inwardly I groaned. Of course she knew—Engdynlor had gotten word nearly a week ago. At least I didn't have to explain it to her.

"No, not anymore."

Lady Sally sent a look Schelli's way, as if to chastise her. They settled, and I asked what brought them to Portsmouth.

"I'm here as your ambassador, don't you remember?" she teased.

"Of course I do. I just—it's really great to see you, both of you. Have you met Linda yet?" I knew she would want to find her old friend as soon as she could.

"No, I was hoping you would show us the way to her house and visit with us."

"If you aren't too busy with your work," added Lady Sally.

"No, no! I needed to take a break from it. It's very boring."

"Oh?" interrupted Schelli, eying the closed books beside her on my desk.

"Yes, too boring to talk about," I replied a little nervously perhaps. "Let's go right now—there are others I'd like to introduce you to—friends of mine.

We made our way to the large-framed house of Linda's adopted family. Linda was old enough to be considered a young adult by troll or human standards. Her family didn't recognize the Princess of course, and told us we could find her at the Ahrens' home.

As we left their house, Schelli spoke, "I didn't realize their houses were so *big*—and the trolls themselves. I guess I knew how tall they would be, but when I stepped off onto the dock here in Portsmouth, I was...very surprised."

"I know. When I first arrived, I felt like they might gobble me up at any moment," I replied.

"*Mark,*" Schelli scolded, "you shouldn't joke like that. Someone might hear you."

"There's no use pretending otherwise. The trolls for the most part have come to expect it. It's just something we have to learn our way around, as we get to know the trolls better." I smiled and added, "Admit it, you were both scared back on the docks."

"*I wasn't*—not at all," Schelli objected.

"Well, maybe a *little*," added Lady Sally, glancing across the room toward the Princess.

"If it was only a little, you were braver than all the delegates," I told them. Lady Sally tried to hold back a smile, but the Princess only frowned. "There's one other thing I should mention—Linda doesn't want others to know of her past in Thraen Kholl. She's managed to keep all but her adopted family from knowing—and the Ahrens, of course."

Before long, we were at the Ahrens' front door. I knocked and Linda answered. Before I could step aside, Schelli pressed past us and flung her arms around Linda.

"*Hrinda*—I mean Sreehabem! It's really you."

Linda's eyes grew wide, as Schelli jumped to reach her neck

in embrace. Smiling, Linda pried the Princess away and held her at arm's length. "Little Schelli…I thought I'd never see you again. You're all grown up."

"*Me?*" Schelli cried, dropping to her feet. "What about *you?* You're taller than my father."

"Well, I would expect that," she said, smiling. "He's not a troll."

They talked on for some time before Tom Junior came to the door.

"Hi, Mr. Mark. Who are these people, Linda?"

"I'll tell you," Linda replied, laughing, "but you won't believe me."

We sat in the Ahrens' living room and were joined by Tom's mother, Phyllis. Linda seemed a little reluctant at first, but she remembered the entire Ahrens family knew her story as she made her introductions.

"Phyllis, this is Schelli and her Auntie, Miss Sally."

Phyllis looked pale. "You mean this is…Your Highness! I didn't know you were coming—"

"Please ma'am, I'm only Schelli today, an old friend of Sreehabem's. Please treat me as you would any of her friends."

Mrs. Ahrens calmed a little, but she plainly felt distressed to have the Princess visit her home unexpectedly. Eventually Sally asked Phyllis if she could help her make lunch, as it was already early afternoon. They left for the kitchen to make sandwiches for the rest of us. Linda ate a sandwich with sliced raw meat, and no one seemed to notice.

Schelli and Sreehabem chatted and giggled like schoolgirls as they caught up with each other's lives. Linda—Sreehabem by her troll name—explained how she had taken a part time job helping Mrs. Ahrens running her household. Soon Yenem and Yureev would be there, as they usually spent their afternoons with the Ahrens. Thomas was out in the barn fixing tools, but soon came in for lunch and met the Princess and Lady Sally for a second time. He wasn't as thrown off as his wife had been, but he did seem different—more polite perhaps. By the time the sandwiches were gone, the atmosphere had relaxed, and seemed closer to a gathering of friends than a royal visit. I wished the Captain and my brother could have been there.

Sitting in the Ahrens house that day, I knew the tranquil mood would soon leave me. I was due to testify in Arnold's trial the next morning, and that knowledge wore at me. So while the rest of the group talked into the afternoon, I excused myself and returned to my room.

I'd already gone over the scene between Arnold and me several times, but I wanted to make sure Arnold and his council wouldn't confuse me. I was nervous and more than a little embarrassed the next day when I was called to the stand.

As I took the witness chair, I saw Bob in the audience. *As if I'm not embarrassed enough,* I thought. I wished for the thousandth time everyone could simply forget what had happened.

My face stung again at the memory of Arnold hitting me. I wore a failing bruise near my nose and mouth: faint yellow with a sign of purple around the edges. The impression his blow made in my mind was more significant. *What did Mr. Davis try to tell me?* I suddenly wondered, chastising myself for not thinking of it earlier. *Something about me trying to hold it in too long? Or did he suggest I should have tried to deal with my anger when it first came up?* I don't know how I hoped those thoughts might have helped me then, as the defending council was about to ask his first questions of me.

My eyes scanned the discussion room; it was as full as it had ever been. I saw Schelli and Lady Sally among the others and I wondered what specifics they'd heard of my scene with Arnold. Then I began to notice angry faces in the tightly packed crowd. Here and there, I noticed Arnold's staunch supporters from town. Their expressions couldn't have stood out more. I glanced at the Chaplain, wearing the blue robe of a judge, sitting in a chair facing the rest of the room. Jonathan Arnold had just finished his statements, and now it was time for me to make my own, in answer to Arnold's councilor.

I didn't know much about trials at that age, but I knew enough to see the one I sat in was different from trials in our world. The accused was only interviewed by the court's accuser. Witnesses against the accused were not interviewed by the court's accuser, though he could interject while the accused's council did.

The Chaplain asked if I was ready, and when I nodded, he called for all to be silent. He had me take an oath to reply honestly, then he let Arnold's councilor begin his questions. His councilor was a man from Oyster Bay named Mr. Veele. I'd never seen him before the trial, and his appearance did nothing to calm my nerves. I couldn't say exactly what it was about him I disliked, but his eyes seemed to gleam with malice, and his voice seemed somehow deceptive to me.

"How well did you fulfill your role as head delegate?" Mr. Veele first asked me.

"Justly, I hope. I did all that was required of me," I answered.

"Were you filling your requirements of a peacekeeper when you insulted Mr. Arnold last week?"

"*Your Honor*," interrupted Lieutenant Phillips, "Mr. Adams is not on trial here—Mr. Arnold is." The Lieutenant, as a representative of law enforcement, was given the job of bringing the charges against Arnold. He seemed quite comfortable in the role.

The Chaplain nodded his head. "He's right, councilor. Continue your questioning."

Mr. Veele shifted his weight as he stood. "You're the youngest delegate head in our kingdom's history. Do you think an older, more mature head could have done your job better?"

"Sure," I replied. "Who wouldn't? The job required an enormous amount of experience and maturity. Even the growth I've experienced since the incident would have been useful to me."

Veele didn't look satisfied with my answer. What was he hoping to hear?

"Did you make any mistakes in your role as Head Delegate?"

"Of course," I answered. "Who doesn't make mistakes?" The crowd chuckled a little. Veele looked uncomfortable.

"Were the remarks you made to Mr. Arnold a mistake?" he asked. The Lieutenant tried to interrupt, but the Chaplain waved his hand at him.

"Yes. I lost my temper and said things that angered Mr. Arnold, when I should have tried to calm him down again."

"*Again?*" asked the Lieutenant. From what I'd learned about courts back home, I didn't think both councilors could ask questions at the same time. I looked toward the Chaplain, and he nodded his head to me.

"Yes, it wasn't the first time I'd had an encounter with Mr. Arnold while he was angry."

Veele seemed to smile while he tried to keep his face blank. "And how did you react those other times?"

"I tried to calm him. Sometimes my role made it difficult."

He motioned with his hand, as if to whisk away my reply. "Then you admit you made a mistake by not calming him last week? And that you fell short in your duties as Head

Delegate?" He spoke quickly, leaning forward as if it would help him hear my response sooner.

"My main duties as delegate head weren't related, but yes, it was a mistake. And I guess that means...yes, I did fall short of my duties." The Lieutenant winced at my words. I glanced over at the Princess. She was glaring at Veele.

"Thank you," Veele said. "Now let me ask you; what is your opinion of Mr. Arnold?"

I paused. I saw Arnold in the tightly packed room wearing a somber face. "He is an important man in the community. I know a lot of people look up to him, and his opinions have an effect on many in Portsmouth. I don't agree with many of his opinions, and for that matter, neither does the King—"

Veele interrupted, "Thank you Mr. Adams, I wasn't asking you to pass judgment on Mr. Arnold just yet; that isn't your job today." He paused a few seconds before continuing. "Do you think he was out of line in his response to your angry words?"

"Yes."

"He was, wasn't he?" replied Veele. "But by how much?" The Lieutenant started to stand, but Veele retreated. "Never mind, never mind. Let me ask you this instead: do you think he *intended* to cause you harm?"

"Well, he probably didn't think of it. He—"

"And if he didn't *think* of it," Veele interrupted, "he couldn't have *intended* harm, could he Mr. Adams?"

"I guess not."

"Thank you, Mr. Adams. Just a few more questions, now," he paused to take a drink. "What did you say to Jonathan Arnold that caused such a powerful reaction?"

I looked to the floor as I began to respond. "Well, he accused me of—"

"No, no!" Veele scolded, "I didn't ask what *Mr. Arnold* said.

149

I asked what *you* said."

"Yes, sorry. I told him he drove his son away. When he—
" Veele started to protest again, and I paused and re-started.
"I asked him, 'Who blames a boy for his crimes?' and 'Who
turns his son against him, and is too much a fool to admit it?'"
I forced my eyes toward the jurors. Those who knew me wore
expressions of confusion or shocked disapproval.

"Did you also curse him to live a life of hatred, and to be
kept by hate from all others?"

"Curse? I didn't—"

"*Did you*—" he cut in, his voice drowning mine out.
"...Did you *say it*, Mr. Adams?"

I sighed. "Yes."

"Do you think it will come true?"

"I hope it never does. I hope he learns forgive—"

"*But*," he interrupted again, "did you know it's already
coming true? Did you hear his wife left him—or wonder why
she's moved into her sister's home?"

"I didn't know...I hope she—"

"Only one more question for you, Mr. Adams." Veele was
turned so the jury and the Chaplain couldn't see his face. His
eyes looked evil, like he was getting away with murder. "Do
you feel...*guilty* about what you said?" The way he said *guilty*
sounded as if he were the judge, delivering a sentence over me.

What will the King say to me? I wondered. "Yes, I do."

"That is all then. May you seek forgiveness from this old
man, this sonless father and wifeless husband."

"I will," I replied in a low voice, before I realized I'd
spoken aloud.

How had he done it? As he returned to his seat, I saw all eyes
were on me. They saw me as the criminal, not Arnold. I half-
agreed with them.

Our Chaplain-judge raised his hand to signal he would

question me. This was also something we didn't have back home: if the judge thought there were facts yet to be uncovered, he asked his own questions at the end of each interview, whether they were questions for a witness, or the accused. They called it an *inquisitorial system*.

"Mark, please tell me," the Chaplain began in his warm, friendly voice, "that is, after you've had some time to collect yourself after Mr. Veele's…performance." Someone snickered in the crowd…the very composed, always-proper Lady Sally.

Mr. Davis continued. "Mark, what was your role here in Portsmouth?"

"Why, to lead the King's Delegation to establish a peaceful human and troll settlement."

"And what made you qualified for this role, in the King's eyes?" I thought for a moment about what the Captain had taught me before I left for Portsmouth the first time.

"Well, it might sound silly…" I started.

"Silly isn't good enough," Mr. Davis interrupted in a serious tone. "Tell us what your heart knows is true." His eyes seemed to peer into me, through my expression and into my mind.

"I was passionate about seeing the kingdom live in peace— to see the trolls and humans stop hating and hurting each other."

"Thank you. And tell me then," the Chaplain went on, "why was this a concern for the King?"

"Because…I couldn't do the job if I wasn't passionate about it. The King is passionate about it himself. I had to learn this before I could be a part of the delegation."

"And being passionate about something, is it an easy thing to do?" he asked.

"What do you mean?"

"Can you say to yourself, 'Self, let's be passionate about this,' and then become passionate about it?" Someone in the crowd giggled—Princess Schelli.

"No, no—of course not. I had to learn many lessons. I had to experience the pain caused by the hatred between humans and trolls. I had to...to *yearn* for peace and forgiveness between our peoples."

"And you did all that in the short time between the war and your joining the delegation?" he asked.

"Yes. It was a busy few weeks." *Laughter.* I looked back up at the people in the room, and saw many of them snickering. They wore smiles. They didn't blame me, I saw. They *knew* me. Their eyes met mine and I saw acceptance. Relief flowed over me in a welcome wave. *Why is their acceptance so important to me?* I thought, *Is this wrong?*

"And after the war, were there some soldiers who hated the trolls...*all* the trolls?"

"Of course," I answered, "*many* people. They fought them in battle. They saw their friends die at the trolls' hands. Some wanted to see the trolls wiped out."

"But you feel so deeply about peace between humans and trolls...don't you hate those soldiers?"

"No, of course not. How could I? They are, most of them, good men—upright, honest, self-sacrificing people. They fought for their families and for their King." I thought back to the old man I'd cared for in Thraen Kholl, and remembered his deep hatred.

"Well then," Mr. Davis continued, "if they wanted all the trolls dead, then don't they stand in opposition to the King?"

"Yes."

"Then explain to me, how can these upright, honest men, these good men, how can they oppose the King on something he feels so strongly about? And why don't you hate them?"

"That's the problem with hatred," I started. "It makes good men desire evil. But you can't have a war without causing hate. I guess it's just one of the evils of war. You've got to guard yourself. You've got to make sure your enemy's hatred doesn't bleed over to you, or then it—" I stopped, unable to speak. This was it; this was a lesson the Chaplain had been trying to show me. Why hadn't I seen it until then? The stories he'd made me memorize—many of them flashed through my mind, and so many of them had lessons about hate spreading from one to another.

The story of the generous man who never passed the lessons of his LifeGrowth to another had held hatred for his first mentor, who was long dead. That's why he never passed his gifts on. And the boy who died in the snow…he hated the other boys in his village, the very ones he was trying to show he was worthy of their respect. And the last story—had I really solved it faster than the Chaplain expected? Or was he surprised I'd missed the second lesson the story was meant to teach me? *But why* now? I wondered, dumbfounded. *Why show me these things in the middle of the* trial? For a moment, I thought him crazy, but at the same time, I stared at him in awe. I was shocked by his strange plan, though not nearly as much as I would be only a few minutes later.

"Mark? Go on, son." The jury and all those in the audience were staring at me, waiting for my response.

"Um…it spreads. The hatred spreads to others. You've got to be diligent to make sure it doesn't infect you. That's what I failed to do, isn't it? Mr. Arnold's hatred for the trolls, his hatred for the King's plans, his hatred for *me*…I let it creep in. I…*I hated him back*."

I stood up. I wasn't *supposed* to stand up; I just did. I walked over to Jonathan Arnold, his gaze trapped in my own. I walked right up to him and put my hand on his shoulder as if

I were a dad reaching out to his son. *Why am I doing this? I'm supposed to be sitting,* I thought. I felt as if my feet carried me without my telling them to do so.

"I'm sorry Mr. Arnold. I'm sorry I said those things. I wanted to hurt you. I wanted to hate you and cause you pain."

And then I was truly amazed. I thought nothing could have surprised me at that moment, standing there, not knowing what to expect. And *still*, Jonathan Arnold surprised me. He stood up and wrapped his arms around me. He hugged me like I was his son, and he cried. He started with a sniffle, while great tears built in his eyes, then he sobbed. He wailed out his own guilt, and admitted he didn't want the trolls to be better than him. He said they *were* now, and he didn't care anymore.

The front of the room flooded with people. Some were cheering, some were shouting angrily. Arnold wailed for his son Kale to forgive him as if he were there. And then, in a daze, I realized he *was* there, squeezing through a crowd that was supposed to be seated, reaching out to his father. Kale's mother was there, pushing through the crowd, weeping and calling out to her husband.

Later I learned Kale had made his peace with his feelings on the trolls *and* his father's banishment. He'd returned to Portsmouth from Oyster Bay when the news of the trial first reached the Bay. If he hadn't been fishing at the Bay, he wouldn't have heard the news in time. As it was, he'd left immediately, taking his own boat back to Portsmouth at record pace. He arrived thirsty and hungry, not having taken the time to prepare for the long trip. He missed the first days of the trial, but made it in time to hear me from outside the building, and to hear his father call out for him.

The room was in utter turmoil. Some of Jonathan's supporters sat in their seats with confused looks on their faces.

Others were shouting, struggling through the tangle of people in the front of the room. Out of the corner of my eye I caught Mr. Veele worriedly slipping out of the building. No one was buying what he had to sell that day. The humans of the jury had abandoned their bench and flooded Jonathan to encourage him and to welcome his son home. The trolls of the jury remained happily in their seats, silently smiling and watching Jonathan.

I looked up at Mr. Davis, the Chaplain, our judge and new head delegate, to see him leaning back in his chair, hands folded behind his head, and wearing a grin from ear to ear. Was this his plan from the beginning? That crazy, genius man—he might have accomplished more in an hour than our delegation had in all the weeks and months since we'd begun.

2.5 Moving On

After the trial proceedings, Mr. Davis met with Jonathan Arnold—without Mr. Veele present. Afterward, Davis told me about their meeting at length. As soon as the two men were alone, Arnold admitted horrible things to the Chaplain: how he'd been glad when Norman died, how he'd plotted with Robert Eastman to enslave the trolls through labor contracts, and even how he'd wished the young Ahrens boy had died, so the townies would be further united against the trolls.

Mr. Davis knew he saw a changed man before him that day, and he told him so.

"But there still remains the need for your sentence," the Chaplain had told him. "I believe the jury will still find you guilty, even after your change of heart. Even if the jury recommends a light sentence, I cannot give you one. It would set a horrible precedence if I gave you no sentence for striking a representative of the King—especially when it wasn't *personal*, but for the very actions assigned to him by the King."

Arnold hung his head low. "I know. And you're right; I am a changed man today. But still…I'm scared."

"Oh? Of what?"

"Of the old me. I know the trolls are our equals now, I can

admit that. But can I treat them like humans? Can I keep myself from thinking I'm above them, in the back of my mind? Can I hold back the hatred, or will it return to me tenfold?"

"Ah. The sentence I have in mind for you may help you with this. It will either help, or drive you again to anger. Only you can choose which." Arnold remained silent, perhaps wincing in anticipation.

"This scale of rebellion can only be met with a serious punishment. I would be lenient to sentence you to a year in a prison camp." David told me Arnold's face reacted as if he were punched in the gut.

"A year? But my wife—and my business…"

"Yes, I know, it would be hard on them both. It may be harder perhaps on your wife, to have seen you change and then leave for a year. However—I now see another solution. In your original plan with Eastman, trolls and humans would have paid each other for manual labor, but in reality, it would have reduced them to a labor class. So instead of sending you to a labor camp, I will sentence you to one year of unpaid labor, working for the troll farmers. You'll spend some time working for each farmer in the troll camp. You will work a full day's work each day, according to the seasons.

"You will be able to live in your home with your wife, and to oversee your business in the evenings, but you will be very, very busy. There will be a financial cost. You'll have to hire trolls to do any manual labor you need done in town, and you won't be paid for the labor you give to the trolls. You will begin to pay back the people you've most harmed."

The sentence was worse than he had expected, but perhaps he understood the Chaplain's reasons. "You are wise, Chaplain Davis," was his only response.

"My highest hope is this: through serving them in humility,

you can purge yourself of any hateful feelings you have left for them. You may be surprised by what you learn. You may form strong friendships with some of your new bosses."

The sentence was officially handed down the next day. Before the jury began their deliberation, the Princess stood to read a note from her father, sent by pigeon after her ship left the Bay. Apparently, the King wanted the jury to know his feelings on the case before they made their decision. I wished Bob had sent news of the previous day's trial to the palace in time to hear back from the King, but he did not.

The Princess read in a bold tone the words from the King. He spoke of his commitment and urgent desire to see his citizens do all they could to encourage peaceful relations between our two peoples. He suggested the fate of the kingdom depended on it—a bold claim which surprised most of the crowded room. The King's message suggested if the trolls were to die out, as his opponents had hoped, the healing the kingdom so desperately needed could never take place. He argued the unforgiveness and hate held by some would fester and spread, until it consumed the kingdom, and would eventually destroy it. I thought again of the story I learned in the Watchmaker's village. The Princess added her own thoughts after reading the King's message.

"I know if my father had heard news of what took place here yesterday, he would be rejoicing now. He would be glad to receive Mr. Arnold as one of his loyal citizens, as a partner in bringing peace between the peoples of our great kingdom." It was all she had to add, but it spoke broad implications to the townies present.

Then the jury gave their guilty ruling, but recommended a suspended sentence, given Arnold's change of heart. As the Chaplain promised, he did not waver. He sentenced Arnold to a full year of unpaid labor to the trolls. Mrs. Arnold was obviously surprised, and her expression was one of joy, to hear her husband would not be sent away from Portsmouth.

Thomas Ahrens threw a large party the next day. It seemed odd to have a party the day after Jonathan's sentencing, but Jonathan's family, and everyone at the troll camp understood. Thomas and Jonathan had once plotted together against the trolls, and then were divided. They were united once again in their desires for the trolls: a complete change in direction for both of them. Everyone involved had something to celebrate, and Thomas especially liked celebrations. He invited the entire troll camp, and many humans from town as well. The Chaplain approved the use of the Delegate's new mess hall for the occasion.

The Princess, the Chaplain and I sat at the table of honor: a narrow table set facing the rest of the room. At my request, Lady Sally and Bob also sat with us. I asked Jonathan Arnold and his family to join us, but Jonathan said he didn't deserve any honor in front of the trolls, and he was right—for the present. I had a feeling this would change, once he got to know some of them personally. Jonathan, along with his wife and son, sat near the front of the hall. He asked to address the group just before we ate. Thomas, as the master of ceremonies, quickly agreed.

Jonathan's speech was one of repentance. He apologized to the trolls, to the delegation, and also to me for the harm he'd done. There were few dry eyes in the hall when he was finished. Norman's wife, Sarah, stood and ceremonially accepted his apology on behalf of the troll community. In front of the entire party, she took the opportunity to teach Jonathan the troll's tradition. Jonathan needed to bow and offer some item of food to Sarah; he used a piece of cake as it was handy. She received it, and ate it in front of everyone.

This signified not only accepting an apology, Sarah explained, but showed she was accepting the same risk we all accept when we offer forgiveness, and trust the forgiven party not to cause us further harm. This made more sense to the trolls, I was sure, who held a deep-rooted tradition to never accept food from an enemy.

When Arnold returned to sit with his family, Sarah thanked the humans for trusting her people, for inviting them and housing them. At the end of her short speech, she told us the trolls had chosen a name for their community. I realized we'd been calling it *the troll camp* all along, and as far as I knew, no one ever thought to give it an official name. And so the old name was put to rest, and the new community *Forgiveness* was declared on that historic evening. Sarah made sure everyone understood it represented the forgiveness the trolls asked of the humans, for the years of war and skirmishes, and the pain and death they'd caused. But it represented forgiveness on their part as well, for the hate so many humans still held for them. They re-named the delegation building the *Hope Community Center* that night, and a lantern was installed over the glass sculpture Thomas had donated to the community. It lit the glass brightly, showing its secret story within, to all who had the heart to see it.

The guests stayed late into the night, discussing the goings-on of their community. Considering my codebooks were nearly complete, I'd already made arrangements for the ship waiting in the harbor to carry me away from Portsmouth the following day, and a carriage to drive me from there to Thraen Kholl. With the Princess on board, I knew I would have good company when I grew bored working on the codes.

I said goodbye to the delegates and other friends, knowing I would leave early for town, ahead of the Princess and Lady Sally. I packed my belongings and was ready to leave before I went to bed. When I woke, I had only to make my bed and carry my bags down to the Thomas' cart, still on loan to me.

It was bitter cold on that last early-morning ride into town, even in the thick coat and other heavy clothes I wore. I realized it would be a worse trip back to Engdynlor. With no fireplace for heat, or ovens to warm food, I dreaded the ride back to the Bay. I imagined shivering and eating cold, dried meat and stale bread. When I entered the inn to see Bob one last time, he knew right away what I was thinking.

"The ride might not be as bad as you think." Since I hadn't yet guessed he'd read my face, I had no idea what he meant. We said our goodbyes and he handed me a small scroll of paper when I left. He told me it was an honest evaluation of my time spent with him. It was embarrassing to read: both for its praise, and for the frank criticisms in the areas where I most needed to grow. He spared no mention of any honest mistakes he thought I'd made. I read the slip of paper on my walk down to the dock. Just as I finished, I was surprised to hear a familiar voice interrupt my thoughts, though I couldn't place it right away.

"So there he comes: all done with the Port and ready for the Bay. Legs so land-y, gonna puke all day!" I looked up to see Captain Knemoller smiling at me.

Are there any other ships but his? I wondered as he came to shake my hand.

"Welcome aboard, my *fine sir*," he said with a smile. "We be a noble ship now, you know." I had no idea what he meant, but I guessed the Princess coming aboard might have brought some prestige to his ship and crew.

"Thanks for having me, Captain Knemoller. How was your wait in town?"

Knemoller scowled. I remembered he didn't like docking very long.

"Cold and bitter. I got some fishing in, but they ain't taking bait now." He shook off his disdain and smiled. "We got an old friend of yours on board. Why don't you go below and say your *hellos* to him?"

Jaren was working in the cargo hold, lashing down fancy-looking chests. I guessed they belonged to the Princess and Lady Sally.

"Jaren—is that you?" I asked. It seemed like a lifetime ago since I'd seen him.

"*Yes sir,*" he exclaimed, turning to greet me. "Ever since you were at the palace last, I took no jobs but the ones Knemoller gave me. I didn't want to miss you again, the next time you needed a ride." He was smiling wide. I set my smaller sack near the stairs and hefted the larger one toward him.

"Here," I started, "let's stow this, then I'll help you with the rest of the tying." I felt like I'd slipped back in time a handful of months, to when I'd first met him. We stowed the luggage and talked about nothing in particular, until Captain Knemoller called him up. When I followed him holding my smaller sack, I was surprised to see Lady Sally and the Princess already on board. They greeted me warmly, and we walked together to the galley. I thought I recognized a member of the Royal Guard following the Princess.

"Is this trip your first time aboard a ship?" I asked the Princess.

"Oh yes. I'd only been in a little row boat before the trip down here. It was much calmer."

"Yes," I chuckled, "I suppose it was. Come to think of it, your ride down here was probably rougher than mine, this far into winter. I hope our trip back to the Bay goes fast."

We talked mostly about her childhood friend. Schelli was already planning her next visit to Portsmouth. By then the ship was moving; we were on our way.

"Will it be soon?" I asked, referring to her next visit.

"No, I don't think so. I'm going to visit some of the towns in Terrezia Plain—the ones the war went through. I want to see how badly they were affected." Though neither of us said it, we both knew she wasn't talking about the buildings destroyed or the farms burned, or even the families torn apart; she was talking of the hate some still held for the trolls.

"How will you teach them?" I asked her. She looked straight into my eyes.

"I don't know." Her lip quivered ever so slightly. "That is, I know what I *want* to say. I want to tell them, if they continue to hate the trolls, they will hurt themselves too. I want to tell them to stop hating and forgive. But no one will listen to me if I say only *that.*"

She's doubting herself, I thought in amazement. My mind raced to a conversation I'd had with Bob, while I cleaned his loft at the inn one afternoon. I remember his words from that day as clear as if I'd just heard them.

Confidence comes from knowing you're working at the task for which you were created. The King has an uncanny knack for seeing these tasks within us, and assigning us to work on that which will best fulfill us.

I felt Bob must have rubbed off on me more than I could've guessed, as I took a patient moment to reflect once again on these words. For a moment, I swore I could hear him speaking in my ear.

"Imagine how bleak life must seem in comparison," he'd gone on to say, *"for those who never serve the King closely enough to receive such an assignment."*

"You don't mean the King has a specific assignment for everyone in the kingdom," I'd asked incredulously, "do you?"

His eyes seemed to sparkle with untold wisdom.

"As many as find themselves in his service, he will have tasks for. Did you think running the kingdom was so simple, the King only uses a few of us?"

I pulled myself into the present. Those words wouldn't help the Princess; she saw the King as her father, not a great leader. *Maybe if she sees why she was* chosen *for her assignment,* I thought.

"Schelli," I started, "what makes you more qualified to teach humans to forgive the trolls more than anyone else?"

"Hmm? I don't see what you're getting at."

"I think you just may be the most qualified person in the kingdom to convince humans to forgive trolls. It's why I suggested making you a Goodwill Ambassador."

"*Aha*—I *thought* it was you," she replied, wearing a sly smile.

"Believe me, I didn't have to argue to convince anyone; the delegation voted unanimously. But, tell me—why do you think we decided you're the perfect candidate for the role?"

"Well, that's pretty obvious…the King only has one daughter, you know."

"You're part of the Royal Family, and that doesn't hurt—but it's *not* the reason."

Her expression changed to one of frustration. "Well, I don't want to play games. If you want to tell me, then *tell me.*" She seemed more insecure than angry.

What does she have to be unsure about? I wondered.

"Schelli, if you don't know this, you must be blind. *The people love you.* Anyone who's ever met you, loves you. Even Sphotch, the ice troll probably loves you. It's probably why he didn't kill you—he couldn't bring himself to do it."

"What?" she replied, dumbfounded.

"Have you ever met someone who dislikes you? I'm not

talking about an enemy of the kingdom who wanted to harm your family, but you personally."

"You're talking nonsense..." As her words trailed off, her eyes unfocused, as if searching for a memory.

"And how could they *not* love you? Beautiful, compassionate and kind to a fault, polite, friendly—you care about people as soon as you meet them, and it shows. You care about *everybody*. Even though it's sure to bring you pain, you do it anyway. People pity you for the pain you'll feel, but they look up to you just the same. I know *I* do."

She blushed. Did I see a tear in her eye? She wrapped her arms around me in a great hug. Suddenly *I* was the one blushing.

"Um...anyway," I stammered into the awkward pause after our short embrace, "this much I'm sure of; wherever you go throughout the kingdom, people will look on you with love. *This* is what makes you most qualified to teach forgiveness. The worst they can do is call you naive and disagree, so you need to show them you're *not* naive. Let them know you understand their pain and the hurt they've endured, and it's *still* worth it to forgive them. It's what *I* would do, if it means anything to you."

She smiled, then hugged me again. "I'm so glad we get to ride back to Engdynlor together," she said. "When I go to visit Terrezia Plain, I think you should come with me." Her eyes seemed to glow, as a sunbeam streamed in low, through the cabin's window that winter morning. It lit one side of her face, and shifted as the ship rocked over the waves. I felt a pang of guilt over the plans she hadn't yet heard.

"*I can't*. I'm being sent on another assignment as soon as we get back to the palace."

"Oh, the Captain can find someone else to do it for him," she said, pouting.

"Maybe he could," I replied, "but I know he won't."

I stood to leave—suddenly it felt too warm in the cabin, though I'd been shivering just a few minutes ago. I needed time alone to think.

Part III

3.0 Clues

With my head full of questions, I wandered onto the deck. It was a short walk as far as wandering goes, and I wished it was longer. The harsh wind seemed to ignore my heavy coat. A chill ran down my spine. I wondered what would become of Jonathan Arnold and his sentence of hard labor. I liked to think he would do well in serving his sentence, and make friends among the trolls, just as the Chaplain expected.

By noon I'd adjusted to the pitch and roll of the waves enough to feel hungry, though not for eating dried meat or stale bread. The wind bit deep through my clothes, as if I wore nothing at all. I thought of the clam chowder I'd once eaten at Oyster Bay, served in a sourdough bowl with a tough, almost leathery crust. I imagined it so clearly, I thought I could smell it. My mouth watered. Hopeful doubt pulled me from my daydream. *Do I really smell it?* I walked quickly into the galley, shocked to find it full of the savory aroma. Paper sheets were laid on the table, and everyone inside was eating hot soup.

"Did they add a real kitchen?" I asked, confused.

Lady Sally replied, "No, they don't have the room for it. But the innkeeper was kind enough to send a pot of hot chowder along with us. It's still plenty warm." She ladled me a thick bread bowl full of the stuff. My mouth watered so much, it made my cheeks and tongue pucker. I sat down to eat, breaking off the rim of the bowl and dipping it in the chowder. The Princess looked pale.

"Not feeling well enough to eat yet?" I asked her. She frowned her answer to me.

I finished my chowder quickly, and ate the cream-soaked bread bowl. Warm and full, I went down to the cargo hold to work on my codebooks. The sea was calm enough for me to rest a plank across my knees, balance one of the codebooks on it, and roll the die on the open book. I used the last pages of the first book to track the symbols I'd already rolled. It was slow going...roll, check, write, write...roll, check, write, write. I only had room for one of the new codebooks on the plank, leaving the other balanced on my lap. The second codebook kept sliding off and falling to my feet, closed. *Writing in both books each time is fine for a real office on land,* I thought to myself, *but it won't work at sea.* I decided I must change the rules a little if I were to finish the codebooks by the time we reached the Bay.

I felt guilty the entire time I spent filling the rest of that page in the first codebook. *I'll copy the symbols to the second book as soon as I finish the page,* I told myself. *This is probably the first time a knight had to roll code at sea.*

I finished the page and carefully copied the symbols to the same page of the second book. *I'll tell the Captain if he asks,* I thought, still unhappy about the tiny change I'd made to the process. Toward the end, it grew so dark, the light from the hatch wasn't quite bright enough to see where I wrote. I hurried to finish copying the rest of the page, unwilling to leave the books unequal.

I stowed my codebooks and climbed the stairs out of the

hatch to watch the sun set. I realized our trip might take longer in the shorter days of winter. I asked Captain Knemoller about it as he came from the galley, smelling like chowder. No doubt he had large gobs of it in his thick beard.

"Might be m'boy, might be. Don't forget the winter wind. 'Tis faster, and *thicker* too. The cold air, you see, she's thicker than the warm winds of summer. She blows *harder*, even at the same speed." His face screwed into an unspoken question. "Don't ask me how!" he added, as if I had. "Them fancy scientists at the palace can tell you."

Surely he's wrong, I thought. *If two winds blow at the same speed, how can one be stronger and one softer?* But when I remembered to ask the science officers at Engdynlor days later, they agreed with him. It would be years to come before I learned *why* they were right.

I saw the sun setting over the ocean in a crisp line of dark blue and orange. Ahead of us there was a great fog. If it wasn't for a rogue wind blowing out to sea, I wouldn't have witnessed what I saw next.

The captain of the Good Ship Explorer whistled at the wind, facing the shoreline. "It's not often you feel *that*. Smell it? There's a strong wind blowing off plain tonight. Not a bit of sea in it. Smells like dirt." When he turned around, he looked right past me, out to sea. His eyes focused on *something*, before he grumbled about checking their course and hurried into the cabin. I followed his eyes and saw a great fire on the third island of the Broken Coast.

It was one of the longer islands, probably the largest. I didn't see the fire directly, but saw the island clearer than ever before. Just before the southern tip, the clouds and fog were flashing orange. I thought I heard a low rumble of thunder in the distance. I pulled a small telescope from the pack I'd kept with me, and pulled it to its full length. Through it, I saw a little more detail.

There seemed to be an enormous crack in the face of the cliff where it rose out of the ocean, just below the clouds glowing brightest. Perhaps there was a small bay there. The cliff face along the beachless end of the island was mostly covered with trees and scrub brush. I wondered how tall the cliff face rose, obscured by the clouds. I watched it disappear in the mist as the winds shifted, and the island was once again covered in fog and cloud. I was sure it was the same island I'd seen topped in a whirlwind cloud, during my last trip to the Bay.

I rushed into the galley where most of the ship's passengers had huddled. A lantern gave dim light to those sitting there.

"Did you see the fire," I asked them all, "on the end of the long island?"

It was as if no one had heard me. Schelli was leaning against Lady Sally, asleep. Her hair fell over one eye and covered her chin. Sally was reading a book by the light of the gently swinging lantern. Captain Knemoller was the only one who reacted, and *he* turned away from me. I approached him.

"You were out there with me. Did you see it?"

"I *might've*," he said over his shoulder, filling his mug with water from the cistern pump.

"Well, did you or didn't you?" One of the older sailors swung his head around and glared at me.

"Boy, there's a time for curiosity, and a time when folks will tell you whatever you ask them. This time ain't n*either*." At that, he shoved past me and walked into the small bunkroom.

"What'd I do?" I mumbled to myself. Lady Sally put her book down.

"Maybe he didn't like your tone. He *is* captain of this ship."

"I know," I replied to her. "Now he's too mad to talk to me—the only other person who saw the fire. You should have *seen it*, Lady Sally. It was far off, but it must have been monstrous to light up he clouds like that. What would start it, if no one lives on the island?"

"Lightning, perhaps," she offered.

"Well, I did hear thunder…" Something about it didn't seem right to me.

"We had some cheese and bread for dinner…would you like some?" Lady Sally sat upright and gently woke the Princess.

I found the bread and cheese in the icebox, probably cooled with glacier ice from Golden Mountain. The icebox was three times the size I remembered, and to my surprise, it also held eggs, milk and fresh meat inside.

"Why's there raw food in here?" I wondered aloud. "There's no oven to cook it."

"You'll see," said Lady Sally. The Princess roused, but looked too tired to speak.

"Oh? Did they think some trolls were coming with us?" I asked, wondering if Captain Knemoller expected I ate raw meat like they did. I knew he wouldn't allow any flame but a lantern's wick on board—if he had his way, there'd be no lanterns either. As it was, we only had *wax lanterns*. They held a candle inside instead of oil, and were made of glass so thick, they couldn't easily be broken.

"You'll see in the morning," she replied. When she saw my sour expression, she added with a smile, "I guess you'll have to get used to feeling curious tonight."

I was nearly ready to turn in, though it wasn't late. I didn't look forward to sleeping in the uncomfortable low bunks in the next room. I couldn't even imagine the Princess and Lady Sally in them.

"Where will the two of you sleep?" I asked. "Not in the bunkroom I hope."

"The Captain—Captain Williams that is—he ordered some modifications built for us." She coaxed the tired Princess from the bench where they sat, and pulled hard on its large planks. I knew there was storage space beneath them, but then I saw the underside of the bench was covered with soft, *pink* upholstery. From the storage space she pulled a stack of thick curtains, thick blankets, and a metal box she lifted with great effort. She set them down and replaced the top of the bench, cushioned side up, and began to hang the thick curtains right down the center of the galley. I noticed hooks in the ceiling I hadn't seen before. When she was done, I was backed up against the cistern, on the other side of the curtain. She unclasped several hooks in a row down the curtain's center, to reveal two curtains, spread apart.

"A *royal suite*," Sally said with a smile. She laid the sleepy Princess down over most of the bench's length and unfolded a blanket over her.

"Where will *you* sleep though?" I asked.

"I'll make do with the rest of the bench. It worked fine for the trip down from Oyster Bay." Finally, she turned her attention to the heavy box. She spun four stays which held the lid in place, then set it aside. The box was filled with wet sand and nearly a dozen glass jars carefully spaced, held separated by the sand. She drew one out, careful not to knock sand into the hole she pulled it from, then emptied it of its dark green liquid, covering the sand on the opposite end of the box. Then she replaced the jar in its hole, and drew another from the opposite end of the box. She poured red liquid from it, thick as syrup, and placed the jar back into its hole. She closed the box and set it on the floor planks in front of Schelli.

"What is it?" I asked.

"Curious still? Touch it and see."

I reached down and touched the metal box, cautiously. It was warm—very warm.

"How'd it get so hot?"

"It will get hotter still," she replied, "too hot to touch, but not hot enough to burn wood. Some of the liquid will congeal in the bottom of the box, and some will evaporate harmlessly into the air. Before then, it will have heated our *royal suite* considerably."

"*Who made it?*" I asked, bewildered.

"A box like this always travels with the Royal Family. They are called *heatboxes*. Don't you remember our trip down from Golden Mountain—back when we first met?"

"You only had stones heated from the fire," I replied suspiciously, "and *they* were wrapped in mud and leaves, not a fancy metal box."

"It was made by the soldiers of the Royal Guard, not by the King's scientists. The Guard had limited resources at the time." She smiled even wider. "This is much more convenient, don't you think?"

I wondered how it worked, but was too proud to ask.

"Well," I replied, "I'm off to bed, too. Maybe I'll sleep off my *boyish curiosity*." As I backed through the curtains and hung them, Lady Sally's expression objected to my tone. It was the second time I'd spoken out of turn—and only a week after my mouth caused so much trouble in Portsmouth. I headed outside the cabin to clear my mind.

Why don't I apologize to her? I leaned into the cold wind and clenched my teeth. *She's probably asleep by now*, I told myself. I pulled the telescope from my sack and searched for the island and the fire, but it was lost in the fog and mist. When I could no longer keep myself from the warmth of my bed, I quietly opened the door to the cabin and crept past the curtain corralling most of the galley from the table. The thick curtain brushed against me until I reached the door to the bunkroom. I found an unoccupied bunk and climbed into it, careful not to hit my head. Using my sack for a pillow, I buried myself in thick blankets and fell asleep. It seemed only minutes before I woke, dreaming of a breakfast fit for kings.

I woke in the way they train scouts to wake; David had taught me how. With my eyes still closed, I laid still, trying to appear sleeping. *And* I *listened.* I thought I could still smell the breakfast of my dreams. *Why torture yourself?* I wondered to myself. The smell became stronger instead of fading. I heard voices: the captain's first mate talking to someone impatiently.

"...get to eat when I say so. Be happy you're not getting *hardtack and jerky.*"

I bolted upright in bed—or at least I tried to. Wincing and rubbing my head, I staggered into the galley. My nose led me true, the first mate was cooking eggs, bacon, and even sausage.

"Did you get a *stove?*" I asked incredulously. Captain Knemoller, the Princess, Lady Sally, and a soldier were sitting at the small table. I squeezed onto the bench, beside the soldier, and stared hopefully at the first mate, whom was just then turning toward us.

"*Never,*" barked the captain. Schelli jumped a little at his outburst. "Begging your pardon, Highness," he added in a more subdued tone, before turning back to me. "It's bad enough having the wax lanterns aboard. They're safer than oil, mind you, but it's still *fire* on a *ship.* The two just don't mix. A cooking stove would be *downright foolhardy.*"

And yet, there stood the first mate with a huge frying pan, filled to the top with eggs, sausage and bacon. He served the Princess first, then Sally and the soldier of the Royal Guard, then the captain, before he turned at last to me and scraped a meager-sized portion onto my plate. He turned to grab more eggs from the coldbox.

I launched into my breakfast, and scraped my plate clean before I gave a second thought of cooking without a fire. I looked up to see the Princess, Sally, and even the soldier of the Royal Guard staring at me. Had I eaten so rudely? If I had, it certainly didn't bother Captain Knemoller. He pushed a mug in front of me, and held a tall bottle in each hand. When he spoke, he sounded awkward, unsure of what to say.

"I knew we couldn't eat such a fancy breakfast and drink only water, so…uh…" His voice trailed off, his unasked question lingering. The soldier peered back and forth, from me to the Captain, but only smiled. Sally and Schelli expertly ignored the uncomfortable moment.

What's Knemoller talking about? I wondered. It was obvious he was about to quench my thirst. *Why doesn't he pour?*

Finally, he shrugged and growled a reply to the unspoken question. "Well, if you're man enough to lead a delegation for the King, no one's going to *accuse me* of treating you like a boy." Without another word, he set one bottle back in front of the Princess, and filled my mug from the other.

Finally, I thought. I woke not only hungry, but thirsty for something tall and wet. I lifted the large mug and downed at least half without taking a breath. It was cold and stung my throat. *Is it some kind of fruit juice?* I wondered. I emptied the mug before I decided its contents were spoiled. I nearly slammed it down on the tabletop, and wondered what to do with the mouthful I hadn't yet swallowed. Then, with my mouth filled and stomach complaining, I found everyone in the galley staring at me. Schelli's expression was one of horror, Sally's one of stern disapproval, while the soldier's and first mate's showed cheery curiosity. Captain Knemoller was frozen, wearing a lopsided grin.

What's going on? I wondered. I swallowed the last mouthful, embarrassed without knowing why. Finally, I spoke quietly into the silence.

"Um...I think the juice is spoiled." No one said a word for a long second, then everyone smiled at once, and the captain let out a great roar of a laugh. He reached around the soldier and slapped me hard on the back.

"That'll put some hair on your chest," he barked, and filled my mug again. I must have looked like an idiot to everyone in the galley. Finally Schelli spoke up.

"*I'm* drinking fruit juice," she said, pointing to the bottle in front of her, "and so is my guard. But *you*, it seems, are having not-a-little *wine* with your breakfast." She giggled once again, and I felt like a fool. How could I have missed it?

I chuckled and tried to act as if I wasn't embarrassed, but no one was convinced. My face was warm and red, and not only from embarrassment. I stayed this way for the rest of the morning, and my legs had a difficult time carrying me around the ship. I was careful to stay far from the sides when on deck, for fear of falling overboard. Finally, dizzy and nauseous, I fell asleep in my bunk sometime before lunch. It was my first taste of wine.

When I returned to the galley for lunch, I finally learned how the first mate had been cooking on the ship. He used a metal box like the one Lady Sally and Schelli used to warm their makeshift cabin at night. He mixed the strange liquids over a small pile of sand he'd set onto the overturned lid of the metal box, and laid a thin metal skillet over it. I wondered if the captain had complained about the heatbox before he knew it would bring him hot meals. Later, I remember these thoughts as if I'd had them in a dream. The captain's wine was not something I was eager to try again.

The rest of the journey was uneventful, but full of good conversation. I spent a lot of time talking with the Princess, surprising myself when I realized how much I'd missed her, or how much she'd grown since we first met. Her role as a *Good Will Ambassador* was changing the way she viewed everything. The passion burning within her was the same passion which burned in her father.

I also spent a lot of time talking with Lady Sally. I became even more impressed with her knowledge and wisdom. *No wonder she's in charge of teaching the Princess.* I realized she was the type of person kings and rulers would find to teach their children. I was surprised to discover in myself a desire to impress her. I wanted her to know of every lesson I'd learned. I held back, telling myself it was foolish pride. Still, my manner changed when I spoke to her. Unconsciously, I began treating her in the same way I treated my mentor, the Captain.

The balance of my time was spent sleeping and completing the tedious work of filling my codebooks. I finished them just before we reached the Bay. I was not surprised to find a small parade there to greet us; this happened nearly everywhere the Princess visited.

That night at Oyster Bay's inn, the Princess asked me to walk her to Beach Row. This surprised me, knowing she cared nothing for the trappings of high society. Of course I agreed, and we left the inn together.

Being well into winter, the wind from the beach bit through our heavy coats. The Row was crowded enough to corral us closely together to keep from losing track of each other.

Schelli was in a fickle mood. She didn't want to stop at any of the restaurants, and obviously didn't feel like talking. Finally we found ourselves in front of the small art gallery where Thomas bought the sculpture of Norman and his son. Without saying a word, Schelli went inside. Not knowing what else to do, I silently followed.

The walls and shelves of the shop were half-empty. This far into winter, any night could bring a large enough storm to wipe out Beach Row. The Princess avoided my gaze, intently studying each painting in the shop. The owner seemed to recognize the two us, but found a way to avoid eye contact.

I found myself drawn to the glass sculptures. There were several left, but one caught my eye in particular. It was tiny— small enough to fit in my palm. When the shop owner noticed my interest, he approached reluctantly.

"Are you interested in this piece, sir?" he asked politely. It certainly wasn't the attitude he'd had toward me when we first met. Inwardly I sneered at his transparency.

"Yes. May I hold it?" He hesitated for a brief second, then nodded his reply. Using both hands, he lifted it gingerly from behind the glass counter where it had lain. It couldn't have weighed two pounds. I took his unspoken warning and turned it slowly over using both hands, searching for a hidden message. I didn't find it quickly.

The glass was completely clear in an outer layer, about as thick as my thumb. Beneath that, it was clouded with milky bands, as if a trail of smoke lingered through the glass. Though the sculpture was egg-shaped, the smoky area within was in a perfect heart. In the center of the piece were tiny colored pieces of glass, barely visible. I lifted it to my eye and strained to see what secrets I might uncover.

I only saw colored blobs, distorted by the glass and smoke effect surrounding them. Soon, my eyes tired and I lowered it, disappointed. Something in the glass flickered as I did so, and my heart jumped. It was only the smallest fraction of a second, but I thought I saw something familiar.

I moved the piece back and forth, close and far from my eyes, searching for what I thought I'd glimpsed. The owner had returned to a remote corner of his shop, but I saw from the corner of my eye a stern look he sent my way. I began to rotate the glass as I moved it near and far, until finally, I found it. I let out a quiet gasp when I did.

The effect was amazing. If I were the gullible type, I would have sworn it was magic. From one direction only, at a certain distance, the surrounding glass became a lens, both focusing the colored bits, and magnifying them. They were people and buildings, in three distinct groupings. The people were far too small to have individual characteristics beyond *human* or *troll*, but their placement and body language told a story I knew too well. It played out three scenes of the day Norman died. One told the story of Norman's house burning, a mob of humans standing around, and Norman's family escaping out the back. In the second, the barn burned while humans and trolls both stood outside, and a tiny spec flew from a window. The third displayed a circle of trolls crowding around a collapsed mother and her young son. There were humans outside the ring looking on, one smaller than the others. My ears felt numb when I realized the smaller human was *me*.

I've never seen its equal, in skill or design. Even the wisps of smoke from the two scenes wound around each other, never quite touching, each a unique shade of pale gray. I marveled at its complexity, wondering how its creation was even possible.

Sometime while I'd been staring into the glass, the shop owner had returned. I asked for its price, unable to find one on the small title card, labeled only *Love's Sacrifice*. When he told me his price, my eyes widened. Gingerly, I returned to the shopkeeper's cautious hands and hurried away. I found the Princess still browsing the paintings hanging all around us. She said nothing, and for the moment I was content to walk slowly beside her. She stopped when we came to the paintings of the Broken Coast islands. Suddenly she seemed deeply troubled. In a sidelong glance, I saw her chin quiver. A single tear rolled down her cheek, then she bolted from the shop. I followed her, wondering what could have had disturbed her. I laid my hand on her shoulder and asked her. Through tears, she told me what I never could have guessed. She *loved* me, she told me, though her tone was angry. At hearing this, my mind began to reel. In a confused stupor, I tried to pretend I had no idea what she was talking about. I didn't fool her.

She told me she hoped to marry a man like me one day, and wanted to raise her sons to be like me. I only stuttered, trying to find words which would calm her, for the moment refusing to process what she'd just said. She told me she knew from the beginning I would leave her; she knew I would return to my own world. I promised to come back, but she cried all the more, and said she wouldn't yet be born. She leaned into me and hugged me tightly for what seemed like a fleeting second, or an eternity—I couldn't decide which. Then she kissed me on the cheek and, still crying, darted into the crowd. Just before I lost sight of her, I yelled out my response to this revelation she'd sprung on me, though I regretted it immediately.

She turned back to me, nearly stumbling. Our eyes locked for the briefest moment, and the crowd closed in around her, hiding her from my sight. People all around stared at me, though I pretended not to notice.

For a while I stood there frozen, dazed and torn. I wonder now, how could I have felt so strong an emotion at such a tender age. Did my memory add to it over the years? When I realized she wasn't walking back to me, and knowing I wouldn't be able to find her in the crowd, I turned and wandered back to the inn.

My head held a storm of conflicting thoughts: my desire to

return home, and all that had become my life in the past months. *Why should I leave?* I demanded of myself, *everything I want in life is here.* But the Princess expected me to go, and for the moment, this somehow sealed my decision.

I felt filled with resolution I couldn't describe; it had no direction. The aimlessness of emotion left me feeling empty. I had a notion I would marry someone like the Princess one day, and then Lady Sally also came to my mind. She was wise and good, and I wished I would someday find someone who was also like her. I had no way of knowing, back in my own world, one day I would. But to be a boy of fifteen and imagining marriage—it seems childish now, but then it had felt as real as anything I knew.

3.1 Last Assignment

The long ride from the Bay to Thraen Kholl was somber. The Princess and I didn't speak to each other. Lady Sally seemed intent on occupying the Princess with her schooling the entire trip. I wondered if she knew what happened the previous day. How could she not? I tried to sleep in the coach, but could not.

When we finally reached Engdynlor, David was there to welcome me. My thoughts fell back to the time when I'd arrived at the palace, and spent my time worrying over David and his latest scouting mission.

David and I talked for hours, telling each other of every event we could remember from our delegations. David was furious when I told him about Jonathan Arnold. He seemed to understand when I told him it was worth it to see his family restored, and his acceptance of the King's plan for a peaceful kingdom. Still, he thought he noticed something different within me. He said it was something quiet, something sad. I couldn't explain it to him and he didn't press me to try.

I met with the Captain just after David left my room. He'd been waiting outside for a while, not wanting to interrupt us. He seemed sad or lonely somehow, but I couldn't yet guess why. I gave him the two codebooks, just as Bob instructed me to do. He smiled while he flipped through a few pages, as if to say he remembered the long hours he'd spent filling his first pair. Afterward, he held one book out for me.

"This is for you—to send us word while you're on your last assignment. You'll be going home soon, you know." He wore a strange expression which seemed to say, *it's for the best*. His voice was distant, as if I'd already left.

"Why? *Why* do I have to go?"

"I don't know." There was uncertainty in his voice. "I only know this is the path laid before you. It's what's required of you. I know it's hard—" I swear his eyes bored right through my soul and he knew my every thought, "but I also know this path is best for *everyone*."

"How can you *know* that?" I railed at him. *Let him read my mind,* I thought, *let him know everything I ever thought—but let him answer my questions too.*

"How can you know it's best for me? What if it's *worse* for me? What if I never find anything better than what I have right here, right now? What if I never find anything even *close?*"

I realized I was yelling, and my throat felt tight. I knew how well known I'd become in the kingdom, how reputable I looked to others. I knew what my life might be if I'd stayed in their world, if I refused to return—*and I wanted that life.* I wanted it so badly, I could *taste* it.

"Be careful, Mark," he said, laying a heavy hand on my shoulder, "be *very* careful, my young friend. I know what you feel. If you've ever trusted me, if you could ever put your faith in what I have to teach you, trust me *now*. Our feelings aren't always right. We have them to help us, even to guide us at times, but they're never meant to control us."

He paused when I looked away from him in anger.

Eventually, I gave him my attention again, and he went on.

"This is your path. It will pay you a *thousandfold* what you think you might have by leaving it." I decided not to think any more about what he'd said until he left.

"And just *what is* this last assignment?" I asked, though I didn't want to hear his answer.

"It's one you may never finish. It comes in two parts: one to be completed in our world, and another to take back with you. The King will brief you and your brother in the morning."

"Why can't you tell me now?" I only wanted to argue with him, but it wasn't going to happen.

"I'm afraid that's for the King to tell you. There will be some details I don't need to know—some involving secrets few will ever hear."

"What secrets are kept from *you?*" I asked, pondering how there could be something the Captain didn't know, a secret the King might keep from him.

"Not many I'll wager, but the way to travel from our world to yours is one of them. The fewer who know of this, the better it is for all. The King will brief you and David in the morning, and on the following day you will leave by ship. If the King is right, we will not meet afterward."

I tried to calm myself. If it was the last time I would see the Captain, I didn't want to spend if fuming like an insolent child. As much as I tried, my anger wouldn't be calmed. I said the words I would want to say if I weren't angry, but they sounded insincere. I can only hope he understood. I thanked the Captain for being my mentor and friend, and for teaching me all he had. I asked if I could talk to him after I met with the King, and he promised I would. He shook my hand, then embraced me. When he left, I laid in bed wishing for sleep.

Sleep didn't come soon enough. I thought of all the people

I'd be leaving behind, especially the Princess. *Why couldn't she have kept her words to herself?* Leaving would have been so much easier. I tried to console myself by thinking of all the time David and I would have together, and of finally being reunited with our family. *Mom, Dad, our younger brother…what do they think happened to us?* I lay in bed wondering so many things, but none of them brought me peace. Each good thought called to mind a painful regret about leaving a world I'd come to love. My thoughts and emotions mixed into a maelstrom in my mind, keeping me awake all night—or so I thought. When I woke, it was late in the morning, and I found I'd merely been *dreaming* I was lying awake in bed. What sleep I had brought me no rest. My mind and heart were tired and felt strange, like I'd gone for days without sleep.

There was a knock at my door; I realized it must have been what woke me. It was a page, sent to tell us the King was ready to see us. Apparently, David's mentor had visited him the previous night just as the Captain had visited me. I changed into clean clothes, and the three of us walked across the palace. We followed the page into the basement, where a soldier took his place and lead us to the deep hall where we'd found the secret room. Arriving at the last turn, the soldier handed his torch to David and told us we'd know where to find the King. He turned around and walked back into the darkness behind us. We shrugged to each other and walked to the place in the wall with the intricate carvings. We opened the secret door in the same way as before, and saw the King sitting in a tall backed chair in the middle of the room, studying a thick sheaf of papers.

The room was different from when we'd last seen it. *Someone cleaned it,* I noticed. The King asked us to sit on the two low stools before him, and we did. After a long pause, he spoke again.

"Thank you both for your loyal service to me and our kingdom. The two of you have brought many changes to our world, changes we are better for having. You will return one day, I know it. I only wish I could be here to see you both when you do.

"You have grown and learned much in your time here. You came as children, but I send you back as men. It will be hard for you to adjust, difficult to accept your old roles in your own world. Be patient, and the skills and lessons you've learned here will help your world too. This is my last assignment for you, one that will take the rest of your lives to honor. You will continue in your loyal service as Honor Knights, even in your own world. You will teach others what we have taught you, and you will *lead*. Whatever role in which you find yourself engaged, be a leader of men, and *influence them*. Bring the New Rule to the hearts of those in your world, one person at a time."

The King paused, as if he thought we might have questions for him. Unsure, I sat there silently, in a fog of uncertainty and doubt.

Tomorrow, we'll be home, I thought. *We'll be children again.* I couldn't have been more wrong, on both accounts.

"But how do we *get back*?" David finally asked.

"There is a gatekeeper, so to speak, who guards the secret of passing from our world to yours. We believe the path from your world to ours isn't constant; it is only present when it need be. But the path *from* here is always open. I kept this secret from you until you fulfilled all that you were sent here to do."

"*Sent* here?" I nearly interrupted, "we came by *accident*."

David glared at me, but the King took my outburst in stride.

"You will see, Mark. Right now, what seems to you like

random chance will be revealed later as intricate design—when your heart is ready. You were sent here through what seemed like an impossible mistake to you. And your return will—"

"But you *lied to us*," I cut the King off in mid-sentence. "You could have sent us back months ago!"

The King paused, waiting for me to finish. I hung my head, unable to rant any more at him. I bit down on my tongue thinking, *why won't my mouth stay shut?*

"I *kept* this from you, I didn't lie to you. Don't you see? I couldn't have sent you back until it is your time. You will come to understand this."

He sat solemnly for a while, saying nothing. I looked up at him through watery eyes. My apology was plain. Only then did he continue, in a voice more quiet than before, his face full of joy.

"*You've fulfilled the last prophecy.* You were the tools that joined the trolls to our kingdom, both legally, and in practice. They are legal citizens with full rights. Angering the old Portsmouth mayor to strike you—who could have guessed this is what it would take?"

The King saw my expression, and stopped me with a look before I spoke.

"I know, you think since *you* didn't plan it, it wasn't planned at all." The King's face suddenly grew long and regretful. "Understand, please—no one is happy you were struck." He rubbed his nose before continuing, as if he could feel my bruise on his face.

"No one could have guessed this act of violence would create a landmark court case, and set a precedence of trolls deliberating a criminal case over a human. Even more unlikely, it brought healing to the guilty in the process. I marvel at it still.

"You must know, I can only send you back now, after

you've fulfilled your last tasks. In our history, *you already have.*"
His face took on a strange expression as he paused for the
briefest of moments. It seemed to suggest a riddle, or a shared
secret. I didn't dwell on it when I heard what he next had to
say.

"So now it is time for you to learn of the Path back. I will
tell you how to find it."

He stopped again, as if to be certain neither of us would
interrupt.

"Deep within the Northern Forest, far off the road
between the towns and villages, lie the Three Brothers. Three
mountains lie a little apart from the rest of the Northern
Range. The second of these mountains is called Perch. In the
forest around its base, live the Sentinels. They are the
gatekeepers who preserve the continuity of the *Path.* Only
they know its secrets, and only they can guide you through it.
They will tell you how to reach it, and anything else you need
to know in order to return to your home."

"You mean…" David started doubtfully, "you *don't know?*"

The King chuckled, and it warmed my heart—but only a
little.

"No," he answered, "and I'm glad I don't. No one can
take from me what I don't have. We *must* protect the Path."

"Why?" I asked, before I could stop myself.

"We believe it's paramount to keep anyone from crossing it
unless they are *meant* to. What would happen in your world if
anyone could pass from here to there?"

David and I looked at each other, confused. We looked
back at him, unsure what hint he thought he gave us.

"Well then, not just *anyone.* What if someone *not human* was
to appear in your world?"

"Whoever found him would be pretty famous," I offered.
The idea didn't seem so horrible.

"Perhaps you are both too young. After all, you've adjusted very well to our world. But how difficult was it when you first arrived?"

I tried to remember the chaos that filled the first days after our arrival. I was nearly convinced I was insane, then, for a while, I was fully convinced I was dreaming.

But it wasn't from seeing strange sights, I reasoned to myself. Then I remembered; we had no idea why we'd felt that way.

"If a troll or some other creature gifted with speech—not human—found his way to the Path, and traveled to your world, the damage done would be catastrophic—to your world *and* to ours."

He paused, and though we didn't speak, our thoughts must have been plain to him.

"You see, people don't like having their beliefs questioned. To have something everyone knew to be impossible show up in your world, if many people learned of it, it could destroy their sense of reality. The affect is too subtle to see in just one person, but across millions, the affect could destabilize governments. New wars could pop up, industries fail. The loss of life could be uncountable. No; what came from this world stays in this world."

"What about us then? Why shouldn't we get to come and go as we wish?" I asked, perhaps a little too certain of myself.

"We didn't choose for you to come here," replied the King. "You were *sent*. How many times have you been in the cavern in your world, only to come right back out when you were done? No, none of us initiated this exchange. It was *meant to be*."

"Wait a second," said David, plainly as confused as I was, "you said it would be catastrophic for *both* our worlds. What could go wrong here if one person went missing?"

"Well," the King began, sitting back in his chair, "do you

think your world's scientists would be satisfied to see something out of your legends appear, with no explanation? They would need to have an answer. They just might solve the mystery of the link between our worlds. And if they learned of our constellations, they might even find we are in the same universe—though I doubt it very much. If they discovered the link, what do you think it would mean for this world?"

At the time it didn't mean much to me. I couldn't see a problem with people hopping back and forth as much as they liked. But in the decades to come, I've changed my mind. There would be many who wanted to go to the King's world, and not all of them would be helpful. No, the kingdom we visited had something special. They don't need a large rush of people from our world any more than we need one from theirs.

"Don't let anyone know you're headed for Perch," the King warned, his tone ominous. "There is a cloud of superstition and fear surrounding it. All humans keep away, fearing what? They don't even know."

The King must have seen my expression, and once again, read it immediately.

"Take heart, young men, I will send another Honor Knight to go with you, to carry on your mission after you return to your home. Your *official* mission, you see, is much simpler and more understandable to the rest of our kingdom. But it is also important. And if—as I expect—you find your way home on the way to accomplishing your *official* mission, the third knight will complete it for you."

"And what is our *official* mission?" David asked.

"Your mentors will explain it to you later today."

My spirits eased a little to know I would see the Captain one more time, though he had already promised it to me.

"More importantly," the King continued, "know this. Only the knight I send with you knows of both missions. He will learn the absolute minimum of your return, but knows every detail of your official instructions, so he can complete it for you. As important as it is, now that the kingdom may finally come together, it's also going to be a cover for your real mission: to return home. If it is at all possible, you will carry out the Sentinels' instructions directly. Only if you must, are you to return to Thraen Kholl, or stop at any other town along the way. It will be best if you can take the Sentinels' secret with you, having as little contact with others as possible."

The King thanked us again, and was about to dismiss us.

"Will we have any time to say goodbye to our friends around the palace?" David asked. My ears burned to hear his answer.

"Yes. I suppose you've said your goodbyes to those at the delegations before you left, but I can see there are others in Engdynlor you have gotten to know."

"Will we get to say our goodbyes to Lady Sally and the Princess?" I asked, fearful I might show something I dared not. His reply crushed me to the ground.

"I'm afraid not."

Why not? How can you stop me? My mind raced and I held my breath. The King continued.

"My daughter and Lady Sally were going to leave for Terrezia Plain at week's end, but the Captain thought it safer for her if they left immediately. Perhaps he thought a storm is coming, or feared a moonless night to travel under."

I don't remember another word he said. Eventually, David and I were dismissed, and we wound our way through the tunneled halls back to the ground level of the palace.

"What are you so down about?" David finally asked. "Aren't you excited we're finally going to go home?"

"Honestly," I answered, "I don't understand it either. I feel like I *should* be excited, but I'm sad just the same." He gave me a strange look before changing the subject.

"You weren't very polite to the King." Of course he'd noticed it.

"My mouth runs away from me, and I don't even know why. What's gotten into me?" I thought David might have choked on something just then, but I turned to find him snickering. *"What's so funny?"*

He tried to look serious enough to placate me, though he couldn't completely hide his smile.

"You *weren't* acting strangely. I was only surprised you didn't hold back in front of the *King*."

"What on earth are you talking about?" I demanded.

"Mark, when have you ever held your tongue?"

"Are you serious?" I asked. *"All the time."*

"Oh my, then it's much worse than anyone could have guessed." He laughed out loud, further irritating me.

"Come now," he said, "are you seriously telling me you've never let an angry thought slip out in the past?"

"Well, no...but it's been *worse* lately. I've been trying so hard, but it hasn't helped." Did I really have to explain this to him? I expected he knew me better.

"I think I see what's happening," David said as his expression turned serious, almost stern. "I learned the same lesson from the Lieutenant. If that's what this is, I won't laugh anymore."

"What are you *talking* about?"

"It's like this. When you climb the ladder of maturity—as the Lieutenant calls it—you begin to see things in yourself you didn't notice before. Or maybe you *did* see them before, but they didn't *bother* you. Or maybe—well, that's the gist of it."

"What are you trying to say?" I didn't like the direction his words were headed.

"You're kind of known..." he paused, fighting back a laugh, "for running off at the mouth."

"Are you insane?" I snapped back.

When I calmed, David began to list the times I'd let my mouth run away, before the delegations even began. Most of them I remembered after he mentioned them, but some I swore he'd made up. *How could I not notice this?* I wondered. I felt like crawling into a cave and sealing it up.

"Well, like I said, you're kind of known for getting yourself into trouble with your words...*almost as much as I am.* I have the same problem. Did you think we're so different?" Strangely, I felt a little better at hearing it. As we walked along the hall, I thought to myself doubtfully, *did David just teach me a life-lesson?* If he did, I might sum it up as: *people usually think they're more mature than they are.*

We stopped at the kitchen to beg some early lunch from the cook. Arriving there, we found an assistant of Eb's, an elderly lady we didn't know very well. She rapped our fingers as we tried to grab a loaf of bread, but seeing how hungry we were, she gave in and set out some meat and cheese as well. We devoured our sandwiches and thanked her heartily. We told her we were leaving for a long assignment.

"Oh yes, I've heard something of it," she said, conspiratorially. "It sounds quite exciting. *Good luck*—and *do* be careful, so far from home and all."

David and I looked at each other in surprise. How did she know more of our official assignment than we did?

We walked around the palace grounds, visiting the stable master, the smithy, many of the soldiers in the barracks, and the few Honor Knights we could find, though we hardly knew them. My heart wasn't in it, knowing the one goodbye I most wanted to give had been robbed from me.

We'd nearly reached our rooms before I realized there was one goodbye I needed to make, even if I didn't *want* to. Something in me needed very badly to see the old man I'd cared for while the Captain was preparing me for the delegation—the same man who cursed me and threw me out of his home when he found I wanted to help the trolls. I didn't know if he would see me, but I knew I had to try.

I'd long ago told David about the man, and I told him then I wanted to say goodbye to him right away.

"Is that wise?" he asked me.

"If he yells at me and throws me out again, it won't be any worse than the last time. Most likely, he won't agree to see me at all."

"Then what's the point?"

"I want to give him the chance—even if I know he won't take it. You don't have to come."

"I will though," he replied. "I'll keep out of the way."

We walked to the old man's home, and I knocked on the door. The young lady who was his caretaker answered. At recognizing me, she stood speechless.

"May I come in?" I asked.

"Yes, yes. *Please* come in," she replied quickly.

We followed her inside. She gave David a curious look, but said not a word. The old man called to her angrily.

"Who's there? Who is it?" he cried from within his small bedroom. He was lying in his bed, as he did most of the time.

"Take courage," she whispered as she ushered us into his room.

I worried how she expected he might react. When he saw me, his face took on a painful expression. It wasn't the look of hate and ruin I'd last seen him wearing—a horrific expression burned into my memory.

"So it's *you*," he said simply, waiting for a reply. When I gave him none, he went on. "Did you change your mind about...*them?*" I saw a flash of hatred pass over his eyes.

"No sir. I'm convinced even more—"

"*None of that talk in here.* I hear enough about them as it is," he said, glaring at this caretaker. Then his face relaxed a little and he sighed. "I'm getting too old for this. Who would have guessed the things I'd endure to see and hear of in my lifetime?"

I didn't say a word, I only looked at him sadly. After a silent moment he went on.

"I heard about the martyr you know. Don't think it changes anything." But it *did*, and I could see in his face he *knew* it. He was speaking, of course, of Norman.

"I wanted to say goodbye to you, sir," I said when it seemed too long a pause. A concerned look crept over his face.

"Goodbye? Where are you going? Are you so afraid to come and see me again?"

"I'm returning to my homeland, far away from here. I may never see you again—or anyone in Thraen Kholl."

"Why? *Why* must you leave?" he asked, visibly upset. When I paused to answer, he cut me off. "No, no, it's all right. I understand. You miss your family. I know the feeling only too well. I think of my family often, all of them gone before me."

He stiffened a bit, as a painful memory surely woke within him. He was straining to sit up in bed. I remember thinking he must have been projecting his own feelings onto me. Whatever he might have sensed in my attitude and expression, it wasn't a longing to see my family. I suddenly wondered again why I'd returned to see him. I knew he wouldn't let me talk about the trolls. The young woman left the room and returned to her tasks, as if we weren't there. David was a statue behind me.

"Uh—sir?" I started, uncertain of what to say. "I just felt I had to see you again…" I wasn't doing a very good job so far. I stumbled on anyway. "I just couldn't leave without seeing you again, not after the way I last saw you."

"Ah, I see," he replied, lying back against his mattress and pillows. "Yes, I was a hard sight to take in, for sure; you saw me at my worst. *If you only knew what they did to me, what they did to—*"

He stopped abruptly. He drew a deep breath as if to calm himself.

"But you don't want to hear that, do you? No, you don't. And truth be told, I don't want to tell it. I'm weary—weary and *old,* from carrying my hatred so long."

What? I thought, hardly believing my ears. *He knows.* He must have seen my surprise. I wanted to tell him to give up his hatred and be freed. I bit my tongue instead. He smiled slightly, and chuckled.

"Too much like the Sergeant. Ah, *the Captain* to you— Captain Williams was once my Sergeant, you see. You're too much like him. It's fine; your thoughts are so loud, I can read them on your face. After a while your Captain also learned not to speak of the trolls to me. Still, it didn't keep me from hearing his words in my thoughts whenever he visited. You're his son, in a way, aren't you?" He saw my eyes widen.

"He's taught you like the son he never had. Or rather, like the son he had too short a time. Oh, you didn't know, did you? No, I can see you didn't. Your Captain has more reason to hate the trolls than I do, *much more,* I say."

The old man's voice grew suddenly from a tired mumble to a fiery pitch as he spoke. His caretaker appeared in the doorway behind me for a moment, but left when he calmed himself.

"*That's* why I hate them—for what they did to the Sarge—taking his family like that. He may have forgiven them, but I hate them enough for the both of us."

He forced the words through clenched teeth, his voice a rumbling hiss. In a moment, he looked back at me, as if he'd forgotten I was there for a little while. My heart felt sick to hear this story of the Captain's past—and curious for the tale's details. Then, another thought occurred to me: just how much had this man's hate cost him? Though he knew it brought him harm, still, he was unwilling to part with it.

"Yes, I know…" he said when he had relaxed once again, "I know it; you don't have to tell me again. I know it only too well."

He relaxed his clenched hands and dropped his head back into his pillow.

What does he know? I wondered. Is he imagining someone else is talking to him?

"Heh heh. The Sarge never liked it either—me stopping him from saying it. I'm an old man, and fragile old men will be given their way. It's what makes life bearable for us I suppose…" He mumbled on, but his words made no sense to me. Eventually, his voice trailed off and he fell asleep. David and I left the room, and I approached his young caretaker. She held her finger to her lips and pointed to the door. She followed us out into the street.

"Thank you for visiting," she said. "He hasn't stopped talking about you since you left. It's been an angry time for him, I'm sure he'll be better after your visit."

"What?" I asked, surprised. "Did he feel badly for yelling at me?" I asked.

"Oh, yes! He knows how harmful his words can be. It's a sad condition. He often rocks back and forth, between hate and guilt. He recognizes the compassion others show him, and yet—I guess it's hard to change when you're so old." I didn't know what else to say to her. I didn't know this woman at all—not even her name. Was she a distant relative of his? Or maybe a hospice worker randomly assigned to him?

David, speaking for the first time in front of her, asked, "Is he always so...angry?"

"Most of the time," she replied. "He knows his hate is the cause of much of his pain. And yet—he's afraid to give it up. It's all he knows."

"Will he ever change?" I asked her.

"Who knows? It's not why I help him anymore. It's enough to give him the chance to change—like you did today. The world is a tiny bit better today, for one person giving another the chance to forgive." She smiled at us. "I know it sounds strange, but it's what I believe. Even if it doesn't change him, even if he *never* changes, *we* change, by offering him the chance." Her face lit up, and her voice grew a little cheerier. "So again, thank you." She reached out with both hands and embraced mine. She held them tightly, as if giving me a hug with her hands. "I hope your journey is a good one."

Pulled back into my thoughts of our impending trip, my eyes dropped. "Thank you. I—I hope it is, too."

She curtsied, and went back into the tiny house. David and I headed back toward the nearest entrance into Engdynlor. David broke our silence.

"He's a very strange old man."

"Yes, he is," I said, sighing. Turning toward him, I added, "Thanks for coming with me."

David punched me roughly in the shoulder, knocking me off-balance. Then he threw his arm around my shoulder and squeezed me sidelong until it hurt. I threw my arm over his shoulder and we walked side by side for a few paces, until he punched me in the shoulder once more, knocking me against the stone wall of a building we passed. I jabbed him in the shoulder with my elbow. It might have been a strange sight for anyone who happened by us, but *we* understood it. *I missed you, brother*, his arms had said. *I missed you too*, mine answered back.

3.2 History Teaches All

When we returned to our rooms, our mentors were waiting for us. We probably would have guessed they'd be there if we'd stopped to give it some thought, but neither of us had wanted to think about it. It was the last time we would see them.

I opened the door to my room and let the Captain in. We sat down: he on the chair near my desk and me on the side of my bed.

"Are you ready for your journey?" he asked me.

"You know I'm not," I answered quickly.

"Then you're still angry about leaving."

"No. Yes," I tried to straighten the thoughts in my head. "I'm still angry about leaving, but I'm *angrier* I won't get to say a proper goodbye to *everyone*." He knew my meaning.

"Sometimes it's better that way," he replied.

"I guess I'll never get to find out," I answered, allowing my anger to grow.

"I'm not only looking out for her. I'm also responsible for *you*."

I was going to give him a snide reply, but held my tongue.

"I don't want to spend my last hours here angry at you," I told him. If I do, I'll regret it for the rest of my life."

"Sometimes these things can't be helped," he replied.

His words surprised me—I expected a scolding from him. I looked at him and saw that my leaving was also difficult for him. I thought of the few times he slipped and called me son. How old would his son be if he hadn't been killed?

"There are things I need to tell you. Some you are ready to hear now, others you will remember later and may learn from them then."

I caught myself trying to think of a sarcastic reply, and sighed instead. I really *didn't* want to be mad at him—and yet I was. I tried to ignore it.

"You're still my mentor. I'd be a fool not to listen to you."

He paused just long enough to smile. I saw a sparkle in his eye, but couldn't be sure it wasn't a tear. Then he launched into a long story of his childhood. It was the third time he'd gone back to fill in details of his youth, having always saved part of the story for another time. We both knew this would be his last chance to tell me anything at all.

"Soon after my father died, my mother became deathly ill. For a time, I was left all alone. The village where my other relatives lived had been destroyed in the troll battles. It had been a hard time in the kingdom for more than a generation by then, and many children were left without relatives—many more than ever before. The King recognized the need for a government program; it was too large a task for any one town or city to absorb.

"An orphanage was created to care for several hundred children from the generation before I was born, and more were added every year. Many more people died in the years of the troll battles than did in our short war, but there was no organized enemy to wage war against. The trolls even fought with themselves; they never united against us."

The Captain's eyes seemed distant. I fought the urge to

speak, and eventually he continued.

"At any rate—where was I? Oh yes. Outside a large farming village, the King ordered a huge campus to be built, to house and raise all the orphans. Each building held all the children of a given age. Most children had been there since they were infants, because an infant is the only human a troll warrior won't kill. Needless to say the orphanage was in a real mess by the time I was brought there."

It wasn't at all obvious to me, but I didn't want to interrupt the Captain. He saw my puzzled look anyway.

"Don't you see? The children weren't divided into groups by age for their own benefit; it was purely an administrative decision. They didn't have enough workers to run the orphanage yet, and the orphanage overseer decided it would be easier to deal with the children if they were separated according to their age. The children lived and learned together. They were given capable and honorable men and women as caretakers, teachers and role models. Not a few knights who had raised their own families volunteered to oversee the orphanage's progress, even though they were badly needed to defend the farming villages from troll raids.

"Even with all the work and oversight, the orphanage had been turning out far too many adults, who in their hearts were still rebellious children. Many of them chose to remain this way for the rest of their lives. Some continued to draw from public funds for decades, oppressed by indolent poverty. Many fell into illegal gangs after they were graduated or released, and were later arrested, further burdening the kingdom. The orphanage's overseer ordered a study to investigate how the carefully planned program had turned into such a failure."

Young and optimistic as I was, I could hardly imagine a way the trend the Captain described could come to an end.

The Captain paused, and I waited patiently for him to continue. My anger toward him was all but spent.

"The children had no families, and the program had intended to provide all the things families provide: food, shelter, learning, role models, and the like. There was one fatal flaw: the program's designers had created the *opposite* of families. Instead of small groups of people, diverse in age, with others to learn from *and also to teach*, the orphans were placed into huge groups of thirty or more children the same age, with only one or two older mentors in each group. With no older siblings or relatives to follow, they turned to their peers: the other children, who needed healthy examples just as badly.

"There was something important missing, something about helping; this much was obvious to the caretakers, and even the overseer. But the effect of gathering together all those children of the same age proved far worse."

"Why?" I finally interrupted. "What's so horrific about being with kids your own age?"

The Captain rose from his memories and stared at me as if he'd forgotten I was there.

Why is this so difficult for him to talk about? I wondered.

"Why," he finally continued, "it isn't a natural state. At no other time in our history have children spent the majority of their time, from infancy to young adulthood, surrounded only by other children of the same age. They didn't have a family of people who were responsible for each other. Neither was their group comprised of people who cared for them, or provided each other with a healthy sense of belonging, of right and wrong. Instead, these groups of same-aged children looked to *each other* for their concept of self-value. They looked to their misshapen groups to find what they valued in themselves, and in life in general.

"The problem with this is *obvious*," he said, his expression pleading with me to understand. "Each child needed to learn these things as badly as the rest, so they had no business teaching each other. It was the blind leading the blind, don't you see? I forget—you didn't see it firsthand. The consequence, tragically, was this: the most important thing in their lives became their own inexpert opinions of each other. Each of them was convinced this strange method of random values was absolutely right; it was self-reinforcing.

"Imagine a child of ten who is utterly convinced nothing in the world matters more than the misguided opinions of other ten-year-olds. How will such a child act? How would he teach younger children to act, should they ever come in contact with him?"

Subconsciously, I looked down in shame—he very nearly described how I'd acted in school as a ten year old. In fact, I couldn't deny I'd acted so differently before I found myself in Terreldor. I had David—sometimes my friendship with him was a safe harbor from the cliques and schoolyard opinions that seemed so trivial to me, sitting in front of the Captain. But other times, the influence of the other kids in our classes drove us apart. When we were younger, if David went to find me with my classmates during recess, his classmates mocked him for *playing with babies*, even though he was only one grade ahead of me. It seemed impossible in my school for two kids a grade apart to be friends. David and I were often forced apart, at least at school. Many of my classmates had no brothers or sisters at all.

The opinions of the other kids in my classes seemed so important to me *then*. At times it seemed as if their opinions were my whole world. I remembered the few kids in my school, who over the years *didn't* care much for the collective opinions of the other children. They were ridiculed or ignored as freaks. I remember the cruel words cast on them, as clearly as I remembered counting myself lucky for not being like them. I realized they were possibly the most mature kids in my classes. I imagined how much worse it would have been if I had *lived* at school, all year long, from infancy to adulthood. I shook my head, subconsciously. The Captain, seeing this, cocked his head with a concerned expression.

"*Mark,*" he began, his voice sounding like reproach. I winced. "Whose opinions are most important in a child's life?"

"I'm not sure what you mean..."

"Whose approval should a child regard—that of someone wiser, who loves him and wants what's best for him, or the random approval of the unwise, who care nothing for his wellbeing, or even his life?"

"The one who loves him," I replied, suddenly realizing I was slowly shaking my head again.

"And more times than not, what have you observed in the schools of your world?"

I paused before answering. I waited until I was sure I could speak without faltering. "We regard the approval of the fool."

Soon my shame turned to anger. Many of my teachers had been honorable examples to me, adults who truly cared for their students. Why had they hidden this from us—why hadn't they shown us the folly of allowing other children to choose our values? I concentrated, trying to force a memory that would not show itself.

Had they? I wondered. *Could they have tried to teach this to me, and I ignored them?*

Neither of us spoke for several minutes. The silence was at first uncomfortable, but as the discomfort faded, I was glad for it. Strangely, it felt refreshing. Eventually, it turned into boredom.

"Were you in the orphanage long?" I asked, turning to him. As I did, I read the expression on his face, and guessed he had not yet had enough silence. I was certain he'd drifted deep into some distant and unhappy thought. A short while later, he woke from his brown study, surprised, as if there had been no pause at all.

"What? No. Before long, my mother grew healthier, and she left the infirmary. I was sent home to her just as she was growing well enough to take care of herself. The effect of that strange habitat had taken root in the already-angry boy that I was. I spent a period drifting angrily, as I told you before. Sometime afterward, my mentor returned from a tour of defending our villages from troll raids, and he found me. Years later—toward the end of my apprenticeship—I spent some time in the orphanage again, trying to help. I learned much more about the problems they saw. I was still there when it was declared a failure by the overseer. He stepped down, and appointed a new overseer—someone with new ideas the old overseer had resisted while he tried unsuccessfully to reverse the same harmful patterns he'd unwittingly begun.

"The results of a long study—undertaken by the new overseer—were soon published, and the orphanage was shut down in a few short years. The new overseer had the difficult task of helping the children already caught up in the problem, as the orphanage was replaced with a new solution."

"What was the new solution?" I asked, feeling for some reason invested in its outcome.

"First of all, they broke up the large groups of age-sorted children into smaller groups. The ages of the groups were mixed—more like a large farming family. In fact, that's nearly what they became. There were a shortage of farmers from the raids and battles, and so it appeared two problems might share the same solution. More volunteers were recruited to join the effort, and groups of eight or ten children were moved into smaller houses where a volunteering young couple became their adopted parents.

"This first step accomplished several important things. In those cobbled-together families, the children learned two of their most important lessons at the same time: whose opinions should matter to them, and how to teach others. In a caring group of people who are responsible for you, you find people whose opinions will help you, not drive you to random or harmful behaviors for the senseless approval of others. The children were made responsible for each other, to the degree they were able. This invited them to *care* for one another. '*Teaching*,' the new overseer insisted, 'is the way our minds best learn.'"

"What?" I interrupted again. "How can you learn by teaching?"

The Captain smiled.

"When you learn a concept, you are likely to forget it unless it is regularly put to use. But when you *teach* the concept to another, you show mastery of it, and are unlikely to forget it. So in this way, the children *learned to teach* in order to truly learn. In their new families, they learned the value in helping others. Part of each child's schoolwork was to teach some of a subject to a younger one. This made their environment more like a family and less like the failed orphanage.

"There was a great shift in the program over the following decade. Some of the children who graduated found mates in the nearby school-homes. Often, they married and immediately adopted their younger orphan-siblings they'd grown close to. When this happened, their adopted parents were free to start another orphan-family, or retire.

"This is what I did after I completed my apprenticeship with my mentor. He knew the failed orphanage was something I'd followed, and was passionate about. In the end, he encouraged me to become a part of the solution. So when I married, my wife and I moved to one of the orphan-villages and adopted a half-dozen children to teach and raise. Before long, we had two children of our own to add to our growing family. Our two eldest, when they found their spouses and were married, built homes on our property and helped expand our farm. Soon, they had their own children, whom our younger children helped to teach and raise." He smiled in a sad way—it was an expression I'd never seen in him before.

"I felt like a king then. We were our own tiny kingdom. And by doing merely what we loved, we were helping to solve the problems of the greater kingdom. It might have gone on for generations, but it wasn't meant to be."

A hush fell over him and his eyes were full of pain. A long, weary tear trailed down his cheek before he wiped it away.

"Was your village attacked by trolls?" I asked, my own throat tight. I remembered a conversation we had before the short war with the rebels. He'd shown me the first two tables and tried to tell me how to trust the King to do what's good for us. He'd hinted back then at the hurt I saw so plainly in his eyes. He nodded in reply to my question.

"It's a hard tale for me to tell, but it's one you need to hear. I want you to bring this story back with you. This, and all the things I've been so privileged to teach you, my son."

We were both silent for a while, but it wasn't as awkward as you might think. Without warning, the Captain regained his story-telling voice and went on, as if the moment was wrapped up and put away for later.

"Afterward, the system of fewer, smaller schools, with children of different ages, all learning from—*but also teaching*—

each other, this system was carried to all the schools in the kingdom. Now even the schools in our cities are divided into small groups of different aged children—each group like a tiny village's one-room schoolhouse. Brothers and sisters are never split up. Their relationships are a great value in their tiny classes. This system required many more teachers, but after the obvious differences it made from our failed orphanage, teaching our children became a highly held value throughout the kingdom."

How odd, I thought. *How strange it must be to go to such a school.* Then I thought of being in school with both my brothers all the time, with a half-dozen others of different ages mixed in. I imagined having my older brother, David, to help me with things he'd learned the year before, and my younger brother, only ten, able to learn from me. I knew I loved to teach him when I'd had the chance. Suddenly I envied these children I was never to meet. In all my time in the kingdom, I'd never even noticed these strange schools. The Princess learned privately from Lady Sally, and the children at Portsmouth had schools like the Captain described, but I assumed it was out of necessity or lack of funding—but by the time I thought of these things, the Captain had started to speak and I was missing what he had to say.

"…And when children are ready to leave the school, they usually become an apprentice to a wise tradesman, or a shop or business owner. The system works well for us, and allows so many more children to see what it means to mature while they learn and grow, instead of being kept separate from their older peers.

"You've explained your world's need for a longer and more complex education, but you've also described a system closer to our failed experiment than anything else I can imagine. I'm not presumptuous enough to think our system would work in your world, but I know it has worked very well in ours. I'm not sure how we would have implemented our system in a place where a child is educated for thirteen or twenty-some years before they *produce*, only to stop learning abruptly in most cases. I only know where we've had success and where we've had failures. The most important distinction we learned is: large classrooms work best for giving and receiving information. This, and: diversity in age *helps*—not hinders—the learning process. If a child can be taught by those who understand this, there is always hope."

He paused, and I waited silently, lost in my thoughts of his sad tale.

"Most of this won't help you now," he finally went on. "As I've said, it's for later. But the point I wanted you to see today is this: to *teach* is to give of yourself. Sometimes it's the most you can do for others. To give them *information* is only to push them along. But to *teach*…to teach, is to show them how to climb! And how high they'll climb—how far they may go—is entirely up to them. *This* is what you must learn in your final assignment, Mark—in the assignment which will last the rest of your days."

"Weren't you supposed to tell me what my *official* assignment is?" I asked with a smile. *My anger for him is gone,* I thought. As soon as I thought it, a pang of sadness fell over me. I remembered I would never see the Princess again. And yet—how did the Captain carry his memories? He'd lost his *entire family*, those he'd loved for years and years. I knew it was much more significant than anything I'd felt just yet. And I was going home, to be reunited with the rest of my family. Somehow his story of families and orphans made me miss my family worse than I had in months. I told him so.

"Thank you for telling me so; I'm glad to hear it. And yes, I'm also here to tell you of your official assignment—I just thought I'd throw that in, just in case the King turns out to be right about your impending voyage home. He usually *is* right you know," he said with a wink. "Your *official* assignment is much simpler to explain…"

He went on to outline the assignment others would hear about. It was time for the King to send representatives to the Animal Coast. This was possibly the time the New Rule would be introduced, and the distant subjects of the Animal Coast needed to hear of it. Many would welcome it. Whatever trolls still lived there would be a problem, but if the King was right, it would be a problem for others to solve. Supplies and helpers were going to be brought to the silent duke, and messages brought to the antelopes of Otlak Plain and the village Peaceful where the Watchmakers lived.

When he was done explaining it to me, he reminded me to encode any messages I sent back by pigeon. He told me it was of utmost importance I didn't send anything before encoding it. Then he handed me a paper tube and told me to open it later. I was almost afraid to take it from him. I didn't want another critique of my performance like I'd received from Bob in Portsmouth, but I should have trusted him beyond that. We said our goodbyes; it felt as if he were dying, knowing I would never see him again. When we were done, he gave me a great big hug, and told me he was proud of me. It was what I remember most of all he said that day, and it took him only half a breath.

Then, alone in my room, I unrolled the scroll of paper expecting to find a long sheet—but there was none. There was a blank page covering a thick patch of leather, rolled into a cylinder. Burned onto one side was a miniature Table of False Reflections. On the other side were tiny versions of the Table of Opposites and Table of Maturity. I kept it buttoned in my pocket the rest of my time in Terreldor.

3.3 Departure

David and I talked late into the night about our return. First we packed all the things David would not leave behind, then went to my room and did the same. We talked each other out of a lot of things we really didn't need.

As we packed, I told David about the strange school system used throughout the kingdom. He already knew some of it, but hadn't heard of its origins. I told him about the Captain's family and what had happened to them. I didn't mention the Princess at all, and when David spoke of wishing he could have said goodbye to her and Lady Sally, I changed the subject.

In a single evening, David and I spent more time with each other than we had in months, but still were so eager to see each other as it grew late. My mind rebelled with the notion we would soon be gone, never to see any of the people in the kingdom again. Logically I accepted the fact, but it was a sterile piece of information in my mind, as if it hadn't yet filtered down into my gut.

I began to miss my parents and younger brother more and more as we talked about our nearing return. I felt better about leaving, but no one could accuse me of being *happy* about it.

David left to go to bed with the morning only hours away. I rolled into my bed, already half asleep. I dreamt of being lost in a mist, caught between worlds. I worried all night such a thing might be possible.

I woke to the sound of someone knocking at my door. *It can't be morning already.* Again, I'd dreamt all night and woke, dreading the long day ahead of me. When I answered my door, I was surprised to see Lt. Underhill in full uniform. David peered from around his shoulder, sheepishly.

"Uh, good morning, Lieutenant Underhill," I said, unsure of what else to say.

"Are you ready to go? We have a coach waiting with some breakfast packed for the ride."

"You do?" It took me a minute to realize the Lieutenant was going with us. I threw on the rest of my clothes and hefted the large sack filled with my belongings over one shoulder, and my knapsack holding little else than my codebook over the other. I hung my sword on my belt, and slung my chain mail over my knapsack. I fell into step with David and whispered to him, "Did you know the Lieutenant was going with us to the Bay?"

David, still acting oddly, said only, "I guess so."

Through the windows, I saw the dim pre-dawn sky. All of Engdynlor was asleep, it seemed. *Why do we need to leave so early?* I thought. With an early winter sunset, the ride to the Bay would take all the daylight hours. Still, I hadn't left *this* early when I rode for Thraen Kholl, from the Bay two days before.

When we walked out through the grand doors of Engdynlor, we found a double row of men lining the sides of our path to the coach.

"Quickly men, into the coach," the Lieutenant whispered to us. As we passed them, the men on both sides kneeled in salute to us. They were the Honor Knights. The last knight we passed was the King. I felt embarrassed to see him kneel. I nearly missed him, without his royal clothes or crown. He was wearing a full set of armor, just like the rest of the knights.

It seemed a thousand thoughts flew through my mind in the few seconds it took us to reach the coach. *What if someone sees them all together? Where is the Captain? So that's why we left so early—so the knights could get together without being seen. Is that the Captain?* I whipped my head around wildly in search for him, but loaded down as I was, it was difficult. I wished I hadn't packed so much.

When I turned to climb into the coach, I saw the Captain out of the corner of my eye. By then, David was at my side, and we were pulling away. I leaned out the window to catch a glimpse of him. I saw him for the last time in my life. He wore a proud smile, not dimmed by the tears I couldn't be sure I hadn't imagined. Inside the coach, the Lieutenant sat across from me. He asked if I was all right.

"Yes," I said, though I certainly didn't feel like it.

The first part of our ride was silent. When we stopped at Kniefel, we ate lunch at the inn. I recognized the innkeeper the Captain had yelled at during the war, on our way to meet the Third. He recognized me, and stopped by our table to strike up a conversation with us. The innkeeper was the last man in the world I wanted to eat with. I knew he didn't care about us; he was only fishing for gossip. The Lieutenant saw the look in my eye as he approached.

"Off on an important mission, sir?" the innkeeper asked.

The Lieutenant dropped his mug conspicuously, breaking it and spilling its contents onto the floor.

"*Oops,*" was all he said, though the glare he gave the innkeeper looked painful. The innkeeper backed away, startled and mumbling.

How'd he do that? I wondered, fascinated. *Perhaps,* I thought, *the Lieutenant has a reputation something like the Captain's.* Though he wasn't as old, I supposed he might look just as threatening to someone he opposed.

"Well men, are you ready to go?" he asked a moment later.

We both took a few more bites of our meals and headed back to the coach. While we turned onto the north road to the Bay, I couldn't help thinking Lady Sally and the Princess had just passed there, but continued west for Carrottop. I stared down the westward road as if I might see them on their way. David nudged me, pulling me from my thoughts. He asked the Lieutenant to tell us a story from his childhood. I turned toward him and feigned interest, but only out of civility. I was in for a rare surprise. The Lieutenant, I soon learned, was quite a comedian when he wanted to be. He had us both laughing in no time.

Most of his stories were about the family he lived near when he was growing up. They had five sons, each as big and strong as an ox—and just as smart. Each story seemed to end in the same way: one of the *oxboys* would scratch his head and wonder aloud some idle bewilderment such as, *Now why'd he go and do that?* After a few of his tales, I felt nearly like myself again.

David and I tried to outdo one another by telling stories from before we'd arrived in Terreldor. They might not have been as funny as the Lieutenant's, but it felt good to remember them together.

It was nearing dusk when we reached the Bay. We dropped our bags at the inn, but I kept my small knapsack with my codebook and a few other valuables with me. The Lieutenant said he was taking us to our last decent meal for a while, and we got back in the coach. The driver dropped us off at the entrance to Beach Row.

Large lanterns lit the way between the shops and restaurants; it was surely the best lit area of Oyster Bay, and probably the entire kingdom. I pondered again at the number of people who braved the cold to walk up and down the popular strand.

As the Lieutenant led us down the Row, I asked if we could walk around before we ate. I wanted to visit the art gallery with the glass sculptures I thought so highly of.

The Lieutenant told us to go ahead of him while he ordered our meals at the restaurant. "It's called the Wading Duck— just a few shops past here. Try to be there in a half-hour."

It was the first time David had been to the Bay. I knew he'd want to see if the sculptor who visited his delegation had any of sculptures left in the gallery. She did; it seemed she'd been very busy. I wanted to show him the miniature I'd seen just days ago, the day the Princess and I had last spoken. As he looked over the glass pieces on display, I found the one I was looking for was missing. I'd been thinking wishfully of trying to trade something I owned for it, if the shop keeper could by any means be talked into it.

As we discussed the remaining sculptures, a quiet mood fell over David. I gave him space and I allowed myself to be drawn again to the paintings. As I stood in front of the one where the Princess had begun crying, the shop keeper approached me.

"Young sir, I have something for you."

I looked at him in surprise. "Excuse me?"

"Your...ah, *revered* friend who accompanied you earlier this week—she left a gift for you." I was quite taken back.

"You mean the Princess?" His eyes darted from side to side, as if searching for someone who might have overheard me.

"Yes. I left instruction with the inn to let me know when

you arrived. I was going to have it delivered to the inn after I closed, but I thought you might visit my gallery again."

He held a small rectangular box, covered with decorated, dark leather.

"I wanted to see if the custom box I had built was satisfactory to you," he added.

I took the box and turned it over in my hands. It was bound by a leather buckle. I unlatched it slowly and opened the box. The lid of the box fit tightly; perhaps it was even waterproof. I stood there in near-shock, staring at the glass sculpture I had hoped against all reason to barter away from the gallery owner—Schelli's gift to me. He wore a satisfied grin.

"I take it the box is acceptable to you?" he asked proudly.

"Huh? Yes...oh, yes. Very well crafted. Thank you, sir. Did she—did the Princess leave a message for me? Did she say anything about...well, about the gift?"

He gave me a knowing smile. "There is a *sealed message* packed away under the lining."

The glass sculpture was snug in the box, surrounded by dark blue velvet stretched over padding on both the box and its lid. I carefully pulled on the velvet from the bottom half of the box, and it slowly slid from its recess. I saw a tiny envelope made of real gold leaf under the soft padding. I quickly opened it, tearing it as I did so. The Princess's initials were pressed into the envelope across the seal, where the gold leaf seemed to have been melted together. There was a folded slip of paper within it, which read:

I want you to take this with you. The shop owner assures me he will craft a tiny box capable of keeping it safe through your travels. It's called *Love's Sacrifice*. The sculptor believes *Love* must sacrifice *Want* in order to be seen—a lesson I am now learning.

In case we never speak again, I wanted you to know I heard you shout after me in the crowd just now. I just couldn't return and face you, knowing you'll be gone so soon. Take care. Be safe. And find all the happiness in your own world we both hoped you'd find here.

Love, Schelli Harrington

I folded the envelope and put everything back into the tiny box just as it had been.

I took the shop owner's hand and shook if firmly. I looked steadily into his eyes and thanked him. Any ill will I'd held toward him was gone. He nodded solemnly and quietly returned to another part of the shop.

I put the box in my knapsack, and stood facing the painting until David found me and suggested we leave for the restaurant before our meals were ready.

On the way, David was quiet. Just as we found the Wading Duck, he put his hand on my shoulder and said in a low tone, "So, do I get to hear about the box later?"

Almost in a panic, I answered, "Yeah—I guess so."

I thought he hadn't noticed anything in the shop, but of course, he'd seen everything. Waiting as long as he had, must have been a great exercise of his patience. I wondered how I would explain it, how much I would leave out. I was happy to put it off while we ate a long and hearty meal with the Lieutenant.

That night as we lay down to sleep at the inn, David brought it up again. Our two small beds were stuffed into a tiny room, barely able to hold them. The lantern was out and the shutters were closed, though there was little light for them to hold back on that starless winter night.

"So...what about the little box in your sack?" he asked. I

couldn't read his expression, but I knew from his voice he'd tried his best to sound patient.

"It was a gift…a tiny glass sculpture I saw the last time I was here."

"Oh? Who from?" he replied too casually, feigning casual interest.

"From *whom*," I corrected, trying to delay my answer.

"You know what I mean," he said, finally showing a little impatience. I wished there was enough light for me to find something in the room to distract me from his questions.

"It's from the Princess."

David shifted in his bed. "Really?" he asked. "Oh…I thought maybe it was from Amelia."

"Who's Amelia?" I asked, hoping he was changing the subject.

"The sculptor. Really, she's more of a glass blower than sculptor. She was still an apprentice during the war."

My mind raced to guess what he was talking about. *Is he making this up?*

"So why did the Princess give it to you?" he asked. "Did she think you might be jealous?"

I thought I was clueless before, but with only a few words David confused me even further. It sounded as if he had everything backwards.

"Uh…honestly, I don't know."

"You know," he went on, "because I already had one of her sculptures, and you didn't." He chuckled, "Remember how jealous you were when the King gave me the mirrors from Eastward and Westward?" His words began to fall into some semblance of reason. "You remember Amelia; I told you about her before."

Of course, I thought. He'd written about the strange young woman who braved the lonely trail up Golden Mountain, to ask permission to meet the ice trolls. I rolled my blankets around me and half-covered my head to save a little warmth.

David told me a long story—though I heard little more than its beginning. I remembered he'd written to me of the day she arrived at *Friendship Hall*, soon after he'd renamed it. He was curious about her, what had driven her to travel alone—barely older than himself—for a remote chance to learn something of the art she'd only heard of in rumors. At times she seemed almost crazy to him, she was so passionate about her art. She was also passionate about the Lyssiltiks living in peace—*alone.*

She was an isolationist. She believed the ice trolls' best hope for peace was for humans to avoid all contact with them. Eventually they struck a difficult friendship. When she returned home, David was sad to see her go, though she had done nothing to make his task easier.

I fell asleep while David was still talking. Under a cover of heavy blankets, I had a better night's sleep than I'd had in a long time.

3.4 On to Rester

The Lieutenant woke us while it was still dark. By dawn we were aboard the ship that would carry us to the North Forest. I didn't realize we wouldn't be taking the Good Ship Explorer, but instead a smaller boat belonging to a local fisherman. When we boarded, the Lieutenant rushed us into the small cabin without introducing us to any of the crew. We shoved off while it was barely light enough to see the harbor buoys.

We only ate once aboard the ship, so I didn't have much chance to miss the warm meals I enjoyed on my last ride from Port to Bay. Cheese and cold beef sandwiches were food enough on that chop; it was a rougher ride than any I'd been on before. The fishing captain and his small crew didn't speak to us at all. The Lieutenant had warned us of this; they were instructed to speak only to him for the length of our journey.

We landed at a rarely-used dock in a bay named Safe Harbor. It was colder even than the icy winds at Beach Row. My nose gave me more pain than anything; it seemed almost too cold for smelling. The winds were fiercer even than any David had felt at Friendship Hall.

Safe Harbor was a large bay. It had a long beach which curved slowly into a half-circle, and a long mountainous island across from it, calming the waters. Together, the beach and opposing island nearly formed a complete circle. It was growing dark fast, but I could see far across the water to the bay's other exit. The Lieutenant explained the narrow strait between the beach and the far side of the island made for horrible tides, which could drag a ship to pieces.

The Lieutenant, David and I left the ship with packs loaded for a day's hike. As soon as we set out, he explained word was sent overland to Rester, the nearest town to Safe Harbor. If they got the message, there would be a coach waiting for us nearby. If not, we would return to the ship and start again in the morning. Either way, the ship would set out for Oyster Bay the next morning.

"How will they know when to come back?" I asked.

"The messenger who brought word to Rester left a present for you: two pigeons."

I wondered who'd planned this trip: the Captain or the Lieutenant.

"Where are they?" David asked.

"In town—in Rester. We won't send them until we return from Perch. That is, assuming the Sentinels' Path is far, and we need the ship to get there."

I had to strain to hear him. Though the wind blowing from the water howled, he insisted on talking quietly. If I had heard him correctly, the Lieutenant had no idea where or how we would enter the Path to our world. Would it be from the very place we would find the Sentinels? Would it be from the jungle, where we first found ourselves? Would it be far out to sea, where no human in the kingdom had ever sailed? My thoughts trailed on until the enveloping darkness distracted me with cold and fear.

Not far from the dock, we found Rester *had* gotten word. Just as we began to lose sight of the lantern at the ship's bow to the scrub brush behind us, we came along an old man sitting on a coach with no light. Without a word, he lit a lantern inside the coach, and though I hoped it would, it made us no warmer. I wished the lack of wind in the coach might give us some warmth, but its cold wooden seats more than made up for the difference.

He stopped at a one-room shack just past the small town. There was an iron woodstove in the center of the hut, with four cots stacked high with blankets, and a pigeon cage. Firewood was stacked near a small table against one wall, under a set of cabinets. The pigeon cage stood on a bench and held the two pigeons sent overland ahead of us. A piece of flannel was draped over the half of the cage furthest from the woodstove.

They were well stocked with food and water, and sat on perches above a large, flat stone in the center of their cage. When I checked on the birds, I felt the stone and it was hot to the touch. I saw another like it on the woodstove, with a pot of stew resting on it. I guessed the old man would keep the pigeons alive until they were needed, though I didn't break the silence settled firmly over the four of us to ask him.

We ate dinner with the old man, and no one spoke a word. When either of us looked questioningly toward the Lieutenant, he only scowled and shook his head.

We went straight to our cots after we ate, and I fell asleep immediately. When I woke, the old man was gone, and there was fresh wood stacked near the door, drying from the warmth of the woodstove. Outside, we found three fresh horses and a donkey. Even then, the Lieutenant wouldn't speak. Just before we left, I went to take the pigeon cage, but the Lieutenant laid a hand on my shoulder and shook his head.

As we prepared to leave, I considered how long it had been since any of us spoke: not since we met the driver waiting for us in the dark the night before. *How creepy it must've been for him,* I thought of the old man.

It had been a cold night in the stranger's drafty shack. Sleeping there had been almost like sleeping around a campfire. My cot was so close to the woodstove, it nearly burned my face, but the half of my body facing away from the stove was cold, even with a layer of thick blankets over me. I was still cold when we left early that morning.

Stepping out of the shack to find our horses, my first thought was one of utter surprise. The sky was clear, the air crisp, and it was *bitter cold.* Though the sun was higher in the sky than I'd expected, and there was no wind to speak of, I felt no warmer than I had the previous night. Along with this first shock of cold air, I got my first real glimpse of our surroundings.

What seemed grim and gloomy the night before, was bright and glorious in the light of day. And though I shivered fiercely, I noticed everything around us sparkled in a gleaming blanket of white. If the crusted snow had been coated with diamonds, it wouldn't have looked more brilliant. Remembering Crystal Caves, I wondered how far to the south and east it was from us.

There were pines all around us: short and brush-like, tall as myself, and also needled giants stretching far above us, holding untold tons of snow on their limbs. Our horses' feet crunched through the snow while I breathed the sharp dry air as shallowly as I could. It would be hours before I felt warm again.

Why doesn't the old man keep his house warmer? I thought uselessly. I wondered if the tiny shack was his home, and felt guilty for not even learning his name. As soon as the cabin was out of sight, David broke the chilly silence surrounding us.

"Where are we going?"

"To Perch, like you've been told before," the Lieutenant nearly whispered his reply.

"But how? We left the road back there," he said, tossing his head toward the cabin. "Is there a trail we're following?"

"No," the Lieutenant replied, "but I know the general direction. Soon we'll be able to see the Three Brothers; they're hard to miss."

"Do you think it will get much warmer?" I asked. Even my voice was shivering.

"Not likely. Don't worry, your saddle will warm up before long. Our horses are working hard, and these saddles were made thin so we can benefit from their warmth. You'll warm it some, too."

I was glad to find him right. We rode slowly as the horses plodded on through the trees. I was almost warm by the time we stopped for an early lunch of cheese and bread. I raced David between the trees until finally I was hot under my thick clothes. I felt much better when we next mounted our horses.

It must have been around noon when I realized we were not on a one-day trip into the woods. Eventually, we came to a clearing where we could see the three mountains. We were already heading up the slope leading to the first mountain, though Perch was too far to reach before nightfall.

"Lieutenant, how far is it to Perch?" I asked.

"Hopefully we'll reach it early tomorrow. We'll have to wait and see—we're not making very good progress so far."

"How will we find shelter tonight?" David asked, as if reading my mind.

"We brought our own. Didn't you notice the donkey?"

Can we really be warm enough in a tent?" I asked, remembering the bitter chill I'd fought all the previous night, despite the woodstove so close to me.

"You'll be warm enough—wait and see."

Perhaps he was trying to teach me patience. I wasn't happy with his answer, but I held my tongue. The trees grew closer together and the snow was very shallow on the ground beneath them. We made much better time for the rest of the day. The ground sloped downward as we passed a foothill of the first of the Three Brothers. In the dense forest of the Brothers' foothills, we stopped to make camp, just as the sun began to sink below the trees.

The Lieutenant pulled the heavy load from the donkey, and began to pull items from it.

"Work quickly," he warned. "Soon it will be too dark to see your hand in front of you. Take these axes and chop down as many of the small pines as you can."

He motioned to the short, bushy pines growing here and there between the tall giants over our heads. We'd learned how to fight with axes, but we'd never used them for wood. I hefted the axe in my hands, remembering the last time I'd held one. I felt much safer in that snowy forest than I'd felt in the Great Dunes, constantly scanning the horizon for trolls.

There weren't many of the short pines near us, and we worked fast to gather as many as we could in the failing light. Once, as I swung the axe hard at the base of a springy tree, the smooth axe handle slipped straight through my snowy gloves. I looked up in horror, hoping my brother wasn't in its path. I knew I should have checked his position before I swung, but in haste, I hadn't.

My heart stopped as I lifted my gaze and saw David's boots a dozen feet away. Time seemed to slow, as I lifted my eyes and saw the axe fly right past his head, narrowly missing him. I heard a loud *crack!* as my axe sunk into the bark of one of the taller pines towering over us.

Did the handle hit his head? I wondered in fear, as David's swiveled back toward me.

"You almost hit me in the—" he started, but never finished.

A white powdery blizzard engulfed him, then spread out toward me and dusted my face and neck. The snow fell from the tall boughs in an inverted mushroom. Everything was white for a second, until the snow settled around us. The axe had missed David completely, but shook the tall pine hard enough to loosen a great pile of snow from its lower limbs.

"*That was incredible*," David remarked, recovering from his surprise.

He walked past me and swung his axe hard at the base of another tall pine. He struck the tree with the flat side of the axe, bringing another upended blizzard down on us. We laughed together, running from tree to tree, each time shaking loose what seemed like a thousand snowstorms onto our heads.

Before long, we remembered the falling night. We ran to gather all the felled brush pines, and brought them to the Lieutenant, who seemed to be waiting for us.

The Lieutenant had unpacked a low tent and set it up among a cluster of brush pines. As we watched, he crafted a quick frame of large limbs over the tent's ridge and propped up all the brush pines over this frame. Following his example, we worked quickly to scoop snow with two large wooden bowls and pile it over the tent. The brush pines, I realized, were to keep the snow in place. By the time we were finished with it, it looked more like an igloo.

David and I worked fast to slip the horses' feed sacks over their mouths. Afterward, we used the left-over brush to start a campfire. The Lieutenant loaded a thin metal pot with snow, again and again, to water the animals. Finally, we sat around the campfire long enough to eat our bread and cheese, and drink as much of the warm water as we liked. I spit out many small needles, which proved impossible to weed out of the snow we collected.

"Careful not to drink too much," warned the Lieutenant. "You won't like getting out of your sleepsack in the middle of the night."

When we finally climbed into our tent, I found myself dreading the cold night ahead of us. Instead, I was surprised at how warm it was.

I must've sat too close to the fire, I thought. But as I took off my heavy coat and slid into my sleepsack, I knew it was something more. My sleepsack felt almost *warm*. Then I noticed the metal box in the back of the tent—just like the ones from the *Explorer*, on my last trip from Portsmouth.

"Wow, I guess all that snow really insulates the tent," David said.

The Lieutenant looked at me and smiled; he could tell I wanted to be the one to explain it to David. I told him about the boxes that followed the Princess whenever she travels. David worried the box might suffocate us while we slept, but the Lieutenant assured him it was safe.

I slept well, but woke the next morning with watery eyes and a painful throat. I learned the hard way my sleepsack was insulated with goose down. I hoped we wouldn't need to sleep in the tent for too many nights, or my allergy might rob me of all my sleep. The Lieutenant hoped we'd make Perch soon, but not as badly as I hoped we would. My nose made the cold air seem worse than the day before.

By the afternoon, I could tell we were approaching the mountain named Perch. The Lieutenant warned us to be alert and to tell him if we saw anything moving in the trees. I wondered if the Sentinels lived in trees, or posted guards in them. Perhaps there were wild animals in the trees, and we would need to defend ourselves. My throat hurt so badly, I was content to only wonder. Soon the Lieutenant interrupted my thoughts.

"The Sentinels are very cautious of those who approach their mountain. We need to let them know who we are as soon as possible."

I scanned the forest around us, letting my thoughts wander. *Will they attack us? What's so special about their mountain?* I wondered if Perch was where we would find *the Path*, as the King had called it, which would take us home. *What will it look like: a door, or perhaps a tunnel?* I found myself wishing the Path was far away. I wanted another journey before we left, despite the bitter cold we traveled through.

Before long the Lieutenant slowed to a stop and whispered a hushed *Halt!* I saw a dark shape pass over us in the trees. I froze as my mind raced. Thoughts of being attacked from behind brought waves of crippling fear. Even my imagined attacks did nothing to prepare me for what we saw next.

3.5 Meeting the Sentinels

A loud *SWOOSH* roared above us, and we were buffeted with a fury of snow and wind. When the snow settled, I saw a beastly monster in front of us. I blinked—once, then twice— my mind still didn't know what to make of it. It eyed us coolly, and while my heart raced, I thought the fierce-looking thing was a *griffon*—not that I'd ever seen one. I turned to my brother, but he only shrugged. I turned to the Lieutenant, but his gaze was fixed on the strange beast.

When my senses returned somewhat, I saw it was a colossal bald eagle. Its fearsome gaze seemed to burn right through me. Its eyes glared *down* at me, though we sat on large horses. It let out a piercing trill, stabbing painfully at my ears. Our horses fidgeted and I tightened the reins to steady mine. I was glad the Lieutenant was between me and the beast.

The Lieutenant spoke clear and loudly—to whom, I had no idea. I wondered if the Sentinels were small as Watchmakers, and rode on the backs of giant eagles.

"We come for wisdom," he said, "for these two weary travelers from another kingdom." The beast cocked its head slightly, as if it tried to understand what he'd said. He said it again, slower and louder.

"I heard you well the first time you spoke," the giant eagle replied. My ears burned and my mind reeled yet again—the Sentinels didn't *ride* eagles—they *were* eagles. Its voice was clear and low, though not raspy. It sounded windy, like a ridiculously loud whisper. Hearing it speak seemed odd, though I'd seen stranger things on the Animal Coast. Trolls were so human-like; their presence seemed to feel normal to me then. Talking animals remained purely surreal. In its strange voice it continued.

"Do you know the punishment for impersonating a traveler from another kingdom?"

"I assume it's death," replied the Lieutenant in a low tone.

"Death it is. And now, you must follow me. Be aware: you are under careful guard and will be attacked if you flee."

With a great gust, the Sentinel turned and leapt into the sky. I was shocked at the way its wings seemed to clutch at the air as it lifted off the ground. It left a snowy whirlwind behind—shaking the lower branches on the trees around us. It turned and swooped over our heads, low enough to shake us again, then flew off in front of us. We followed, but were far too slow to keep up. It disappeared into the trees above us, and flew over our heads many times before it perched on a large fallen tree before us. It let out a painful screech as it landed. We approached it slowly, our horses resisting their reigns.

"You will wait here," the Sentinel said. "I am a Low Father, posted in watch. I have called down a High Father, and Mentor to my people. He will come to speak with you, and you will answer him."

He looked away from us, ending all possibility of our questioning him. Not long after, an even larger eagle landed on the same fallen tree, nearly blowing me off my horse. I held my breath until I realized he wasn't going to bowl right over the three of us. I blinked snowflakes from my eyes, tossed up from the ground in the violent gusts from the bird's great wings.

The dead log they rested on was larger around than my horse's girth, but their feet had no trouble wrapping nearly around it. The second eagle, the *High Father*, looked very similar to the first, but it seemed to move slower and more carefully. His feathers were the same mottled dark brown, save for its head, which was white as the snow surrounding us. It wore a golden chain around its neck.

"You must answer my questions," the larger bird said. David and I looked at each other. The larger Sentinel's eyes darted back and forth from David to me.

"Are you two the travelers?" it asked.

"Yes," David answered. I held my breath, hoping they would believe us.

"And you?" It stared directly at me. I felt weak under its gaze.

"Yes, sir."

Only then did it turn to the Lieutenant.

"And do you represent the King?"

"Yes," he answered resolutely.

"You may leave now."

"I'm sworn to take the travelers to the Path," the Lieutenant protested, then added in a softer tone, "...if they need transportation to find it."

"You don't know the location of the...*Path* then?" asked the larger Sentinel.

"No," he replied. Then almost as an afterthought he added, "If I knew the way, I would not have troubled you to show us." The Sentinel didn't answer, but instead left an awkward silence hanging in the air.

Is the Path farther up the mountain after all? I wondered. *If it's far from here, would he have asked whether the Lieutenant knew where it*

239

was?

Finally the larger Sentinel spoke again. "You may wait out of earshot. Follow Briquidia and wait beside him. Then your wards will join you once again."

The smaller of the two eagles lifted into the air, dusting us with snow once more. It landed perhaps a hundred feet away. Reluctantly, the Lieutenant followed. On his way past us, he spoke in a low tone.

"The King approved your answering any question the Sentinels ask. Nothing you know needs to be secret from them." His voice sounded unsettled, which did my nerves no favors.

"I am Saupender," the larger Sentinel began. "I am a High Father and Mentor of the Sentinels. What are your names?"

"I am David, and this is my brother, Mark," David answered. I was content to remain silent.

"And what have you done in our world...Mark?" So much for silence.

"We've done...many things. We've been here for almost a year. We found the Princess held prisoner, and freed her. We joined the King's army and fought in a short war. We led delegations of peace to the two troll communities."

"And what offices do you still hold in this kingdom?"

I was about to answer *delegates*, but we weren't delegates anymore. The King said we were on our last assignment, one that would take the rest of our lives.

"We are Honor Knights, um...noble...*bird?*"

David screwed his nose up and glared sidelong at me. *Noble bird*, he mouthed silently. My ears burned with embarrassment. Had I not tried to embellish my reply, it might've sounded impressive.

"And what do you bring back to your own world...David?" Inwardly, I sighed with relief. After my last reply, I was glad to have the focus shifted from me.

"The teachings of the Honor Knights," David answered.

"Very well; you are the travelers. Tell me, Mark: what world do you come from?"

I tried to think of an answer that would make sense to him, and also a way I could say it without fumbling my words.

"Um…Earth?"

He nodded slowly.

"What year was it when you left?" he asked. I answered him, only to receive another thoughtful nod.

Is he still testing us? I wondered. *Would he know if I lied?*

"It will take us days to reach *the Path*, as your friend called it. I can only show you the way; I cannot allow you to create or follow any map to reach it. Did you travel by ship, David?"

"Yes," he answered, "and then nearly two days riding through the snow."

"That will make it more…difficult," Saupender replied. "You must go to your ship before I guide you to the *Path*."

I looked around; it was already dusk. I saw David noticed it too.

"We can't get there tonight," he interjected, "we need to make a warm place to sleep, or we'll freeze."

"We can help," Saupender replied after the briefest pause.

He trilled deafeningly, and the other Sentinel, Briquidia, returned to us. The Lieutenant followed behind him. The two Sentinels carried out a rapid, songlike conversation.

"Tie your beasts under those low trees," the shorter Sentinel commanded, extending his long wing to a group of trees with dense limbs, low to the ground. "Protect them with what coverings you have. You will be warm where we will take you."

Take us, I worried, *what does he mean?* David and I looked at one another, then to the Lieutenant. He shrugged, dismounted, and began to unpack the donkey's load. David and I led the horses under the low boughs and took their bits from their mouths. David tied their reins to the trees while I walked back to get the donkey.

I looked over to the Sentinels, a dreamlike fog brewing in my head. *Is this really happening?* I felt a dizzy reminder of how I'd felt so long ago, back on the Animal Coast. I nearly tripped, carrying out the Lieutenant's orders without giving thought to what I was doing. Then we were ready: each carrying a knapsack and our swords, the Lieutenant also carrying a sack from the Donkey's load. It was getting dark, and I hoped we wouldn't have to hike far. I wondered if we would freeze, despite the Sentinel's assurances. How well could a giant eagle understand human physiology?

It became immediately apparent they intended to *carry* us to our destination. I studied their large talons fearfully. Could they carry us without crushing us—or shredding us with their fearsome claws? The Lieutenant suggested fashioning rope slings for us, and I was grateful for it. He tied a loop around each of our waists, then secured them at each end to the great eagle's ankles—if they are called that. Before long David and I crouched side-by-side, under Saupender's belly, while the Lieutenant crouched before Briquidia, the smaller Sentinel, holding his packs in his arms.

The Sentinels lurched into the air, nearly flipping us upside-down. David and I wriggled to right ourselves as Saupender flapped furiously around the clearing until we lifted above the tallest trees. I couldn't see Briquidia and the Lieutenant, but guessed they were directly behind us. With his feet tucked in, we were pulled in close to Saupender's belly. I felt a sneeze coming on, as we were pillowed by colossal feathers. I expected them to be far smoother and softer than they were. David and I tried to speak, but neither of us could hear the other. The icy wind bit through my clothes, stinging my face and knees the worst.

We soared high over the woods surrounding Perch. I was able to make out two small towns—I had no idea which ones. As suddenly as we'd risen, we dropped down to the mountain's base. I saw no clearing in front of us, only tall trees before the base of a cliff. When I was certain we were going to crash, Saupender dropped below the last of the treetops just before the cliff face. As he dove, we were tossed around violently and I was again grateful for our safety lines. I had no way to see clearly, but felt certain we dropped down a dark shaft in the cliff face. We landed in a dark cave with the failing light of the sun behind us, and a dim unknown light far ahead of us.

To say we *landed* is somewhat generous. We were dropped on our hands and knees and nearly crushed by the Sentinel's belly. Then he rose far off the ground, and we scampered out as far as our safety lines would allow. We quickly untied ourselves and ran to one side of the great bird. The Lieutenant was doing the same behind us, mere silhouettes in the dim light seeping into the long tunnel. I looked around, taking in our new surroundings.

I found no simple mouth to the cave, only a gaping shaft behind and above us. The cave didn't look natural, and I saw no stalagmites or stalactites. *How could they dig through stone?* I wondered. It was perhaps thirty feet wide and at least three times as long before it curved out of sight. There was little snow or wind inside, but it was not exactly *warm*. Saupender told us to follow him closely and began an awkward gait along the tunnel under the mountain. As we walked farther along the tunnel, a dim yellow light grew brighter, and the air grew warmer. When we rounded the corner, we were struck by a troubling sight.

A colossal cavern lay before us: big enough for many Sentinels to take flight, with room to spare. It was lit by a large fire in the center, which sent smoke into the cavern's unseeable ceiling. The cavern's sides were blocky cliffs, with giant steps cut into the stone. It must have held a hundred or more Sentinels, complete with nests and perches all around. Not all were as tall as Saupender, but I saw a few who seemed even larger.

I heard a brook and my eyes searched it out. It sprang from the cliff wall furthest from us, off to the right, and ran across the floor of the cavern before disappearing in a large block-shaped stone at the cave wall to our left. The stream seemed to be clouded in fog, and it divided several times on its way before it converged at its drain.

I heard squawks, trills and whistles echoing throughout the cavern. Two more Sentinels landed hastily before us, and began an angry-sounding conversation with Saupender. Apparently, Briquidia had found Saupender out flying, and no one in the cave expected us.

After a short conversation in their strange language, Saupender led us to a level area near the cliff wall where the stream appeared. We set down our things on a stony platform, about ten feet square. I saw steam rising from the stream, and I knew why the cavern was so warm.

By then I was sneezing fairly violently, buying the unwelcome attention of many nearby Sentinels. The Lieutenant cut two small bits of cloth from the sleeve of his undershirt. He wet them from his canteen, and told me to pack them as tightly as I could into my ears. I did so, doubting it would change anything. Soon after, I stopped sneezing and my nose began to clear.

Saupender gave the Lieutenant instructions I couldn't hear. As David stood listening, I turned to the back of the stony level I guessed we were to sleep on, and found a pile of downy, oversized feathers. Allergies or not, it seemed I would either sleep on feathers or on hard stone. Warming quickly, I pulled off my outermost layer of clothing and used it partially to cover me, and partially as a pillow as I lay on the mat of feathers.

Later, David told me Saupender claimed it had been centuries since a human had been allowed in their underground lair. If he'd told me right away, I'm certain I'd have been too tired to care.

Soon, Saupender left, and the Lieutenant motioned me toward him. He spoke directly into my ear to give me instructions. He pointed to the far end of the cave, where the brooks converged and disappeared. He told me I must hike down to the stream's drain when I needed to relieve myself. He handed me some bread and hard cheese. The bread was getting stale, but its crust was more chewy than crunchy, and in my hunger, I was glad for it. We walked cautiously to where the stream sprang from the rock, and filled our canteens, scalding our fingers somewhat as we did so. David and the Lieutenant sat and talked.

Unable to hear them, I quickly became sleepy. My throat was sore and my head ached; it was not a welcome place for someone with a feather allergy. Sleep couldn't come fast enough for me. Part of me knew seeing and exploring such a strange place was the chance of a lifetime, while the rest of me couldn't care less. As I let my consciousness ebb, I wondered the questions I would have liked to ask the Sentinels. *Who carved the long tunnel? Who made the stone platforms in the giant cavern? Who made the fire, and who keeps it burning? Is there a natural gas spring at its center?*

It was just as dark when the Lieutenant woke me. My throat was raspy and sore. Briquidia stood before us, waiting for us to follow her. We put on our heavy coats and wool leggings, already anticipating the cold. I left the cloth in my ears and was content to follow them without speaking. As we rounded the corner of the tunnel, I turned and took one last look at the great cavern. I paused, trying to burn a picture of it into my mind. My head pounded with each step, and I knew I wasn't ready for the cold waiting for us. I wished for more time and energy to learn of the Sentinels. I hoped David had felt curious enough to explore while I slept.

At the shaft we'd entered the previous night, I saw it was indeed morning outside. Saupender was waiting there and the rope we'd used was still lying on the tunnel floor. The Lieutenant tied us into our sling again while Saupender stretched high over us. The Sentinels barely spoke, and what little they said was missed by me. As much as I wanted to learn about them, I wanted to feel healthy again even more. The wads of cloth stayed planted firmly in my ears.

Before I was ready, Saupender jerked us painfully into the air. There was little room in the cavern before we needed to rise straight out through the shaft. I closed my eyes and held my breath, wishing the throbbing pain in my head would leave. Each time the great bird flapped his wings, we were tossed up and down, bouncing painfully. I was grateful for the intermissions when Saupender stretched his wings, and we glided, teetering over unseen streams of air. The passing minutes felt like hours before we reached the small clearing where we'd left the horses.

They looked no worse for their second night in the cold. I'm sure they appreciated our sleepsacks and blankets. David started making a small fire. It took me a moment, but I guessed his purpose. I found the pot near the donkey where we'd left it, and began to fill it with snow.

The Lieutenant was talking with Saupender. Briquidia took

flight and left us: a foreshadow of what I couldn't yet know. I took one more look at him, a *Low Father* to the Sentinels. I already wished I'd stayed awake longer and learned more about them, no matter how sick I felt. Just then a wave of nausea swelled over me. I needed to eat something soon.

Finally, the donkey and horses were watered and fed. Only after we were packed and ready to leave, did Saupender take flight. As he did, I noticed a long black branch sticking out of the snow. It looked as if it had gotten tangled on Saupender's claw, and I wondered it if had cut him. I rode near to check how sharp it was—but it wasn't a branch after all. It was a giant wingtip feather, torn free from Saupender, perhaps, by the violent flapping needed to carry us.

I jumped off my mount, forgetting for a few seconds how much my head hurt, and pulled the feather out of the snow. With the quill resting on my boot, the feather's tip reached far over my head. I knew I had to bring it back with me—at least as far as the ship. How could I let it go to waste? David and the Lieutenant were waiting. They rode over to me, watching me inspect this rare treasure. For something causing me such pain, I was pretty enthusiastic about it.

David tried to call me back to reality, shouting to be heard. "Leave it, Mark! Do you really think we can take it home with us?"

"Probably not," I answered, "but I'd like to send it back with the Lieutenant as a gift."

"Mark," the Lieutenant said, barely loud enough for me to hear, "we can't advertise we've been to Perch. Folks are superstitious about the Sentinels, those who believe in them."

"Can I wrap it with pine branches and drag it behind me?" I pleaded.

"I'm afraid not. It's too recognizable. Who could mistake it for anything other than a giant feather?"

My mind raced for a way to hide it. I pulled out my knife and hacked at the thick barbs radiating from the hollow center shaft.

"Can I cut the feather down to only the center...uh, rod?" I asked, desperate to bring something of it back. The Lieutenant sighed.

"It's called a calamus. And *yes*, I suppose so. Why don't you sheath your sword in it so it looks like it has a purpose. And *hurry*; we need to cover a lot of ground today."

I cleaned most of the barbs from the calamus, and cut off quite a bit of its tip. I was left with a strong, lightweight hollow tube about four feet long. I left the rest of the great feather in the snow and mounted my horse again. Why did I fight so hard to keep something that had brought such pain to me?

I tried to keep my mind from my headache as the horses tromped through the crusted snow. It made it difficult to walk...a few inches of fresh powder over a hard crust with crystallized, crumbly snow beneath it. It had caused me an extra dose of pain when I'd trampled carelessly after the feather. The crust had not only forced my pant legs up over my ankles, but scratched and chilled my legs at the same time.

The tracks we'd made on our way to Perch were plain and easy to follow. We ate our breakfast and lunch while we rode. Fully stale bread and frozen cheese—not my favorite. We stopped at the area where we'd camped two nights ago—only a day's ride from the driver's shack. We had plenty of time to make camp, using the same brush pines and piled snow, and to tend to the animals. It was not quite dark yet, and we had nothing left to do. David asked—loudly—if I wanted to *beat the trees again*, as he put it. I shook my head slowly, trying in vain to keep my head from throbbing worse.

The Lieutenant saw my pain and cooked an extra pot of

snow for us to wash with. I went first, removing the makeshift earplugs from my ears. I tried to wash all trace of the feathers from my hands, face, hair and neck. When I was done, I ran into the tent and slid into my sleepsack as fast as I could. We left our heaviest clothes outside at the Lieutenant's suggestion, to keep out as much dust from the feathers as possible. I wrapped the upper half of my body in a blanket, inside my sleepsack, and I hoped it would be enough to protect me from its down filling. *Why couldn't I be allergic to something else?* I asked myself for the last time that day.

The tent was warm from the metal box, and the thick layer of snow and branches for insulation. The Lieutenant came in quite a while later than David had. Crowded together in our small tent, he rolled onto his side and handed me something.

"Here, chew on this for a while," he said, handing me a small item. I nodded in thanks and took it, though I had no idea what it was. It looked like a clump of dirt—no, not quite, it was more like bark scraped from a tree. "It will help your head feel better."

"How did you know?" I asked. I'd made a point of not complaining about my headache.

"Your face showed your pain so clearly, I felt it myself," he said, smiling.

"What is it?" I asked, dropping it into my mouth.

"Well, it's not candy, if you're wondering about its taste. It's willow bark—I was lucky to find some. It helps take away headaches. Just make sure to spit it out before you doze off."

I thought he was joking, but I fell asleep and woke twice before I remembered to spit it out. I didn't know if the willow bark helped much or not, but I slept better than the previous night. In the morning, I woke in a state of confusion. I'd expected to be in my bed in the delegation building. It took me a while to orient myself. Our tent in the middle of the frozen North Forest seemed alien to me. I felt more like I'd just arrived there, straight from Portsmouth.

What is this strange feeling? I wondered, trying to make sense of it. Then the tiniest shard of memory flashed through my mind, and it felt so close, so familiar, lying in our tent felt even more foreign than when I'd woken. I'd been deep asleep, in a powerful dream. I tried hard to remember it—any details at all.

Why are my dreams always like this? I asked myself. A fleeting thought was all I had left of a dream which felt so familiar, I could've sworn it was real and our trek into the forest was imagined. As we packed our camp and prepared to leave, I tried to remember the dream again. I felt like a few more pieces fell into place, but I couldn't be sure; I still couldn't remember anything like a scene or plot. Perhaps it was one of those dreams made of thoughts and feelings rather than pictures and scenes. Not until we stopped for lunch, did the scant pieces finally fall into place. Immediately I knew why it felt so familiar; *it was a dream I'd had before.*

There were high walls of water on both sides of our ship. They didn't fall, though they tossed our ship like a cork. Looking up through a dark fog, I saw the outline of an eagle. It seemed to hang perfectly still in the air, never flapping or turning. Just before I woke, the eagle dropped something on top of me.

Did it mean anything? My emotions in the dream seemed fearful, not the comforting feelings you'd expect from something so recognizable. My thoughts sped along ahead of me. *Why does it seem so familiar?* I wondered. The answer came to me immediately; I hadn't repeated a dream I'd had once, nearly a year ago—I'd dreamt it many times before.

After remembering more of my dream's details, it felt commonplace and I easily shrugged it off. After all, how unusual is it to dream about a bird or a ship? I rode beside David for a while and tried to ask him questions about the Sentinels' great cavern.

Just as I'd hoped, David had explored the Sentinels' cave, and asked plenty of questions—especially about our quest. We wouldn't see Saupender again until we were back on our ship, and out of Safe Harbor.

As we packed our loads, David surprised me with news I hadn't even hoped for. Briquidia had told him some of the Sentinels' history. Once we mounted our horses, he tried to explain the mystery of the fire in the cave, and the carved rock, but our voices were quickly strained from talking loud enough to be heard over the crunching of hooves through icy, crusted snow. I fell back into line, behind David and the Lieutenant, content to know I could ask David more about the Sentinels later. I stuffed the cotton rags back in my ears, hoping my headache might go away.

Part IV

4.0 Onward from Safe Harbor

The rest of our ride passed without event. We made good time, riding mostly downhill. We reached the old man's shack in the afternoon, plenty of time ahead of sunset.

The tiny cabin was empty, though the fire was still burning and a warm pot of stew bubbled temptingly atop it. The Lieutenant confirmed my guess; the old man had been watching for us, and left when he first saw us approaching. I was glad we'd be able to talk without him. The pigeons seemed fine, and I swapped the cold stone in their cage with the one on the woodstove, nearly scorching my gloves.

We ate the stew in gulps. The Lieutenant told us we wouldn't see the driver again until our ship had arrived at Safe Harbor, and warned us not to speak to him when he arrived. I felt like we'd become *untouchables*, like some sort of condemned prisoners no one but the Lieutenant would ever speak to.

After we ate, I unpacked my codebooks and encoded a message to send back to Engdynlor. The Lieutenant had reminded me to tell Engdynlor to send our ship back to Safe Harbor. While I busied myself with the message, David and the Lieutenant visited the only shop in Rester. They bought new clothes and wraps for all three of us, at quite an expense. They also bought three new sleepsacks, ones that were filled with wool instead of down.

When they returned, the Lieutenant told us to remove our clothes and throw them out of the shack, along with our sleepsacks, still rolled and sitting in the corner. At his suggestion, we sponge-bathed with the hot water we'd melted from snow on the woodstove, and even soaped and rinsed our hair. We hurried into our new clothes and directly afterward, into our new sleepsacks, and under the covers already on the cots. The Lieutenant stoked the fire in the woodstove and turned the damper wide open. Though the water was nearly scalding and the fire hotter than ever, the air and floor were still cold enough to leech away any heat I might have expected from them. We made a soapy puddle around the stove, for the Lieutenant to stand in as he washed after us. The shack had a dry floor of packed earth when we arrived, but after our washing nearly a quarter of it had turned to mud.

"Is it worth all this trouble just because I'm allergic to feathers?" I asked the Lieutenant.

"Of course it is," he replied, sounding genuinely surprised. "You may need your strength on the Path ahead of you. We know close to nothing of it. As it is, I'd rather not send you on your way sick." He noticed my smile, and added, "It's not the only reason for the measures we took. Your brother and I left our wraps outside the shop today while we were inside—"

"We stripped right down to our pants and undershirts," David interjected.

"—and I'll burn our old clothes and sleepsacks before our driver returns. No one needs to know our journey got us covered with feathers from head to toe—not with the strong superstitions held in Rester. The men aboard the fishing ship, they will learn as little of our visit with the Sentinels as possible—though I'm not sure how I might keep them from seeing Saupender."

I felt better to hear he had more to consider than my allergy. Still, I wondered which would have caused more surprise for those in the shop: two men covered with feathers, or two men walking in from the cold in nothing but pants and undershirts.

"Be sure your new sheath is well hidden," he added as an afterthought. After being reminded how important it was no one suspected we saw the Sentinels, I knew he shouldn't have let me bring the giant quill.

Still chilled from our sponge baths, David and I stayed in our cots the rest of the evening. As soon as I woke the next morning, I sent the second pigeon with an identical note asking for our ship to be sent.

That day we had little to do but rest and talk. I was already feeling better, but nonetheless, the Lieutenant gave us foul-tasting teas to drink. He told us they would help our bodies fight off colds and allergic reactions.

Between turns to the woodpile outside, I pumped David for every detail of his time in the Sentinels' cavern. I chided myself again for missing such an opportunity.

As David had been told by Briquidia, the Sentinels had labor agreements with other intelligent animals. They paid raccoons in fresh meat for their service in anything requiring a delicate touch. Beavers helped them by cutting wood for their fire, and in turn, the Sentinels kept their predators' population in check. Daring Sentinels swooped down from the sky and dropped their cut logs just uphill of the fire. As it turned out, the cavern had no true roof, and if it hadn't been overcast, we might've seen a small circle filled with stars overhead.

It's a good thing it didn't rain, I thought, wondering if we could have survived the night if it had.

Unbelievably, the tunnel into their cave was carved by raccoons, through soft rock, with iron tools supplied to them by humans. *How many had it taken*, and *how long did they work*, David had asked Briquidia.

"Many animals worked for many years," he told David in reply. It wasn't a very satisfying answer.

Why do they even need a tunnel entrance, I thought, *if the cave has no roof?* There must've been a giant sinkhole farther up the mountain.

"Did you find anything else about the *Path*?" I asked David.

"*We begin by sailing south, out of the harbor,*" David recalled. "*And the trip will take five days or more.* That's all we know."

"Five days?" I asked, incredulously. "We could sail all the way to *Port* by then."

Another cold night in the shack gave me something to look forward to. It had been warmer in the ship than the drafty shack, extra blankets or not.

All our things were packed and ready. The next morning, before there was light enough to see, the driver woke us with a loud rapping on the shack's door. In only minutes, he was driving us to the dock at Safe Harbor. He took us right up to the dock, and I wondered why he'd stayed hidden in the darkness when we first arrived from Oyster Bay.

The fishing captain didn't seem pleased with the Lieutenant at all.

"I can tell you our heading only after we leave the harbor," was all he said.

The Lieutenant went straight for the crow's nest, and remained there until he could see Saupender, flying high above us. He flew so high, no one on the ship could have guessed he was larger than any eagle they'd seen. The Lieutenant gave the men on the boat their heading, but warned it would change frequently for reasons he couldn't explain. We sailed all day long, straight for Oyster Bay.

When it was dusk, the Lieutenant instructed the boat's crew to go into the cargo hold while David and I sat on the single hatch. Then he waved his arms wildly and let out a shrill whistle I wouldn't have thought possible for a human.

We watched as Saupender dove from on high, and landed expertly on the deck of the ship. While his wings were spread, they were wider than our small ship. No doubt the crew had fanciful guesses about the strange sounds they heard above them.

The Lieutenant told the Sentinel he needed to go ashore for supplies. Saupender agreed, but stipulated only the Lieutenant could leave the ship.

The Lieutenant asked Saupender if there was anything he could bring along for him. I heard his reply as a whisper, through the biting wind.

"I could use a few goats—a mule would be better. I may not find beasts-for-eating along the way."

I was shocked—could Saupender really eat several goats before we reached the Path? I realized I'd had no idea what the Sentinels might eat. I hoped *beasts-for-eating* meant they couldn't talk. A shiver ran down my spine as I wondered if they ever further extended their diet.

We arrived at Oyster Bay long after sunset. The crew grumbled as the Lieutenant left us. Soon, crates and water barrels were delivered to our slip on the docks. Three small goats and a young pony mule were also delivered and tied to the berth. I might have imagined it, but they seemed troubled. The men who left them didn't say a word. Finally, the Lieutenant returned, carrying a sack and a cage filled with pigeons.

Will Saupender eat the pigeons after I release them? I wondered.

At the Lieutenant's insisting, the crew shoved off and

anchored near the edge of the bay, far from the docks. Of course he couldn't tell them our destination; they knew no less than he. Every instruction he gave the crew was met with more resistance. I worried the crew might turn mutinous.

We continued south, and I began to wonder if we would sail past Portsmouth to Athangust, at the southern tip of the kingdom, and beyond. The Lieutenant would certainly face mutiny if he tried to take them far from land.

Each day Saupender led us from a high altitude, and never far from shore. Each evening the entire crew went below while another animal went topside, never to be seen again. Saupender swooped down and plucked each of them, then flew off to find a place to eat and sleep in some secluded spot along the coast. The young mule went first, and made far more noise in its departure than the goats. A vicious rumor was born of this; the sailors created stories of strange sacrifices the Lieutenant made to the sea each night. I was shocked to overhear this, but could say nothing to correct them. The Lieutenant thought it better than if they guessed the truth. On the third night from Oyster Bay, the Lieutenant sent me and my brother below with the crew, and we spent an uncomfortable half-hour pretending not to notice their glares.

The Lieutenant called us back on deck in time to see Saupender do something unexpected. He circled the ship several times, then flew straight out to sea. My eyes followed him to the longest island of the Broken Coast. He disappeared somewhere in the mist the island seemed to wear as an eternal cloak. Soon after, the Lieutenant called the crew up from the hold, and asked the two of us to follow him below. The last goat was in the hold with us, and while it bleated, I wondered what it suspected of its fate.

"This is it," the Lieutenant told us. "We'll anchor near the island's beach, and I will row you ashore in the morning.

Then the two of you will follow Saupender the rest of the way to the Path…"

"You mean…*alone*?" David interrupted. "We'll never see you again?"

"Well, not *alone*," he replied. "You'll have your brother to keep you company." He smiled weakly. If he was trying to lighten our mood, it wasn't effective. He sighed and laid his hand on David's shoulder.

"We knew it would be so; I never expected our journey to take as long as this. You've been a good apprentice and student. I'm proud to have taught you."

An awkward silence hung over us. I deliberately broke it.

"You mean the Path is on the island?" I asked suspiciously.

"He wouldn't say. Perhaps he'll carry you to the Path from there. In a way, I almost expected this island might have something to do with it. There are many legends about it, and superstition surrounds it—just like the forest around Perch."

Immediately I thought of the paintings of the Broken Coast in the gallery at Beach Row—especially the one the Princess stood beside the last night I saw her. Did she somehow know?

"Did he say *anything else*?" I asked.

"Oh yes, I'm afraid he did."

"Bad news?" David asked.

"Well…I'll let you be the judge. Saupender said you can only bring ashore those things you can carry easily, and enough supplies to make camp for a few days. Any remaining supplies will remain in our world. Only what you wear can go through the Path to your home. In fact, he warned against wearing anything which might hinder you…no swords or armor. He'll be able to protect you, though I doubt very much you'll see anyone on the island."

"Why can't I take my knapsack?" I asked defensively.

"I don't have any answers for you. I only know what Saupender said; no sacks or bags will go with you." He paused for a moment. "Look—I don't know why he has this rule, but I think you'd be wise to heed him. Out of all of us, he's the only one who really knows anything about the Path. He claims it will be a *rough ride*."

"So…we'll have to leave *everything*," I mumbled.

"*Almost* everything," David added.

"After you've been gone for five years," the Lieutenant told us, "you'll be legally classified as dead. Your properties will be distributed by a will, if you leave one. Why not draw up a will now, and use it to give away whatever you can't take?"

If I hadn't known the Lieutenant through David, I might've suspected him of trying to profit from our situation. At first his words sounded horrible to me, but not long after I was smiling at their implications. It seemed fitting, after nearly a year of studying the Three Tables, to be practicing so literally the act of *giving it away*.

I thought of my gilded mirror set and remembered how badly I'd wanted David's when he first received his. If there was anything I wanted to bring of the items that couldn't survive a *rough ride*, it was that set of ancient mirrors. I didn't know whether to call it poetic justice or irony. *Maybe I finally learned my lesson*, I thought, realizing I felt no pain in knowing I couldn't bring them.

David and I used the rest of the night to go through our things and find exactly how much we could fit in our pockets. For certain, the tiny glass sculpture in its leather and wooden box was going in my overcoat's largest pocket, even if it was the only thing I brought. David's decorated field scope fit nicely in the pocket of his inner jacket. We each had our leather rolls with the Three Tables burnt onto them; they took almost no room at all. Our apprentice knives were an easy choice for both of us; we already wore the belts which held them. The stalactites from Crystal Caves were so small we slipped them into a pocket without thinking. I also chose the giant catfish tooth, the maps I'd copied or drawn myself, my antique medal from the King, my patch of snowsnake pelt from Oyster Bay, and the watch my grandmother would soon give to me when I turned sixteen. David also took his dagger, and a handful of rocks and crystals he'd collected during his travels.

"Now who do we give the rest of our stuff to?" I asked him, looking at the pile of things we would leave behind.

David had a wooden trunk the size of a hatbox he hadn't shown me before. He opened it and showed me a beautiful glass sculpture. It looked like the blue glacier ice soon to be sold across the kingdom, according to David's own plan. But there were swirls of darker blue within it, though I couldn't tell what they portrayed. He smiled when I asked him what the sculpture showed.

"That's a secret for those who see it plainly," he replied.

It wasn't the sort of answer I appreciated. I tried, but wasn't able to coax a better one from him.

"I'm going to give this to the Princess," he told me. "I hope she meets Amelia and they become friends one day."

I first planned to give the Sentinel's giant quill to the Captain, but decided against it. He wouldn't display it; he wasn't the type. Knowing it would mean so much more to Bob the Birdman, I decided to leave it to him. Since he was an Honor Knight, the Lieutenant might actually allow me to pass it to him. David left his Eastward and Westward mirror pair for Amelia, and I left my set for the Princess.

I had to leave *something* for the Captain. I hesitated for the briefest moment before I removed the ancient medal from my shirt pocket and added to the things I'd leave behind. It was a gesture I thought he'd appreciate.

I wanted to leave something for Sally too, but what did I have left? My main sword and armor would go back to the armory. Would she think anything of the decorated sword I received as a reward? Not likely. The Princess would hate seeing it in Lady Sally's room if she ever visited her there. No, my decorated sword would go to the Chaplain. As peaceful as he was, I knew my gift would not offend him. He'd treat it as it was intended: a reminder of the time we'd spent together.

Still nothing for Lady Sally, I thought. Just then I remembered the tiny medals we'd both received from the Watchmakers back in their village. I felt lucky to remember those tiny medals. If I hadn't remembered, I would've unwittingly left them in the knapsack they were tied into. I cut the hair that held them to the ring in the sack, and plucked two more hairs from my head. I made a tiny paper envelope from extra paper in my codebook and placed my tiny medal inside it. I wrote *Sally* on the envelope, knowing the Captain would deliver it for me. David tied his medal to the small piece of leather he'd already packed, using a small hole meant to hang over a nail.

David left some of the larger crystals he'd collected to his mentor, and his decorated sword to another lieutenant, who had served in the delegation high up on Golden Mountain. His Medal of Bravery he also left to his mentor.

And so we had all our possessions either in our pockets or in the neat stack in front of us as we sat in the cargo hold, lit only by a wax lantern. These knickknacks and mementos didn't look like much for all the stories they had to tell. We labeled them with their recipients' names, using string and little slips of paper I tore from the outside margins of my codebook, still in my knapsack.

After packing the items into a spare trunk in the hold, we

went to the bunkroom. I fell asleep immediately. Again I dreamt of the Sentinel flying high above me, lying flat on my back. It was very close, but rising away from me quickly. My dream turned into a nightmare, as I plummeted toward distant ground. I woke just before I struck, clammy and breathing heavily. I hoped the trip would end soon.

4.1 Long Goodbye

Early the next morning we climbed in a small dinghy and headed for shore. We didn't exchange goodbyes with the ship's crew, and I'm sure they didn't miss us. My stomach was knotted as it often is when getting up hours earlier than normal—an unpleasant dose of worry and sleepiness, this time mixed with a dash of fear. I didn't want to remember such details, but I do; I remember them all too well.

We sat in silence as the Lieutenant rowed. I shivered, sitting on the cold plank seat while a biting wind blew off the water. Shivering didn't help my mood at all. Finally, David broke the silence.

"I can't believe we'll never see each other again."

"Many adventures lie ahead of you, surely more important than learning from me," the Lieutenant replied with a strained smile.

"I don't think I'll ever agree with that," David said.

"You will eventually; it's part of your last orders. Teaching what you've learned is more important than learning itself. After all, what good is knowledge and wisdom if it doesn't affect others? If we don't embrace teaching others, we become libraries closed to the public, of no use to anyone."

"I know you're right," David said slowly, hanging his head and speaking softly.

It was painful for me to watch, and it made me glad I'd already said my goodbyes to the Captain. I wanted badly to give them the privacy they deserved.

The only sound to be heard was the wind and waves, and the burble of the caged pigeons I brought. When we reached the shore, the Lieutenant jumped into ankle deep water and pulled the bow of the boat onto the beach. He helped unload our sacks. They were lighter for all the things we left on the ship, but included some items the Lieutenant had carried on our trek to Perch. He stood still as if wanting to say something. I carried my bags farther up the shore, more from a desire to remove myself from the awkward situation than from kindness.

What did the Lieutenant want to say in private? Maybe he gave David an evaluation like Bob gave me. If he did, I was certain David would not like me to overhear.

I looked to the south, wondering anxiously what the journey ahead held in store. Dark brown jagged boulders jutted up from the sand ahead of me, about halfway to the western side of the narrow island. Back to the south, the beach seemed to stretch on for untold miles before it finally disappeared into the cliff faces onto which we could not have rowed.

Do we have to hike that far? I wondered. It looked just how I remembered the painting at Beach Row: steep cliffs rose out of the water all around the southern half of the island, and formed the base of a small mountain, its top hidden in troubled clouds. Just above the waves, dark rocks were swallowed up in greenery. It was so far away I couldn't tell whether the green was from evergreens, or low grass.

Surely, I thought, *any grass should have died off this late into winter.*

Just before the mountainside disappeared into clouds, it changed hue from a dark green to a lighter, yellowish color. I wondered if the color shift was a trick of perspective.

When I turned back to the boat, I was alarmed to see the Lieutenant launching the dinghy back toward the ship. I ran over to where David stood waving, and I shouted, *"goodbye,"* across the beach and waves.

David yelled after him too, "We'll come back—*I promise.*"

The Lieutenant smiled and shouted back to us, "I know— *you already have."* I wondered what he meant for a second until I realized he spoke of our second trip they expected us to make to their past. I shuddered at the paradox, and my foggy memory of tiny Watchmakers.

As we turned from the beach, David carried a heavy canvas sack with something heavy and blockish inside. I saw his eyes were red.

"He gave us the heatbox." He spoke so quietly, I barely heard him.

"Oh." What else could I say? "I suppose Saupender will be here soon."

"The Lieutenant said to walk south along the beach until we see him. We need to reach the mountain before dark, or we might freeze."

We began hiking toward the mountain at a worried pace. My imagination struggled to conceive feeling any colder than I already felt. I carried both our sacks and the caged pigeons while David carried the heatbox. Before long, I knew it was too much weight to carry for any distance. We emptied the sand from the heatbox and wrapped the glass jars with the few pieces of spare clothing we had. It was so light, David carried it along with his sack, while I took my own and the pigeon cage.

It was hours before we saw Saupender. He flew low over our heads, then rose and glided down near the base of the mountain. He remained there for a few minutes before taking flight, rising as he continued south until he vanished into churning clouds. His message was clear: walk to the place where he had landed.

The snow wasn't as deep as I'd expected it. It was hard packed over dead beach grass with a thin layer of powder on top. In some places the powder was gone, and in others it piled up in drifts, high enough to hide all traces of the tall dead grass. The ground swelled beneath our feet as we rose above the beach, and we eagerly anticipated the trees and tall boulders we saw ahead of us at the mountain's base, and the protection from the wind we hoped they would provide us.

It was dusk when we reached the first trees. I was disappointed to realize we were less than halfway to the southern tip of the long barrier island. When I tried to guess how far we might have left to go, I saw how distorted our view had been when we'd first landed. I knew the other end of the island could be much farther, even farther than it looked from where we stood.

"This could take us a *week*," I muttered.

"I hope it doesn't," David replied. "Even more, I hope Saupender tells us where we're headed soon. I want to know if we're going to hike all the way to the other end of the island or not. Maybe we even have to leave the island to find the Path."

"How can we? We don't have a boat," I wondered out loud.

"Maybe he'll carry us, one at a time."

"Then why not carry us *now*?" I was tired and worn. All I could think of was home.

We assumed we would stay at the trees' edge for the night,

and so we began to set our small camp. We pitched our tent under a low pine growing where the first sharp rock rose from the grassy plain. The rock was fractured, with infinite quarter-sized air pockets all through it. I hoped our trek wouldn't take us over any rock like it.

We started a small fire and set up the heatbox. Refilling it with new sand was more troublesome than I'd imagined. I lifted the thick cloth which covered the pigeon cage to check on the poor birds. They were alive, but far from lively. I gave them a small dish of melted snow and some feed. The wind was picking up, and I was grateful for the protection the low pines offered. Sitting near the fire and talking of home, I began to relax. Suddenly, a great gust of wind blew sparks into our faces, nearly blowing us over. It was Saupender; he'd finally come.

He walked near to us in his strange manner, and told us we'd need our sleep, come morning. Immediately, we asked him where the Path to our world was.

"South. At the southern tip of the island." Finally, an answer—even if it wasn't a welcome one.

"How far is it?" I asked.

"A few days' walk for you." Sensing our disappointment, he continued, "It's not far...but it's a difficult climb. Steep and sharp rocks, and thick forest await you." His words did nothing to improve our mood. We had many questions for him, but he wasn't willing to give us further answers. Before long he interrupted us.

"I must leave now. There is little food on this island and I must hunt again. Follow the mountain, along its foot, away from the mainland. I will meet you tomorrow."

Before either of us could reply, he turned and strutted away before taking flight. I realized this was a favor to us. He caused quite a wind, but nothing like the gust from his landing.

When I woke the next morning, I found tiny rays of light peering in from holes burned into the tent's canvas, from the sparks he'd sent us when he landed.

The night was cold, but we kept warm enough. Pouring out the hot sand from the heatbox felt wasteful. The snow wasn't much deeper between the rocks and low trees—or maybe it *was* deeper, but packed hard enough we couldn't tell. We tried to walk as close to the mountain as possible without hiking up and down the swells along its base. It was hard for the first few hours, half-crawling over the dangerous rocks Saupender had warned us we'd need to cross. It was a tiring and cautious hike. The thick forest beyond them was a welcome relief.

We wound our way through the dense firs and pines, sometimes nearly turning around before correcting our path by the sun, a mere bright spot in the clouds before us. The trees grew taller until we couldn't see the shape of the mountain through them. Finally, we came across a small lookout where I could see westward, down to the water. I saw no beach below us, only water below the trees and craggy rocks. David's eyes must have pointed in the same direction.

"I can't tell if the beach disappears completely," he said, "or if it only looks like it from here."

"It must...we saw the cliffs going right down into the ocean from the ship, below the mountain."

"Then we should start climbing the mountain now," David said, matter-of-factly. "It isn't too steep here, but if we go much farther, it might be. I don't want to back-track."

"But what about Saupender?" I replied, "He said *stay off the mountain*, and he'll find us. He might not look for us on the mountain."

"He never said *stay off the mountain*," he argued.

"Yes he did...he said to follow the mountain toward the

far side of the island."

"He *said*," David replied a little louder, "we should follow the mountain by *hiking along its foot*. The foot of the mountain is still part of the mountain." His logic was sound, but I didn't want to admit it. "Well then," David pushed when I didn't reply, "Do you have a better idea?"

"No, but it doesn't make you right."

"You'll see when he finds us tonight."

David turned away and began hiking uphill. I followed him, my frustration brewing. An hour passed without a word. Soon we reached a level area clear of trees, and a steep cliff edge directly ahead of us. Getting as close as I dared, I peered at the treetops far below us. David set his load down and pulled out our dwindling food supply.

I backed cautiously away from the cliff's edge and sat on a snow bank to rest. I wished many times I could have traded my pigeon cage for something twice as heavy and half as bulky. Still, the steeper terrain was far easier than hiking over the craggy rocks.

After a quick meal of bread and cheese, we continued uphill. We skirted the cliff until we were far enough from it to stop me from worrying about losing my footing and flying over its edge. We crept higher up the mountain until our legs ached. It was different from walking, hiking up such a steep slope. I wondered what caused such a violent change in geography—a cliff so large and long, it was as if half the mountain had been wiped away by a giant eraser. I wondered if volcanoes or shifting plates far underground were the culprit.

Again, we waited until it was dusk before we stopped. We found a tiny level area between trees and pitched our tent at its edge. With no sand around us, we filled the heatbox with dirt, which was surprisingly easy to dig up after we cleared away the snow and a shallow layer of frozen moss. The moss came up in a thick layer, and I imagined the clumps looked like green-frosted chocolate cakes. I remembered back to our first night on Golden Mountain, when we used moss to keep us warm. From that memory, my mind returned to our heatbox. We only had two sets of jars left.

Just as the previous night, Saupender arrived a short time after we started the small fire we'd lit to melt snow and warm us. This time, the shower of sparks was even worse. We turned our backs to the fire to shield our faces. I realized our clearing didn't leave much room for the great eagle to land. As he approached the last few paces on foot, I padded out a glowing ember on David's back, and he did the same to me—in more than one place. I hoped our coats would be warm enough for the rest of our trek.

"The time is getting close. Tomorrow I will carry you the rest of the way."

"You can *carry us*? Why did you make us hike for two days?" I asked before I could stop myself. If Saupender took my question as rude, he didn't show it.

"Arriving early wouldn't have helped you. You would only have to wait two days longer until the correct Path is open for you."

My heart quickened in anticipation. *Finally, some answers.* David spoke before I could put my question into words.

"What do you mean 'the correct Path'? Is there more than one? Do they lead to *other* worlds?" Saupender's answer couldn't have been more frustrating.

"You will have your answers tomorrow."

"How will you take us?" I asked. "Can you carry us both at once?"

"Yes. We will arrive with plenty of time to spare. You must leave everything here when I return for you. Take only what you wear through the Path." I didn't know if he had any idea how many things we'd stuffed into our pockets, and I wasn't about to bring it up.

"What time will you return for us?" David asked.

"There will be several hours of light left when we leave here tomorrow."

I asked another question I hoped would tell us something more of the Path.

"Will you carry us *through* the Path, or only to its…entrance?"

"You will learn this tomorrow," was the only reply he gave us.

"Nice try," David hissed under his breath.

Saupender turned to leave, but then paused and spoke again.

"I'd like for you to help me before you sleep. Then, I have a story I will tell you."

It seemed a strange way to ask for help, but we both answered we would do whatever we could. I thought about his words, wondering why his sentences always seemed half-done to me.

"Add the rest of the wood you gathered to your fire," he answered, "then cover it with rocks."

We did as he asked, though rocks were not easy to find in the failing light. Our hands tingled with cold before we had a fair pile of rocks over the embers of our fire. Saupender sat near the fire, but not near enough for a spark to jump out and touch him. I guessed a spark hitting his feathers might be more dangerous than hitting my bare skin.

David and I sat near the fire, remembering the story he'd promised us. I wasn't sure it would be worth the sleep it would cost me—I was getting very tired.

"I want to share a story of eagles with you. Not

Sentinels—I speak of eagles the size of hawks, not sentient."

"We understand," David offered, prompting him on. Saupender glared at him in such a way, I was glad I'd resisted my urges to interrupt him. After a tense minute passed, he continued.

"Eagles are graceful creatures just as well. They are noble animals. If you study them you will find lessons they can teach, even to your own people." He looked as if he were done.

Is that it? I thought to myself. *Does he expect us to glean some sacred truth from so few words?*

I held my tongue, remembering his painful glare. His patient speech frustrated me. Years later I came to believe the Sentinels spoke much less than humans do, to offer each other time to reflect on what is said. If this is correct, it was wasted on me that night.

He turned his head nearly all the way around, then snapped back to meet our gaze. He looked as if he might speak again, only to leave another healthy pause. While we waited, I guessed why he wanted stones in our fire. As it burned down to coals, the stones would hold the heat. He meant to sleep near us.

"When they begin to reach adulthood," he started without warning, "an important part of their growth is to care for the molting elders."

David and I exchanged glances when Saupender paused yet again. We considered asking him to continue, but said nothing. Whether or not Saupender understood our expression, I don't know.

"A few decades after eagles mature, they go through a period in which they lose their feathers. They are trapped, unable to fly from their perches, high on the faces of cliffs where the sun strikes them. They cannot hunt or wash, and they are not pleasant to be near. But the maturing eagles of their aerie sustain them. They will hunt for them and drop prey onto the tiny ledges where their elders are trapped. Only in this way can the elders survive their mature molt."

Just when I thought he was done speaking, he shifted his weight, and anticlimactically, he finished his tale.

"Even though they are not *people*, they know this moral. It is a lesson to the sentient peoples of our kingdom—to offer help when you can, and to humbly receive it when you must."

I felt uncomfortable when he was done. *Will he start talking again?* I wondered. *How long do I have to wait?*

When I thought it was certain he wouldn't speak again, I stood and stretched. His gaze was fixed on some distant thought of his own. Not sure of what to say, I looked at David. He returned my gaze with his own silent question. His eyes complained, *what do you want me to do?*

"Thank you for sharing this lesson with us," I said, unsure of my words. "I will remember it and…think more about it later." I searched for a phrase which might make my words sounds more important, but none came. "Um—I'm very tired and will leave you to rest," was the best I could manage.

I nearly dove into our tent, as quickly as manners would allow. I noticed a strange smell in the tent. Before I found its origin, David followed.

"Hey," he whispered, "thanks a lot for helping me out back there."

I only smiled, then I realized he couldn't see me in the dark. By then our fire was only coals under rocks.

"He's so *strange*," I offered. "Why does he talk like that?"

"He's harder to talk to than anyone I've ever known," David agreed.

Then it was David's turn to notice the earthy smell which had filled our tent. We followed our noses to the heatbox. Its scent was so strong I could taste it. And then we knew why sand was used for filling the box instead of dirt. Not long after, our warm and odorous tent carried us quickly to sleep— a welcome end to a cold and weary day.

4.2 The Path

When we crawled from the tent the next morning, Saupender was gone. Knowing we had until noon or thereabouts, we got ready at a leisurely pace. I coded quick duplicate messages and sent all but two of the pigeons to carry them to the palace. Feeling like the codebook had been a huge waste of effort, I used a separate page for each message.

I tore each used page from the notebook and used them to light a fire from embers buried in rocks and shallow ash. Realizing I had no more use for the codebook, I tore out the next sheet and folded it around the two last mini-scrolls, onto which I would encode my final messages. I tossed the rest of the codebook into the growing flames. I would carry the last two pigeons and the last two pages—front and back of the single sheet—with us when Saupender carried us to the Path. When I saw Saupender far off in the sky, I wrapped the remaining pigeons each in half my scarf and put them gingerly into the pockets of my coat. The codebook I'd spent so many hours filling was nothing but a single sheet of paper, folded and buttoned into the pocket of my trousers.

When Saupender landed, we were ready for him. Knowing he might object to our bringing blankets, we tied them around our coats. We didn't know how literal he might prove to be when he said we could take nothing but what we wore. We both remembered how cold the ride had been the last time we were carried by a Sentinel. We also knew we'd be waiting, perhaps for several hours, after Saupender carried us.

"Are you ready?" the Sentinel asked us. We told him we were. "And what of your little friends?" he asked, staring at the empty pigeon cage.

"I sent them back. All but two—those I want to send just before we enter the Path," I said, wondering for the thousandth time what the Path might be. I worried we should have loaded our pockets down with food and canteens instead of the few treasures we'd chosen.

"Very well," Saupender replied.

He lifted his body up as high as he could, to let us tie a sling between his two feet, just like the Lieutenant had. Not too short—or we'd be banging our heads into his belly the entire way, and not too long—or he'd drag us on takeoff and might beat us to death with his wings.

I felt numb as I tied the rope to his right leg. David was busy doing the same to his left. Then, before I had a chance to regret it, we lurched into the air and Saupender was beating his wings like a great machine. It was frightening to be close to those wings, beating so violently, but soon after we were soaring—following some unseen current of air, I guessed. We pitched and banked, sometimes dipping or rising in the air. I shuddered every time we did so. *Did I tie the knots well enough?* I wondered.

We soared over the mountain until I saw it went much farther south than I'd guessed. We *still* weren't halfway to the southern tip—not by a long way. In fact I couldn't even *see* the southern end—it was covered in dark clouds, swirling and boiling. I thought I saw flashes of lightning coming from its center. It looked like a thunderstorm and a tornado rolled into one.

What if we're hit by lightning? I worried as we entered the clouds.

I was terribly cold when we first took off, but it seemed I'd gotten used to it. The cloud was moist, and felt almost...*warm*. It *was* warm, or the wind-whipped skin on my face was playing tricks on me. I hardly had time to think of it as we rushed headlong through the clouds. I felt we might crash into the mountainside at any moment, and yet we didn't.

Saupender beat his great wings harder and harder as we flew at a dizzying speed, jerked around by every tiny dip or drop in the wind surrounding us. Then we seemed to hit a wall in the storm, and I was pushed up, hard into the downy belly over us. It took a moment before I realized we had landed. The wind around us was so fierce, it felt like we were still flying high in the air. But instead, I found myself on a slippery pile of shattered slate. If not for the many layers of clothes we wore, we might have been cut badly, for all the times we slipped.

Saupender told us to leave ourselves tied to one of his legs so we wouldn't be blown away. I tried to answer him, but I was overcome by the roaring wind all around us. David and I stood to one side of the giant bird, still tethered to his left leg. He made his way to a tall vertical wall as we struggled to follow him—we were at the bottom of a stone cliff. It was dark and the clouds were thick around us, despite the rushing wind. I found something bothering me, and it was some time before I realized what it was—*I was hot.*

I pulled the blankets from my coat, and though I tried to hold onto them, I lost them to the wind. David followed suit, but flung them carelessly away, seemingly glad to be rid of them. We followed Saupender uphill, along the cliff face, until he entered a crack or narrow cave in the cliff. It was utter chaos, and at no time since we'd entered the clouds had I been able to see more than a few feet away. I smelled the ocean air, but also a strange odor I couldn't identify.

We followed Saupender into the cave—really more of a fissure, but it was large enough to hold the three of us. It gave us shelter from the wind, allowing us to hear each other.

"What next?" David yelled.

"Now it is time for Mark to send the rest of his messengers."

"Why?" I asked, "Is this cave the *Path*?"

"The Path is only a short walk from here. We will wait here until it is time."

"Time for what?" David asked. "What aren't you telling us?"

"Anything else I have to say is not for anyone in this world to hear. I will answer your questions only after the remaining messengers have been sent."

"*Let them go*," David yelled to me, even louder than was necessary for me to hear him.

"I need to write the messages first," I said, pulling the last of the codebook from my pocket. When I unfolded the single sheet of paper, the tiny roll of paper for the final coded message nearly slipped from my hands into the wind. I stuffed the tiny roll into a pocket and picked up a smooth piece of slate from the cave floor.

The slate was wet, and the light—if you could call it light—was dim. The wind tried to pry the codepage from my fingers. I dried the slate with the inside of my coat as best I could, and folded the codepage in half, laying it on the slate. I wrote a quick message on the top margin of the page and started to circle the symbols which would encode it. When I unfolded the page to see the rest of the symbols, I nearly gasped. The symbols were wet and running on the page. The slate wasn't dry enough to save my precious code. Instead of using a new page to repeat my final message, as was customary, I would have to use the same page to encode my second scroll. I crossed out some words in the message to try and fit more information in the second copy.

I carefully transcribed the symbols for the first message before I began encoding the second. I only encoded a few short words when I saw something horrific in my page of symbols. The wind tore beads of sweat from my forehead, and some dropped onto the fading page. Sweat from my brow stung my eyes.

"What's taking you so long?" David shouted.

"The symbols—*I think there are repeats*," I answered. I felt even worse after saying it aloud.

"So what?" David was as impatient as I was anxious.

"It can't have any repeats—it means there's a *mistake in the code.*"

"So?" David replied unsympathetically. "They'll be able to figure it out."

I knew it wasn't true. Surely the page in the codebook I'd left with the Captain couldn't have the same mistakes...surely I couldn't have missed it twice. I remembered back to the time I spent so carefully filling the pages of code, checking and double-checking...and then I remembered a time I impatiently rushed through my codewriting—the last few pages I filled under the dim light of Captain Knemoller's ship. I went back to check, and found repeats in the section of code I'd used for the first message. I ignored them, knowing there was nothing I could do to fix it. Why had I taken a shortcut? I cursed myself under my breath, wishing for the impossible.

I still had the second message to encode. I wanted very badly to skip the code altogether and write my message in plain words, but I remembered how the Captain had warned me not to do so in any circumstance. I transcribed the circled symbols, trying to ignore the repeats as I silently counted them anyway. Twelve repeats in as many words. Would it make any sense at all? I went back and added the letters RPT to the end of the first message, which meant I would send a copy with another pigeon. I removed the first pigeon from my coat pocket and sealed my faulted message in the tiny tube attached to its leg. I tossed it high into the wind and it was sucked out of the cave immediately.

I looked back at the un-encoded text of the second message. I'd abbreviated the message so badly, I worried it might not make sense to anyone else. I read it to David and asked if he thought it made sense.

"What? I hardly heard a word you said."

The wind was picking up. Saupender interrupted us.

"I didn't mean to imply our time was limitless," he said.

I looked down at the codepage. I'd used up all the dry symbols; there was nothing else I could do. I sent off the last pigeon in a rage. I hoped it wouldn't make it off the island. What a horrible legacy for me to leave in the kingdom: proof I couldn't follow the simple instructions to fill a single codebook. I fumed at the idea.

I tried to calm myself by reasoning the information wasn't very important to the King. After all, he didn't want to know the secrets of the Sentinels—but I was fooling myself. I wanted to let the King know we made it—or at least we'd made it so close to the Path. I screamed in frustration after the pigeon, long gone into the swirling cloud outside our crevice.

"*Finally,*" David cried, uncaring of my frustration. "Now," he turned to Saupender, "what is the Path?"

"The Path is the way you will reach your home world. You

already know this."

"*I know we know that much,*" I shouted. "What *is* it—a door, a tunnel? Is it a hole in the ground we jump into?"

"I don't know exactly."

David and I screamed at once. Could the Sentinel be so frustrating by accident? He went on, oblivious to our tempers.

"I only know you must fall through it. It's in the air."

"In the *air*?" I ranted.

"What are you talking about?" David screamed, already in a panic. A moment later I wished he hadn't asked. I rather Saupender would have lied to us, or forced our hand.

"It's in the air, just over the volcano." Our eyes froze on him, and neither of us said a word. As if repetition would help, Saupender added, "You jump into the air over the volcano to reach the Path."

4.3 Path of Horror

I felt dizzy. I reached out, clutching only air, as I fell backward, slipping on the wet slate and shale. I blacked out when my head struck the ground. When I came to, I was in a steam bath, bathed in a dark red cloud. A booming clamor filled my ears. Through sounds of explosion, I heard David yelling, as if in the distance.

"...wait, wait...I think he's waking! *We still have time.*"

"Very little. Are you ready?" It was the deep, windy voice of Saupender.

"I am, but Mark isn't. Let me explain." David slapped my face—*hard*. "Mark, *listen*—we're on the ledge. We have to jump off of it, to pass through the Path. Are you ready?"

"What?" I asked, "Jump off the cliff? I thought we were already at the bottom." I tried to stand, but David's arm held me down.

"*Not yet.* Yes, we *were* at the bottom of a cliff, where Saupender landed after he carried us. But that cliff was only partway up this mountain. We brought you to the ledge— we're at the end of the island."

Saupender tried to help explain.

"What you assumed was one island is really two. A deep

chasm separates them, with a volcano in the strait between them. It's what makes the steam and clouds. A whirlwind covers this place at all times, hiding the Path." He spoke as if his words made sense, though I couldn't tell why. When their meaning sunk in I fell back, clutching at the jagged stone behind me.

"David, *listen* to me. You have to listen to me—*just listen!*"

I clawed at my brother and grabbed his face, pulling him in close to me. He feigned calm, though his eyes betrayed his thoughts. He looked at me as if I were a raving lunatic. I was, actually. I felt sanity's gentle grip sliding away. I stared into David's face as though it was through a long tunnel. Time seemed to freeze as a horrible understanding settled over me. This was the island I'd seen burning, from Captain Knemoller's ship. It wasn't a forest fire on the island, it was a live *volcano*. The thunderclaps I'd heard were explosions from within it. The painting of the island in the shop at Beach Row—it wasn't imaginary, we were standing on it. The rumors about the island we'd heard...Captain Knemoller's unwillingness to talk about it...they all slid into place.

This was the crazy superstition these people held about the island—they believed the volcano held some magical power. How many people did they believe they'd *sent back*, only to drop them to their death from this ledge? It was a nightmare from which there would be no waking. Randomly, I recalled the nightmare I'd had months ago, about a tornado off a cliff's edge.

I tried to explain all this to David. He shook his head.

"No, they're *right*. Think about it Mark—how did they know so much about us? They knew what we would do before we even thought of it. Think of the *prophecy*."

"No, you don't know, David. *I went back*. I read the rest of the prophecy after the King said we shouldn't. It was *insane*.

They *had* to be written after we did those things. This has to be…*a test.* Yes, *they're testing us.* They want to see whether we're gullible, or if we can decide not to go."

"You're talking nonsense, Mark. Why did you read those pages? The King knew they would make you doubt. Why didn't you listen to him? *Just look at your wrist.*" David grabbed my left arm from his face and pulled back my sleeve, all the while shouting. "Here, see this? What is it? How did it get here? This watch is all the proof you need. We will make it back home. Grandma still has to give it to you."

"No," I yelled back, "you told them. You showed them your watch—they made a fake copy for me, just like yours."

As we shouted back and forth, Saupender trilled out a loud shriek; it nearly deafened me.

"It is time now. You have no more time to argue, you must go *now.*"

"David, just wait and think this through—just give me a second to explain—"

Saupender leapt into the air and grabbed the wind in his wings. It ripped him off the ledge at a terrible speed, and he swirled out into the whirlwind. As I turned to watch him disappear I felt David's arms wrap around me from behind. *"Trust me,"* I heard him shout. I kicked back at him, wriggling to get away.

"Stop it, you're going to—" I felt his forehead strike the back of my head *hard.* Sharp pain spread over my skull, radiating from where I'd struck the rocks just a little while ago. Things began to go dark as my muscles gave way. My arms and legs felt *heavy.* I began to fade before the panic kicked in again. As David carried me to the ledge, sharp and painful reality surged back over me—just as we went over. I screamed like a maniac all the way down. David kept his hold on me, all the while yelling, "Trust me, trust me, trust me…"

4.4 Unwelcome Returns

I was lying in a bed with white sheets and blankets in a plain room. *Saupender saved us,* I thought. *We failed the test, but he snatched us out of the air.* I knew we must be back at Engdynlor, or in some nearby infirmary. I closed my eyes and breathed a great sigh.

I recalled the dizzying fall, and then being violently jerked backward...and then, nothing. My head was swimming in a fog. I was horribly tired and confused. I guessed the jerking sensation in the air had been Saupender snatching us with his great talons. *Where's David?* I wondered. *Is he all right?*

I tried to sit up, but couldn't. I struggled against something. I was lying on my back, with sheets and blankets tucked tightly around me. Were the sheets really so tight I couldn't sit up? I began to notice subtle differences from what I expected in the room. Too much of the furniture was metal—and shiny metal—chrome plated chairs like I'd never seen anywhere in the kingdom. There was a great mirror at one end of the room, built into the wall like a window. On the adjacent wall was a white door with a small pane of glass. The glass had the crisscross pattern of metal wire within it— safety glass. My head began to spin. I struggled to turn my head far to one side, and I saw a shiny metal pole resembling a coatrack. It held a bag of clear fluid, with a tiny tube leading to the edge of my bed, where it disappeared beneath my covers.

I should've realized what these clues meant, but my mind was sluggish and wouldn't cooperate. I tried to point my thoughts in one direction, but they fled chaotically like sparks from a fire. I became convinced the traitorous Duke of Enthicia had captured me, and was holding me for ransom. I yelled for help until I was hoarse. Finally a nurse in white clothes rushed into the room with a needle in her hand, and jabbed it into the tube hanging from the bag of liquid. This is the only recollection I have of the first several days after we returned.

When I next woke my brother was in the same room, sitting in a bed beside mine.

"*Finally.* I thought you might never wake up," he said. My head throbbed painfully.

"*Where are we?*" I asked, my mouth feeling numb.

"*We're home.* Well, not exactly. We made it back through the Path, and we're in some kind of hospital."

"Why? Were Saupender's claws too hard on us? We were burned by the volcano?"

"*What?* No. Mark, listen to me. Saupender didn't come *through* with us. We made it *back home*. I *told* you to trust me. Sorry I had to head-butt you, and pull you along. I wasn't coming back without you." Finally, what he said began to sink in.

"You mean…we're *home*? *Home* home?"

David chuckled. "Haven't you been listening? We've been just as confused and forgetful as when we first *left* home to begin with."

Just then a man wearing a white lab coat over a light blue shirt walked into the room. He had a stethoscope around his neck.

"Good morning, Mark. How do you feel?"

"Uh…not so good. I feel dizzy, and my stomach hurts."

"Sorry about that. The nausea is an unfortunate side-effect. We'll give you some food soon—it might help."

"Side effect? You *drugged* me?" My mind reeled, again suspecting the duke.

"We're *treating* you. You've been through an awful lot these past few days."

"*Past few days?* How long have I been here?" I asked excitedly.

"You arrived from the ER about four days ago. You and your brother were *not* in good shape."

"What's wrong with us? Were we crushed? Were we burned?"

David interjected, "I told you, Saupender didn't—"

The doctor also interrupted. "David, I warned you of the dangers of discussing your hallucinations with your brother. It won't help either of you recover—"

In turn, I interrupted the doctor.

"What do you mean, *hallucinations?*"

"Firstly," began the man in white, "please calm down. Getting excited *certainly* isn't going to help." He paused to watch my reaction to his words. I could see I wasn't going to get any information unless I played by his rules. Silently, I cursed him for desiring to control my feelings.

"All right, I'm calm," I said, drawing my words to a slow pace. "Now, I guess you're calling the past *year* we spent *in another world* nothing but a long hallucination?"

"Yes, I'm afraid that's right. You and your brother have had some memory problems in the past week. According to your parents, your actions became stranger and stranger for a period of days before you both went missing...while visiting your grandmother it seems," he said, reading a chart.

"Yes," he went on. "There was a police report filed for your disappearances, but the very next day you were found in the woods behind your grandmother's home. Both of you were incoherent. They told us you kept talking of strange hallucinations in the short times you made any sense at all. You've shown symptoms of both retrograde and anterograde amnesia since you were found. Your parents brought you to the emergency room of the county hospital, and you were given some medicine to calm you. You were transferred here the following morning. Your conditions worsened and you were both sedated again. You've been mostly sleeping from that point until now. Your brother woke up feeling a little better yesterday, and we thought you'd do better to wake up with a familiar person beside you. We thought you might benefit from being together, but if you insist on talking about your hallucinations as if they are real, I'm afraid we'll have to separate you."

Later I postulated great theories of this man in white, specifically about his desire above all to impose his will over mine, and redefine reality in his own terms. In my confused mental state, I wished only for my sword, or perhaps a stout battle axe.

"You think *nothing happened?* You think we haven't been gone for nearly a year?" I asked, fighting to keep myself calm.

"You certainly were *not* gone for a year. You were barely missing long enough for your parents to file missing person reports with the police. Like I said, you were found the next day."

"But...but I can *prove* it! Where are our clothes? Didn't you look in our pockets? Where's my watch?" I tried to pull my arm from my bed, but found I was still bound under my covers.

"Don't, Mark," David interrupted. "Just calm down and listen for now."

"Yes," replied the doctor, "Listen to your brother. He too told us of a watch you found...from the *future*. It doesn't exist. You were found by your parents, not far from your grandmother's house, and wearing only your underclothes. You were dirty and dehydrated—and covered with scratches. You looked like you'd taken a tumble through a briar patch. We thought there might have been foul play, that you were kidnapped and hurt or drugged. But other than the blow to the back of your head, and the bruise on your brother's forehead, there is no evidence of either. Your brother said he was forced to hit your head with his own...do you remember that?"

"Yes, of course I do!" I remembered to act calm. "He had to hit me in order to get me through the Path."

"A path?" the man asked excitedly, clicking his pen. "Was it a path in the woods?" David shook his head, as if our conversation was a waste of time.

"No, the *Path to this world*," I answered. "The Sentinel brought us there. He..." I let my words trail off when I noticed the doctor wasn't listening anymore.

"What about the injury to your head? Did someone else strike you? Did you fall? Why did your brother hit you?"

"To get me to come along," I shouted. "I thought he was crazy, but he was right." Again, the doctor's eyes examined me coolly, but he seemed to ignore my words. "I *did* fall down. I hit the back of my head on the rocks, and then I passed out."

"All right then, you passed out," the doctor repeated, clearly excited. "How long were you out? Did you think you were in a different world when you woke up?"

"No, no. I was still in Terreldor *then*. I was only out for...what—a few minutes?" I looked over at David, who had his arms crossed in front of him, shaking his head. *Don't bother*, his face said plainly. "When I came to, we were at the ledge. Saupender was there, but he flew off. Then David pulled me off the cliff with him, into the Path."

"Saw Penner? Can you repeat that? Were you near an airport? Did this...*Mr. Penner person* harm you in any way?"

"No, no. Saupender was our friend. Well, sort of—if we'd stayed, I'm not sure he wouldn't have left us to die on the island. He's a guardian of the Path—and they don't have any *airports* there. He was a Sentinel. You know, a giant eagle. He could talk."

That's when I first understood the look in his eyes. Of course they wouldn't believe us—they *couldn't* believe us. In my drugged haze, I recalled the words of the King, the last time we saw him. I ignored the doctor as he talked on and on about head traumas, amnesia, and hallucinations. I remember thinking, *if we'd only remembered being away a few days, he'd probably convince me.* I wondered how long we'd be in the hospital, and where our parents were.

When the doctor stopped talking I tried to sit up, and I found once again, I was restrained.

"You know, it sounds kind of silly when I say it out loud. It seems so *real* though. I feel like Saupender was just here beside me—a giant, talking eagle who could carry two people at once. But it can't *all* be a dream...*we remember the same things.*"

David bolted upright, a look of shock on his face. I went on.

"I mean, we were both hit in the head—me on the back of mine, and David in the forehead. We know *that* much happened. And we know we both passed out. Maybe I dreamt all this stuff up while we slept. How long ago did you say this was?"

The doctor smiled as if I'd begun to see the light.

"You were found unconscious with head traumas four days ago. You've been in this hospital for three days."

I felt like a traitor as I looked over to David—but his surprised look was gone. Of course he'd figured it out.

"I just don't know," he said, "They *both* seem real. Maybe I was only dreaming, and maybe we really *were* in some far away world for a year. But sitting here now, I don't *feel* any older. How could we be gone a whole year without Mom and Dad missing us? And they said we were only missing for a day... It's all so *strange*." David buried his face in his hands.

"Where are Mom and Dad?" I asked. "They'll know if we were gone for a year or a day. They can settle it. No offense doctor, but I don't even *know* you. For all I know, *you* kidnapped us, and drugged us too." The doctor smiled.

"That's just fine—a very healthy suspicion of strangers. I know it seems confusing now, but your parents will explain the same facts to you. Hallucinations can be *very* disturbing."

I saw his expression change. He believed he was helping us, but some part of me felt he believed he was *winning*—and it was winning which pleased him most. He stood over me.

"Let me loosen your restraints. You were thrashing about when you first arrived, you know." He pulled back my covers and I saw I was wearing a strange kind of shirt with sleeves that reached far past my hands. The ends of the long sleeves were tied to handles under the mattress.

"Where are our parents?" I asked again, trying to sit up.

"Not just yet," replied the doctor. "About sitting up, that is. You'll be very dizzy for a while and will probably want to sleep most of the time. I'll have your parents notified you are ready to see them. They'll be very happy to hear it."

A nurse entered the room and gave me water and soda crackers. The doctor seemed about to leave.

"Is there anything you need? Can I have something sent to either of you?"

"The hallucinations seem so real in my head," I lied, hoping my eyes didn't betray the enmity I felt for him. "But when I started telling you about them," I went on, "they sounded ridiculous. I'd like to write down as much as I can remember about them. I think it might help. I feel like my mind is bursting with memories of some strange faraway world."

The doctor looked skeptical for a second, but then he nodded.

"Yes, I think that might help," he lied in return. "I'll have a notepad and pencil sent in." Much later I would learn he feared we would present with hypergraphia, though he never attempted to confirm a diagnosis.

"*Me too*," David called after him, wiggling his hand symbolically, as if he were writing in the air.

The doctor turned to him and nodded. He was at the door and about to leave when he spoke again.

"It might take some time before you feel like your normal selves again. Your heads have been through quite a lot this week. We'll keep you on the medications for a while—they will help you from getting too worked up about anything."

He paused, and seemed as if he were going to ask a question, but decided against it. "Your parents are still working with the police to discover where you went missing. If you remember anything about where you were, anything in *this world*, be sure to call for a nurse and tell her right away."

The pencils and paper he promised never arrived. As soon as we were alone, David looked me straight in the eye and said, "I feel better already. I was afraid I was the only one of us to have such strange memories."

He got up from his bed and walked around the room. He told me how he'd woken up the day before and seen our parents. They looked so worried, he told me. He spoke quickly, and interrupted me every time I tried to talk. When I stopped trying to reply, he stood over my bed.

"I'm very tired," he said. "The medicine they have us on keeps me asleep all the time. That stupid doctor is giving us way too much of *something*. He should lose his license."

I was shocked at his insults…what if they were listening? David turned away and spoke in low tones.

"The last time I remember falling asleep," he continued, sounding very reluctant, "I woke up thinking I was in a different world." He let an awkward pause stretch out, then said, "Can you scoot over, and let me sleep in your bed?"

"OK…" I replied, wondering what had become of my brother. I wriggled to the edge of my bed and he climbed on top of it. No sooner than he did, he lay on his back and pulled the blanket over his face. I thought I heard him say something, and strained to hear him, holding my breath.

"Close your eyes," he whispered. When he added, *"trust me,"* I nearly laughed out loud. It was the last thing I'd heard him say before we fell through the Path. I closed my eyes and pretended to yawn. "Listen carefully," he whispered very quietly.

He went on to describe how I was to act if we were ever to be released from the psych ward.

"Don't try to tell Mom and Dad. Don't let on you know we really left our world. Don't act surprised if Mom and Dad look younger than you remember them. Just play along and remember: they might *never* let us out of here if they think we need to be cured of *psychotic delusions*. When you feel angry and want to shout the truth out loud, remember this—places like this are *expensive*, and they bill by the hour."

"Hey David," I said aloud.   He stiffened but didn't otherwise respond. "Hey, wake up. Do these hallucinations seem as real to you as they do to me?"

David relaxed and pulled the covers from his face.

"It's scary how real they seem. But talking about them helps. They sound so *ridiculous*, otherwise I might believe them. I remember seeing talking animals, and *trolls* even."

"*Me too*...were they green?"

"Some were, and some were brown."

"Yeah...and some were even *blue*. One of the blue ones bit me on the neck and gave me a terrible scar...but I don't have a scar now, do I?"

We talked back and forth until we fell asleep.   The doctors—there were several—felt it was helpful for us to talk about our hallucinations as long as we agreed they weren't real.

We saw our parents the next day, which was harder than I'd expected. To finally see them again but have to lie about our journey, felt worse than I could have imagined.   And something else was different...they treated us like *children*. We'd grown into positions of authority in Terreldor, but our parents doted over us as if we were sick babies. I reminded myself they believed we had some mental disease, and things would feel different once we were home. I should have heeded the King's warning.

We lied so well, the doctors let us return home in a few days. David and I agreed to hold our tongues until our parents stopped bringing us back to the hospital for our weekly appointments.

There was one great consolation with our being released from the hospital. Since my parents hadn't brought him into the psych ward, we finally saw our little brother, and it was a welcome reunion indeed. I noticed Josh seemed shorter than

I'd remembered him, and this triggered a troublesome thought lurking in the back of my mind.

We certainly *were* gone a year, and in that time we'd grown in maturity, but we'd grown *physically* as well. How could our parents miss such an undeniable proof? They *had* to notice we were taller. David had grown more than I had, so while he was barely taller before we left, he stood at least six inches over me after we returned from our strange journey. I found some pictures taken just a few weeks before we'd left, and pointed one out to my mother how the picture showed the two of us side-by-side. She offered a nervous laugh in her reply.

"Oh, you're just standing on higher ground," she said dismissively. The next day when I looked for the picture again, it was gone.

David and I made a habit of talking about such things only in the woods behind our house, as if the doctors were still spying on us. The day I noticed the picture missing, I told David during one of our walks.

"I think Mom and Dad know a lot more than they let on."

"I don't understand it," David answered, "but I think you're right."

"Why? Why would they let the doctors try and convince us we'd gone insane, when there's nothing wrong with us? They had to know it would hurt us."

"Maybe they think the truth would hurt even more."

In the end, I found David's suggestion was right. When I asked questions along these lines in front of our younger brother, all color drained from my mother's face. I could tell she was worried I would scare him somehow, or even worse, infect him with some of my apparent insanity.

After a few weeks, we stopped seeing the psychiatrists at the hospital. David and I cornered my dad on the ride home from our very last visit.

"Dad," I started cautiously, "what would you say if we told you we lied to the doctors…and we're still convinced we were in another world for a year?"

He paused. Not a worried pause, but a cautious one—perhaps as if we'd caught him trying to trick us. And that, of course, was exactly what we *believed* we'd done.

"I'd say it would be a dishonest thing to do, especially for the long time you would've been lying. But we're just talking hypothetically here, right?"

David interjected.

"There's a lot more at stake, Dad, like our sanity…and our *trust*…and the total lack of concern on *some people's* part about how we turned up missing for an entire day in the first place."

This was, of course, a tricky subject. My parents seemed to believe we must have been walking in the woods one day, when we fell and hit our heads. They seemed to think we just wandered around the woods in some delusional state for a night and a day, losing our clothes in the process. There were a lot of holes in this theory. The largest being, a search party they organized missed us for a night and a day, but our parents found us unconscious, and quite close to our grandparent's house just after the search party ended.

We waited for our father's reply. We waited quite a while. Finally, he turned off the highway and pulled onto a side road. He parked the car at the curb and turned off the engine. Even then, he didn't speak right away. Finally, he let out a heavy sigh and began to speak.

"Some things, boys, are better left as they are." He paused again. Was he testing our patience? I resisted the urge to speak.

"Let's pretend you *were* convinced you left our world—and you fell through some cosmic wormhole and landed in another dimension, or some other universe—or some other far-fetched notion."

Actually, it sounded pretty accurate to me—*suspiciously* accurate. David and I had arrived at the same conclusion, but never mentioned it to him or the doctors. He went on.

"Let's pretend you believed this was true. Where would this belief get you? And how would it *harm* you? You could never prove it happened. Believe me; *no* amount of proof would convince most people. Most would consider you lunatics or frauds. Either of those reputations would hurt you, and they would take a long time to escape. They *could* land you in a mental ward for a very long time. And they would certainly cause emotional stress—maybe even psychological harm. It's not easy being called a liar or a lunatic throughout your entire adolescence."

He spoke with such conviction, I immediately believed he spoke from personal experience. *What could have happened to him as a teenager to give him such feelings?*

"If you believed you'd gone through some fantastical journey," he told us, "traveling back and forward in time, what could possibly motivate you to convince anyone it was true?"

David tried to interrupt him at that point, but Dad waved him quiet.

"Just a minute—hear what I have to say first, both of you. If you learned things which affected you, then so be it. When it comes down to harsh reality, it doesn't matter how you learned them—from delusion or from unbelievable circumstance. Take life's lessons as they come, and don't worry about the manner which brought them to you. Believe me, taking such a stance can only hurt you. And it might even stop you from doing the things you want to do in life—maybe even the things you're *supposed* to do."

David and I stared blankly at each other. He sounded as if

he was telling us we couldn't allow ourselves to be labeled lunatics, or we might not be able to carry out our last assignment from the King. He never heard us describe these things. In fact, he seemed very uncomfortable whenever we'd tried to bring up our *hallucinations*.

Does he know? I wondered, and *how?*

"So please," Dad went on, "if you have any such notions, keep them to yourselves. I don't want to see you go through the pain it might otherwise cost you."

Then, just as unexpectedly as he stopped the car, he started it and continued on our drive home.

I felt a deep disappointment in my father for a long while. Even to suspect he shared this amazing, other-worldly experience, but never know, was a great frustration to me.

Afterward, if we ever tried to point out how we'd grown taller while we were missing, he would only give us a shorter version of the same speech—and always in private. We'd *gone missing*—as we later called it—in early summer, so by the time we went back to school in the fall, our growth wasn't so suspicious to our schoolmates. Joshua, our younger brother, once mentioned the *time we grew taller*, but he got such a glare from our mother, he never mentioned it again. Despite several efforts, we were never able to get him to talk about it.

I don't know if it was some deep rooted need to have my father believe me, or a desire to feel we shared such a rare experience, but I fought a daily temptation to try and get him to open up. Several times I gave into this urge, and none of them fared well. I began to feel a barrier growing between us, one I was doomed to continue building upon as long as I couldn't resolve these feelings.

To my greatest frustration, we continued to suspect our father knew we'd truly been gone nearly a year. More and more, we began to suspect he'd been to Terreldor himself, but there was no way of *knowing*. Even if we one day returned as adults, there could be no records of our father having been there. For if the King had been right, any trip our father made in the past would be in the kingdom's distant future.

Finally, on a Sunday visit to our grandmother—our father's mother—David and I happened to find ourselves alone in the room with her.

"Was there ever a time," I immediately asked her, "when Dad disappeared for a few days? Or when he grew a few inches, almost overnight?"

"Oh, no," she replied. "Your father was a very good boy. He would never run away." She didn't understand, it seemed, but then, she looked up at the ceiling as if she were recalling a distant memory.

"He *did* grow really fast the summer before we left the farm."

"He did?" I asked excitedly.

"*How* fast? How much taller was he?" David added.

"Oh, I don't know…it was so long ago. And he *did* seem to have grown, almost overnight. I think he'd been slouching, and then decided to sit and stand correctly one day." Unexpectedly, our grandmother's face grew sad.

"That was a hard year for your father. A new school, making new friends…he wanted so badly to fit in. It was after he started making up his *stories*. Kids can be so cruel, you know. *What's the harm in making up stories*, I always said to his father. They were so odd, no one could have believed them. He wasn't *lying*, you know—just *pretending*. I still remember one night he came to me and asked why I didn't believe him. He seemed so sad, as if he expected I should have pretended along with him. He didn't bring it up much after that."

She wore a somber face for the rest of the day, and

wouldn't talk any more about our father's childhood.

When David and I had a chance to slip outside, we went straight into the woods, where we couldn't be overheard. When we were sure we were alone, we talked right over each other.

"*He really went,*" I said. "How could he not tell us?"

"*Who would have guessed it?*" David added.

I was overjoyed. All my feelings of frustration toward my father had dissolved. At last I knew we shared this amazing journey—something few others in all of history every could. Even knowing he wouldn't discuss it was bearable, knowing we had this extraordinary event in common.

David wanted to press him further, but in the end, we decided against it. Dad had been so adamantly against talking about our journey, over the past year, we knew he wouldn't give us any further answers. I stopped short as something troubling occurred to me.

"But if he was there like us, why didn't Grandma notice him gone for a whole day—or longer?"

"Actually, it makes perfect sense," David replied. I waited for him to continue. "We were supposed to return at the very moment we'd left our world."

"*What?*"

"When you were unconscious, just before we returned, Saupender told me about the Path. I found out the Sentinels know a lot about the Path, but they rarely talk to humans about it."

"Well, what did he say?"

"He told me the Path is different at both ends. He said each end is fixed, but moving."

"You mean it's broken, so it moves?" I interrupted. David frowned.

"No, not *broken*. This end is fixed...like it doesn't move.

But it's also moving."

"What sense does that make?"

"Be quiet and you'll find out," he said, glaring at me. "Its *location* is moving, but the timeline it carries people to, *that* is what's fixed. Not *fixed*, as if it always takes people to the same exact time, but there's a relationship between the time in *our* world and the time in *their* world. Our timelines are flip-flopped."

He saw my expression and tried again.

"Each point in time from our world is linked to a point in time in their world, but the relationship is backwards and *tilted*...or something like that. I'm not explaining it very well."

"I can agree with that."

David paused a moment, just to tease me.

"It's like this: Say we crossed from our world to theirs, and met a sixty year old man. If we came right back home to the same time we left, and *then* waited in our world for three more years, we could travel to their world again, and see that sixty year old man *as a baby*. For every year in our world, twenty years pass in their world, but backwards. It's just like the King told us."

"I'm not sure it makes sense," I said, "but go on. What about the other end...does it work the same way?"

"No. The other end is fixed in space, meaning it doesn't move around; it's always just over the volcano. Saupender said the time-space rift actually *creates* the volcano, and the whirlwind above it—whatever that means. Anyway, the location is fixed, but the timeline it carries you to—*that's* the part that's moving. This is why it's guarded so heavily. If enough matter moved through the Path in one direction, it could destabilize both worlds, but even if that doesn't happen, letting people use the Path unrestricted would allow us to *travel through time*. We could've returned to *any* time in our world.

That is, if Saupender would have *let* us, and told us when to jump."

"How is that possible?" I asked.

"I have no idea; I only know what Saupender said. He told me the Sentinels were *made* to guard the Path. Think about that—not that they're *forced* to guard it, but they were *designed* to. He says they sense fluctuations and waveforms within the Path. It's like a *sound* to them. They have something in their brains tuned to hear some waves the Path gives off, and they know what time in our world the Path will bring you to, as it changes from moment to moment. This is why we had to go through at just the right time. He said they even *heard* us travel through the Path when we first arrived in Terreldor, a year ago."

"Did you make this up?" I asked doubtfully.

"Do you think I could have? No, Saupender told it all to me. Why do you think I was so set on us going through?"

"What does one thing have to do with the other?"

"Don't you see? As guardians of the Path, they can only let people travel to the same period of time they came from—in our world that is. He said they have no choice. Maybe Saupender promised his leaders—I don't know. But one thing was certain, if we'd waited any longer, we would have died."

"*What?*"

"You heard me right. Once we knew so much about the Path, we *had* to go through it. And when you stood there arguing with me, we were missing our time to go through. If we'd waited any longer, there would've been only three possible outcomes for us. We could stay in their world knowing the secret of the Path, we could go through the Path to the wrong time—you know—to some other time in our world. Neither of those is acceptable to the Sentinels."

"But you said there were *three* outcomes…"

"Yeah, but first realize, those first two would both bring us *death*. Saupender wasn't leaving us; he took to the air to swoop back down and *kill* us. It was the only other outcome he could accept." I went pale for a moment.

"He would have killed us?"

"They're not murderers, Mark. They're *guards*. It's what guards *do*." I let the idea sink in for a minute. Something still didn't seem right. David brought it up before I could. "The third outcome, was for us to pass through the Path at the right time, which we did—barely."

"So what does this have to do with Dad going and getting back at the same time?"

"Well, Saupender was supposed to tell me the exact time to jump off the ledge with you. But you woke up just when we were supposed to jump. Then you started arguing, and I knew we were missing our time. If we jumped right when he meant us to, we would've arrived at the same exact time we left. But we missed that point, and were about to miss our chance for good. Didn't you think I was being a little *forceful?*"

My hand reached up to touch my cheek. I raised my other hand to point at David.

"You...you *slapped me*," I recalled suddenly.

"That's right. I knew every second you stalled, we were a second closer to our deaths. Like I said, Saupender didn't abandon us. He took to the air so he could circle back and pluck us off the ledge—then drop us too low to find the Path."

I realized my mouth was hanging open. David didn't wait for a reply.

"We either jumped and *maybe* we'd make it home, or we stayed and faced certain death."

"But—we could have hid from him. We could have stayed—*and lived*."

"This is *exactly* why I didn't explain it to you; I knew you'd argue. Even if we could've hid from Saupender—which isn't likely—there's no way we could have made it to our tent and blankets by nightfall. Remember how far he carried us?"

"But we could have stayed on the cliff—*it was warm there.*"

"For how long? We would have died of thirst or hunger. And think about this…Saupender could have easily flown to our tent and supplies and destroyed them. He made sure you had no pigeons left to call for help—and we were on an *island*. No, Saupender had it all planned."

I had a surprising flashback. The scenario David painted for me was the same as the choice we'd been forced to make when we first arrived. After we crossed Otlak Plain and climbed Golden Mountain, we found ourselves faced with a choice at the Winter Palace. We heard strange noises inside, and even suspected danger, but we didn't have the supplies to make it down the mountain in either direction.

"Our choice was made for us," I said under my breath.

It reminded me of something the Captain once told me. David let me ponder for a moment, and I almost let it go. Then, suddenly, a new thought occurred to me.

"*Wait a minute*," I said angrily, "you said we knew the secret of the Path so Saupender couldn't let us stay. That's not true—I was unconscious when he told you all of this. He could've let *me* stay—I hardly knew more than the Lieutenant."

David looked away from me, but kept walking.

"That's the problem, isn't it?" he mumbled.

He let an awkward silence hang between the trees as we walked. Did he really know all this and take me back anyway? How sure was he the Path was real? I thought of the Princess, of the Captain, and the world we'd left behind. I grabbed his shoulder and spun him around to face me.

"How could you make such a choice for me? How could you rob me like that?"

"There's no guarantee he would've let you live," he argued. "Do you think he would've just picked you up and taken you to Engdynlor? If he allowed you to stay, you could've found a ship one day and returned to the island. You could've returned later and made it through the Path to some other time—Saupender couldn't allow that."

"But you didn't think of all this, up on the cliff that day, did you? You just *took* me."

"*So what if I did?*" David demanded. "*That's what we went there for.*"

"Admit it; you didn't want to leave me."

"*Fine.* How do you think *I* felt? Could I go home to Mom and Dad and tell them some crazy story about a faraway world at the end of some time-path, and then say, 'oh, and by the way, Mark is never coming back—he's gone forever'? Do you know what it would have done to them—what it would have done to *me?*"

We walked through the woods in silence for a while. Finally, after I'd calmed a little, David spoke again.

"Admit it, Mark. You would've done the same thing."

I only grunted. He was probably right, but I was far too angry to admit it.

"Besides," he started, "aren't you..."

His voice trailed off as if he changed his mind. It didn't matter; I already knew what he was thinking. *Aren't you glad we're back home?* And I knew why he'd held back—he wasn't sure how I would answer. And neither was I.

I thought about what it would have been like to stay. As my mind was filled with those useless musings, I noticed David had stopped dead in his tracks. We were there—the place where it all began. Before us stood the great bent oak, growing out of the giant boulder at the foot of the hill. Without hardly a thought, I jumped over the sprawling roots, ducked under the lowest branch, and stepped up to the cave's opening. When I realized what I was doing, I turned back to look at David. Still frozen, he looked at me with a painful expression on his face.

"Saupender said..." he began to protest.

I looked back into the cave. I thought about the Princess, but also the King and the Captain. Could I really go back to them both and tell them I refused my last order? I did a quick calculation in my head. We'd been back for about a month...twenty months ago in the Captain's world would be about a year before we arrived. He wouldn't know me, *or* suspect I was the one from his prophecies.

I looked back at David as I took another step into the cave. He wasn't moving. I looked once more from the cave to David, and ran inside.

I fumbled my way to the back—it wasn't far—and felt along its wall on both sides, from front to back. Nothing happened. Slowly, I walked out of the cave and headed back. It was growing dark, and I found David standing by the oak, waiting. We spoke very little on our walk back.

4.5 The Future Comes Slowly

We went back to living our old lives, more or less. It was a difficult adjustment, as the King had foretold. Dad seemed to give us more slack. He gave us more room to make mistakes, and generally trusted us to make right choices—and most of the time we did. He gave us more responsibility than he ever had before, and often it shocked or even scared Mom. Still, it was nothing compared to the responsibility we'd been given by the King.

Living a normal life felt good at first, almost a relief. But both of us eventually came to the same reaction: we were bored. What was worse, our time in Terreldor had ruined us for most of the things which had seemed so important to us before we left.

We got very involved in school. For a while, I was convinced I wanted to be a lawyer. I joined the debate team, and studied negotiating further, and also public speaking. David didn't join debate, but he studied similar topics, and became very interested in politics. He was convinced it was his best chance at making his mark in our world.

David went to college a year before I did. I think he already had his doubts when he left, but during his first year, he confided in me he was abandoning politics altogether. I thought he was giving up. I didn't understand for another year, when I was halfway through my first year of pre-law. One day I just *knew*—it wasn't what I wanted in life. I couldn't feel passionate about it. I wouldn't change the world as a lawyer—and I deeply wanted to change people's lives.

The next summer, David and I went home to work and save up for the next year of college. We were talking about the reasons we wanted to change our majors, when Dad said something which got my attention.

"You boys grew into men long before you left for college. You trained your younger brother up in many things. You affected many of your friends and classmates at school. You helped people who needed helping, and many times gave advice that shocked me to hear coming from the mouths of teenagers.

"Why do you think your *careers* will change people? Don't you see? It's *how you live your lives*. It's the relationships, and the effect you'll have on everyone you come in contact with. I think you both ought to stop worrying about what jobs you'll have, and realize you'll make your marks in this world no matter *what* your professions are. Why not look to your passions for the job skills you'll need to learn in school? Honestly, I think you have more to teach some of your professors than they have to teach you."

It was a blessing to hear his praise, but it was his confidence which mattered most. Once I realized it was my *life*, rather than my *job title* which would affect people, I was free to let my talents choose my areas of study. At some point years later, David told me he'd discovered the same thing from those words of wisdom Dad gave us. So in my sophomore year of college I studied engineering and management, never forgetting the Captain's admonition to lead others for a greater chance to speak into their lives. David became interested in business and marketing and changed his major also.

When we both returned home for Christmas that same year, my attention once again focused on our *second journey*—the one the King and Captain saw as having already taken place in their timeline. It began with a conversation David and I had one late night, staring into the fireplace.

The story of the Chaplain, the head delegate I'd left in Portsmouth, pointed my mind back to the idea of our future return. For some reason, I couldn't shake the memory of Chaplain Davis's story.

He'd experienced a life change when he joined the army at the age of thirty. The Chaplain never spoke of his previous life. When I thought of the inventions he'd made before becoming a Chaplain, I saw a pattern. All his inventions would be fairly easy to *re-invent* from memory, provided you'd used them before, and possibly had some local artisans to help. Most of them were just becoming popular with others in the kingdom while we were there.

The list was long: eyeglasses, bifocals *and* compound microscopes, screwdrivers, paper clips, safety pins, thumb tacks, potato chips, crayons, life preservers, pencils, barometers, Braille, pasteurization, and even a Morse code transmitted by reflecting sunlight between hilltops. Many of these inventions had different names in Terreldor, but were unmistakably the same. When I shared the list with David, he laughed.

"*That's impossible,*" he said. "No one could invent all those things."

I countered with Leonardo da Vinci's example, though David claimed his was a much smaller—and less varied—list.

The items made of glass lenses were the least likely of the bunch. Perhaps Chaplain Davis had worked with a glass blower. In our world, these same three discoveries were made centuries apart. David was certain the Chaplain stole his inventions from our world.

When David returned to school, he spent all his free time researching those who invented the same items in our world, and the societies they lived in. Sociologists had even created complex theories suggesting a single society or generation could never come up with more than a few of the Chaplain's inventions. One man creating a thousand years' worth of inventions in a few years was more than strange; it was unbelievable.

Moreover, I'd become friends with Davis during our stay in Portsmouth. He was an intelligent man, but he didn't fit the profile of any inventor David read of. He didn't like to tinker while I knew him, and was content in taking his time with menial tasks. The more we studied the problem, the more difficult it became to believe the Chaplain's claims.

David said it best when he wrote to me in a letter: *it's as if he was a revolutionary super-inventor for a few years, then never thought like an inventor again.* For a while I still insisted this was possible, given his LifeGrowth, and multiple transformations. Then David shared with me some books in which he read of *da Vinci doubters*—those believed he'd had help. One historian theorized Leonardo had stolen his inventions from the East, merely re-drawn them and claimed them for himself. If one could believe da Vinci had received emissaries from Asia, the theory fit quite nicely. There are records and drawings of all the inventions in da Vinci's many notes—drawn less beautifully and in two dimensions—which pre-date the great artist, some of them by centuries. Even more telling—in Asia, the same inventions occurred over many years, and were recorded by different inventors.

Eventually, we were both convinced the Chaplain had

taken a one-way trip across the Path. This fueled my search for dates and timelines to fit our theory. I knew Patrick Davis was thirty when he first joined the King's army, and he had used the name Patrick *Ulrich*. I knew he was in his early fifties when I met him, so he'd been in Terreldor for at least twenty years when we'd arrived. If that was *all* the time he'd been there, he must have left our world about a year after we returned. I was excited to share my theories with David the next time we met in person.

"He would have left our world about three years ago," I explained.

"Could it really be?" David wondered aloud. "We could've met him again, only *twenty years younger*."

Since I had no idea what kind of life he'd led before he'd taken the Path, we had no easy way to search for him.

"How many Patrick Ulrichs could there be?" David asked next. "And how can we find a list of all the adults who turned up missing three years ago? Is there some kind of national *disappeared list?*"

David looked for many lists while I searched with renewed enthusiasm to find another way to the Path. According to the King's records—the ones I supposedly wrote—David and I visited their world as adults about a hundred years before our first visit. In that same time, five years in our world would have passed—and we'd been back in our world for four years already. I was sure we had only one more year to find the Path. David, on the other hand, looked at our second voyage as the King did—it already happened in their world, so it was an absolute *certainty* we would return.

I began to wonder about the types of cycles which might govern *our end* of the Path. I began by guessing the Path would return to the cave in the woods near Grandma's house about five years from the day we'd stumbled across it. I also guessed the Path's cycle would have to do with celestial bodies, though I had no evidence to support the idea. I took a course in astrophysics, but its equations and theories had little application to our problem. The only thing I gleaned from the course was a vague idea that the Path might indeed be a wormhole connecting two points in space-time, inspiring a wild guess on my part. I began to view our end of the Path as a pinhole in time-space, which would be affected by large gravitational shifts, like the proximity of the moon and sun to the Earth.

I was disappointed I hadn't found anything concrete. Mainly as a distraction, I began to study solar and lunar cycles. I learned neither cycle matched our calendar exactly, though the moon's cycle was much further off than the sun's. I counted off five solar years from the date we left, and then counted off sixty moon phases. They didn't match up of course—the two dates were off by quite a bit. There was, however, a lunar event on the exact day, six solar years after the day of our first trip. The moon would line up with several planets, including our own, and larger than normal tides were expected in many parts of the world.

Maybe it's a hundred and twenty years between our two visits on their side, and six years on ours, I thought. It wasn't until I looked at the solar and moon phases on the day we disappeared four years ago, I was convinced. There was in fact, the same overlap in the solar and lunar cycles back then. I assumed I'd discovered the exact date of our destined trip back, and it was roughly two years away.

I wrote David to tell him the good news about my calculations. I didn't mention the date, just to see if I could pique his curiosity. He wrote me back saying:

Why did you go through all that trouble? Don't you remember my broken watch, under Engdynlor? It was frozen at 10:35 AM, and the date was Wednesday, March 15th. The next time March 15th falls on a Wednesday is the year after next. We go back in two years.

I doubted his simple method, and blind faith in the broken watch we found, but when I checked his date against mine, I nearly shouted aloud. Both our methods had come to the very same day.

Meanwhile, David had been doing some research of his own. He'd found more than one organization which kept lists of missing persons. He checked lists from the FBI, the Red Cross, the State Police from each state, and many Comptrollers' lists of unclaimed bank accounts. His biggest breakthrough was after he wrote a voluntary research paper on locating missing people for an English class. He found most government offices were much more helpful to a student doing a research paper than they were to someone who couldn't give them a good reason for their questions. Soon after, he learned if his letter was written under his English Department's letterhead, and mailed from the University's mail office, the recipients nearly always gave him the information he asked for, provided it was legal for them to do so.

I was sure the Chaplain had to come from the United States, judging simply from my memory of his accent. Sure enough, David found a Patrick Ulrich in his late twenties, who had gone missing from a suburb of Philadelphia, about three years ago. He was a postman, and he'd been discharged from the Post Office when he failed to report to work for two consecutive weeks. During spring break, David and I drove to Philly to visit the post office where he'd worked, to see if any of his co-workers remembered him well enough to describe him.

One of Patrick's old co-workers had a picture of him, taken at a Christmas party. It looked very much like him, in a skinny, restless sort of way. I explained I was a friend of his from a few years back, and asked what he could tell us of his disappearance.

"Well," his old co-worker said, "it certainly was unexpected. When he didn't show up for work, I stopped by his apartment. No one was there, but I kept checking back every week or two. Eventually, his things were put out in the parking lot, and his apartment was rented out to someone else."

"Did he seem like he was thinking of leaving?" I asked.

"Well, it was hard to tell with Pat—he was an impulsive kind of guy. He talked about joining the army sometimes, but I never thought he'd do it. We all wondered what happened to him when he disappeared. Do you know?"

David shrugged his shoulders. I told him the truth.

"That's what we're trying to find out. I haven't seen him in four years." Patrick's old coworker wished us luck.

4.6 Hope of Return

Two years later, we found ourselves counting the days until our hopeful camping trip. I was in the middle of my last year of college. David was changing jobs to move nearer to our hometown, and planned some time off before he started with his new employer. We were all set for another trip through the Path.

We'd bought tight-fitting packs and stuffed them full of the things we would need the most: dried energy bars and other survival food, clothes for cold and warm weather, notepads, and some items requiring little space we might find useful in trading. We packed pencils, cheap colorful crystals, hand-wound flashlights and cigarette lighters, to name only a few. And of course, we packed different seeds capable of growing a nearly impenetrable wall of thorns we would need to give to the Watchmakers. Multiflora Rose, wild brambles, and dried blackberries known to grow well in shade, took little room and added close to nothing to the weight of our packs.

We didn't know how long we would stay in our second trip to Terreldor. Truthfully, I wasn't convinced I would return home. After we'd discovered Chaplain Davis had made a life for himself there, I knew it was a possibility. If the King wouldn't let me stay, perhaps his reigning predecessor would.

Just in case, I'd studied a whole new set of inventions, different from the ones the Chaplain had brought over. I didn't discuss any of this with David, certain he'd only disapprove. Any inventions I brought to Terreldor's past should have been present when we were there last. I didn't worry about the problem, but I knew David would object to bringing anything I couldn't prove was already present when the Chaplain made his trip.

We knew it was possible, even likely, we'd return to our world a year older, or even more—and with temporary amnesia. For this reason alone, I didn't enroll in any classes for the spring semester. Thinking like a student, I knew I wasn't likely to pass a course after taking a year-long break halfway through it. With nothing to do from Christmas to March, I had plenty of time to prepare.

I didn't tell Mom or Dad I wasn't returning to school right away, not until we were home for Christmas. They were very surprised, and more than a little concerned.

"I don't understand it," Mom said when I told them. "You're doing well in school, and I thought you were enjoying it. You're nearly done. Why not wait until you graduate, and take some time off before starting work? You're not thinking of dropping out, are you?"

"No, nothing like that," I replied, "I just need a little time to sort some things out. You know, to re-group a little. I'll be better prepared to finish school, and more focused on interviewing when I'm finished."

"I have to agree with your mother," Dad added. "What do you need to *sort out?*"

Just then, our younger brother Josh walked into the room. He was starting high school the following year.

"Can I take a semester off too?"

I squeezed his shoulder forcefully and he slapped me hard on the back—our rough-and-tumble form of brotherly love.

"Sorry, kiddo," I teased. "Junior high doesn't allow for sabbaticals." Dad was still staring at me, waiting for an answer. David avoided everyone's gaze.

"Uh—well, there's *plenty* for me to sort out," I muttered. "What I want to do with my life, what my values mean to me, and how I can better share them with others. I want to do some real thinking on what I've accomplished so far in life, and how I'm doing with the goals I want to reach." Dad jerked his head back in surprise.

"I don't think you're supposed to wonder about all that until—well, until you're at least *my* age." The stern look had left his face, and he soon replaced it with a smile. "You boys have always been mature for your age—all three of you. But Mark, I still don't understand what you'll do between now and next fall."

"Well," David started, "before I start my new job, I've had my heart set on going on a spring camping trip up in the old woods, and Mark wants to join me. Afterward, he'll find a summer job before all the other kids get out of school."

"Why can't I go?" Josh complained.

"How about going with us on a pre-trip, to test out our equipment?" I asked him. "We want to go for an overnighter to try our gear in cold weather." Josh smiled while Dad plied on.

"Are you sure this is wise? Most kids who take a break from college never finish; I'm sure you know this." His concern had returned to his brow.

"I know Dad, but really—I'm *eager* to graduate. I just don't mind delaying it for a semester. This will be a nice break from school, and from job interviews. I'll do better at both after taking the time off."

"I don't understand it," Dad said, smiling. "You're not even worried you might not finish school, or have trouble finding a job afterward? I'm not sure you're supposed to be so...*calm* in your last year of college. I was stressed nearly out of my mind."

Eventually Mom and Dad were agreeable, even if they weren't excited with the idea. There was one more item to address—one possibility we couldn't responsibly ignore. We had to acknowledge the possibility one or both of us might meet our death in a more savage, less sheltered world. With this thought on our minds, the same week while we were all home for Christmas, David and I tried to pull Dad outside for a late night walk. Josh was asleep and Mom was working in the kitchen.

David and I had already been talking about how we could bring it up. When we asked him to go on a walk with us and handed him his coat, he looked into our eyes, and his face grew somber. For a passing moment, he seemed distracted, or perhaps regretful. He took his coat and hung it back up.

"Not just yet, boys," he said, gravely. "There's something I need to talk with you about—out in the garage."

David and I stared at each other, at a loss for words. We followed him into the garage. Without saying a word, he pulled on the dangling string which lowered a folding staircase, and disappeared into the storage attic. A few minutes later, he backed slowly down the staircase, easing an old steamer trunk after him. I'd seen it before, and wondered what reason he had for bringing it down. I'd never seen it opened, but knew it held Mom's wedding dress and some things belonging to Great-Grandma.

"Boys," he began, his voice more dire than before, "there are tough choices parents have to make while they're bringing up their children. For me, some were harder than others. *This* choice," he said, tilting his head to the old trunk, "was the most difficult of them all. I still believe I did the right thing, but I've regretted it, just the same."

"What? If you chose right, why do you regret it?" David asked.

"And what does it have to do with Mom's wedding dress?" I added.

"Doing the right thing isn't always easy. And sometimes it causes pain—for you, and for others. That's when the right choice is easy to regret. And it has *a lot* to do with Mom's wedding dress…or rather, it has a lot to do with the fact that there's no dress in this trunk at all—and there hasn't been for half a decade." David and I exchanged confused glances.

"Dad," I said, "You're not making any sense."

"Not yet. Why don't you pull up a seat?" he said, nodding toward the stools in front of his cluttered workbench. "This is going to take a while."

We pulled them near and sat. Our breath made tiny clouds, lit by the single light bulb hanging over the workbench. Dad shoved the mess on the workbench aside and threw the trunk onto it. He worked a key through its lock as he spoke. For the first time in six years, he spoke of our trip. He told us once again how badly he thought it would hurt us if we tried to convince others our tale was true. He'd hoped we'd believe it was only a dream.

"But I had no idea you'd done so much there," he said, sadly. "I didn't want to offer you any encouragement to believe what you felt was so real. So, we hid things from you. We told some untruths. Yes, *we lied*. We believed we needed to lie to protect you from…so much pain."

His face grew long as his voice lowered. I saw a single tear fall from his eye.

"We told the police and the psychologists you'd been acting

strange for days before you went missing. We also told them we found you in your underclothes. The truth is, you were acting perfectly normal that Friday when we drove to Grandma's house—and all the days before. We found you fully clothed in the woods behind Grandma's. You were both babbling incoherently from the jump, and you were wearing *these*."

He opened the trunk, and to our surprise, we saw the heavy winter clothes we'd been wearing when David drug me over the cliff's edge and into the Path. David and I tore through the trunk until we'd found our inner clothes and the bulging pockets we hoped we'd find.

I found the leather-bound case holding the tiny glass sculpture. We found our old leather sheets with the Three Tables burned onto them, David's field scope and decorated box, his tiny medal from the Watchmakers, our belts with apprentice knives in their buckles, various stones, two tiny stalactites, the giant catfish tooth, my maps, David's dagger, a patch of white, furry pelt, and my watch—the same one I was wearing on my left wrist. I held the two up to each other and stared at them. Then I opened the box holding my tiny sculpture and pulled out the note the Princess had written when she bought the sculpture for me. The gold leaf envelope had melded shut, then torn back open. The folded paper was stuck together and torn unrecognizably, as if someone had tried to force the two halves apart.

I looked back toward my father and saw his eyes welling with tears. I didn't know whether I wanted to shout at him accusingly, or hug him and thank him for returning these most valued possessions to us. Torn between gratefulness and anger, between resentfulness and forgiveness, I chose the better pair. David did likewise. Without thinking, I pulled David's watch from the trunk and tossed it to him.

"You'll need this…*in the future*," I said nervously, wondering what Dad would think of it.

Then I swapped the watch on my wrist for the one in the trunk. The older would stay in our world. The newer one had to go back with me, so I could leave it in Terreldor, for me to find a hundred years later, then bring back to…put back in the trunk… I felt dizzy.

Dad's eyes were misty as he spoke.

"Your trip was also painful for me. I'd come to believe my own experience in the cave was only a dream. *This*," he said, waving his hands before him, "forced me to believe again."

"So you *did* go through," David whispered, as if speaking aloud might undo it all.

For a moment he only shook his head. We waited patiently as time seemed to stretch. My mind raced, exploring the possible responses he might give us.

"I might as well tell you," Dad finally started. "I was only a boy—not much older than Joshua. Grandma and Grandpa's farm isn't far from where Grandma lives now, you know. This was before they sold the farm and moved into town. I was so mixed up afterward—after the jump back. My father punished me again and again for lying. All my friends thought I was crazy or stupid. I'm certain now it was the real reason they sold the farm. Though it was only a few miles from town, the move put us in another school district. I had a chance to start over."

David and I looked back and forth at each other, full of anticipation.

"This—it still isn't easy for me. Even now I can only talk about these things as if they *might* be true. Part of me has called this something from my imagination for so long, I can't fully accept the truth. The rest of me—well, you understand what I'm saying."

We both nodded, unsure of what to say. Dad didn't seem much like himself, talking to us that night.

"Then you'll have to excuse me if I don't want to talk about my experiences with all this. It was hard enough to bring this chest out of the attic. It was so easy to stuff it away and forget about it. Your mother—don't mention a word of this to her, *please*," he urged us.

Only after we nodded, did he continue. "She saw the way you were dressed. She knew *something* of what was happening. She grew up not far away from here. When she married me, she knew of my delusions—or experiences. At any rate, she knew of the stories about me as a child. Times were different back then. If someone was…mentally unstable, they were seen as *defective*. After we'd been married for a while, I tried to tell her about the cave in the woods down the railroad from the farm, but she would hear nothing of it. 'We live in the *now*,' she said, 'The past doesn't matter. Let's not dig it all up.' Even today, it would be too painful for her to hear any of this again."

He paused and sighed, his eyes focusing on a distant memory. Before long, he continued.

"When we found you two a day after you disappeared, not far from that same cave, we brought you into Grandma's house and stripped off your clothes. Your mother went straight into Grandma's attic and emptied the first trunk she found. She told me to put all the things into it, and I did. I told myself it was better for you—and mostly, I still believe it was. You don't know the pain I went through—the years of questioning my own sanity, all the while being accused and ridiculed."

"So why bring this up now?" I asked.

"Well," he said, waving a hand over the contents of the trunk, "isn't this why you're going camping up in the woods near Grandma's?" David and I shared a confused glance, unsure of what to say. "As soon as you mentioned it, I knew. Mark, you're taking the semester off, and David, you're changing jobs. How much more convenient it would be if you returned looking just a little older than when you left. It might hide a year's worth of aging, just like when we had you finish school from home, that spring six years ago. It all fit too well. My question to you, is *why?* Why would you go *back?*"

We explained to him as briefly as we could, how we were expected to return, and how it had already happened as far as the King and other knights were concerned. Dad seemed interested in hearing only the barest of details, as if telling him too much would injure him. It scared me to see him act so strangely.

When we were done, David mentioned we needed a way to prepare Mom and Josh for seeing us looking older when we returned—and a way to say a possible goodbye, should the worst happen. Dad promised to help with those expectations for Mom, but he was at a loss on how we might approach the issue with Josh. In the end, we spent as much time with our youngest brother as we could in those few months. When we brought him on our camping test-run, I took it as our chance to bring it up.

I told him David and I had a rare medical condition which could cause us to age a little faster every now or then. He thought I was joking, but when I mentioned it happened once when we were younger, he grew serious.

"Is that..." he paused, as if unsure whether he should continue. "Is that why you spent so much time in a hospital when I was little?"

"Yeah, almost six years ago," I told him. "I wasn't sure you'd remember. There's also a very small chance that...well, *the worst* could happen. We're almost past the age when that could happen to us...but until I turn twenty-two, it's still possible. I just wanted you to know how much I care for you, and how lucky I am to be your brother, in case something happened and I missed the chance to tell you again."

David walked in halfway through the conversation, and decided just then to speak up.

"The same goes for me. You need to know the way I feel, in case the worse should happen to *either* of us."

No one spoke for a moment, until David broke the silence in a boisterous tone.

"But the chances of that is so *tiny*, it's not worth worrying about. We just wanted you to know how we felt, and now you do. So let's forget about this morbid talk, and start the campfire."

David and I turned to the pile of dead branches we'd collected, but Josh remained still. I noticed first, and turned back to him.

"What's wrong?" I asked.

"Do...do I have the same problem?" Josh asked in a troubled voice.

"*Certainly not*," I assured him. "You would've shown symptoms years ago—by the age of ten, at the latest. Ask Dad about it sometime if you like." I made a mental note to explain the conversation to Dad, in case he *did* ask.

He seemed a little somber the rest of the day, but he let the topic go. It was as ready as we could make him, I guessed. I don't know what Dad told Mom, but before we left for our week-long camping adventure, she sat us down and told us nearly the very same thing we'd told our younger brother. It ended with a teary-eyed declaration of how blessed she felt to have us as her sons.

We hoped to make it back through the Path on the same day we left, knowing this time what to expect. Just in case, we talked to Dad about what he might do if we returned late. He promised to check the forest around the cave every day after we left. If we came back in as bad shape as we'd been in six years ago, we'd have our Dad there to take care of us—this time with no police or psychiatrists.

We planned to set a campsite near the cave entrance a few days early, and spend most of those days inside the cave—just in case the date I'd calculated was off by a little. We brought candles and lanterns to light the cave, and brought books and a deck of cards to keep ourselves occupied.

The night before we left for the camping trip, I could hardly sleep. We'd prepared as best we could, but I still thought of things I would've liked to add. As it was, we'd been able to stuff a tremendous amount into our small packs. Our kits included enough dried food to keep us alive for weeks, waterproof matches, warm winter clothes, two flare guns and flares, lightweight rope, snares, fishing line and hooks, a wire saw, some fourteen-gauge wire, and small pliers. The last two items were added at Dad's insistence; he'd always claimed he'd fixed more with a bit of stiff wire and a pair of pliers than anything else. Of course, we wore our belts with our apprentice knives hidden in the buckles, though the leather straps were longer than the originals.

In the morning, I busied myself going over my pack while I waited for David to show. He'd found an apartment near his new job, not far from our parents' home.

"Be careful...and *be wise*," I heard from behind. I recognized the gravely bass as Dad's voice, just after he woke. The phrase played over in my mind as I turned around, and I realized this farewell wasn't only shared by my brother and I— it had been my father's custom all along. I hadn't heard him say it in years; how could I have forgotten?

"Thanks, Dad. I know you don't agree, but I feel strongly I

must do this." He put his hand on my shoulder and nodded, looking deep into my eyes.

"I know, son," was all he said in response. It seemed odd to me at the time, but what else could he have said?

Twenty minutes later, I was in David's car. He drove us to Grandma's house, and parked behind the garage. She expected us, and knew we'd stop by to visit at the end of our trip. She was confused about the timing—she found it unfathomable someone would want to go camping so early in the spring. With everything on our minds, we didn't yet want to bother inventing reasonable-sounding answers to her questions.

As we walked through the woods, we talked nervously. We were weighed down with gear: both items to bring through the Path, and also items we meant to leave behind in our campsite. I was worried we'd picked the wrong date, while I think David was more worried we'd guessed it correctly. We knew it would be a couple of unnerving days, sitting in the cave waiting for the Path to take us. Of course, the Path *could* already be there. We might slip on through as soon as we crossed the cave's entrance. Or, the Path might not even be in the cave, but somewhere nearby.

"Did you bring the notebooks?" David asked.

"Of course." How could I forget? I'd told David I wanted to bring log books, for us to write in before *and* after the Path took us. We planned to log a quick entry every two hours during the daytime after we reached the cave. In this way, we would know roughly when we made the trip across. If we were conscious on the other side, but phasing in and out of amnesia, the notebooks also might give us a record of it, to read later.

It was a longer hike than I'd remembered. We walked close together, wondering more about what the Path might look like.

As we'd done a hundred times before, we talked about what we'd do when we got there. We knew we were going back to help the Watchmakers, but how exactly would we go about it? There were too many variables we wouldn't know until we arrived. Eventually David changed the subject.

"Hey, look," he said, "it's the bent oak. We're almost there."

He was right. I wondered if we might see something strange in the cave, like a glowing light, or something surreal, like a black hole. As I rounded the tree and ducked under its lowest limb, my ears tingled with anticipation. I thought I heard a rock fall inside the cave, and wondered if the stone walls inside might appear to be caving in where the Path began. As I rounded the entrance, my flashlight cast a bright beam into the cave. I nearly stumbled in shock when I found someone inside.

"Hello? *Who's there?*" I demanded.

"Hey," the voice called back, "easy with the lights, you just about blinded me."

For a second, my heart seemed to stop, and my flashlight dropped to the ground.

"Well, Mark, don't blind him," David said, entering the cave's mouth behind me.

"They're finally here?" I heard from farther back in the cave.

David's voice seemed to be coming at me from two directions—which of course, it was. Louder, I heard, "What do you have to eat? We're *starved*."

I grabbed my flashlight and shone it once again on the man in front of me—the perfect image of a slightly older, dirtier, and scruffier *me*.

"It's about time," my elderself said. "We've been in here

for two days with hardly a thing to eat. Now let's open those packs of yours...I seem to remember we packed quite a bit of food we didn't need on the other side."

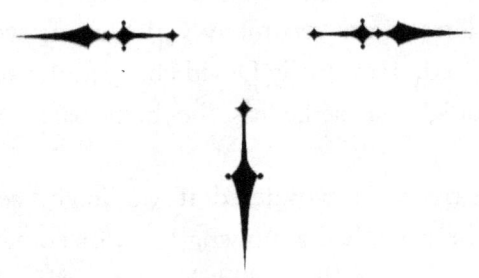

The Three Tables

Table of False Reflections
Worthy and Honorable Characteristics, and their Pale Imitations

Boldness: Stand against strong opposition for what is right	**Rebellion**: Stand against what is right for your own preferences
Freedom: Glorious, unnatural & precarious state where citizens are free do right w/o gov't interference	**License to Wrong:** Abuse of freedom to do wrong, exploiting gov't restraint from defining morals
Love: Consistently & reliably choosing to provide for another, promoting every facet of their lives; desiring strong, healthy relationship	**Lust**: Need to have selfish desires filled by another, regardless of the other's needs
Compassion: a. Allowing/providing what's best for others at own expense. b. showing mercy out of love. c. willing sacrifice to create chance for others to choose right	(Negative) **Weakness:** Lack of ability to make hard decisions or to show strength. (Deceitful) **Feigned Compassion:** deceitful by intent & practice; leads to distrust
Submission: Understanding & operating in your position in chain of authority	(Negative) **Timidity:** lack of boldness & strength (Deceitful) **Feigned Submission:** submit in words & public actions only: leads to disloyalty & treachery
Selflessness: putting others & their needs above yourself & your own needs	(Negative) to disguise selflessness as a **weakness** (Deceitful) **false selflessness**: hidden pride, leads to selfishness
Leadership: (servitude) serve those who follow you, imbue them with your values & give them opportunity to choose to follow. Preferable to supervision, which teaches nothing	**Manipulation**: motivate others to do your will through fear, greed & other wrong or hurtful desires
Conviction: desire to cease wrongful conduct: results in true behavioral change	**Guilt**: causes shame, does not foster change, leads to separation or loss of relationship

Humility: accurately understanding yourself & your abilities	(Negative) **Insecurity**: Self-doubt, often combined with a crippling fear of failure (Deceitful) **False Humility** (a type of pride)
Strength: the degree to which you reliably oppose wrong & stand for what is right	**Anger, bullying, forcefulness** all used to assert your will without regarding how it affects others
Forgiveness: freeing someone from the wrong they did to you; choosing not to recall the pain or damage caused. Dismisses retribution, not punishment	(Negative) **Weakness**: lack of resolve or ability to take revenge (Deceitful) **Feigned Forgiveness** leads to hidden unforgiveness
Loyalty: Integrity in relationships, duty, & commitments: prevents betrayal	**Unreliability**: Reduces relationships to brief alliances motivated by greed, masked by deceit & ripe for betrayal
Wisdom: Degree experience, knowledge, & insight used to make decisions. Joined to maturity & humility. Demonstrated by choices & actions, not professions or claims	**Knowledge**: Result of learning. Without wisdom, knowledge cannot lead to wise action. Alone it leads to pride; doesn't prevent foolishness
Peace: Contentedness, lack of worry or stress: does not infer a lack of productiveness	**Lethargy**: lack of productivity or meaningful action. Often joined to lack in boldness, strength, & concern. Exposed to manipulation
Patience: Self-discipline over whims & fleeting desire	**Stubbornness**: Willingness to bide time until easier to assert will over others. Reflects selfish desire
Honesty: Integrity displayed in words & actions. Fulfilling commitments & duties	**Well-planned Deception**: Practiced deceit, hard to discern. Prevents loyalty & reliability

Table of Opposites

Honorable Characteristics and their Opposites

-a quality's false reflection often leads to its opposite-

Humility: accurately understanding yourself and your abilities	**Pride**: traits stemming from the deep-rooted (and often hidden) belief in every man that he is better than others
Compassion: a. showing mercy out of love. b. sacrificing to create opportunities for others to choose what is right	**Judgment**: desiring Justice over mercy for others; desiring to see others punished **Indifference**: disdain or lack of care for others, holding no value for their lives or growth.
Wisdom: Degree experience, knowledge, & insight used to make decisions. Joined to maturity & humility. Demonstrated by choices & actions, not professions or claims	**Foolishness or Recklessness**: decisions or actions utterly lacking useful thought, knowledge, and values. Disregards consequences and scorns reflection and forethought
Love: Consistently & reliably choosing to provide for another, promoting every facet of their lives; desiring strong relationship	**Hatred or Indifference**: counting as irrelevant, selfishly discounting inherent value of, desiring destruction of a person or group
Forgiveness: freeing someone from the wrong they did to you; choosing not to recall the pain or damage caused. Dismisses retribution, not punishment	**Judgment**: holding someone responsible for wrongdoing, enacting punishment or retribution
Self-forgiveness: willingness to receive forgiveness for your wrongs, to release guilt for your actions following Conviction	**Self-condemnation**: inability to release guilt, usually from a lack of Conviction. Imitates piety or duty, fosters no change
Loyalty: Integrity in relationships, duty, and commitments: prevents betrayal	**Dissention and Betrayal**: sown in distrust and selfishness, inability or refusal to recognize authority
Generosity and selflessness: Sharing coupled with Contentedness, or the peace accompanying having enough	**Greed and Poverty**: perception of not having enough, regardless of possessions or lack thereof. Constant desire for More, irrespective of reality

Peace: contentedness, lack of worry or stress: does not infer a lack of productivity	**Restlessness or Discontentedness:** mental or emotional state of dissatisfied unrest. Married to anxiety and stress
Submission: understanding and operating in your position in a chain of authority	**Rebellion:** refusing to recognize your position in a chain of authority; feigns ambition, robs peace, prevents contentedness
Conviction: desire to cease wrongful conduct: results in true behavioral change	**Arrogance:** Refusal to or unwillingness to recognize the need to change, rebellion combined with resolve

Table of Maturity

Worthy & Honorable Characteristics, & Childish Behaviors they Replace

Mature Characteristics	Childish Characteristics
Helping others advance, selflessness	Comparing others to self out of jealousy
Compassion, willing to sacrifice to give others the opportunity to choose right	Passing judgment, anger and hatred
Contentedness, joy, willing to suffer for good	Fits of anger or self-pity when selfish desires aren't fulfilled
Patience & Longsuffering (contentedness, happiness, & elation proportion; willing to bear hardships for a cause)	Focus fixed on short-term gain, impatience, expecting constant elation or entertainment
Service, and giving	Self-centeredness, inability to see beyond Self, taking
Leadership: Allows room to grow & choose. Leads to loyalty. Gives away authority, trains others to take place. Gardener leader.	Controls others through fear, leads to resentment and disloyalty. Holds onto control. Watchmaker leader. Imparts nothing.
Humility, giving attention to others	Pride, bragging, needing attention of others
Learning priorities from father/ mentor	Rebellion: Orphanhood, no relationships or responsibilities
Controlling emotions enough to make responsible choices	Letting emotions and desires control you
Teaching path of maturity to others; giving it away	Never learning path to begin with; holds others back from finding path through negative example
Conviction, learning shortcomings and changing	Guilt, shame, shortcomings grow to insecurity, never grow past them

The Six Levels of Moral Behavior
Distributed across Three Moral Planes

Others Plane
Fear of Punishment
Anticipation of Reward

Self Plane
Desire to Conform/ Become Accepted
Recognition: Governance Helps All

Beyond-self Plane
Recognize morals as larger than ourselves—containing
universal, self-evident truths, beyond what immediately
benefits the individual
Moral of Ultimate Love and Truth: moral not motivated by
fear, but sacrificial love

*"No one can comprehend a plane of morality above the highest plane
in which he operates." – Chaplain Davis*

Excerpts from C. M. Hibbard's online reviews on iTunes, Kindle, Nook, & Smashwords

"[Hibbard] takes the reader on a thrilling ride…a journey of suspense and adventure." -*Susan Mahoney*

"An original idea and thought-provoking story." -*J. D. Howard*

"A gripping read." -*Sandra Hicks*

"Amazing insight." -*Parul, Amazon user*

"Interesting story with unexpected turns…beautifully written." -*Nook user*

"I would love to see more books by Hibbard." -*Maya, Amazon user*

"So much meaning it leaves you asking what's important in life."
-*DebbieS, Amazon user*

"A must read."-*Larry B. Gray*   "Amazing!"-*Odetta, Amazon user*

"Leaves you wanting more!" -*Diskson Magombedze*

"Excellent, meaningful book." -*MinisterAsh, iTunes user*

A Word on the Typesetting

I had *Terreldor: The Long Path Home* set in 12 point Garamond and printed on cream paper—both deliberate choices with the reader and environment in mind. By far, the easier of the two choices was the paper.

The most hazardous chemicals used in the manufacture of paper are the chlorine compounds used in the process of bleaching it white. Cream paper is not only easier on the eyes with its utter lack of glare, it's easier on the environment.

Garamond is considered among the most legible of all typefaces, but it is also heralded as one of the most *green* of the major fonts in terms of ink usage. With such a highly readable font, a 12 point typesetting is effortless to read.

A Brief History of the Garamond Type

The name Garamond describes a collection of humanist serifed typefaces named after the letterpress punch-cutter Claude Garamond (1480–1561), though it is clearly a misattribution. Sixty years after Garamond died, Jean Jannon issued a typeset in France with several similarities to C. Garamond's, though it was unquestionably a new work with undeniable intrinsic value. It is this typeset today's Garamond fonts most resemble.

The French government raided Jannon's office and stole his new typefaces, which were then forgotten for two full decades. When they were next uncovered, they were chosen by the Royal Printing Office as their standard type. Eventually this office evolved into the French National Printing Office, which officially adopted Jannon's type in 1825, erroneously crediting it to Garamond.

New Garamond fonts have poured in throughout the 1900s, predominantly based on the original work by Jannon—even the so-called Garamond-revival fonts. Typographical scholar and journalist Beatrice Warde famously corrected the misnomer in 1925, but by then, the nomenclature had already become permanent.

An inordinate number of popular book titles published this century have chosen Garamond, but its usage isn't limited to the literary world. Its extreme popularity has crept into nearly every corner of modern life.

When Apple launched the Macintosh in 1984, it developed a proprietary version of Garamond for its introduction. This Garamond dominated Apple's marketing and became a major part of their brand recognition for nearly two decades.

Nintendo chose italic Garamond in 1985 to describe the versions on their 1985 game consoles. Fifteen years later, Nintendo named a character Garamond—a successful author—in their RPG video game Super Paper Mario.

Though using a common font for a corporate logo can restrict trademark laws and protections, Abercrombie & Fitch chose a Garamond typeface for their famous logo, which is why it looks so familiar to you as it is printed on this page.

The same can be said for Neutrogena, who has proudly imprinted their Garamond logo on their famous bars of soap for decades, as well as their other products and accompanying packaging.

As the Garamond typeset approaches its 400th birthday, it seems there is no sign of slowing for this classic font. It may prove just as popular in another 400 years.

Embark on a New Journey:
Return to Terreldor
A New Series Coming Soon

New release notifications: email <u>publishing@Terreldor.com</u>

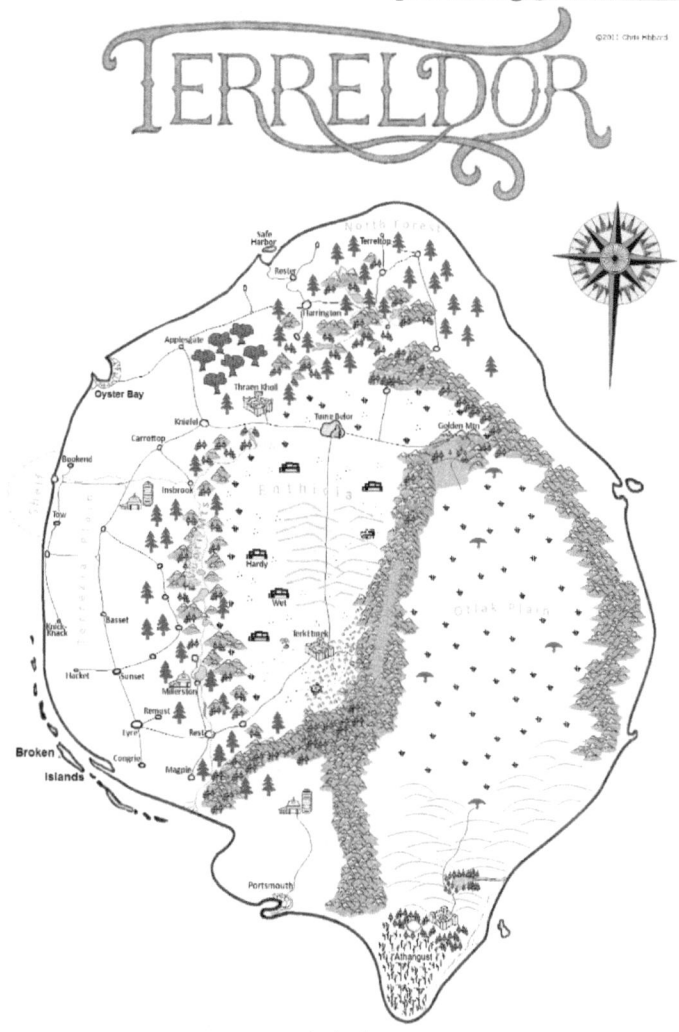

Chris M. Hibbard

www.ingramcontent.com/pod-product-compliance
Lightning Source LLC
Chambersburg PA
CBHW020328180626
46812CB00001B/102